A private eye is hired by a famous television comedian to seek out a mysterious stranger.

A business analyst for a mining operation travels off-world on a mission to investigate the sightings of a monster.

A politician calls a meeting to renegotiate a supernal contract with an enigmatic salesman.

But he's no stranger, not a monster, and hardly an enigma.

He is…

THE DEVIL YOU KNOW BETTER.

THE DEVIL
YOU KNOW
BETTER

Edited by R.J. Carter

Critical Blast Publishing
1097 Preswyck Drive
Belleville, IL 62221

Cover Art and Design by Bobooks
First Edition June 1, 2022

0 9 8 7 6 5 4 3 2 1

ISBN-13: 978-0-578-39020-8

DEDICATION

It is said the evil that men do lives after them.

Surely that must apply to angels as well.

CONTENTS

ACKNOWLEDGMENTS

This book would not exist without the faith and trust of the contributing writers who rose to the challenge armed with the greatest weapon ever devised by man: imagination.

FOREWORD:
THE SECOND COMING
OF SATAN

The Devil made me do it.

It's not that the first volume of *The Devil You Know* wasn't good enough. With twenty authors delivering twenty kick-ass stories, there was no reason we couldn't just sit back and say, with no small amount of pride, "We did that."

And perhaps that seed of pride was all that was needed. It is, after all, one of the seven deadly sins. So perhaps it was pride. Or, perhaps, it was that our erstwhile protagonist simply wasn't done with the stage and insisted on an encore.

Every writer and actor knows: the villain has the meatiest part. And villains don't come any bigger than the Prince of Darkness himself. The schemer, the conniver, the corruptor: the very personification of all that is evil. And yet, from at least a literary perspective, we simply cannot get enough of the eternal adversary.

1

And so here we are with yet another collection of tales that will shock, awe, astound, and amuse, all spotlighting that inglorious bastard, The Devil.

We're taught that the wages of sin is death, but we find there's a cost unaccounted for in Tim McDaniel's *Sin Taxes*. Later, Lena Ng whips up one hell of a four-course dinner for the damned in *Hell's Kitchen*. And Nadia Steven Rysing takes readers to a deep space mining colony to investigate a debilitating wave of superstition in *Salt Gets in Your Eyes*.

Sometimes he wins. Sometimes he loses. Always he enthralls.

You may think you know who he is. But after reading these twenty tales of terror, fantasy, and science fiction, he'll be someone very different.

He'll be The Devil You Know Better.

— R.J. Carter, Editor

THE DEVIL CAME TO ROOST

Hart D. Fisher

The devil came to roost
making a home in my heart
driving down a rainy side street
cheap wine taste on my tongue
grease running across the windshield
soiling the fall leaves
and when he cracks a wink
he says there's a little piece of god in everybody
a mean animal place
in every orphan's eye
worn through over time.
Tapping out a Camel
the devil says he needs a new face
one without the sad little grin
a face full of thorns
not one like mine
a weary beaten thing

a china doll mask
pliable
yet brittle.
Under a cloud of smoke
the devil says I have an ugly face
something he saves for old widows
a cackle for the corps
and he slaps his leg,
like it was funny
his breath sizzling the smaller hairs
teeth like angry diamonds
bit sharply into the filter.
Spitting it onto the floor
the devil said if only there were no god
he'd be able to retire
spend his days getting golden in Barbados
his nights fucking blue haired old ladies until dawn's first
kiss
but he was stuck in the 9 to 5
the same old grind
since the beginning of time
just another working joe
stiff in the joints
nickel and dimming a lotto slide
also coming up a loser.
After the third cigarette
the devil leaned back slow
whispered from across the smoldering seat
"you're just too barren for me,
pull over to the side"
And I did.
Looking at him in my mirror
a split forming down the center
I pulled away slow
leaving him by the side of the road
water spattering his boots
each droplet an angry sigh.

But I took his words with me
each one a painful treasure
full of world weary truth
good for nothing
and worth less.

ABOUT THE AUTHOR

HART D. FISHER is the author of *Poems for the Dead*, *Still Dead*, *An American Horror Story*, editor & publisher of *Sex Crimes* plus writer/director of the feature film, *The Garbage Man*.

He is also the creator of the American Horrors tv series (created in 2008 for the Global Broadcast Company), the True Crimes tv series, the American Horrors Intermission tv series, is a co-creator of the tv series Groovey.TV with Guinness Book Of Records winner Groovey Newville, creator of the horror anthology comic/tv show *Flowers on the Razorwire* (in development) and is most noted for the creation of the infamous Jeffrey Dahmer comic book biography published by his notorious publishing house, Boneyard Press, with his original series of books *Dark Angel*, *Bill the Bull*, *Flowers on the Razorwire*, the Dahmer Comics & *Babylon Crush*.

AD MAJOREM
SATANAE GLORIAM

Damascus Mincemeyer

London, England, 1898

The flames were all he knew.

Long had the fires of perdition incinerated everything that could be called man; his past, his life, even his own name were lost to the fiery abyss. The reasons for his damnation were gone, too, eaten away by every carnivorous lick that had reduced his soul to ash.

Yet there had been a dawning, a rising through the embers, and he found himself among a writhing horde of gnashing teeth and flailing limbs, all of them moving upward through the pit to a destination unknown. And above it all the Voice spoke to each of the million screaming souls, clear above the chaos:

The time has come to war with The Creator, to turn His world to blood and dust, it said. *You are the hordes of Damnation, and shall fight to the last, from the clay of the earth to the gates of*

Heaven.

Then the flames were gone. No, not gone. Different. Fire still surrounded him, but now there were streets and carriages and buildings ablaze, the wailing agony of men and beasts symphonic in the night.

He stood there, the Nameless damned soul, the taste of sulfur in his mouth, bewildered by the anarchy around him.

Forward, the Voice urged.

And the Nameless One obeyed.

♉

Calvin Woolery stood in the open doorway of the narrow terraced house, watching the night sky above the city's West End dance with flames.

"The line at Hampstead was breached last evening," Martin told him, thumbing through *The Times* at the parlour room table, so fresh an edition the ink was still practically wet, his usually jovial tone sober as he read. "They say the VRC have fallen back to a position in Regent's Park and have all but abandoned St. John's Wood and Paddington, and there's another line retreating back through Bethnel Green and Spitalfields to bolster up the police contingent along Brick Lane." He rapped the paper with a knuckle. "This article claims the Sappers will burn all the bridges to prevent the enemy from crossing the Thames if necessary. I tell you, lad, if those Russian bastards reach the Isle of Dogs, they'll have us by the inexpressibles then, no question."

Calvin said nothing, though his uncle's assessments held truth--the Isle of Dogs was the main hub of London docks, a short march from where they were in All Saints Poplar, and a shining strategic target for the enemy force besieging the city. It was also a powerful indicator of the desperation in the struggle if the Royal Engineers were indeed considering demolishing spans across the river.

Martin set the paper aside, ripping a chunk of bread from the moldy loaf on the table and emptying the last wine from a bottle into his glass. "Come and eat, Calvin. We might as well enjoy what little we've got left."

"I'm worried about Anne." Calvin said. Martin laughed.

"The one thing I'm decidedly *not* concerned about in all this is that daughter of yours. She's the most head-strong woman I've ever met, besides your aunt, that is. You made the right choice sending Stuart and James to Brighton with her."

Calvin's fingers brushed against the Webley service revolver tucked in his waistband. At one time he'd been robust, but a decade in the regiments and that old spear wound from Rorke's Drift had transformed him from youthful soldier to middle-aged dockworker before he knew it, and that was before his wife Louisa had been eaten alive by consumption, leaving him with three young mouths to feed and little money to do it with. When the current calamity began, his primary instinct was to protect his children, but sending them south had been a difficult choice, despite what the papers said about the protective zone the military had established there.

From outside, another round of screams punctured the night, followed by the distant rumble of artillery. Martin went to the window, watching a herd of panicked people rush down the street. He withdrew a pipe from his vest, tamping it before lighting up. "I tell you, lad, I always knew the Russians would make a move on us one day. Tsar Alexander just couldn't resist Queen Vicki's plum pudding, so to speak."

Calvin looked at his uncle. "I don't think the Russians are capable of launching an attack on this scale. On the continent, against France or the Germans, yes. But not here."

Martin frowned. "Don't tell me you're one of those who think the enemy's some phantom army of the Devil. I thought you level-headed enough not to believe in such superstitious nonsense. From my worthless drunk of brother I'd have expected it. But not you."

Calvin bristled at Martin's casual condemnation of his father, even if the description was apt. "I don't know what to think, uncle. But it doesn't seem God's hand is in this."

Though the newspapers loudly championed the military response to the invasion, there were conflicting reports as to the nationality of those launching the assault upon Britain's shores. Many assumed, like Martin, that it was the Russian Empire making a violent power play, or even a surprise French attack. But there were other, darker, rumours whispered by those who had actually seen the enemy first-hand. Tales abounded about sinister soldiers with charred flesh and burning eyes, monstrous creatures so perverse they could have only come from a Bosch painting, about beings that belched brimstone and could turn river-water to boiling blood and men to bone with a mere touch. And despite the press' refusal to acknowledge the tales, Parliament had hastily formed a new cabinet ministry consisting of a cabal of England's most notorious occultists, psychical researchers and ritual magicians, an act giving weight to theories of the enemy's otherworldly origin. Despite that, Martin still only laughed.

"Heard a fellow when I was out today swear up and down a cadre of vicars and priests had set out to bless the Thames. Mad as hops, he was. I mean, it would take a blessing from the bloody Archbishop of Canterbury himself to just combat the stench from that miserable river." Martin looked to his nephew, his laughter fading. "Chin up, lad. Anne and the boys will be fine. You'll see." He put his pipe out. "Maybe we should try to get some sleep."

Martin waited a few minutes, but Calvin didn't budge from the doorway, and eventually he sighed, going upstairs alone.

♉

Something stirred within the Nameless One as he marched with the legions of the Damned; around him whirled a cataclysm of burning shops and collapsing houses, the bodies of the slain mingled among the wreckages of carts and cycles, carriages and omnibuses, yet there were things in his surroundings that triggered memories from a time before the flames claimed his soul, words and places that seemed somehow familiar: Shoreditch. Liverpool Street Station. Bishopsgate. Gracechurch Street.

Amid such destruction there remained, astoundingly, pockets of defiance; a detachment of riflemen had staunchly erected a stubborn defensive perimeter along Cannon Street, complete with securely nested Maxim Gun. As the Damned approached, the riflemen opened fire with well-practised aim, but though they howled as bullets struck them and their charred flesh bled sparks of fire, the Damned did not die, and proceeded forward despite the onslaught, obsidian-tipped blades and halberds in hand.

More insidious were those commanding the hordes, things the Damned themselves would have difficulty recognizing as having ever been remotely human: the demons. All of them were different, yet similar in their hideousness--some were tall and thin with ten heads and twenty hands, while others were squat creatures with rows of sharp teeth and bones protruding from mottled, raspberry-like flesh; there were those that shrieked and collected the skins of their victims as trophies, even as their compatriots whipped the Damned forward with tendrils of fire.

Unlike the Damned, the demons had names, whispered in the heads of the infernal infantry: *Beleth. Amdusias. Leraje. Eligos.* Those, and dozens more, were the Earls and

Dukes of the Abyss, the generals of the dark crusade upon the earth. The Nameless One saw his own commander appear in the midst of battle astride a viper the size of a horse, directing the offensive: Haborym, who appeared as a handsome man in body, but possessed three heads--one of a serpent, a man, and a cat. In its hands the demon carried a lit firebrand with which it sprayed flames so intense upon a group of retreating riflemen they disintegrated into white ash. The sight was a horror even to the Nameless, but Haborym's heads bellowed with unholy laughter.

Once the line had been breached and the rout began, the Damned poured down Cannon Street, driven by the Voice and Haborym's ruthless prodding, and at first the Nameless did not know to what end the assault was for until he saw the baroque dome of St. Paul's Cathedral rising from beyond the thick billowing smoke.

$$\text{♉}$$

A pounding on the front door woke Calvin with a start and he lurched from the chair he'd nodded off in, hand automatically pulling the Webley from his waist before he was fully on his feet. The grandfather clock in the parlour room's corner read half past three, which told Calvin he'd slept barely twenty minutes, yet despite the lateness of the hour the room was lit with a soft amber glow from the flaming sky; under other circumstances the way the furniture and decorations were illuminated would have been picaresque, but as it were it seemed an ill omen.

There was another furious hammering at the door, followed by muffled cries for help that had become all-too-common since the attack upon London began. But not every entreaty was necessarily genuine: Calvin had witnessed his fair share of looters and ruffians taking advantage of the chaos. Calvin walked to the closed door, grip tight on the revolver.

"Go away!" He shouted. "We've no food or water here!"

There was a pause, then another plea, one that took Calvin by surprise: "Father? Father, let us in. Please."

"Anne?" Calvin asked, turning the knob almost involuntarily. Part of him remained cautious, but his daughter's voice was unmistakable; when the door was open Calvin saw Anne standing on the step with a group of strangers, all of them looking ragged and filthy and exhausted. When Anne had departed two days earlier, she'd been in her finest dress, hair coifed neatly beneath a bonnet; now her clothes were torn and mud-spattered, her teenaged face bruised and scratched.

Calvin pulled his daughter close, but the embrace was short. One of those behind Anne, a bloodied, grey-headed vicar, tried to shove through the door. Calvin blocked him, raising the revolver.

"My daughter may stay. There is no harbour for the rest."

Anne glanced at the vicar, then to Calvin. "Please, Father, let them in. You don't understand what we've been through."

Calvin scrutinized the refugees. There were five all told: besides Anne and the vicar were a heavyset fellow in an expensive matched derby suit and a bowler hat and a woman who looked like a typical East End factory girl clutching a small boy. Two others he expected in the group, however, were nowhere to be seen.

"Where are your brothers?" He asked Anne, the hesitation before she spoke telling Calvin everything, and his heart sank.

"They're...They're dead, Father," she finally admitted, tears streaking down her face. "We made it no farther than Brentwood. Somehow those...those *demons* circled around and cut off the rail lines and roads out of Havering...I tried to hold onto Stuart and James, but there was too much commotion, too many people. Stuart stumbled and was trampled, but James...Oh, Father! It's too terrible to speak of!"

Anne buried herself, sobbing, in Calvin's chest, and slowly he lowered the Webley, motioning for the refugees to enter. Once they crossed the threshold, the man in the derby suit immediately went to the bottle of wine on the parlour room table, frowning when it proved empty. He tore a piece of bread from the half-eaten loaf, ate it, and was about to rip another when Calvin told him, "For the child first, sir."

He bristled, but begrudgingly did as he was told. The factory girl came over to Calvin, soot marring her otherwise attractive features, saying, "Don't pay no mind to Mr. Cornthwaite, sir. He told us he's from Hamstead and his whole house done burned down," she patted her scruffy boy on the head as he devoured the bread, and Calvin felt a pang. "My name's Margaret, by the by. Thank you for the shelter."

Martin's voice called out then, "What's all this ruckus, lad? And who are these people in my house?"

Calvin's uncle came down the stairs in his nightclothes, staring at the newcomers; when he spotted Anne his face drooped. "Anne? I thought you and your brothers would be well away from this madness by now," he glanced around the parlour. "Where *are* your sons, Calvin?"

"The devils took them," the vicar said, sitting down. "Just as they'll take us all."

"Devils?" Martin sneered. "Did they have horns and pitchforks? Perhaps the Russians will employ leprechauns and wood nymphs as hussars next."

The vicar furiously launched from the chair. "Do not mock me, sir! My entire congregation in Ipswich was massacred right before me not more than a week ago, from spinster to infant all! So do not presume to tell me our adversary is anything but from Satan's own dominion!"

"And do not presume to come into my house, an uninvited stranger, voicing such rubbish!" Martin roared back. The vicar shouted again, but Calvin heard the argument as if it was from far away. His only thoughts were of his sons, neither yet ten and already gone from the world, and he glanced at the hand holding the revolver; it trembled uncontrollably.

"Quiet! Both of you!" He yelled, and the two men silenced. "This is no time for division. Anne says these invaders are inhuman as well, uncle, and I believe my daughter."

"Is there no way out of the city then?" Martin sounded fearful for the first time. Calvin looked at Anne.

"By what way did you return?"

"Through Dagenham and Canning Town, but the whole of Barking and Newham are clogged with people, and the police have been unable to stop rioters and arsonists from burning half the buildings."

"I've seen much of that here, too." Calvin said.

There was a frantic cry from the street. Calvin went to the window; outside, an overstuffed wagonload of people clattered by, one of the passengers yelling, "Tower Bridge is on fire! Tower Bridge is on fire!"

The vicar tossed his hands up. "It's all over for us now!" He collapsed back into the chair, rocking back and forth, repeating, "It's over. It's all over."

"Get a hold of yourself, man," Martin chided, whispering to Calvin, "I want this madman out of my house!"

Before Calvin could reply, a dull rumbling, deeper than any artillery barrage, shook the ground; the windows in the house rattled, plaster from the ceiling broke loose, and the grandfather clock tipped on its side in front of Margaret and her child. As the quaking ceased Mr. Cornthwaite pointed out the cracked windowpane.

"By God! Look!"

In the distance a pillar of fire soared into the night, reaching higher than anything Calvin had ever seen.

A heartbeat later it began raining fire.

♉

There were many jewels coveted by the demons in their black campaign, none more so than those places dedicated to the reverence and worship of their great enemy, The Creator. Ever since the Incursion began it was the triumph of triumphs for the infernal commanders to capture, and spoil, and desecrate the churches and temples and mosques they came across. From quiet country chapels to vast Gothic abbeys, all offered delight, and the greater demons competed with one another for the chance at violation each presented, and if worshipers and holy men were discovered within, the pleasure only increased.

So it was in London there was no greater prize than St. Paul's. The cathedral was so awe-inspiring, so resplendent in its features that it became a lusted-for object, and Haborym was determined its legions would possess it after dislodging the defenders from Cannon Street.

The Damned surged up St. Paul's Churchyard and Newgate Street and stormed Ludgate Hill, finding thousands of The Creator's devoted cowering inside, those frightened or foolish enough to seek refuge from the invasion in His house and offer supplications that turned to screams as the Damned began their massacre.

Despite the boldness of the Inferno's war upon the world, there remained firm rules even the demons had to obey. Unlike the souls it marshaled, Haborym, being born of the nether-realms, could not set unholy foot upon the sacred ground to celebrate its victory; instead, the fiend commanded the Damned to use the blood of the slaughtered in the creation of a seal upon the cathedral's central nave to deconsecrate the area, allowing Haborym access. Once inside, the demon reveled in its small conquest, repeatedly striking the main altar with its firebrand, and soon the ground began to quiver, then split and fall away as a fiery chasm opened, spewing smoke and churning magma.

As the floor gave way, the walls shook, columns crumbled, and the dome itself cracked; the two towers of the west façade were failing as the fissure widened, sliding into the pit, and soon the whole of the cathedral disappeared like a ship sinking into an ocean of fire. There followed a series of ever-more violent spasms from the crevice where St. Paul's had stood, the quaking intensifying until a spire of flame erupted heavenward, bursting and showering incendiaries upon the portions of London thus far unscathed by the legions, and from the well-to-do estates of Greenwich and Blackheath to the immigrant enclaves and silk weaver's sweatshops of the East End, the city began to burn.

Dawn came, but the sky remained black, the sun blotted by the volcanic smoke from the wound in the earth Haborym had opened, and the Damned regrouped.

East, the Voice commanded, *So that The Dragon may soon come.*

♉

The terraced houses and shops and pubs all along Poplar High Street were ablaze. Everywhere, people desperate to escape the quick-moving flames swarmed into the road; fire brigades were overwhelmed, and soon lawlessness reigned throughout All Saints.

Calvin Woolery gripped his daughter's hand tightly as they rushed from his uncle's burning house, dodging a mass of carts and cabs and cycles. All around, the din of hysteria assailed the senses, and to Calvin the noise of the flames as they claimed building after building was like a thousand chariots beating together over stones. Close behind, Martin, Mr. Cornthwaite and the vicar staggered to the sidewalk; Martin, robe hastily thrown on over his nightclothes and carrying an armful of possessions, angrily protested the evacuation.

"My house! Damn the Tsar to hell!" He shouted, waving a defiant fist in the air; a second later a man on a bicycle collided with him, both of them tumbling to the ground, the assortment of coins and silverware Martin held scattering across the pavement. The man who'd struck him was dressed in a railway porter's outfit, and he scuttled to his feet, seething.

"Bloody Christ, you old bastard! Get out of my way!"

He grabbed his bicycle, still swearing as he rode off. Calvin hoisted Martin up; next to them the vicar raised arms to the still-black sky, then dropped to his knees, wailing, "This is the Revelation! The Day and the Hour has come! Mercy! Mercy on us all!"

Calvin reached for the vicar, but Mr. Cornthwaite intercepted his hand.

"Leave him, sir," he said, "The man's mind is gone. Just leave him."

Calvin hesitated but eventually turned away, rapidly losing sight of the vicar amid the crowd. Behind him there was a creaking from Martin's house as the roof caved in upon the upper floor, showering the street with cinders. Calvin dodged a chunk of falling masonry, but Margaret and her child were not so lucky; in the panic they had not fled quickly enough and the buckling front of the building crashed down upon them, the pair disappearing under the flaming rubble.

Martin unleashed a slew of obscenities, thrashing as Mr. Cornthwaite pulled him away from the blazing remains of the house and back towards Calvin.

"This is intolerable!" Martin yelled, angry tears rolling down his cheeks. "Where are we supposed to go? *Where?*"

Calvin had no answer to the question; his only immediate thought, like everyone else's, was escaping the maelstrom, but he possessed little in the way of an actual plan until Mr. Cornthwaite said, "The ferry from the Isle of Dogs to Greenwich might still be running. The roads south were passable yesterday afternoon."

"It may work," Calvin agreed, but before he could take a step something landed with aplomb on the street beside him; the way it wriggled and flopped he didn't recognize what it was, but then another hit the ground a yard away, flapping wildly and on fire, and Calvin realized what they were. *"Pigeons,"* he said, watching the flock of birds, their wings ignited by the inferno, fall from the sky. "The pigeons are on fire..."

A hot, rank breeze started up; the air in the East End always smelled foul from the noxious odors of factories and tanneries and the docks, but there was something else tainting the wind that now rankled Calvin's senses: the overpowering stench of sulfur.

"Make way!" Someone in the crowd shouted. "They're coming! The devils are coming!"

In the distance there was a shrieking made by neither man nor beast, a cacophonous, tortured howl, and from far down the burning street a figure appeared through the smoke, charging headlong into a throng of people, brandishing a long, sinister blade, quickly followed by a second attacker, and a third, before an entire host of them swarmed Poplar High Street like locusts, hacking and slashing at all in their path, their screeching worse than any Zulu war cry Calvin had heard. At first glance they looked like men, but their skin was blackened and blistered, eyes ember-red, and around their necks were collars of flame, linked between each like a chain, and to Calvin the lurid tales of demonic invasion seemed abruptly real.

Mr. Cornthwaite stumbled past Calvin and ran, but made it no more than a dozen paces when the closest of the skirmishers caught up with him, plunging its blade into his back. He gasped, blood spewing from his mouth, and Calvin instinctively fired the Webley at his attacker. The demon--what other word was there for it?--reeled from the closeness and force of the shot, a sputter of quick flame spurting from the wound, but the thing did not fall, only merely staggered a step before rebounding, withdrawing its weapon from Mr. Cornthwaite's fallen corpse and slashing at Anne. She screamed, and Calvin pushed her away, firing point blank at the creature; there was second burst of fire from its flesh, but the thing's momentum was too great and it tackled Calvin to the ground, the Webley slipping from his grasp.

Despite its ghastly appearance the attacker was no stronger than Calvin, but its skin was hot to the touch, its breath reeked of brimstone, and as they wrestled Calvin grabbed for the weapon it held, his own flesh searing when it brushed against the blade, and he swore from the pain.

The creature brought its weight to bear upon Calvin, its face coming so close to his that he could clearly make out features--the heavy brow, that off-center nose, the cleft chin--that seemed familiar to him despite the inhumanity of its guise. Yet only when Calvin's gaze locked with those burning eyes did he truly realize what he was struggling with; Martin noticed it at the same time, and Calvin heard his uncle feverishly cry, "Good Lord, it can't be! *Stephen?* It *can't* be!"

Until then the creature had been intent on driving its blade into Calvin's chest, but abruptly it relented in its assault. Lowering the weapon, the attacker looked down at Calvin even as it straddled him, and their eyes met again; this time Calvin saw not fury, but despair deeper than any bottomless pit.

The lull lasted only a moment. Shoving the brute back, Calvin snatched the Webley from where it had fallen, lashing the creature's skull before scrambling upright and practically dragging Anne with him down the street, Martin trailing close behind.

They went along blindly, turning down bystreets and alleys, wherever the fire wasn't, but as they neared Bow Lane and All Saints' Church, Anne stopped, slumping against a gas streetlamp.

"I can go no further," she rasped, face suddenly pale.

"Nonsense," Calvin pulled her up, shocked when his hand come back smeared with crimson; Anne quickly collapsed to the sidewalk, the spreading spider-web of blood splotching her soiled dress from the wound in her left side visible to Calvin. The demon's blade had found its mark after all.

Calvin tried to scream, but his mind was too numb, too full of the horrors that had been so swiftly thrust upon him, and he fell to his knees, frantically cradling Anne. Weak, she touched his face.

"Take me to the church, Father," she whispered, "I need to be cleansed of my sins..."

"You have committed no sin, Anne," Calvin said, burning tears welling up in his eyes. "If there's any sin here it belongs to me, for my failure to protect you and your brothers."

"Oh, but Father, I've done terrible things," Anne coughed, bloody spittle dotting her chin. "I did not tell the whole truth at the house. Stuart was indeed crushed by the crowd in Havering, but James...I knew there was no way out of London, knew we were all going to die horribly, and I thought surely you were already dead, Father. I just didn't want poor James to suffer, so we walked to the Thames...and I drowned him. Sweet boy he was, trusted me right up to when I held his head under the water..." Her voice grew faint. "I *murdered* him, Father. I wanted to protect him from those demons, and God above, now I'm going to *become* one..."

Anne coughed again, gurgled and choked, her body writhing in Calvin's arms before the life slipped out of her and she slackened, eyes open and staring yet seeing nothing. Calvin knelt there, the numbness spreading throughout him before he summoned enough strength to lift her body.

"Where are you going, lad?" Martin asked.

"She wanted to be in the church," Calvin replied. "That's where she's going."

Martin shook his head. "It's bloody pointless, lad. That milksop vicar was right. We're finished. *All* of us. Londoners. Britain. Everything. There's no salvation for anything now..." he pulled at his thinning hair. "I never thought The Devil and Hell more than pabulum to frighten the flock, but now I know how wrong I was," Martin grabbed Calvin's jacket. "That...that *demon* who attacked you and Anne--did you *see* its face, lad?"

Calvin nodded. "Yes. But it's not possible. It *couldn't* be *him*. You said so yourself."

"But it *was,* lad. I'd recognize my own brother anywhere, even after fifteen years in the grave," Martin's grip tightened. "That was *Stephen*. That was your *father."*

Hell had been cunning.

For untold millennia the Kings of the Abyss designed their campaign against Creation, and it had been decided early on that drafting the endless multitude of condemned souls as foot soldiers to spearhead the attack was essential, and much time was spent organizing the legions in such ways that the Damned would be intimate with their surroundings, so they would better know the terrain, the cities and villages, and the people with whom they were to war.

So it was when the Nameless One marched eastward after the destruction of St. Paul's that the memories of his past life became more vivid with each step. With no need for rest, or food, or any other worldly succor, the Damned pressed relentlessly on past Tower Hill and proceeded down the Ratcliffe Highway through St. George's Street East, and flashes of existence, like shards of glass, pierced his mind. First the visions came randomly, but as the column of dead souls moved unencumbered through High Street, Cock Hill and Broad Street to Limehouse and then to Poplar High Street, they became more intense and increasingly unpleasant, filled with the mean-spirited spitefulness of a life lost to drink and senseless violence, the reasons for his recruitment into Hell's invading force slowly making themselves clear.

It was as the legions entered All Saints Poplar that the Nameless realized he was where everything began and ended for him: *this* had been home. Was that not The White Hart, the pub that had claimed so many of his nights, now burning to the ground? And there--was that half-collapsed rubble the brothel he had repeatedly abandoned his wife to visit, and where his life had finished with a knife to the gullet?

There was no time for reflection despite the revelations; the sepulchral intonations from the Voice drowned all else with its constant urge--*forward, forward, forward*--and he could not help but obey, finding himself in the vanguard of the attack as the Damned stampeded into a crowd of alarmed civilians.

A house collapsed nearby, a handful of people narrowly eluding the falling ruins; one of them was an elderly man, white-headed, another portly and dressed in an expensive suit, yet a third man among them stood clasping a revolver, shielding a young woman from the debris; despite his shabby dockworker's clothes, the Nameless could tell this one was no stranger to battle.

The large man, however, was not so steadfast; as the Damned gained ground he ran, and the Nameless set after him, wolf to hind, thrusting obsidian blade through his spine. Before the corpse could even fall the dockworker opened fire, the bullet's sting enraging the Nameless, and he lashed out at the woman the dockworker protected, catching the girl by surprise and driving his blade under her left arm, between the ribs. The dockworker fired again, but the pain only further fueled the Nameless' ire, and he hurtled towards the man, both of them going to ground with crushing force, the revolver clattering out of the dockworker's hand. Together they were a jumble of limbs, and the Nameless swung his blade down, but the man grabbed his wrist, the pair wrestling to control the weapon.

As the dockworker strained under the weight of the struggle, the Nameless caught a glimpse of the man's eyes. Those eyes--*those eyes!*--where had he seen them before? From someone in his earthly life to be sure, but who? A friend? An enemy? No--*NO!* They were closer than that--a part of himself, were they not? Indeed, there they were-- the eyes of a son, grown to manhood and looking back at him.

From the sidewalk, the Nameless heard the elderly man cry out, "Good Lord, it can't be! *Stephen?* It *can't* be!" And that, too, sounded familiar.

Martin. His brother. But he hadn't been old before, had he? And that name, Stephen--why did it feel so wont?

Something roused in the Nameless that he had not felt since his unholy resurrection, and only rarely before that, and for the briefest of moments he remembered the boy who was now a man: Calvin. In his mind the Voice goaded him to kill, but the memories supplanted compulsions to perform another atrocity atop the ones he'd already committed, and he let the weapon fall to his side, simply staring into his son's eyes, wondering--was there recognition, a spark bridging the gap between living and dead? If there was it did not show, and Calvin retrieved the fallen revolver, striking the butt end against the Nameless' temple before escaping down the street, pulling the woman and Martin with him.

Watching them flee, The Nameless stood, looking then at the obsidian blade, thoughts of the innocent blood it had shed suddenly disgusting to him, and he threw the weapon down even as his fellow Damned rushed past, still eager for mayhem.

A gravity overcame him, like the very ground was trying to swallow him whole; somewhere deep within he knew what was coming and why, and all the horrors he had inflicted, both in life and afterwards, were washed away in one final kaleidoscopic wave and the last fragment from his existence fell into place, even as the Voice berated him.

You have failed us, soldier of darkness. Mercy has no place in Hell, and by showing such you shall burn until nothing that can be called man remains.

The tone was furious, yet even as the flames of immolation kissed him, the dead, damned soul tried to speak while his unholy vessel was dragged back through the embers into the furthest recesses of the Abyss. When the unquenchable fires began to engulf him once more, the words were lost, but Stephen Woolery was at last no longer nameless.

The churchyard surrounding All Saints' was a large garden enclosed by railings, its perimeter lined with trees, from the centre of which the church itself rose impressively, unscathed by the ruination surrounding it, the ionic columns of the portico supporting a steeple that towered over the terraced houses on adjoining streets.

A mass of people had assembled seeking safe haven, filling both interior and exterior beyond capacity with frightened fugitives praying to a suddenly distant God. Together, Calvin and Martin maneuvered through the crowded churchyard, the weight of Anne's body draining to Calvin's arms, though he barely felt the pain; his only goal was getting her inside--a futile gesture, but one that to Calvin signified the final act he as a father could perform for his daughter.

A man in a filthy coachman's uniform clawed at Anne's dress when Calvin and Martin passed, his eyes crazed as he tore at the fabric. "The body of Mary, all for me?" He said, repeating, "Pretty, pretty, pretty."

Martin shoved him back, but the coachman only laughed manically. Calvin didn't even look twice; the wounds to his spirit were too vicious for him to care. He just kept walking, up the steps and into the church itself.

Inside All Saints' were grand galleries on all sides and a raised, ornate cast-iron altar positioned in front of a cracked stained-glass window. As in the garden, people packed the building, stuffing each pew and kneeling on the floor in every available space, weeping endless lamentations. Despite the desperation, there was a strange, calm atmosphere inside the church, palpable to Calvin as he made his way toward the front altar, where he laid Anne's body on the floor. He knelt there, looking at her attractive, blood-speckled features, knowing that she, and Stuart and James too, would never enjoy life as he had, never grow to adulthood, marry or have children of their own, and the thought sickened him.

"My *father* killed her," Calvin said to Martin as he stood, the words unbelievable even as he spoke them, though he knew they were true.

"Your father was a brute. You and I both know that," Martin replied. "It doesn't surprise me a jot his soul ended up where it did."

Calvin could not argue with his uncle's statement; his father *had* been a brute, the man's meanness the keystone of Calvin's youthful memories. Before his mother's death from typhoid she had borne the brunt of his father's rages, and afterwards Calvin sought escape from the cruelty in the regiments, a place where, ironically, the harshness of his father's abuse had bequeathed a survival instinct that served him well.

"Will Anne be one of those demons like him, I wonder?" Calvin asked.

"Your daughter wasn't like Stephen."

"No, but you heard her. My father was many things, but murderer wasn't one of them, and if *he* is one of hell's soldiers, what will become of *her?*"

Martin somberly shook his head. "I...I don't know, lad. I truly don't."

Outside there was another rumble, perhaps from artillery, perhaps from something more wicked, and a chorus of uneasy screams rose from the assembly. Calvin was no theologian, and religion had never been a major facet in his working-man's life, but he had no doubt that Hell--whatever it proved to be--was responsible for the battle ravaging London, though whether the city, or Britain, or the world would survive whatever apocalypse had been unleashed was not for him to speculate. His war was over, and he had lost on all fronts. What happened from now on out, to himself and to England, was inconsequential. His daughter had confessed to murder, yet out of mercy, not malice; Calvin had killed, too-- willingly, if not eagerly--countless times in Africa. Did that mean *he* was damned? He glanced at the Webley. How many times had he fired that weapon in anger on the battlefield? How much blood had it shed?

"Do you believe in the Devil now, uncle?" Calvin asked. Martin slowly nodded.

"I've no choice, not after what we've seen."

That hollow numbness spread throughout Calvin once more, and he closed his eyes; opening them again, he could barely see Anne's body through the bitter, burning tears. "If the Devil truly is real, I pray he guides my soul steadier than God ever did," Calvin said, "For if my daughter is to be damned, then so shall I."

Quickly Calvin raised revolver to temple; from far away he heard his uncle scream, but before Martin could stop him, Calvin pulled the trigger, a white heat searing his final thought in the ether.

♉

Day, night, day, night; sky black as pitch, hour slipping into hour, few were able to distinguish between the two.

Despite the damage done to London, there remained flickers of hope in the resistance to the Incursion; the

Royal Engineers following volunteer forces retreating south of the Thames demolished each span across the river, from Tower Bridge to Blackfriars to Albert Bridge, in a bid to buy time for reinforcements moving up from Woking.

Soon after, the Damned, having advanced through All Saints Poplar and Blackwall, made their way to the Isle of Dogs, the legions wading into the waters only to find their infernal flesh blistering and melting as if the Thames flowed with acid, the sulfuric stench of their dissolving bodies thick on the wind, and Haborym recognized the ploy with equal parts rage and bemusement: the river had been blessed, and the entirety of the Thames now ran with holy water--a crude spiritual blockade, but one that was nonetheless effective, however temporarily.

Yet even as commanders on both sides reorganized and counted casualties, the fires of perdition opened and more souls from the abyss blossomed, black roses upon the earth, all of them moving upward through the pit to their ultimate destination.

And the Voice spoke to them, clear above the chaos:

The time has come to war with The Creator, to turn His world to blood and dust, it said, *You are the hordes of Damnation, and shall fight to the last, from the clay of the earth to the gates of Heaven.*

Then the flames were gone. No, not gone. Different. Fire still surrounded them, but now there were streets and carriages and buildings aflame.

Among them a soul stood, confused, the taste of brimstone in his mouth, bewildered by the anarchy around him.

"Forward," the Voice urged.

And Calvin obeyed.

ABOUT THE AUTHOR

Exposed to the weird worlds of horror, sci-fi and comics as a boy, DAMASCUS MINCEMEYER was ruined for life. Now a writer and artist of various strangeness, he's had stories appear in numerous anthologies, including *Fire: Demons, Dragons and Djinn, Earth: Giants, Golems and Gargoyles, Air: Slyphs, Spirits and Swan Maidens, Hear Me Roar, Bikers Vs The Undead, Monsters Vs Nazis, Mr Deadman Made Me Do It, Satan Is Your Friend, The Devil You Know, Crash Code, On Time, Trigger Warning: Hallucinations, Appalachian Horror, No Anesthetic, Death In the Deep* and many more. He's also had a (now out-of-print) collection of short fiction, *Where The Last Light Dies*, released by (the now-defunct) Deadman's Tome publishing, and spends his free time watching movies that he reviews for Critical Blast and fiddling around on Instagram @damascusundead666.

JUSTICE

Rose Strickman

"Nathan," said Edward, cigarette shaking in his hand, "I had the dream again."

Nathan Danvers sighed and leaned back in his chair, puffing his own cigarette. "What dream?"

"The one I've told you about!" The China plates rattled as Edward lurched forward in emphasis. "I've had it every night for over a week now!"

Nathan eyed his friend through the smoke. Before this business with the dream had started, Edward Sullivan had been a smooth, dapper individual, as befitted his position as Morning Falls's leading grocer: his hair oiled and combed, always neat in his suit, eyes bright and movements energetic. Now his suit hung off a frame gone thin and spare, his eyes were ringed with shadows, and his unshaven face was haunted. Nathan couldn't help glancing around the dining room of Ellman's Restaurant, hoping no one they knew was eating at any nearby tables.

"The dream about the tree?" Even to his own ears, Nathan's tone was dry and unsympathetic.

"You wouldn't sound like that if you'd had it yourself,"

31

snarled Edward. He nursed his cigarette, eyes brilliant with anxiety. "I wake up, or think I've woken up, by the tree— you know, the one we always use. It's always night, but I can see the tree. And the tree…*talks*. It recites every name we've ever written on it. I can't move as it talks louder and louder. And behind me there are people…people coming nearer and nearer." He trailed off, face going gray, eyes blank. "And—and I think there are people *in* the tree," he continued at last. "Every night I see them just a bit clearer. Two people sitting in the branches of the tree, watching me. And one of them…"

"One of them—what?" Nathan said when the silence stretched too long.

"I think one of them isn't human," Edward whispered. "I think one of them is…the Devil."

Despite himself, a shiver ran down Nathan's spine. He shook it off with a laugh. "The Devil!" He waved his cigarette, smoke wreathing in dismissal. "Edward, you're a grown man. It's just a *dream*."

"It's not just a dream." Edward's hand was shaking again. "It's…it's Nicholas Hopkins's spirit haunting me. I'm sure of it. He wants revenge."

"Revenge?" Nathan scoffed. "Nicholas Hopkins? How could he want revenge? We didn't do anything wrong. He talked back to a white man. That couldn't go unpunished. He knew that, as well as anyone."

"I know, I know," Edward said. "But Nathan—"

"No buts, Edward old man." Relenting, Nathan reached across the restaurant table to pat Edward on the shoulder. "Look, I think you may need a rest. Why don't you let Andrew run the grocery and take Mrs. Sullivan to the shore for a few days? Get some sea air. It'd do you a world of good. You'd come back fresh as a daisy."

"Maybe." But Edward's voice was a low, unconvinced murmur, and he avoided Nathan's eye.

Nathan sighed, stubbed out his cigarette, and signaled the waiter. "I'll pay for lunch, all right? You head home and get some rest."

"All right." Still Edward stared at the white tablecloth, not looking up as Nathan settled the tab with their server. "Eight nights," he said suddenly.

Nathan froze midway through standing up. "Pardon?"

"I've had the dream every night for eight nights," said Edward. "Tonight will be the ninth."

Despite the humid dining room and warm river breeze coming through the open windows, Nathan felt a chill. "Don't see why that's relevant," he said, forcing a bracing cheer into his voice. "Go *home*, Edward. Get a nap."

Edward nodded, still not looking at Nathan, and stood. Nathan guided him out onto the wide, open porch wrapped around Ellman's Restaurant. The finest dining establishment in Morning Falls, it overlooked the wide clear river, now lush with summer greenery, the trees bending down to kiss their reflections in the water. On so still a day, they could hear the distant thunder of the falls downstream. An emerald-green lawn ran down to the shore. In the middle of that lawn stood a huge old oak tree.

Edward stiffened and reeled back, stumbling against Nathan. "Nathan—!"

"What…?" Nathan followed his friend's horror-stricken gaze down the lawn, to the great old tree.

There was someone standing under it, he saw: a small dark someone. A colored woman, Nathan realized with a shudder of unease and distaste, one of the few left in Morning Falls. Nathan struggled to place her; he was sure he knew her from somewhere…Amanda, he remembered. Amanda Hopkins.

Another shiver ran down his spine. Amanda Hopkins, widow of Nicholas Hopkins, the last colored farmer in town, dead these two months. Amanda stood tall, staring unblinking at the two white men on the porch, and the summer breeze stirred her long pale dress, the apron she was forced to wear in public as a colored woman. Her gaze was unflinching, almost insolent, and Nathan felt anger stir in him.

He strode down the steps toward her. "You shouldn't be there, wench!"

Unbelievably, a faint smile touched her lips, proud and contemptuous. "Mr. Danvers." She gave a slight curtsy. "Mr. Sullivan."

Nathan glanced back over his shoulder to see Edward shaking like a leaf on the porch, bug-eyed as he stared at Amanda. Furious now, Nathan wheeled back on her— only to find her gone. The tree stood alone, leaves shushing in the breeze, shadows puzzling themselves over the lawn.

"Nathan!" Nathan whirled around again, to see Edward standing stiff as a board, staring at the tree with wide, horror-blanked eyes. "Nathan, do you *see?*"

"See what? Edward, get a hold of yourself!" Nathan ran back up the porch, wooden steps pounding hollow under his feet.

"The Devil." Edward's eyes were fixed on the tree, his face a terrible pasty gray. "It's the Devil in the tree. She's *summoned the Devil*, Nathan. And now he'll kill us all."

Nathan grabbed Edward by the lapels and shook him like a terrier with a rat. Edward gasped and sputtered, but he did tear his gaze from the tree, staring at Nathan in beseeching bewilderment and terror.

"There is no Devil in that tree," Nathan hissed. "There is no ghost, no curse. Your damn dreams mean nothing, Edward, and if you don't get a hold of yourself, I am going to get Dr. Armitage to commit you to a sanitorium. Now come on, I'm taking you home."

Edward whimpered but put up no resistance as Nathan, seething with rage and embarrassment, yanked him off the porch and led him down the street, back to his home and wife and away from the murmuring tree.

♉

Nathan heard the news the next morning.

He was lingering over his coffee, smoking a morning cigarette and perusing the latest newspaper from Portland, when the telephone rang. His wife Eleanor, who had been fussing about in the kitchen, bustled into the hallway to answer it.

"Hello?...Oh, good morning, Sarah...What!...Oh, no...Oh, Sarah, no...Have you called Dr. Armitage?...Hold on, honey, we'll be right there...Oh, Sarah...Yes, don't worry, we'll be there as soon as we can."

Eleanor hung up and rushed into the breakfast nook. "Get your jacket on," she ordered. "We're going to the Sullivans'."

"What for?" Nathan asked, though he had a sinking feeling that he already knew.

Eleanor confirmed his worst fears. "It's Edward. He's dead. Sarah found him dead in his bed this morning."

☿

The Sullivan house was in a subdued uproar when Nathan and Eleanor arrived, Sarah sitting sobbing in the front hall, her housekeeper and a few neighboring women murmuring over her. Eleanor shouldered through the crowd and Sarah nearly fell into her arms, wailing with tears. Upstairs, Nathan could hear men moving and talking: apparently someone had already had the presence of mind to call Dr. Charles Armitage and Police Chief Liam Prescott.

"What happened?" Nathan knew he sounded brusque, but his heart was pounding with a strange fear. "Mrs. Sullivan, what happened?"

"I-I f-found him this morning." Sarah's voice slipped and stuttered, her face white with shock. "We've b-been sl-sleeping separately. Since he started having n-nightmares. I th-thought he was taking too long to come down to breakfast. So I went in and—and he's dead! Bed full of leaves."

An icy prickle ran over Nathan's skin. "Leaves?" His voice came out high-pitched, shaking. Eleanor shot him a sharp, interrogative glance from her seat next to Sarah.

"Mr. Danvers?" Liam Prescott stood on the stair, badge glinting in the morning light streaming down from the window. "Could you come up here?"

Still cold, Nathan left the women and headed up the wide, dark-wood staircase. Liam's face, wreathed in the smoke of his cigarette, was grim as Nathan joined him on the landing. "There's something you need to see," Liam said, in a voice too low for Sarah or Eleanor to hear.

Nathan followed him down the carpeted corridor, past the paintings and photographs hung on the walls, into the small, papered room where Edward's body still lay. Dr. Charles Armitage, standing by the bed, stepped back for Nathan to see.

Edward's eyes were still open, staring at the ceiling with an expression of horrified shock. His face was frozen in a white rictus, his fists still clenched on the patchwork quilt, rucking it around his legs. And—Nathan's heart lurched— there were indeed leaves scattered in the bed, some of them fallen onto the rug. Green summer oak leaves.

"We don't know who might have put the leaves in his bed," murmured Liam. He stubbed out his cigarette. "But...show him, Charles."

The doctor took hold of Edward's jaw and tilted his head back, showing a red, abraded pattern on the corpse's throat. The twists of a rope, dug into pale flesh.

"He died of strangulation," Charles said. "Everything I've found points to it. But...we can't figure out *how*."

"He must've been kidnapped and hanged." Nathan was amazed by how calm his voice sounded. "Then they returned his body here."

"That's just it," said the police chief. "I can't find *any* signs of that happening. There's no hint that someone approached the house, no signs of a struggle—except in the bed, of course. Mrs. Sullivan says she heard nothing."

"Maybe the kidnappers hid their tracks?"

Liam made an impatient noise. "He was a grown man, Nathan. There's no way anyone could have abducted him without *some* sign that they did so, even if he was drugged. But there's nothing. From everything we've found, Edward was…hanged in his bed."

Hanged. The word echoed in the three men's ears like the clapper from an ominous bell. They eyed one another, fear lighting their faces.

Nathan pulled himself together. "We're being ridiculous," he said. "Jumping at shadows. There's some perfectly logical explanation. Meanwhile, we can't have this hurting the town chapter. We'll get these leaves cleaned up and hide the—the marks. Charles, you tell the ladies that Edward died of a heart attack or some such. Liam, you and I will tell the others in the chapter what happened and that someone might be—going after our chapter. Someone might be targeting us."

"But who?" Charles still looked fearful.

Nathan shook his head. "I don't know."

Across the bed, the shadows of tree leaves danced and swayed.

♉

"You don't look so good," said Eleanor that evening. She placed another slice of pie on his plate. "Eat something."

"Thanks, honey." Nathan gave his wife a wan smile. He hadn't gotten any work done at his legal practice, but spent all day roaming the town apprising chapter members of Edward's death. He could have called them up on the new party line—the chapter had paid for the town to have one installed—but didn't want to risk anyone listening in. The

37

story was bizarre enough, without rumors spreading and no doubt exaggerating the facts.

The other chapter members were shocked by Edward's death, but no one seemed inclined to accept Nathan's suspicions. "Are you *sure* it was a rope brand you saw?" more than one man said. "It could've just been a rash. Edward wasn't in the best of health. And how could *oak leaves* have ended up in his bed?" No one wanted to believe that Edward's death might have been foul play, and Nathan had a hard time believing it himself. After all, how could a man be hanged in his own bed?

"It *is* terrible, what happened to Mr. Sullivan," Eleanor continued. "Poor Sarah. I hear their sons are coming down from Seattle to help her settle the estate. After Sarah comes out of quarantine, of course." She shivered. "I thought the flu was over."

"Me too," Nathan murmured. Dr. Armitage had done a good job of disseminating misinformation on Edward's cause of death. It hadn't taken much convincing: memories of the Spanish influenza were still raw in Morning Falls. People had stayed away, and there was no danger of the coroner contradicting the official medical report: he was a member of the chapter too.

"God rest his soul," Nathan said. "And let's hope the influenza isn't back again." He finished off his pie and stood, pushing his chair back. As he did so, a noise sounded: a long, low creak.

He froze. "What was that?"

Eleanor looked up from clearing the table. "What, dear?"

"That sound." Nathan listened hard, but heard nothing more than the wind outside. "Like a...rope creaking."

Eleanor stared at him in concern. "Maybe you'd better go to bed, dear," she said at last. "It's been a long, hard day for all of us."

"Yes." Nathan erected a smile that felt fake on his own face. "You're probably right, honey."

Eleanor *was* right, Nathan decided later, as he and his wife were preparing for bed. It had been a long, hard, tragic day, and he was exhausted. No doubt he'd imagined the noise. Nathan snuggled into bed with Eleanor as she turned out the lamp, and was soon asleep.

The dream began with the rushing of leaves.

The wind sighed through luxuriant leaves, a long, languorous sweep. The tree branches waved above Nathan's head, alternately hiding and revealing the moon. Nathan stood before the tree, the night a rush of wind around him, and listened to the sighing of the tree.

…Henry Cottom…Juan Rodriguez dos Santos…James Wulf…

Ice coursed through Nathan's veins. It was talking, he realized through the rising terror: the tree was talking. The wind was shaping words out of the branches. It was shaping names.

…Tom Elliott…Eduardo Gomez…

At every name, Nathan's terror spiked higher, but he could not move, could not speak. He prayed desperately that the tree would not speak the final name.

But it did: *Nicholas Hopkins,* moaned the leaves and the wind, and a great sob rang out, the tree shivering with its force.

It was then that Nathan became aware of the two figures in the tree branches. Two figures, silhouetted in the night, sitting in the branches, staring down at him. One of them, the smaller, seemed human, but the other—the *other*—

Nathan awoke, a scream clawing his throat. The dark room spun around him. His pajamas were stuck to his skin with sweat. He struggled, kicking at the blankets, and Eleanor awoke, switching on the electric lamp. "Nathan! What is it? What's the matter?"

"Eleanor!" Nathan clung to her, sobbing like a child. The terror had followed him out of the nightmare, washing around his room in a malevolent flood. "I saw…the tree…"

"What tree?"

"I…I…" Nathan took one steadying breath, then another. "It's nothing," he said, his voice almost normal. "I—had a nightmare." The fear was receding now. He broke away from Eleanor gently. "I'm sorry for waking you, honey. Here, my pajamas are sweaty…"

Nathan avoided Eleanor's eye as he changed into clean pajamas, but he sensed his wife's concern and alarm, and he could not feel easy himself.

He did not sleep again that night.

♉

The next morning, Nathan was scratchy-eyed from lack of sleep, his head pounding. He did not have a good day at the office, unable to concentrate on the contract he was supposed to be reading, unable to respond to his colleagues' questions and comments. Unable to stop his eye from drifting to the window, with its view of the river and the forest beyond. The trees.

"Mr. Danvers?" Nathan jumped, blinking up at the concerned face of his clerk. "Are you all right?"

Nathan forced a smile. "Yes, I'm fine." He stood. "I think I just need some air. I'll grab lunch at Ellman's. You hold the fort here."

"Yes, sir." The young man still looked worried, but stood back as Nathan headed out of the office.

Outside, the day was warm and sticky. Nathan walked down the street, careful to keep his steps jaunty and nod to any leading townsmen he passed—all chapter members, of course. He must keep up his standing with the town and chapter, especially in this moment of crisis: he would not look weak.

At Ellman's, however, he found his footsteps curving away from the path to the front steps. He headed down the lawn, the river gleaming beyond. And the tree.

He slowed to a halt beneath its branches. It was a still, windless day, the distant falls droning, so the leaves lay silent, but its shade was deep and cool. The great bole, patterned with moss and lichen, loomed in a patchwork of light and shadow.

Nathan circled around the trunk to the bald patch on the other side, the place the chapter had stripped of bark, to gouge the list of names into the living wood. He read them all, one by one. Nine names, with *Nicholas Hopkins*, the newest, at the bottom.

Nine names. Why did that disturb him so? Nathan cast back, to Edward's frenzied descriptions of his nightmares: *I've had the dream every night for eight nights. Tonight will be the ninth.* And on the ninth night, Edward had died.

The wind hissed through the leaves.

The hair on Nathan's neck stood up. *There was no wind.*

He whirled around, breath catching in his lungs. And met the dark gaze of Amanda Hopkins.

She was clearly out shopping, her purchases in a basket under her arm. But she now stood on the lawn watching Nathan with the slightest trace of a smirk on her lips.

"You—!" Nathan lunged at her, only to pull back at what a ridiculous picture that would make: the town's leading lawyer charging at a colored widow.

Amanda's smile widened, as though reading his mind. "Good day, Mr. Danvers," she said, crisp and clear. "My condolences for your friend Mr. Sullivan."

And she turned on her heel, leaving Nathan alone under the tree.

♉

That night, the nightmare returned.

The tree chanted the names, nine names of nine men hissed out in a curse of leaves and wind. Nathan stood frozen with terror in its shadow, glimpses of the moon like a stabbing silver knife. And the two figures silhouett against the sky leaned forward, eager and fascinated, as behind him Nathan heard approaching footsteps—

Nathan managed not to scream as he woke, but it was a near thing, and he still woke up Eleanor. Perhaps his lack of sleep, and Eleanor's anxiety, accounted for the odd noises he kept thinking he heard the next morning: the creak of a rope, the low whisper of voices outside, always disappearing whenever he tried to concentrate on them.

"Nathan?" Eleanor, in the middle of placing breakfast before him, looked at him in concern. "What's the matter, dear?"

"Nothing, honey." Nathan gave her a quick smile as he sipped his coffee.

Eleanor wasn't fooled. "It's *not* nothing. This is the second night in a row you've woken up with nightmares. What's the matter?"

"Nothing!" It came out sharper than he'd intended, and Eleanor drew back, blinking. "Sorry, honey. I guess I'm just a little worn out."

"We all are." Eleanor came around the table to hug him, and Nathan, too weary and unnerved to resist, leaned into her soft warm side. "It was terrible what happened to Edward. The influenza, back again!" She shook her head, moving away. "I just pray there isn't going to be another outbreak."

Nathan felt a pinch of guilt at lying to his wife. "Yes, let's all pray."

"Still, life's got to go on." Eleanor bustled about, continuing with breakfast. "I hope I can hire a maid again soon," she muttered. "Someone affordable. Now that all the coloreds and Mexicans have left town, there's only white folks left."

"That's a good thing," Nathan said shortly.

"I know, dear, but whites are so expensive. I hear the Tomsons have gone already. There's only that widow woman left now, and once she's gone…"

That widow woman. The words rang in Nathan's head like

42

a bell. The widow woman. *Amanda Hopkins.*

Nathan leaped to his feet. Ignoring Eleanor's cry, he barely paused to grab his hat and jacket as he tore out of the house and dived into the automobile.

Morning Falls's colored and Mexican neighborhoods had once comprised a thriving area on the edge of town, full of neat cottages and little shops. But the chapter had done its work, and now the shops were shuttered, the cottages boarded up, already falling into ruin. Nathan drove past falling-down houses, rusting gates, weed-grown fields, to the final farm, on the other side of the river, at the very edge of the vast, ancient forest.

Amanda sat, grand as a queen, in her porch swing. Her face broke into a wide, white, sardonic grin as Nathan cut the engine and strode out. "Mr. Danvers. I thought I'd be seeing you."

Nathan stamped up the path through her garden. The massed scent of her herbs and flowers filled the air, contrasting with the heavy green scent of the forest beyond and making Nathan dizzy. But still he pressed on, driven by rage and a deep, nameless dread. "You—you— What have you done, witch?"

Amanda sucked on her teeth, leaning back to gaze at her porch ceiling. "You know, all those stories about making bargains with him," she murmured. "They're all wrong. You don't actually have to make a bargain to get his help, Mr. Danvers. You just have to ask in the right way."

"Who?" Nathan demanded in fury and confusion.

Amanda fixed her gaze back on him. "You know." Her grin widened.

The Devil, Edward's voice seemed to whisper in Nathan's ear, carried on the wind, in the whispering trees. *She's summoned…*

"The Devil." Nathan could only whisper it. Ice coursed through his veins. "You—you've called up the *Devil?*"

At this, Amanda Hopkins' smirk disappeared. She

stood up, looking down at Nathan as though he was some loathsome worm that had crawled out of her cesspit.

"Let me tell you something about the being we call the Devil, Mr. Danvers." Her voice was soft as a death sentence. "He is an angel still, and, like any angel, was created with only one intent, one absolute purpose. And that purpose wasn't evil, Mr. Danvers. It wasn't darkness or suffering or sin. It was *justice*. The Lord of Hell exists to punish evildoers. To deliver God's justice. And you and your precious *chapter*—with your white robes and your crosses and your evil tree—have certainly earned that justice." Her eyes flashed then, with a fire that was not of Earth. "Nine men," hissed the witch. "Nine innocent men you murdered, including my husband. Nine nights each, for *all* of you. Satan's justice has already taken Mr. Sullivan. Now he'll take you. You've already survived two nights, Nathan Danvers. Seven more and your time is up!"

"You…" Nathan tried to lunge at her, but she fixed her inhuman eyes on him and weakness and dizziness crashed over him like a Pacific wave. He staggered away, head spinning. He couldn't breathe. He stumbled back toward the car, unthinking, wanting only to escape.

"Yes, run away!" jeered Amanda. "Run back to your fine house, your polished silver and lace curtains! But you cannot escape what's coming, no more than Edward Sullivan could. You cannot escape the justice of Hell!"

Her laughter rang loud in Nathan's ears as he started the automobile and tore out of the ghost neighborhood in a cloud of dust.

♉

"We need to do something about that Hopkins wench," said Nathan the next day at lunch in Ellman's Restaurant.

After another night of Devil-ridden horror, he knew he had to act. If he did not remove Amanda Hopkins, he was doomed. But he would need the chapter's help, and so he needed to frame his request in just the right way. If he told the truth—that Amanda had summoned the Devil out of Hell to drive Nathan to his doom—no one would listen. While the chapter frequently likened their enemies to the Devil, and saw Satan's work throughout the modern world, none of them would care to admit that any of their number would be vulnerable to such an uncanny, unlikely thing as a curse. So Nathan, forcing his brain to work through the fog of exhaustion and terror, thought through his plan most carefully.

"Why's that?" Charles Armitage forked some eggs into his mouth. Around them, Ellman's buzzed with the lunch rush, and tobacco smoke hazed the air.

"That Negress…insulted me," Nathan said. "And she spat on Edward's memory. She said he was facing Hell's justice."

An angry murmur ran around the table, occupied as it was entirely with chapter members. "She can't get away with that," said Liam, stubbing out his cigarette in rage. "Any insult to a white man is an insult to *every* white man!"

"And she's sitting on prime land there." Timothy Evenfield, the largest landowner in town, had a speculative gleam in his eye. "No widowed Negress has the right to hog land all to herself."

"Exactly," said Nathan, pleased he didn't have to point that out himself. "We've all benefited from the colored town emptying out. We've bought us some fine property, ready to redevelop and benefit the white people of this town. Why should we let one old woman stand in our way? She's got no business staying here in Morning Falls. Or even Oregon itself."

"And Edward's funeral is in just a few days," Liam said, a ferocious scowl crossing his face. "We can't let one wench dishonor his memory like that. It would be an insult to him."

Another murmur of agreement. Nathan hid a smile. It

was all going even better than he'd hoped.

He let the other chapter members exchange a few more furious murmurs, their anger and disapproval heating up, before continuing. "So we're all agreed then? That Negress has to go?"

"Yes!" Liam threw down his napkin, and the others all raised a brief cheer.

"Tonight, then," said Nathan, joy and relief coursing through him. "We'll all go out and get her together."

♉

As night fell over the town, the forest an onyx shadow and the first stars wavering into view over the murmuring river, an automobile, its headlights turned off, crept up the dirt road, toward the faint lights of the Hopkins house. The driver cut the engine, and several figures, ghostly in their white robes and blank white hoods, climbed out.

They mounted the porch and kicked in the door. They needn't have bothered with such violence: Amanda had not locked her door. She stood in the front room, fully clothed, arms folded as her uninvited guests streamed in.

"I knew you'd come," she said.

"You know why we're here," said one of the intruders, voice slightly muffled under his hood. "You know what you've done. Now you'll face justice!"

Amanda Hopkins burst out laughing. The intruders drew back, milling, suddenly uncertain, as her laughter went on and on, loud and jeering.

"Oh, yes, *justice!*" she cackled, and put up no resistance as the intruders swarmed around her, bound her hand and foot, and dragged her out to the waiting car.

♉

Nathan stumbled home as dawn was breaking gray over the treetops, exhausted and euphoric. He threw aside his robes and crashed onto the sofa, too tired to go upstairs. Fleetingly, he wondered if the nightmare would come back, but then sleep fell over him like a wave of darkness, bearing him away.

Nathan awoke hours later, as the sun was slanting brilliant through the windows, to a sense of disbelieving peace. He lay on the sofa, blinking at the ceiling, listening to Eleanor puttering in the kitchen, and joy welled up in him. He hadn't suffered a single nightmare. The curse was truly gone!

Nathan bounded to his feet and ran into the kitchen, throwing his arms around Eleanor's waist. "Hey! What's all this for?" she giggled as he kissed her on the cheek.

"Can't I kiss the woman I love?" chuckled Nathan

She giggled again and turned in his arms to embrace him fully. "It's good to see you well again, my love," she murmured against his mouth. "I'll launder your robes."

Later that day, Nathan went into town, his footsteps brisk and jaunty, and headed straight to the park by Ellman's Restaurant. It was a pity, he reflected as the tall, lush oak hove into view, that the chapter had been unable to hang Amanda Hopkins from the tree, as was proper. But the chapter had never delivered justice to a woman before, and, as Liam had pointed out, it was unclear how the town would react. Best to keep it hidden.

Still, the sight of the tree, with its nine names carved into the wood, raised Nathan's spirits. He stepped into its shade and leaned an arm against it, regarding it with affection. Here was the visible symbol of the chapter's power here in Morning Falls, its power and protection and security. Amanda might not have met her end here, but she was buried outside of town, her body cold, and Nathan Danvers was safe.

There came a harsh caw overhead.

Nathan looked up to see a large crow hopping through the branches, flapping its wings and staring down at him with beady eyes. It cawed again and leaped to a lower branch, cocking its head and fluffing the feathers around its neck.

Nathan scowled, annoyed that his happy reverie had been disturbed. "Get!" He looked around for a stone to hurl, but found nothing. Meanwhile, the crow croaked again, harsh and mocking.

"Damn bird." Nathan turned away, fighting down a surge of unease. He was safe, he reminded himself. The witch was dead.

Behind him, the crow watched him go, eyes black and bright in the shelter of the tree.

♉

Nathan had another blissful sleep that night, and the next. He attended Edward's funeral the next day with a sense of heady relief and warm safety. The witch was truly dead, he thought, looking around the clean, whitewashed church, and he was surrounded by his own people. Indeed, the whole business was already starting to seem foolish and far-fetched. Amanda Hopkins hadn't been a witch who could summon the Devil; she'd just been a bitter, delusional old widow. Edward had been an idiot for allowing her to drive him to an untimely death, and Nathan had been equally foolish to even entertain the notion of her Satanic power. Standing up with the rest of the congregation before the flower-decked coffin, the pastor's voice sonorous in his ears, Nathan even felt a wriggle of guilt for Amanda's fate. But, on the whole, it was for the best. Her land and property would enrich the worthy in the town, rather than one lone colored woman. And her malevolence had certainly influenced Edward's death.

As the congregation sat down again, a muted caw rang out. Nathan turned his head to see a crow sitting on the windowsill, bathed in summer sunshine. It cawed again, voice muffled by the glass, and hopped.

"What is it, dear?" Eleanor, next to him, looked over too. "Oh. Just a crow." She frowned at him. "What's the matter, Nathan?"

Nathan forced himself to look away. "Nothing, honey." And it *was* nothing, he reminded himself, facing the pastor once more. The witch was dead and her evil, real or imagined, was gone forever.

♉

"…So the Hopkins estate is cleared up," Nathan finished his piece at the next chapter meeting. "Mrs. Hopkins died intestate, so there is nothing to stop Mr. Evenfield from buying her property. Assuming the judge agrees." He couldn't restrain a smirk, and a knowing laugh ran through the cigarette-hazed dining room of Ellman's Restaurant: the county judge, though he belonged to a different chapter, was one of them.

"Very satisfactory," said Liam, grinning around his smoke. "Congratulations, Mr. Evenfield. I trust we'll be seeing a corresponding rise in your donations to town charities, and your membership dues."

Timothy looked a bit disgruntled, but nodded. "Of course."

"Well," said Liam, "I think that about wraps it up. Thank you, Mr. Ellman, for allowing us the use of your dining room after hours."

William Ellman bowed courteously. "Anytime, Mr. Prescott."

"Before we go," continued Liam, interrupting a general rise to get to their feet and gather their jackets, "I think we should observe a minute's silence for Mr. Sullivan. He's only been nine days dead, after all."

A chill of alarm ran through Nathan at this. For a moment he couldn't think why, but then he remembered: Amanda had promised him nine nights of torment before his own death. This was the ninth night. He shook off the disturbing realization: he hadn't had a single nightmare since they'd disposed of the witch. Clearly the curse, if there ever was one, was neutralized.

Silence fell over the dining room as all the men, Nathan included, bent their heads and fell still, thinking of Edward and his tragic death.

The laughter rang like a gunshot.

The hairs stood up on Nathan's neck, and he jerked upright, staring around the restaurant for the source of the loud, mocking, derisive laughter. Around him, other chapter members sat upright too, cursing, and all eyes turned to the open window admitting a warm night breeze. There on the windowsill sat a single crow, almost invisible against the dark. Now that he'd identified the source of the laughter, it sounded much less human: it was clearly the crow staring in and cawing.

William bustled over, waving a towel. "Get out, bird!" He snapped the towel at the crow, which flapped away into the night, still cawing, still laughing.

Nathan sat frozen, staring after it. It was the same crow. He was certain of it. The crow that had been in the tree, and at the church. This was his third sighting. And something told him he would see the crow again.

Get a hold of yourself, man. Nathan fought down the fear, just as he had during his brief stint in battle during the Great War. He lit another cigarette, taking a deep soothing drag. *Nothing is going to happen. It's just a crow.*

Still, he was jittery as the meeting broke up and he headed out into the night, back to his house. The night's shadows hung deep and heavy over the town, the moon a mere curved sliver in the sky. But nothing happened on his way home. Eleanor had even left the porch light on for him.

Nathan let himself in and headed upstairs, quietly, so as not to disturb Eleanor. There was light under their bedroom door, but when he opened it, Eleanor was asleep, her mouth slightly open, her book slumped down in her lap. Nathan gently removed her book, careful to mark her place, and undressed quickly. "I love you, honey," he murmured, kissing his sleeping wife before turning off the lamp and settling down.

As Nathan's breathing evened and he fell still, a pair of wings fluttered at the window. The crow swooped in to land on the sill. It peered in, head cocked, eyes bright, waiting.

♉

Nathan stood before the tree.

It sighed and moaned in the night wind, clawing at the moon. Nathan stood frozen, staring. Trapped.

The tree took another gusting breath of wind. There were two figures silhouetted in its branches, Nathan saw with a paroxysm of terror. One was a crow, small and dark and feathered against the moon. The other…

This is a dream! he thought, mind skittering like a frantic insect. *Wake up!* But he couldn't wake, couldn't move, couldn't do anything at all as the tree began its dreadful chant:

…Henry Cottom…Juan Rodriguez dos Santos…James Wulf…

The crow winged down to a lower branch, where it sat, eyes bright as it stared down at Nathan. Carved into the wood, the names blazed with infernal fire.

…Tom Elliott…Eduardo Gomez…Ari Cohen…

Behind him, in the vast shadowed night, he could hear footsteps approaching. Multiple footsteps. Multiple men approaching.

…Sean Hennessy…Zachary Tillman…

Nathan knew the next and last name. His terror and dread gave him voice—"No!"—but the tree was merciless:

Nicholas Hopkins.

At the sound of her husband's name, Amanda assumed her human form again, shedding her feathers, emerging

51

like a butterfly from a black cocoon to stand over Nathan, eyes blazing with triumph and hatred. "Did you really think you could get rid of me, Mr. Danvers?" she asked, and cracked a loud, cawing laugh.

"Witch…witch…" Nathan heard the crazed, uncontrolled fear in his voice, but could do nothing to stop it. "We had every right…We did nothing wrong!"

"Oh, really?" Again Amanda's eyes glowed with that inhuman fire. "Well, why don't you ask them?"

Nathan whirled around, to find himself surrounded by a ring of white.

White robes, white hoods. Blank white masks, with only two holes cut for eyes. Robes that Nathan himself had worn. The robes of the chapter, of the Ku Klux Klan. But the sight brought no relief, no joy, only a sense of trapped panic, even as the first robed figure raised his hands to remove his hood.

It was no white man under that white hood, none of Nathan's friends or colleagues. The face underneath the hood was dark, his eyes burning with the same fire as Amanda's. The name fell into Nathan's mind: Henry Cottom. The very first man the town chapter had left hanging from the tree, sacrificed to inaugurate the Ku Klux Klan in the town of Morning Falls.

"Justice," said Henry Cottom, voice loud and clear.

Beside him, the next man took off his hood, revealing the face of Juan Rodriguez dos Santos, a Mexican storeowner who had refused to sell his shop and get out of town when ordered to by the Klan. "Justice," he said.

One by one, the men all removed their hoods, revealing the faces of colored men, Mexicans, Jews, Catholics, all those the Klan chapter had killed on the tree, and all spoke the same word: "Justice."

Finally, the last man raised long, elegant hands to lift off his hood. Nicholas Hopkins fixed his blazing stare on the shaking Nathan. "Justice," he said, and the word rang through Nathan, tolling his doom.

And then Nathan was turned around again, facing the tree, and he watched as the second figure stepped down, floated down, and he beheld at last the countenance of the entity Amanda Hopkins had summoned.

It was a man—no, it was a woman—it was both and neither. They were beautiful beyond all dreams of beauty—they were hideous enough to drive a mortal to insanity. Their wings were darkness and fire. Their horns curled in hair that was sable and flames and blood. Their body was perfect beyond perfection—it was a nightmare of monstrosity. Their eyes opened onto the abyss and the full glory of Heaven.

They were an angel. They were a demon. They were the Devil.

The Devil spoke.

You have sinned greatly, Nathan Danvers.

From somewhere—he had no idea where—Nathan found strength for a single word: "No."

Yes. You have spilled innocent blood.

The Devil's words stripped away all the lies Nathan had told himself, revealing the truth he had so carefully avoided for so many years: he had killed innocent people, and he'd enjoyed doing it. People who had committed no crime. People with souls like his own.

You have corrupted your immortal soul with evil and hatred.

Nathan remembered Klan ceremonies, the bloodthirsty excitement, reveling in the righteous hatred coursing through him. The flickering light of torches, of a blazing cross. The bulging eyes and protruded tongue of Henry Cottom, kidnapped from his own home and sacrificed on the branches of the oak tree for the sheer brutal imagery of it.

You have stolen the property of others, and driven families into exile.

The smug, covetous laughter of the Klan members as they divided Amanda Hopkins's property among themselves, theirs only because they had murdered her.

The non-white families of Morning Falls, packing up their automobiles and driving away forever, persecuted out of their homes.

You have used my name—the name of one of God's angels—to mask your own evil.

All those meetings, with all the chapter members crying out that the Devil had gotten into the town, the government, the Oregon State Legislature, and must be cast out with fire. Small, angry, evil men screaming that they must cast out the Devil.

You have spread your evil among others.

The townsfolk looking the other way, complicit in corruption and violence. Families taking pictures of themselves standing next to the murdered bodies hanging from the tree.

For justice was I created, and so justice I shall deliver, said the Devil. *The voice of a wronged and wounded soul summoned me, to beg for my judgment. And my judgment is this, Nathan Danvers: for your crimes, you have earned the greatest punishment. Your soul shall be cleansed of its sins in the fires of Hell until such time as it shall be pure once more.*

And the white-robed figures closed in, nine pairs of hands seizing Nathan, nine men hoisting him up, screaming and sobbing, as Amanda let the noose fall, dangling in the infernal light of the pit that had opened up at the tree's roots, a pit of darkness and fire, that rang with the screams of billions of tormented souls, billions of sinners, billions who had earned their just punishment with hatred and bloodshed and evil, even as Nathan had earned it, even as Nathan's head was forced into the noose, tight around his throat, and he was held suspended on the very edge of the cliff, the nine men waiting one last moment, one moment that lasted for eternity.

Do it, said the Devil.

And the nine men let go.

☿

The summer morning dawned bright and sunny in Morning Falls. Squirrels scampered, dogs barked and birds caroled from the trees. The sunlight touched the windowsill, touched the coal-black crow waiting there.

Movement within the house, as one of the figures in the bed—but not the other—stirred and woke. Eleanor Danvers stretched and, smiling sleepily, reached over to wake her husband.

Moments later, her screams cracked loud, blasting through the open window, sending a flock of sparrows spiraling into the sky. The crow, however, did not move. It waited, watching, as Eleanor, dashing aside green oak leaves, screamed and sobbed and shook the body of Nathan Danvers, trying desperately and futilely to wake him.

Only then did the crow flap away, with a single caw of satisfaction, and the air of one whose task was not yet done.

ABOUT THE AUTHOR

ROSE STRICKMAN is a speculative fiction writer living in Seattle, Washington. Her work has appeared in anthologies such as *That Hoodoo, Voodoo That You Do*, *Sword and Sorceress 32* and *Monsters in Spaaaace!*, as well as e-zines including *Luna Station Quarterly* and *Aurora Wolf*.

She has also self-published several novellas on Amazon. Please see her Amazon author's page at www.amazon.com/author/rosestrickman or connect on Facebook at www.facebook.com/rose.strickman.3/.

SIN TAXES

Tim McDaniel

Tommy "Toad" Tozer sloshed some more vodka into his glass. He thought about putting some ice in it, but it hardly seemed worth the effort, doomed as he was to an eternity of torment. Instead he slumped back into his chair and looked blearily over the patio at Roxroy Dinham, silhouetted against the last of the dying light as the sun set into the sea. "Sure you don't want some more?" he slurred.

"Oh, I'm doing fine, thanks," Roxroy said with an easy smile, his teeth white and even.

"You've been sipping that goddamn drink for an hour."

Roxroy just looked out over the veranda. "Beautiful night, isn't it?" He was sitting in a cushioned white wrought iron chair, at a matching table, looking at the horizon, where the sun was painting clouds with final blazes of red and yellow. "You've sure got a wonderful view here, Toad."

Toad sat his glass down heavily. "What the hell are you talking about? You're just next door. You got the same damn view."

Roxroy smiled at Toad. "You're right here on the

57

bluff."

Toad looked around. "Yeah." He took up the glass again for another long drink. His unwashed hair hung limp on his damp forehead, and his pores exuded alcohol fumes. A plastic surgeon would have a problem knowing where to start on his features, with his lump of a nose and close-set, shifty eyes -- but even they seemed stamped with a deep gloom.

"Something bothering you tonight, Toad? I don't think I've ever seen you so morose. Maybe you just miss Shalah. Is she still in Paris?"

Toad set the glass down and stared at it. "Nah, she got back from the shoot this afternoon," he said. "She's sleeping off the jetlag."

"Ah, the tough life of a supermodel. But she can't seem to stand being away from you for too long. Misses you, I guess."

"Yeah. She always comes back." Toad looked sideways at Roxroy. "I got that, at least. She always comes back. The other women, the forgotten birthdays, the topless-only rule, none of it gets to her. She always comes back."

Roxroy looked away. "She's an amazing woman," he said, his face wooden.

Toad chuckled without amusement and his upper lip curled in a cheerless smile. "You know all about that. You want her. Don't think I don't know. You're just crazy about that cute little piece of ass I've got up there."

Rox blushed and looked away, while Toad chuckled louder. "Well, you got the girl," Rox said. "You got the mansion, the money. So what's eating at you?" He took a delicate sip at his drink.

Toad took another drink, his amusement at Roxroy's expense evaporating. "Why the hell not say? What you gonna do? OK, then. Here goes. The Devil's got me by the balls, Rox. He's got me by the fucking balls."

"Some kind of business problem?" When Toad didn't answer, Roxroy continued. "It'll blow over, Toad. They always do. I've never seen anyone with your luck."

Toad laughed. "Luck!" He raised his glass. "Here's to luck. Luck's got nothing to do with it. It's a contract."

"A contract that even you can't wriggle out of? Hard to believe such a thing exists."

"I made this contract a long time ago," Toad said, staring into his glass. Then he looked up at Roxroy and chuckled. "I guess you musta wondered where I got..." he waved a hand around at the palatial mansion "..all this. A guy like me."

"Well, I guess we've all been a little curious, Toad. You've done very well for yourself." Roxroy leaned forward in his chair, his nostrils flaring just a bit.

Toad chuckled again, and took another drink. "I guess it can't hurt anything now," he said. "Might as well tell you." He stared at the outline of his dim reflection in the glass table.

"So?" Roxroy said, after a moment.

Toad roused himself. "I made a deal, a long time ago, Roxy. A deal with the devil."

"Really?" Roxroy licked his lips. "With whom, exactly? The Mafia? Some drug cartel? Spammers?"

"No, it's just like I said, damn it. The devil. Horns and forked tail, the whole bit. The goddamn devil. Only he called himself Stan." Toad finished the drink, and set the glass carefully down. Then he flicked it with his fingers and set it skittering across the table and off, to smash against the gray brick floor.

"I guess I don't know what you mean, Toad."

"How thick can you be? I made a deal with the devil, get it? And tomorrow afternoon, at one o'clock, he's showing up to collect. My soul. Which means I have to die at that particular time. You got it now?"

"Are you saying that you actually made a deal.."

"With the devil. That's exactly what I'm saying."

"I see." Roxroy brushed at his blonde hair, biting his lower lip, then took a breath. "What were the terms? I mean, what all did you get from this deal?"

"What did I get? This former part-time pimp, hustler, whatever, now I've got it all. I worded that contract real careful. I got a big fat pile of money right off, and I got women, health. Business deals that can't fall through, no loopholes nowhere. Oh, I had that damn guy! He kept trying stuff, you know? Kept squirming, talking fast. But I pinned him down. Just because I am what I am don't mean I didn't have smarts. Like, not only do I get the girl, she stays with me no matter what. I pinned him down on that. Got it in writing." He absently rubbed a scar on his thumb.

Roxroy sat back. "So.."

"But there was a time limit. There is always a time limit. I guess that's one thing that can't be changed. I got twenty-five years, and then... Hell, I was a kid. Twenty-five years? That seemed like a lifetime. Shit."

Toad stood up, swaying unsteadily on his feet. "I guess I'll go to bed. You can stay here, finish your drink, whatever. Trash the place if you want to. I won't care after tomorrow afternoon."

"No, I'd better get home. I got some things to do." Roxroy was on his feet, full of sudden energy. "Maybe I'll see you tomorrow, Toad. Good night."

"Yeah."

♉

"Who the hell is it?" The doorbell rang again, and Toad, wearing only his red silk robe over his flabbing body, rubbed his eyes. "I'm *coming*, already!"

He looked through the peephole, then drew back and opened the door. "Rox? Hey. What the hell are you doing here so early in the morning?" He ran a hand through his greasy hair.

"It's past nine, Mr. Tozer." Toad now noticed that behind Roxroy were several other men, all in dark blue suits, all with briefcases. Rox himself had changed from his customary shorts and Hawaiian shirt into an identical suit. "May we come in?"

"Who is it, honey?" Shalah called from the upstairs jacuzzi.

"How the hell should I know?" Toad called back. "What the shit is this?" he asked Roxroy.

"Mr. Tozer, there's something we have to discuss with you."

"Oh, what the hell. Come on in."

The men filed in, Roxroy at their lead, and took positions on the Italian-leather sofa.

"You, ah, you want a drink, Rox?"

"No, Mr. Tozer. Not while on duty. Please have a seat."

"'Duty'? What's this 'Mr. Tozer' shit, Rox?"

"Mr. Tozer, we've never been accurately introduced. I'm Roxroy Dinham, Special Agent for the Internal Revenue Service." Rox flashed his ID.

"The IRS? I thought you were in real estate."

"That was my cover, Mr. Tozer. The IRS has been interested in you for quite some time. And last night you finally revealed the source of your income."

Toad looked from one man to another. They were opening their briefcases on the coffee table, pulling out papers. "What is this, a joke?"

"Undeclared assets are no joke to the United States government, Mr. Tozer."

"Hey, all my businesses are legit!"

Rox looked at him. "Yes, and that initial 'fat pile of money', Mr. Tozer?"

"Hey, I know my rights! The IRS can't dig deeper than seven years. I got that money twenty-five years ago!"

"Normally, that would be correct, Mr. Tozer. However, in the Belial-Truman Agreement of '52, it was agreed that in cases of supernatural or deitic involvement, we could dig as far back as we need to."

Shalah came in, wearing nothing but a towel around her hips, and every man's eyes swung towards her. Every man's eyes except those of Toad, who had buried his face in his hands.

"What's going on?" Shalah asked.

"Don't worry, Shalah," said Rox. "We know you haven't done anything. You'll be fine. In fact, perhaps we could discuss your future. Tonight? Over dinner, say eight o'clock?"

Shalah looked at him blankly.

"I gotta call my lawyers," said Toad.

♉

They sat at the long dining room table, Roxroy and his fellow agents on one side, and four of Toad's lawyers on the other, pushing papers back and forth and talking in legalese about liabilities and undeclared assets and hefty fines.

Toad sat at the head of the table, a hand propping up each jowly cheek, a defeated downturn in his mouth, his eyes gazing blankly. Shalah -- fully clothed now, though most of the Bible Belt would disagree with that assertion -- stood behind him, her hands on his shoulders. Although, as always, she displayed like twin trophies her prize-winning breasts, her eyes were sorrowful.

Roxroy was sitting closest to Toad on the left. He tore his eyes away from Shalah, who had hardly glanced at him all morning. But that would change. And just maybe, in their future life together, Roxroy could convince her to maintain that topless-only rule that Toad had devised, though maybe only on alternate Saturdays or something instead of daily; unlike Toad, Rox as a man who appreciated moderation.

"Listen, Toad," he said quietly, leaning towards him. "You might as well call off your dogs. They're getting nowhere. There's no way you can weasel out of this."

Toad shifted his head to stare at a spot just behind Rox. "What difference does it make?" he said dully.

"What are you talking about?" Rox asked. "Don't you get it? We've got you. And it's far more than the initial undeclared gift. All of the business profits stemmed from that, and everything is now taxable. You'll be paying us back for year upon year. The profits from all of your companies and investments will go straight to the IRS. You'll be working for us the rest of your life."

"The rest of my life," Toad said. "Ha!"

As if that was a cue to a cosmic stage director -- and perhaps it was -- there was a sudden crash of indoor thunder, and a flash of light, bright as a welding torch, in the doorway to the living room, and a sudden reeking ball of dense, choking smoke -- a smoke from an overloaded crematorium, with a whiff of burning tires and (of course) brimstone.

And from the midst of the smoke and fire strode a shape -- a horned and cowled figure eight feet tall, skin a burnished red-orange, twin horns on its head, and a fringe of beard, obsidian and oily, around its mouth. Its eyes were yellow with tiny black pupils, gleaming with malevolence. He was naked except for a cloak, black lined with red satin, and the dense matted fur covering (most, though not enough, of) his groin continued down the impossible goat legs, shaggy with unwashed fleece.

The being swept the room with a gaze, and chuckled, a deep and mirthless sound.

"Stan!" said Toad in relief. "Thank God you're here!"

"Toad Tozer," the creature said. "The time appointed has come. Your death is at hand, and eternal agonies for your soul!"

"Whatever," Toad said. "Just get me away from these vultures." Toad stood up and straightened his jacket, looking awake and almost cheerful. Roxroy stood up too, and put a protective arm around Shalah. To his gratification, she clutched his lapel in terror, her eyes wide.

"Well, gents," said Toad, "you heard the man. I gotta go." He looked at Roxroy and grinned. "And so I guess you won't be garnishing my wages or taking away my profit margins, Rox, my dear old double-crossing friend. Nope. I'm way past all that! I had a good run, and at least I kept you guys from grabbing my stash. And now I'm ready to go."

He turned to face the creature. "Well, Stan, let's do it."

Stan threw out a hand towards Toad. "Very well. But it is a bit of a disappointment that you aren't cowering and pleading."

Roxroy had been told; he should have been prepared. But he was stunned for a moment. Then he found his voice, thin and uncertain as it was, as Toad and his keeper vanished in a roar of smoke and stench. "You can't escape the IRS that easily, Toad! We'll still take everything you have! We'll…" he trailed off into the empty air.

Then, before the smoke cleared, the demonic form had reappeared in the doorway, Toad behind him.

"Did you say you were from the IRS?" Stan asked.

Rox could only nod, sure that his outburst would result in an eternity of unimaginable pain for him, with hot fireplace pokers and implements with sharp, rusty edges.

"And you want to keep Toad here, alive?" Stan took a step towards Roxroy, branding a footprint into the white shag carpet.

"Y-yes," said Roxroy. "You see he, uh, he owes us money. An awful lot of money."

Stan's eyes glittered. "You will garnish his wages? Investigate his businesses? Scrutinize his dealings? Interview his mistresses?"

"Of course."

"He'll be ruined? Impoverished? Disgraced, and perhaps even embarrassed?"

"That's right."

"Then by all means, keep him!" said Stan, smiling. "I can wait my turn!"

Shalah left Roxroy's side and hurried to hug Toad, who seemed to not even notice. Instead he turned to Stan, aghast. "But we had a contract!" he said. "And the contract means I gotta go now! I can't crawl like a worm for the next forty years for these buzzards! You can't do this!" Spittle was flying from his mouth, and he collapsed to his knees.

"Sorry, Toad, I really am," Stan said. "But I have to extend our contract, to show the IRS some professional courtesy. We're in similar lines of work, and I deeply respect their achievements. They can make your life a living hell."

Toad whimpered.

"Thank you, uh, Stan," Roxroy said.

"My pleasure." With a swirl of his cloak, Stan turned away. "Later, Toad. I return now to my domain."

"One moment," Roxroy said, and Stan turned back to face him. "May I ask, are you a resident of this state, Stan?"

Stan laughed with a rumble. "I am," he said. "I reside in all corners of this universe, and beyond."

"I see. Do you have a business license?"

"A what?"

"A business license. I mean, you've been taking souls as stipulated in your contracts for, I would guess, quite some time. What would you estimate the value of these souls to be, in current dollars? We'll need to know that, in order to calculate your tax burden, you see."

Stan walked over the table. He stood, glowering down at Roxroy, then pulled out a chair and sat. "You would dare to do that -- to *me?*"

Rox gave Shalah one last, despairing glance. He wouldn't get the girl after all. But back to work. The amount he was about to rake in would make him quite a hero in the Service. There would be groupies.

"I'm sorry, Stan," he said. "But the IRS doesn't extend professional courtesies, not even to you. And I'm going to need to see some W-2's."

ABOUT THE AUTHOR

TIM MCDANIEL teaches English as a Second Language at Green River College, not far from Seattle. His short stories, mostly comedic, have appeared in a number of SF/F magazines, including *F&SF*, *Analog*, and *Asimov's*. He lives with his wife and dog, and his collection of plastic dinosaurs is the envy of all who encounter it.

His author page at Amazon.com is https://www.amazon.com/author/tim-mcdaniel and many of his stories are available at Simily.co.

THE KINGMAN DEAL
Troy Riser

1.   IN THE HOUSE OF THE DREAM GOD...

Uri Cohen had a long, restless night the night before and dozed off on the short, private flight from the city to The Paradise, his new client's hotel in the Catskills. Cohen had a strange dream while he slept, not a jumbled memory or a wish-fulfilling fantasy or a nightmare from the war, nothing like that.

In the dream Cohen was someone else, somewhere else, another time and place: leaf-thatched mud brick huts strung along the riverbank, the Holy Euphrates hidden from sight by high reeds as thick and tall as small trees, the sun a blinding hot yellow disk high in the sky, with heatwave ripples and shimmer rising off the rocks on the high ground, the permeating reek of rotting bodies filling his nostrils, a stench so cloying he could taste it at the roof of his mouth. The bodies of the fisherfolk littered the ground, but not randomly. These people had been arranged, he saw, executed in place so as to show the way, a line of corpses pointing like an arrow to the north—wait, no, not *like* an arrow; they *were* an arrow, with two of the bodies set at angles at the end to make the head of it. How the killer did this—and footprints showed only one killer—he didn't know. The victims had been unbound, on their knees. From their posture, they had knelt in the dirt and offered up their throats willingly.

Sorcery, then. The priest had been right. He ordered his men and the priest to stay behind and make sure the dead stayed dead while he and his driver reconnoitered ahead in the chariot. In the dream, the way was slow but steady on the hard-beaten path, but they had gone barely a league when the donkeys on the string, already skittish from the stink of blood and rot, became too balky and stubborn to go on, at which point he and his driver left the chariot behind and took up the trail on foot, bearing only spear and bow. They had gone only a short distance when his driver, Dagrim son of Jubalesh, paused and pointed to a plume of billowing black smoke rising up in the distance and said, "My lord, look!" Somewhere not far-off he heard a child's voice cry out, "A demon! A demon in the wilderness!"

2. THAT MOUNTAIN YOU SAW...

And then Cohen woke up, jarred awake by a sudden lurch of the plane, a single-engine Piper Comanche, as it caught in a crosswind. Cohen had a bad taste in his mouth and the beginnings of a headache, and it took him a moment to orient himself, remember who and where he was and why he was there. The dream had unsettled him. *A demon in the wilderness.*

So real, he thought. *Too* real.

The pilot (whose name Uri Cohen never caught) was still talking, unaware Cohen had dozed off. The pilot had talked nearly nonstop for the duration of the trip. A Yankees fan, the pilot was caught up in the home run chase between Maris and Mantle like seemingly everyone else in New York, to the point Cohen, a fan himself, was tired of talking about it and hearing it talked about. The pilot's voice was Brooklyn-accented chatter, noise, static, so Cohen tuned it out, letting it merge with the near-hypnotic drone of the engine and allowing his focus to fall on the heavily wooded mountainscape below.

Cohen was tall and lanky and broad in the chest and shoulders, making the cockpit close and cramped, and he was grateful the flight was almost over. Cohen had offered to make the drive from the city himself but his new client's Manhattan attorney, a small, nervous, expensively dressed park squirrel of a man named Klein, had insisted. Klein had been hazy on the details but his boss' problem, whatever it was, was urgent, and the advance had been big enough for Cohen not to care about details. Business, usually brisk, had been falling off for reasons he had yet to fathom, but now the lease to his office in Queens was paid. Betty was paid. Rent was paid. His car payment was paid. All was right with the world.

3.   A 1954 PACKARD CONVERTIBLE IS A WORK OF ART...

They landed in a small airstrip on a flat field south of Liberty, with a barn-sized single hangar and an old surplus Quonset hut serving as a radio shack in lieu of a tower. It would make sense, Cohen supposed, for Kingman to offer hops to and from the city for high-end clientele. Or maybe, Cohen thought, it served as a private airstrip for Benny Kingman's exclusive use. Kingman was a TV star, after all. His variety show was wildly popular. Kingman could afford it.

The pilot U-turned the plane at the end of the runway and taxied alongside the radio shack. A car was waiting close-by, an ebony black V-8 Packard Caribbean convertible with the top down so Cohen could glimpse its interior, the rich red leather of its seats. Cohen loved beautiful machines and this, Cohen thought, is a beautiful machine.

This is art, he thought.

A woman wearing a plaid button-down shirt and jeans and calf-length riding boots stepped from the radio shack while Cohen was taking his luggage from the storage well behind the cockpit. She was young—Cohen guessed about his secretary Betty's age, twenty-five or -six, petite where Betty was tall, wide-hipped and compact where Betty was angular and leggy, a shoulder-length brunette (tied back in a ponytail) where Betty was a bob-cut blonde. The confident, fluid way the woman moved was familiar.

Like a dancer, Cohen thought.

When the woman got close he looked at her hands first, a soldier's habit. Her fingers were unadorned with rings, her nails cut short, unpolished. Cohen glanced at her rounded, brightly pretty but not quite beautiful face. No makeup, not even lipstick, and Cohen's curiosity was piqued. The young woman didn't fit with what he knew of Kingman, notorious as a ladies man according to Betty. Betty had assembled a dossier when the job came up and had showed Cohen a sheaf of magazine and newspaper clippings. Most of the photos featuring Benny Kingman had been taken with glitzy starlets on his arm, all of the women glamorous, shapely, beautiful and blonde. Kingman had a type. This—she—wasn't it.

"Mr. Cohen? Alma Boch," she said. "I'm Mr. Kingman's niece."

Alma Boch sounded European, with a clipped, lilting, boarding school British accent, not a hint of New York in it. She flashed her even white teeth in a friendly, almost shy grin and her grip was firm and dry and he could feel the callouses on her palm he had half-expected to find there. He saw Alma had been sweating, with flecks and strands of hay in her hair, barn dust on her shirt and jeans. He imagined her in a stable of horses, mucking out the stalls with the hired help.

"Call me Spike," Cohen said, taking up his briefcase and valise and heading to the Packard, putting his bags on the floorboard in the back.

Alma slid in on the passenger side and put on a pair of round, pink-framed sunglasses she took from the glove compartment. "Keys are in it, Spike," she said, giving him that sunburst smile again and nodding at the Packard. "I saw the look you gave her. I think you might be in love."

The Packard started effortlessly, the big engine rumbling to life like a big jungle cat waking from a nap. Alma started to give directions but Cohen cut her short with a closed-mouth grin and a slight shake of his head. Cohen had seen the country from above coming in so he knew the topography. Interpreting aerial photographs had been one of his jobs during the war. His instructor at the SOE station at Gardener's End, a spinsterish, no-nonsense, middle-aged woman with a thick Yorkshire accent—she suffered no fools—would've been ashamed if he couldn't make it the few miles to The Paradise.

Neither Alma nor Spike spoke much on the way but it wasn't an uncomfortable, socially awkward silence. More like a sharing of the quiet, Cohen thought. He wasn't sure why he felt so at ease with this woman—she had the feel of an old friend—but he decided not to wonder or worry about it. Cohen had clicked with people before: that feeling of instant sympatico. It had been like that with Barry Carlisle, his old partner, Betty's father. It had been like that with Rachel, his late wife. Cohen glanced at Alma and saw Alma had been watching him in turn. Caught, she turned away quickly, red-faced. She's feeling it too, he thought, this whatever this is, this easy familiarity, this sense of connection.

Alma said something he couldn't hear over the engine and the wind.

"Sorry? What was that?"

She turned and looked at him. "I said, 'We could just

keep driving, you know. Just go where it takes us.'"

Cohen, startled, was at a loss. He started to reply but shook his head instead and focused on the road.

She laughed. "Admit it, you're tempted."

4.   THE VALET IS A VALET...

Cohen found his way to The Paradise and pulled up to the lobby entrance, stepped from the Packard, and handed off the keys to a uniformed, brightly smiling valet, and took a quick look around. The place was bustling, with couples and families streaming in and out of the double-doored entrance, people talking, children laughing. He looked up. The predominantly glass and brick main building had a vaguely pyramidal shape to its design, thrusting up from the ground and into the sky, dominating the landscape and clashing with the gently rounded hills ringing the grounds. This neo-modernistic ziggurat style felt out of place here but Cohen supposed its shape made a certain kind of sense given what he knew of Benny Kingman. Everything the man did, all Cohen had seen so far, had been flashy and exaggerated.

The rich aren't like us, Cohen thought. Good for us.

Cohen had been half-expecting Klein, Kingman's Manhattan attorney, would be there to meet them but the big, middle-aged man in the light gray, double-breasted suit looked nothing like a lawyer. The man sent to greet them looked, Cohen thought, like a retired prizefighter or soldier, his craggy face seamed with deep-cut lines, his nose broken at least once, his skin browned from a life in the sun. Cohen also noted the way the man surveyed the crowd, his stocky body still but his eyes roving, taking in his surroundings. A soldier then, a bodyguard. Cohen did some quick taking in of his own of the busy lobby and spotted two more men who didn't fit, who had the look: tall, clean-cut, athletic men lounging by the doors, one in a business suit, another in tennis shorts and shirt and shoes, a gym bag at his feet. Cohen could guess the contents of the bag.

Cohen wondered at the tight security. Kingman's a comedian, not a head of state, he thought, suppressing the urge to speculate, play out the possibilities. He didn't know enough yet. Cohen didn't, he admitted to himself, know anything.

Kingman's man introduced himself. Like many truly dangerous men in Cohen's experience, the big man was outwardly warm and genial, his voice a deep, gravely basso. His name was Leon Urbanski, call him Ski. Cohen could tell Ski liked that Cohen called himself Spike. Cohen guessed it was because Ski thought Spike was a kid's nickname Cohen had kept as a memento of the old neighborhood.

"You look like a Spike," Urbanski said, holding up a finger to a uniformed bellboy, who hurried over and took Cohen's luggage. They followed Urbanski behind the reception desk to a small service elevator at the end of the hall. The three of them crowded inside. Once inside, Cohen noted the quality of its fixtures, its carpeted floor and brass furnishings. Not a service elevator, a private elevator, Benny Kingman's private elevator.

"You made my men in the lobby, didn't you?" Urbanski said.

Cohen shrugged, suppressing a grin. "Three, counting the desk clerk. Desk clerks don't usually come that big. I wasn't sure about the valet, the kid who parked the Packard."

"The valet is a valet," Urbanski said. "He's a good kid."

Cohen didn't press Urbanski on why a television comedian needed a phalanx of armed bodyguards. If they wanted to tell him, they would tell him. If they didn't, he would find out on his own.

5. THAT ZANY, MADCAP KING OF COMEDY HIMSELF...

Aside from the two additional bodyguards flanking the massive oak desk, the first thing Cohen noticed about famous entertainer and TV personality Benny Kingman was Benny Kingman wore lifts, platform shoes. The shoes were expertly made, his trousers tailored to hide them, so it was something most would miss at a glance but Cohen wasn't most and spotted it when Kingman stepped around his desk to shake Cohen's hand. Kingman moved almost at a crouch, with a barely contained, manic energy, his mouth showing large white teeth fixed into a monkey-like grimace Kingman no doubt hoped exuded a happy-go-lucky confidence. It didn't work.

You're trying too hard, Cohen thought.

Close up, Cohen saw the man was wearing makeup. Not much, just a flesh-colored foundation to smooth the lines and obscure the shadows under his eyes, but it was there. Cohen didn't know entertainment types too well. Maybe this was normal.

"I've heard great things about you, Spike," Kingman said, clapping Cohen on the shoulder, giving it a squeeze while pumping his hand with the other. "When I reached out to my friends, they told me 'Benny, kid, You need a fixer. Get Spike, call Spike. You got a problem, he's the guy.'"

Cohen bristled inwardly at the term *fixer* but told himself to let it go. Cohen also didn't like people he didn't know putting hands on him, but he let that go, too.

Kingman motioned to the wet bar.

Cohen shook his head. "A little too early for me, thanks."

It was ten in the morning. Cohen hoped Kingman wasn't drunk—or worse, *a* drunk. Drunk clients at the first meet were typically a bad sign. Cohen couldn't—wouldn't—deal with alcoholics no matter how much money was involved. It was always messy and never worth it.

Kingman clapped his hands together. "Okay, folks, I need to speak with Mr. Cohen privately."

"You sure, boss?" Urbanski said. "I posted my boys in here for a reason."

"I'm sure, Ski," Kingman said. "Give me the room."

What reason? Cohen thought, picking up genuine concern in Urbanski's voice. Cohen had ran high-profile client security details before. Such assignments had been he and his partner Barry's bread-and-butter when they started out, guarding UN officials and dignitaries, the occasional corporate executive.

What are they guarding against?

After Urbanski and his men had filed out, Kingman motioned Cohen into one of the seats in front of his desk. Kingman's own chair behind the desk was high-backed black leather, the armrests organically extending from the frame, shaped in such a way it made Cohen think of the folds of an origami bird.

Kingman said, "You know Irving Frankel, right? I mean, him and me, we're not close-close. Our wives play in the same bridge club, do charity work together. We play golf together. I hate golf, stupid game, but what can you do? I heard the inside man for those mob guys was his own son-in-law. That true?"

"Clients count on my discretion, Mr. Kingman," Cohen said. "I never name names or talk specifics."

Kingman relaxed, leaned back in his chair, and steepled his fingers thoughtfully. "Good, that's good. Discretion is important. So is trust. I need to know I can trust you, Spike."

"I always play it straight with my clients." Cohen said, thinking *Cut to the chase, funny man*. Cagey clients were another bad sign.

"Yeah? Okay," Kingman said. "Like I said, I asked around. I heard all about you, all kinds of stuff. You know what I heard? I heard you were a big-time war hero. That true?"

The sudden shift in tone and topic caught Cohen off-guard. He gave Kingman his usual response.

"No, not me. I was a supply officer stateside," Cohen said.

The supply officer story usually worked because Cohen knew enough about logistics to speak the language. He looked down at his shoes. "I wanted to go overseas, I put in for it, but I guess the Army thought I was needed right where I was."

Cohen tried not to overplay it. If someone at the gym asked about the old bullet hole on his back, Cohen would explain it away as a hunting accident. The burn scar running from the underside of his left wrist to the bend of his elbow was spilled grease, clumsy me. Only his late wife and a few other women had seen the zipperlike bayonet scar on his upper thigh. Cohen had been careless on that mission, overconfident, sure the German was dead, and had paid for it. But this was part of his life he never talked about—couldn't by law talk about for another 30 years—yet somehow Kingman *knew*. This little schmuck *knew*.

Kingman smiled his toothy showbiz smile and went on as if he hadn't heard. "That ain't what I heard. I heard you jumped behind the lines, scaled the wall of a castle—a castle! Killed this high-ranking Nazi and then shot your way out of that place like a regular one-man army. I mean, Oy vey, pal! What a mensch! Like a hero in a movie! Hard to believe."

"Not so hard to believe," Alma said softly.

Cohen barely heard her. He was seething. Whoever had given this story up to Benny Kingman had altered details just enough to deny a security breach. Only a tiny handful of people even knew about that mission and most in the know were dead. Wild Bill was dead. Barry was dead. Kovarovski, their Polish contact, was dead. Codename Plain Jane was dead—years after the war and from natural causes no less, a surprise to everyone who had known her (and probably even Jane herself).

Leaving only Wendell Choate at State, Cohen thought, where *State* meant *CIA*. The sudden, drastic drop-off in his business, the troubles with the bank loan and the lease, the unanswered calls to formerly faithful clients, it all made sense now.

Choate's been a busy boy, Cohen thought. Choate had directed him here, herding him like cattle through the chute. And he was using funny man here as a cutout.

Cohen's assessment of the situation took only moments. It was his gift.

Cohen looked coolly across the big desk at Benny Kingman. Kingman, who had been sporting a goofy gotcha grin, sobered when he saw Cohen's expression. His manner became conciliatory, apologetic.

"Oh, hey, Spike, sorry. Nobody likes talking about the war. Those were terrible days for all of us, terrible. I lost family over there. We all lost…so much. I didn't mean to bring back any bad memories."

Cohen kept it cool and calm. "So what's your story, Mr. Kingman? How can I help?"

Kingman rummaged in drawer of his desk and produced a thick manila folder. He slid it over to Cohen, who picked it up started going through the photocopied pages. The bulk of the contents were pictures, some professional, some amateur. Locale varied: high society soiree-type social events, formal ballroom affairs, parties, musical performances, clubs, cafes, coffeehouses, restaurants. He recognized many of the faces: famous show business personalities like Benny Kingman, sports figures, politicians, the jet set crowd. The documents, what few there were, were handwritten surveillance logs noting places and times, tying them to the photos by number. Cohen had kept such logs, himself.

"What am I looking at?" Cohen asked. He had no context.

"More like *who*," Kingman said. "Check out the common denominator: tall, dark-haired, well-dressed—he's there if you look."

Cohen looked and—after a moment—found the man just as Kingman had described: a tall, dark-haired, fashionably and expensively dressed Caucasian male always on the fringes, never at the center. The dark man was like a skittish relative in a family group shot. One thing jumped out: none of the pictures clearly showed his face, either full-on or in profile, with all blurred as if his face—just his face and nothing else—was in constant movement. Cohen noted it and kept going, riffling through the photographs, and then suddenly stopped.

"The Inaugural Ball last January," Cohen said aloud.

Benny caught Cohen's surprised expression. "The one with Jackie? Yeah, that stopped me, too."

High up enough to be invited and close enough to kiss the hand of the First Lady, Cohen thought. This explains CIA involvement. But why use Kingman as a cutout? Why me?

"He calls himself de Lumière," Kingman said, his voice low and conspiratorial, almost a whisper. "*Porteur de Lumière.*"

"Light bearer, right," Cohen said dryly. "Obvious alias. Odd he would be so brazen about it. French national?"

"Nobody knows where he's from," Kingman said.

Cohen closed the folder and put it back on Benny Kingman's desk. "So what do you need from me?"

"Find him for me," Kingman said. "Find this de Lumière." The way Kingman spat the name caught Cohen's attention. Whatever this business was about, it came off as personal, at least to Kingman.

"So that's it, that's all? Just find the guy, nothing else?"

"Yeah, that's right: just find the guy."

Play it out, Cohen thought. He tapped the top of the folder. "This isn't nearly enough, Mr. Kingman. The more you give me, the more effective I can be."

Kingman was becoming visibly agitated; rather, more agitated than Cohen guessed was usual. In his head Cohen pictured a sputtering dynamo, shooting sparks everywhere.

"So find more," Kingman said. "You advertise as a problem solver, yeah? So solve the problem, figure it out. Be the fixer they say you are."

That word again, Cohen thought, disliking Kingman more by the minute. "Say I do find him, then what?"

Kingman said, "Then *bupkes*. You find him and you tell me where he is and what he's doing. Then you get paid the balance. We'll take it from there."

Cohen shook his head. "That won't work."

"'That won't work'? What do you mean, 'That won't work'?" Kingman took a deep breath and started to go on but Cohen raised his hand to cut him off.

Cohen leaned forward in the chair. Some of his pent-up frustration started showing through as an edge to his voice. "You know that fun little war story you told about me? The people who shared that highly confidential information with you apparently want de Lumière, too. These are serious men, Mr. Kingman. Their involvement tells me this is serious business. I need details. What's he to you? What's he to them?"

"Hey, look, I swear I don't know what people you're talking about, Spike," Kingman said. "I'm not in this with anyone. I talked to people, sure, like my pal Frankel. He's the one who gave me your name. I had my guy Ski check you out. Who wouldn't? But these people you're talking about, them I don't know."

Cohen studied Kingman closely. The comic's confusion seemed real enough but Cohen couldn't be sure. Benny Kingman's shtick wasn't Shakespeare but it still made him technically an actor. He did skits. He played roles. A poker player, Cohen knew Kingman had tells—everyone does—but Cohen didn't yet know the man well enough to read them.

"Talk to me, Benny."

Several seconds of silence passed. Kingman started to speak, then stopped. Finally, he let out a deep breath and said, "You religious, Cohen?"

"Not religious, no," Cohen said. He didn't elaborate.

"Then you won't believe me," Kingman said. "I mean, it's happening to me and even I don't believe it."

Cohen saw where this was going—the very name of the target gave it away—and felt a grudging admiration for Wendell Choate at CIA. Exploiting a flake like Benny Kingman as an unwitting cutout for an off-book domestic operation was a stroke of near-genius.

"This de Lumière, he isn't a man," Benny Kingman said. His pudgy face was pale, the makeup sweated away, and his eyes were wide and frightened. After a moment, Kingman collected himself, taking a deep breath and exhaling slowly, relaxing his grip on the edge of his desk. "He's the Devil," Kingman said. "THE Devil, the real deal. I don't mean it as a figure of speech."

Cohen kept his face impassive. "That's new."

"It's true," Alma said. "He's telling the truth. The Devil is real. It's all real."

Kingman's face reddened. "You laugh or smile or smirk or so much as roll your eyes at me, Cohen, and you're finished, we are finished. I won't be laughed at." Famous TV funny man Benny Kingman caught himself as the irony and import of what he had said struck home. He barked a bitter laugh. He looked about to cry.

Cohen thought, They think this de Lumière character is the devil, no, wait: THE Devil. Bemused, Cohen thought for a long moment how to play it. This wasn't all CIA pretext. Unless someone touched-up the photographs (always a possibility), de Lumière existed. He was real.

Cohen looked up and saw Kingman and his niece Alma staring at him expectantly, gauging his reaction. Cohen said, "Look, Benny, you're the client. I never laugh at a client. I also never laugh at five grand. So go ahead, I'm listening. Leave nothing out."

6. IN WHICH BENNY KINGMAN SELLS HIS SOUL FOR A FEW LAUGHS…

"I got my start here," Benny Kingman said. "I mean, not *here*-here—I built this place—but you know what I mean."

Cohen said, "You went from Borsht Belt comic to sudden, overnight success. I know your story, Benny. Everybody knows your story."

"I was going nowhere," Kingman said, going on as if he hadn't heard. "Writing my own material and to be honest, looking back, my stuff wasn't very good. I had solid delivery, okay? The timing was there. But it was like my act was…" Kingman trailed off, searching for the right word.

"Embryonic," Alma said helpfully.

Kingman made a so-so gesture with his hand. "It was missing something. I was young. I didn't know what I didn't know, you know what I'm saying?"

"And then de Lumière came along," Cohen said.

Kingman nodded. "Not so much *came along* as always there. I was playing clubs all over back then: New York, Atlantic City, Philly, even these little podunk towns that only know Jews from The Bible. They loved me in those places. And that's when I started seeing him, this de Lumière, always there, every night. He's a very distinctive-looking guy."

"Was he alone?"

Kingman shook his head. "He always had his people with him."

"His people? An entourage?" Cohen said. "Men or women?"

"Both," Kingman said. "They really stood out."

"Stood out how?"

"Clothes, the way they sat, the drinks they ordered, the way they talked and moved—artsy, East Village beatnik types. And Greek god beautiful, you know what I mean?

Perfect-looking." Kingman paused, searching for the right word. "Symmetrical," he said. "They started showing up almost every night at nearly every venue I played. Another thing, too: none of them ever laughed. Who comes to comedy clubs every night and never laughs? That should've tipped me off right there."

"And then de Lumière made his approach," Cohen said.

Kingman said, "This guy never *does* anything, you know what I mean? He's got these people—I guess they're all on his payroll—and they do for him. So no, this guy doesn't *approach* anybody. You go to him or his people come to you. In my case, he sent a girl. She came to my dressing room, pretty young thing, perfect like all the rest. She didn't say anything. Just handed me a plain, brown-wrapped box and walked away…" Kingman trailed off. Frowning, he swiveled on his big chair and looked out the west window of his office. The window took up most of the wall and gave Kingman an unimpeded view of the forests and hills. Cohen could swear the man was striking a pose. This is, Cohen thought, Benny's Thoughtful Look; rather, what Benny thought a thoughtful look looked like.

Cohen broke the moment. "Stay with me here, Benny. What was in the package?"

Unable to sit still, Kingman got up from his fancy bird chair and began to pace the office, his hands clasped tightly behind his back in a way that made him seem almost birdlike, a fat pigeon on a wire.

"Jokes," Kingman said, "500 typewritten pages of jokes, skits, sketches, funny stories, observations—you know, slice-of-life kind of stuff. Audiences eat that up. Catchphrases, comebacks, monologues, you name it, it was there, pages and pages. All new, nothing I'd ever seen before, none of it stolen and all of it good, the best material I've ever seen and you know what? It was mine."

Kingman flopped back in his chair. When he spoke, there was an almost plaintive note in his voice. "I mean, it read and sounded like something I would've written if I had any real talent. It was in my voice, only I didn't do it." Kingman shook his head. "Hard thing to describe."

Listening to Benny Kingman, Cohen realized the only way he could make this work would be if he treated this as just another case and this de Lumière character as just another shady operator, which he knew to be the truth, anyway.

"So no talk about payment?" Cohen said.

"Not right then, not at first. Then things started happening."

"Your career took off," Cohen said.

"Like a rocket," Kingman said. "A studio casting agent out with his wife caught my act in Newark and liked what he saw and got me that part in *Penny For Your Thoughts*, that Marty Schaumberg musical—not a bit part, either. I'm not a song and dance man but I did okay. People knew my name and my face after that. Offers started coming in."

"You were on your way," Cohen said.

Kingman nodded and then leaned forward and put his face in his hands, his elbows propping him up. His hands were trembling. "You could say that."

This is a performance, Cohen thought.

Then Kingman's secretary knocked softly at the office door and came in. Cohen didn't turn to look at her but he caught her scent as she breezed by.

Honeysuckle, he thought. Lilacs. Something else he couldn't identify or define, a lingering, earthy musk he guessed was the actual smell of her body.

Kingman's secretary was, he decided, the most beautiful woman he had ever seen—Hedy Lamarr movie star beautiful, only blonde, with long, luxuriant yellow-blonde hair the color and shine of molten gold.

Now this is Benny's type, Cohen thought, remembering Betty's research.

Kingman's secretary made her way around behind the desk to Kingman and handed him a handwritten note. She wore a conservative, buttoned-up floral print summer dress that went below the knee, but the outlines and curves of her figure came through, her full, perfectly shaped, rounded breasts straining at the buttons as if any moment they would burst forth full of promise. When the woman looked up and glanced his way and smiled, Cohen saw her lips were luscious and red, naturally so, without lipstick, and her eyes were a striking light blue.

Aquamarine, her eyes are aquamarine.

To his right, Alma Boch snorted through her nose and chuckled softly in amusement. Embarrassed by his reaction, Cohen turned and caught Alma's glance, saw her roll her eyes and silently mouth the word *men* in mock exasperation.

Kingman's secretary said, "I know you wanted no interruptions, Mr. Kingman, but it's Mr. Rausch on line three. He says it's 'vitally important, critically important' that you pick up." Her voice alternated from lightly melodic to husky and low when imitating Rausch, the man on the phone. Cohen thought he caught a faint French accent just under the surface, just a hint, but there.

"Thank you, Giselle. Sounds important!" Kingman said loudly, as if delivering a punchline onstage. Cohen noticed Kingman's focus was solely on his secretary, his features fixed in an expression Cohen could only read as adoring.

Like a lovestruck schoolboy, Cohen thought, and on the heels of that, *You're one to talk.* Alma's voice, he thought. He turned and gave her a puzzled look, pointed to his ear. *You say something?*

Alma shook her head and shrugged. He thought he saw a smirk but couldn't be sure.

Kingman picked up his telephone, his hand over the mouthpiece of the receiver, and looked up at Cohen. "Tommy Rausch is my agent. I've got to take this. We can pick this up again later, yeah? You've got a room? Everything you need?"

Cohen was tempted to insist Kingman finish his story,

see their interview through—so much more Cohen needed to know—but he let the temptation go and rose to leave. He needed to sort things out, separate the threads, figure out his role in all this, what Choate wanted from him. He saw Alma had risen, as well.

"I'll show you to your room," Alma said, her expression unreadable.

Cohen followed her from the office, feeling oddly out-of-sorts, similar to the way he had felt when he had first awakened from the dream earlier, on the flight in. Maybe, he thought, it was the strange turn everything had taken since he had arrived at this place. His surroundings felt unreal, detached. It was as if the dream on the plane was still going on, only the time and place and faces had changed.

Cohen considered calling Betty from the pay phone downstairs in the lobby. The urge to hear a voice he trusted was strong. Betty was real. None of this seemed to be.

7. ALMA BOCH OPENS UP...

Urbanski and two of his men were waiting next to the common elevator across from Benny Kingman's office suite. Aside from a neatly uniformed maid pushing her cart a few doors down in the hallway, there was no one else around, no guests—which is strange, Cohen thought, given this is July, the height of the season. The place should be packed.

"You want I should put one of my guys on your room, Spike?" Urbanski said.

Stepping onto the elevator with Alma, Cohen gave a rare smile and shook his head as the door closed. He knew Urbanski probably worked for Choate but couldn't help but like the big man. He and Urbanski were roughly the same age and Cohen had the sense his new friend Ski had been through it as he had been through it. They didn't know each other but they understood each other. It was like that. It was also true Uri Cohen had killed people he liked, one of them a friend. But that had been war and he wasn't at war, not anymore, and no way was Choate putting him back in it. He would find this de Lumière character, which was presumably also Choate's objective, and have done with it. Done with them.

"She likes you, you know," Alma said as they stepped from the elevator onto the second floor. "I could tell. She does that lingering come hither look of hers when she's interested."

Cohen looked down at the floor, puzzled for a moment. "Who? What? Oh, right: Giselle, the secretary."

Alma laughed. "Yes, Giselle the secretary. I know I should be jealous since all women are—look at her—but she's actually very nice." Alma stopped in front of the door to room 214 and held up the key. "I took this from the front desk clerk—"

"—Who isn't really a front desk clerk," Cohen said.

She nodded and unlocked and opened the door. "Who isn't really a front desk clerk."

Cohen ushered Alma inside and closed the door behind him. The room was surprisingly large, with a writing desk and a wet bar and a color television. His suitcase was on the floor beside the bed.

Cohen said, "Look, you seem like a good kid. I like you and I'm pretty sure you like me back. Let's be straight with each other. I heard you in there. 'The Devil is real'? You buy that? Serious question."

Alma didn't respond right away. She walked to the nightstand and turned on the bedside lamp since the curtains were closed and the light was dim. She sat on the edge of the bed, her back straight and her legs close together and her arms crossed as if holding herself, as if she were cold. It wasn't cold.

She said, "I've met him, de Lumière."

"Through your uncle?"

She nodded. "Indirectly. He came by The Paradise last Fall when they were finishing up construction. To check on progress, I guess. I don't know."

Cohen nodded, his suspicions confirmed. "So all of this Devil talk is just Hollywood fog machine? Which makes de Lumière what? Your uncle's business partner? Funny it didn't come up. Your uncle—"

"—is a frightened little man out of his depth," she said, interjecting. "He would've told you. He was going to tell you. I'm telling you now," she said.

"And that bit about the magical manuscript, the amazing material that made his career, comedy gold?"

"All true," she said.

"I find that very hard to believe." Cohen walked to the wet bar and poured a drink, a scotch double straight-up. He hadn't eaten breakfast. The liquor burned going down and he grimaced from the taste. He turned to Alma. "In the stories, the Devil deals in souls, yeah? So what, this Devil is big into real estate? Was that the deal? Is that what this is all about, Alma, ownership of The Paradise?"

"Not ownership, Spike," she said. "None of this is what you think. It's hard to explain."

Cohen was about to press her for more but the telephone on the nightstand started to ring. Cohen strode quickly to the phone, hoping it was Betty. He picked up the phone and held up a finger in a *wait* gesture to Alma, who had gotten up from the bed and was standing behind him.

"Betty?"

"No, not Betty, Spike. She's Barry's daughter, yes? I've seen photographs. Pretty girl. Takes more after her mother, I think."

"Choate," Cohen said. His intense dislike of the man came through. He made no effort to hide it.

Choate chuckled on the other end. "It occurs to me I'm the only person left in all the world who knows how you got your nickname. I've often wondered: did you keep it after the war out of sentiment or was it because your real name sounds too Jewish?"

"More memorable," Cohen said. "People don't forget a Spike."

Choate laughed. It was a phony laugh. "No, they won't forget a Spike. To the point, I'm here at The Paradise as well. It's been too long. We should catch up. Let's meet in, say, fifteen minutes? The shuffleboard court, I think. It's a nice sunny day outside."

Cohen closed his eyes and visualized the hotel's layout: restaurant leading to courtyard leading to tennis courts. Shuffleboard courts adjoined the tennis courts. A public place, Cohen thought, an open space, with people around and multiple points of egress.

Cohen said, "Guatemala was a long time ago, Choate. I was sore at first but I got over it. I no longer want to kill you."

"I think I can be excused an abundance of caution where you're concerned, Spike. Indulge me."

"One more thing," Cohen said. "I spoke with Kingman's niece. She tells me your man de Lumière is likely her Uncle Benny's silent partner. Was that what put you on to Kingman?"

There was a slight pause on the other end. Finally, Choate said, "You spoke with whom?"

"Kingman's niece Alma, Alma Boch."

"This might be a problem. Our mutual friend Benny Kingman doesn't have a niece, Spike. He's an only child. I know this with absolute certainty."

Cohen's head jerked away from the receiver. He pivoted on his heel to take in the room. Alma was gone.

As if she were never here, Cohen thought.

On the phone, Choate was speaking, his vaguely patrician voice sounding tinny and far-off. "Twelve minutes, Spike. We can discuss whatever problems have come up over cake and lemonade."

8.   HE WHO SAW ALL...

The Browning Hi Power pistol and shoulder holster rig Cohen had packed in the false bottom of his suitcase were gone, and so was the slender valise he used for notes and so was his knife—or what he used as a knife for close work, an antique French infantry spike bayonet. Rachel had hated Cohen had kept it; hated that part of his life he never talked about and woke him up screaming. And now his gun and the knife were gone and meeting Choate unarmed had the feel of a very bad idea. Cohen scanned the room and took in the wet bar, the ice bucket, the ice pick, yes. It wasn't much but he would make do. He took the corkscrew, too. You never knew, he thought.

Cohen listened at the door before opening it and when he opened it he opened it carefully. There was no one in the hall but a maid pushing her cart from room-to-room— the same maid he had seen on Kingman's floor earlier.

Not right, Cohen thought. Too quiet. There should be people here.

Cohen knew he should be hearing noises, voices, children. Instead, except for the maid, the entire floor appeared deserted. Cohen was unnerved by the silence.

What have you done, Choate? What is this?

On the second floor, Cohen took the stairs down to the lobby, avoiding the elevator.

Another word for elevator is *trap*, he thought.

The lobby was empty: no staff, no guests, no dogs or children, nothing, but he could feel the prickle of hair standing up at the nape of his neck, an itch at the small of his back that told him he was being watched. It wasn't superstition. He had learned to trust his instincts and trusting his instincts had saved his life. Cohen glanced at the parking lot outside. From his vantage he could see three cars parked close to the entrance. Two were ordinary, a black Chevrolet Nomad station wagon and a Ford box truck. The third was the Packard convertible.

Cohen had somehow known it would be out there even before he looked.

I could bug out right now, Cohen thought. Just go.

Cohen could hear Barry Carlisle's Southern gentleman voice in his head: *Fight only when the odds are with you. No shame in retreat.*

His best friend Barry had been an excellent tactician, the man with a plan, always cool and calm, detached and professional.

Not me, Spike thought.

"I'm the guy from Queens with an icepick in his pocket," he said aloud in the empty lobby, to whatever might be listening. "Step up now or stay out of my way."

"You would fight them with an icepick?" Alma said.

Cohen hadn't heard Alma come in. For all he knew, she had just appeared from nowhere, *poof!* She was standing behind the front desk with her arms casually folded on the counter. He saw she had bathed, changed clothes. Like Giselle, Kingman's secretary, Alma was wearing a light summer dress now, with pretty pink polka dots to match her pretty pink sunglasses. She took off her sunglasses and placed them on the counter.

So I can see her eyes, Cohen thought, and flashed on a memory from his Lake Ontario days during the war: 'Our attention is naturally drawn to the eyes, those riveting windows to the soul, which is why one should always watch the hands.'

Speed and brutality are key.

Cohen approached the front desk warily, the icepick out and in his hand. He stopped a few inches from the edge of the counter and noticed she didn't back away, putting him within arm's reach.

"Who are *they*?" Cohen said. "Better, who are you? What's going on? Where is everybody?"

She said, "Wrong questions, Spike. You should be asking who are *you* they would bend and twist the nature of things to bring you to this place. We have no time for any of that."

Faster than Cohen could follow, Alma lashed out and took him by the throat and lifted Cohen straight-armed from the floor and then pulled him across the counter like a suit pulled from the rack. She held him suspended at eye-level, his legs buckled beneath him. Cohen started to raise his weapon and stab the iron-like bar of an arm that held him but she goosed the grip on his neck as a warning, nearly causing him to black out. Cohen had the sense of immense strength held in careful check.

"Drop the weapon, Beloved. I would not want to kill you in the act of saving you. Again."

Cohen was dazed but still thinking and aware. Alma's face was inches from his own and he saw her features had changed. Her features were rounder, her skin darker, her forehead higher, her lips fuller and more pronounced, her eyes wider and more heavily lidded. Even her voice was different and she seemed taller, no longer petite.

"I know you," Cohen said. "I've seen you in dreams."

"I know you too, Beloved." Alma drew him closer and caressed the side of his face with her free hand. "I would spare you this if I could."

With that Alma kissed him on the lips and at first all he tasted and felt was her, a taste like honey and salt, a green scent like fresh-cut grass, and her name wasn't Alma but Inanna and he had a vision of a massive, true-arched temple and in front of the temple she was standing alone on an elevated dais surrounded by a multitude, her arms raised in a blessing—and then the vision was gone and a darkness enveloped him. There was silence in the dark like the holding of a breath and then suddenly a great blinding blue light, followed by a near-overwhelming, kaleidoscopic succession of images and sounds and smells and sensations as dozens—hundreds—of different lives played out from birth to death, each in turn. In one, Cohen saw himself in the orange-reddish glow of a burning pyre of an ancient altar, cutting his way through a mob of robed acolytes to close with a mad sorcerer-king. In another, he was a knight in the Holy Land making a stand at the entrance to a cave carved into the likeness of a monstrous beast with a wide-open, ravenous maw, holding it alone against a horde of mindless, rotting undead stinking of blood and offal. In yet another, he was a lawman in the American West, lying prone in prairie grass with his rifle behind cover of his dying horse, a flurry of bullets thudding against its carcass, his gut-shot deputy screaming in agony only a few impossibly far yards away. It went on and on, each life marked by pain and loss and fierce, unremitting struggle. Cohen's own turn finally came and he saw, felt, experienced his younger self, Spike as he was, killing the SS major whose uniform he took to fake his way into the camp at Sered using Bavarian-accented German and Plain Jane's perfect papers, his then almost boyish face coldly devoid of emotion as he came up snake-silent from behind and snapped the man's neck with a corkscrew twist of his bare hands so he wouldn't bloodstain the uniform. Plain Jane complained when they stained scavenged Nazi uniforms.

And then Cohen came to himself, to the moment, the here and now. Alma-who-is-Inanna was still holding him close, her lips slightly parted as she pulled away from their kiss.

"What are we to each other?" he asked.

"You worshiped me once," she said. "In your first life, when you were Lugalurday, king of Uruk. I was a goddess then, Queen of Heaven. You prayed I would never forsake you. I promised I wouldn't. I haven't. Here I am."

"What am I?"

"You guard the gate of this world," she said. "You have done so for over 6000 years."

"Do I ever say no to this?" he asked.

Alma-who-is-Inanna shook her head. "Not yet, but you can if you want—quit, I mean. No one will stop or hurt you if you do. You have a choice, always. All of us have a choice."

"I saw myself—felt myself—dying over and over. Do I ever survive this?"

"Not yet," she said. "But maybe today we get lucky."

Alma-who-is-Inanna handed Cohen a butcher knife, one he guessed she had taken from the kitchen of this place. Cohen recognized it as a cimeter knife, with its long, slightly curved, razor-sharp blade. It was heavy and balanced. It felt good in the hand.

"A gun would be better," Cohen said. "Urbanski and his men are all armed."

She nodded in the direction of the corridor leading to entrance of the adjoining restaurant. "Those are not men waiting yonder. Bullets only annoy them. Decapitation works. So does dismemberment but it takes longer."

Cohen held up his knife. "This knife," he said, "Is it magical?"

"It is a knife," she said. "You stab with it. You slash with it. You cut off heads with it. You are Lugalurday of Uruk, Uriah Kemp out of Missouri, Uri Cohen of Queens and dozens more. Everything they are, everything they know is within you. Now go out there, Spike, and kill them all."

9.   CAKE AND LEMONADE...

After it was over in the restaurant, Cohen stepped outside and emerged into bright sunlight and saw Wendell Choate seated at a patio table next to the shuffleboard court, just where Choate had said he would be. Choate's outward calm, his attitude of studied nonchalance, must have taken enormous effort of will.

Even in the heat, Choate was wearing a tweed jacket, a crisp, white, buttoned-down oxford shirt, a red paisley tie, sharply creased black wool trousers, and immaculately shined black leather dress shoes. With his horn-rimmed glasses, Choate looked like an Ivy League professor, say, or an actuary. Cohen knew Choate lived with his mother in a brownstone in Georgetown. Cohen knew Choate liked birdwatching and stamp collecting and chess by mail. He also knew Choate liked it up-close and personal with a 13-inch Italian switchblade he kept in a drop sheath sewn into the lining of his sports jackets. Choate liked it face-to-face with his targets so he could watch the lights go out in their eyes as he killed them—or so he had once confided to Cohen. The two men had been working together then, hunting Sergei Ivanov's team in Villa Nueva, and Choate had assumed Cohen liked killing, too—killing for its own sake, killing for pleasure. Cohen didn't.

Choate said, "You're late, Spike."

Cohen, soaked in blood, some of it his own, his hair matted with it, his clothes crusted with it, his face and arms and hands painted with it, took a seat opposite Choate and put his hands on the table so Choate could see them. "I got held up," he said.

"I can see that," Choate said.

Cohen, who knew Choate as well as anyone could know Choate, detected no fear in his voice.

Whatever else he might be, the man is no coward, Cohen thought.

"Where's Benny?" Cohen asked.

"A failure of nerve," Choate said. "He worries you might hold a grudge, so right now Benny Kingman is flying back to New York—with his secretary, of course."

"Giselle," Cohen said, remembering her scent.

"Yes, Giselle. I would very much like to be there when she shows Benny her true face, but one can't have everything."

The two sat in silence for a long moment, their hands flat on the table, waiting for the other to make the first move.

Finally, Cohen visibly relaxed and slowly raised his hands. "Before we get to it, there's something I've got to know, a few things actually."

"I'm game, Spike. What is it you've got to know?"

"That Bay of Pigs fiasco a few months ago? That you?"

Cohen noted Choate's reddening face, the nervous drumming of man's fingers on the tabletop.

"It *was* you, wasn't it?" Cohen went on. "Your plan? Your baby? I thought so."

"It wasn't my fault," Choate said, his voice a near full octave higher. Cohen had struck a nerve. "We were promised air support…" Choate trailed off, the muscles of his jaw bunching. Cohen thought he could see veins pulsing in the other man's temple but maybe only imagined it. "The plan was perfect," Choate said.

Cohen kept his voice level and steady. "I know you, Wendell. We're not friends but we've ran missions together, fought side-by-side. You're nobody's true believer. So what did he offer you? What was your price?"

Choate exhaled audibly through his nose and leaned back in his chair. "Just between us, yes?"

"Sure, Wendell, just between us."

"He promised to make Bay of Pigs unhappen," Choate said. "A new reality, Spike, one where Nixon wins, we keep the element of surprise, the bombs hit their targets, and Castro winds up against a wall."

"And you're everybody's golden boy, man of the hour, is that it? That's what all this is about, you erasing a stupid mistake?"

Choate laughed. This time his laughter was genuine. "Barry was the one with vision between you two. He always had an eye for the big picture, but you? Not you, Spike. You think too small. You've always thought too small."

Cohen shrugged. "Barry was the best of us. But we were talking about you, Wendell. There has got to be a quid pro quo. Your new boss, this de Lumière, what does he want?"

Choate gave him a sly, predatory grin. "You, Spike. You are his price. Must say, I know you've made powerful enemies over the years, myself included. I had no idea such enemies extended into other planes of existence."

Cohen shook his head and leaned forward. "Wendell, look, a friend told me something, something that stuck. She said we always have a choice—and she's right: we do. You and me, we don't have to go through with this, whatever this is."

"Just walk away?" Choate said.

"We both walk away, Choate, no harm no foul."

Cohen could see Choate working through it. He looked like a high school kid trying to figure out in his head the cube root of 18.

"Look, Wendell," Spike went on, locking his gaze with Choate's. "I know what you're thinking. You're thinking you can take me—and you know what? You might be right. You've always been very quick, very precise, and me? Look at me, bleeding out all over the place. I'm nearly done. So yeah, maybe you're right. Maybe you *can* take me."

Choate was opening his mouth to respond when Cohen shot him twice with Urbanski's pistol from under the table, both shots exactly angled to go just under the sternum and into the heart. The impact threw Choate backwards in his chair, the back of his skull bouncing off the concrete of the shuffleboard court with a loud *pok!* Cohen got up from his chair, limped to where Choate was lying, and stood over him, looking down. Choate was staring up at the blue July sky, his mouth opening and closing like a fish thrown up on the dock. Cohen figured the man had 15, 20 seconds to live, tops.

"We'll watch the lights go out together, Choate," Cohen said.

10. POUR COLD WATER TO REFRESH HER HEART...

Alma bathed and bound his wounds in a stream in the

woods near The Paradise since water no longer ran through its pipes. The hotel was disintegrating, falling into rapid ruin. Whatever power had powered the illusion of it had been cut off. The roof was collapsing as they watched.

When Cohen had seen what was happening to the hotel, he had sat up in alarm. Laughing, Alma had pushed him back into the grass, either guessing or knowing why Cohen was so suddenly upset. "Your precious Packard is fine," she had said. "You, on the other hand, need stitches, clean bandages, antibiotics, disinfectants. There is a small town west of here—I forget its name. It has a drugstore. We must go soon."

Alma had retrieved his suitcase from the hotel before the floors fell in, and with it a change of clothes. She stood him up and helped him dress and then, draping his arm over her shoulder, half-carried, half-dragged him to the waiting car. Cohen noticed her strength was no longer that of a goddess. Whatever had powered Alma Boch's transformation had withdrawn. She was human again. Cohen found he liked that she was human again.

It was twilight by the time they were ready to leave. Alma started the Packard but they didn't go right away. They watched while the last remnant of The Paradise fell in upon itself as its support beams oxidized and disintegrated, a process of decades happening in moments. Only rubble remained and Cohen suspected even that would be gone soon, then only dust, then nothing at all.

"He's still out there," Cohen said. He didn't phrase it as a question but the question was implied.

"Yes, he is still out there," Alma said. "He roams, 'going to and fro on the earth, walking up and down on it'—his job, apparently. But we hurt him, yes. Manifestations like this—" Alma nodded at the devolving wreck of The Paradise—"require enormous energies. He is wounded, weakened."

"Can he die?"

Alma shook her head. "Think of him as a bad idea, the

god of bad ideas. Bad ideas never go away entirely. They always come back one way or another. He is like that, a thousand different names for all that is selfish and stupid and cruel."

Cohen winced as he arranged himself in the passenger seat, trying to find a position that didn't hurt. "We need resources," Cohen said. "First thing we do after I get fixed up, we get back to the city and find Benny and squeeze him for everything he knows and every cent he's got. Shouldn't be hard. He thinks I want to kill him."

"Don't you?"

"Maybe a little," Cohen admitted.

"And after Benny, what then?"

"You know *what then*. Then we hunt de Lumière."

"It won't be easy, Beloved."

Cohen remembered his dream, an arrow made of corpses pointing the way, daring a king to follow, and in the dream the king had taken the dare and followed.

"I don't want *easy*," Cohen said. "I never did. None of us ever did."

ABOUT THE AUTHOR

TROY RÍSER is an award-winning fiction writer and accomplished fine and commercial artist. His work has previously appeared in the first book of *The Devil You Know* anthology series with the horror story, *Love and the Forever Machine*. Another horror story, *Pick Trick*, has been accepted for inclusion in the Winter 2022 issue of *Cirsova* magazine. He's currently at work on an as-yet untitled science fiction novel and an animated horror short film, *king_in_yellow*.

SWORD OF FIRE

Stanley B. Webb

Blasted stone ripped the First Man's bare soles.

Dead thorns tore the First Woman's naked skin.

Adam and Eve fled from the Garden of Eden until they could flee no longer, then they collapsed and shivered in each other's arms, awaiting God's final judgement.

Adam cried to Heaven, "Have mercy on us, Jehovah!"

Eve cried, "I did not want to disobey, the serpent made me do it!"

Then, a pair of wolves trotted up from the Garden, bearing raw, brown, furry things in their jaws. The wolves dropped two fresh deerskins beside the humans, then trotted away.

Adam said, "We'll cover our bodies with these."

"Revolting!"

"Less revolting than nudity!"

A third wolf came, with the serpent trapped in his jaws. The wolf dropped the reptile, gagged, and then returned to the Garden.

Eve screamed at the serpent. "I'll murder you!" She leaped up and stomped at him with her bloodied feet.

The serpent slithered away from her. "Don't blame me, *you* chose to eat of the fruit of knowledge."

"You promised that we would become like God, and now He has cursed us to die this day!"

Eve grabbed a shard of stone and threw it at the serpent, who retreated into a fissure. Eve found a dead branch. She limped to the serpent's refuge and jabbed the stick in at him.

The snake screamed, "Adam, control your wife!"

Adam felt no love for either companion, but greater was his rage toward Eve. "Leave the serpent be!"

Eve jabbed again. "But it's all his fault!"

"It's his fault that *you* are cursed to death, but it's your fault that *I* share your fate! Shall I kill you with a stick?"

Eve stopped, then collapsed in tears. "Let me live through my final night."

"This day need not be your last," said the serpent. "You just saved my life, Adam, so now I will help you to acquire the other fruit."

Adam sneered. "We've eaten your curse of knowledge, and now we know: we've traded an eternity of innocent joy for shame, hatred, and death!"

"I said the *other* fruit, the fruit of the Tree of Life, which bestows immortality. Eternal life will make all of your pain worthwhile. I will help you steal back into Eden."

"Don't trust that worm," said Eve.

The serpent said, "My name is Nahash."

"I don't trust him," said Adam.

And yet Adam's fear of death weakened his skepticism. Adam did not want to become dust again. The very thought made his body shudder, and he could think of naught else. Finally he addressed Nahash.

"Jehovah will stop me."

Nahash replied, "He has departed from the garden now."

Adam queried, "What about the cherubim that He left

to guard the gate?"

"The cherubim are there to warn you off, but they will not hinder you."

"The sword of fire will hinder me!"

Nahash said, "I'll think of a way for you to evade the sword."

Adam considered.

Nahash said, "You're already cursed to death, another disobedience can't make your position worse than it is now."

Adam nodded. "You're right, let's go."

Eve cried out, "Do you leave me here to die alone?"

Adam told her, "I will return."

Nahash led Adam down the slope, coiling among the rocks and briers. Adam followed carefully, wincing at each step. His soles made a trail of blood all the way to the gates of Eden.

The two guardian cherubim were frightening to look at. One was a man-faced lion, and the other a similarly deformed bull, both possessing enormous wings.

The cherubim shouted in unison. ***"Beware!"***

Adam balked.

Nahash coiled himself and said, "Simply walk between them."

Adam made a step forward.

"BEWARE!" the cherubim bellowed, but they did not move.

Adam approached the gate.

The sword of fire, wielded by no visible hand, darted from nowhere and stood across Adam's path. Its blaze made his sweat pop.

Nahash hissed, "Dart to your right!"

The sword blocked Adam.

"Now to your left!"

Again the sword thwarted Adam.

Nahash said, "Make as if to go both ways, confuse it!"

The sword parried Adam's every move.

"Duck under it!"

Adam dropped to his belly and crawled forward, but the sword laid itself on the ground before him. The dust bloomed with flames. Adam slithered backward.

"Get up and leap over the sword!"

Adam clambered to his feet and jumped. The sword lofted beneath him. Adam checked himself in mid-air, twisted away from the sword, and fell a-sprawl. He scrambled back from the gate.

The sword hovered before Eden's portal. Its flames crackled.

Nahash said, "Call Eve to help. The sword cannot block two places at once."

Adam cupped his hands around his mouth, and shouted toward the barrens. "Come down here, helpmeet!"

A long time passed before Eve obeyed, and she muttered under her breath.

The First Couple challenged the gate simultaneously.

The sword flashed back and forth so rapidly that it seemed to be *everyplace* at once.

Nahash scratched his head with the end of his tail. "This is more difficult than I expected." The serpent crawled off.

Adam shouted after the snake. "Where are you going?"

"Away to think."

"But we're *dying!*"

"I'll return before the day is done."

Adam and Eve retreated into the barrens. They took shelter behind a jagged rock and held each other. Flies swarmed on their raw skin garments.

The sun set behind Eden.

The serpent did not return.

Eve wept pitiably. "Don't let me die cold."

"What can I do?" Adam said in frustration. Then, and idea came to him. "Make a pile of dead wood." He stood and turned away.

Eve grabbed her husband. "Don't leave me!"

Adam gently loosened her grip. "I will return. I promise."

He descended to Eden's gate with a dead stick in his hand.

"Beware!" the Cherubim cried as he passed.

The sword of fire met him. He thrust forth the stick. The sword struck. The dry wood caught aflame.

Adam returned with the flame, and used it to ignite Eve's woodpile. She sat close to the bonfire.

Eve smiled. "You've done it, husband!" Still, her smile was sad.

Adam felt proud. He sat with her, and although the flames provided ample warmth, he still held her, for he also was sad. He missed the life that he should have had.

Eve cuddled under his arm. "I'm sorry Adam, we've lost the world and it is all my fault."

He felt a vicious, triumphant urge to gloat over Eve's confession, but the tears in her eyes changed his mood. Adam felt no urge to spend their last night in vindictive hatred. "It's the serpent's fault."

"Yes." She squeezed him tighter. "We've lost Eternity, but we still have each other."

They sat together by the fire until it had burned down to red embers, then Eve laid their deer skins out as bedding, and they consoled each other in the dark.

♉

Adam threw the putrid skins aside. He disentangled his limbs from Eves and rose, swatting the flies from his body.

The sun burned white-hot on the eastern horizon.

Adam squinted, then opened his eyes wide. "Eve!"

She awoke with a startled gasp. Eve grabbed the deer skin back over her naked parts. "What?"

"Tomorrow has come, and we still live!"

Eve's eyes widened. She dropped the rotting skin and

rose into Adam's embrace. "Jehovah has forgiven us!"

Nahash said, "Not so, you simply misunderstood Him."

They both grabbed the hides to cover themselves.

The serpent lay beyond their dead fire, his lidless eyes fixed upon a rat who sniffed around the bloodied rocks.

Adam said, "Jehovah said that we would die yesterday, but we live today, so He must have forgiven us."

"Jehovah's temporal perception is different from yours: a thousand years is as a day, and a day is as a thousand years."

"So we will live for a thousand years?" Adam laughed joyously. "That is nearly eternity!"

Nahash asked, "Will you still think so after 999 years have passed?"

Nahash struck and sank his fangs into the rat. The rodent voiced one agonized squeal, then it fell dead.

Adam and Eve left Nahash to his breakfast.

They traveled more to the east. The barrens ended. They discovered a green valley and set up camp. Over time Adam built a house. Eve taught herself to grow crops. Adam domesticated wild sheep.

Every seventh day he sacrificed a lamb on an altar of stone, and prayed for Jehovah's forgiveness.

At night he lay with his wife.

"This is not Eden," he said. "Life is hard, but it is good." He patted her round belly and grinned. "You've gained weight in spite of your labors."

Eve giggled. "This isn't fat." She pressed his hand to her belly.

Something inside her moved. He startled back. "What is it?"

"A son, made of you and me."

Adam felt awed by what they had created.. "A new life!

His name will be Cain."

ૐ

Adam went out to tend his flock the next morning. He found his lambs cowering in terror.

Nahash had slithered out from the barrens.

Nahash said, "I have made new plans for how you can thwart the sword of fire."

Adam regarded the serpent for a time. "Thank you Nahash, but we are content with our thousand year day."

"You can't be serious!"

Adam nodded. "We have gained a different sort of immortality. Our first child is on his way. Someday Cain will have his own children, and they their own children. Eve and I will live on through them."

Nahash muttered, "This is the woman's idea."

"It's our idea. Now be gone, worm."

"As you wish, mortal."

ૐ

Cain birthed with a nightmare of blood and pain. Eve screamed during the whole ordeal. Adam feared for her life, but afterward she held the baby in her arms and smiled.

"He's beautiful!"

Adam frowned. "He barely looks human."

Cain soon learned to walk, then to speak. He followed his mother while Eve worked in her garden, and played in the rich earth. Adam wanted Cain to oversee the flock with him, but the child took no interest in the First Man's work. Adam continued tending his sheep alone. He listened from the distant pasture while Eve and Cain laughed and talked together, and he felt envious. Still, he reasoned, perhaps this was normal behavior for a child of Man. Adam had no way to know. Cain was, after all, the first human child.

On one evening, Cain toddled to the stone hearth in the house that Adam had built. Cain tugged at a rock. The stone fell loose and nearly crushed the child's toes.

Cain said, "Rock!"

Eve gasped and carried her son out of harm's way.

Adam said, "Be more careful boy, you're making your mother's hair turn gray."

Eve said, "It is time that makes our hair turn gray."

"Our hair?" Adam plucked a strand from his own head, and saw that it was gray. He shuddered. "How long has it been since Eden?"

Eve shrugged. "I do not count the days."

Adam had not counted either, but he tried to now. How much time had passed? Five years? Ten? One hundred? Whatever the span was, it had passed swiftly, like the winking of an eye. Would a thousand years seem just as brief at the end?

"I'm going for a walk," Adam said.

"We'll come with you."

"Not today."

He climbed into the barrens, to the slopes that overlooked Eden, where he sat and brooded.

After a time he said, "Are you near, serpent?"

Nahash slithered out from a fissure. "I'm always near."

"You were right. The passage of time only makes me fear death with greater passion. Will you still help me to acquire the fruit of life?"

"I will. I have an excellent plan. If you approached Eden's gate in disguise, you might fool the sword of fire."

"What is 'disguise'?"

Under Nahash's direction, Adam cut two forked branches and lashed them at his temples with wiry vines. He then collected a double handful of thistledown and used pitchy sap to adhere the fluff to his buttocks. Adam crouched on all fours, with his skin garment draped across his back.

Nahash said, "You look exactly like a buck deer!"

Adam crawled down the slope toward Eden's gate. Rocks bruised his knees.

"You're moving too purposefully.," said Nahash. "A real deer would stop frequently to graze."

"Upon what?"

"The foliage of those thorn briers."

The leaves tasted bitter and made him feel dizzy. Green sludge dripped from his chin. He made his slow way down to the gate.

"Beware!"

"You're just a deer, ignore them."

Adam proceeded onward between the cherubim.

The sword of fire pounced and lopped off his wooden antlers. Adam's hair ignited. He leaped upright and ran away screaming, beating at his head. He did not stop until he had reached the safety of the barrens. Adam threw down the antlers' remains, then yanked the thistledown from his rear. The sap adhered tenaciously to his skin.

"Ouch!"

Nahash slithered across the rubble. "We'll try a different disguise next, perhaps an ostrich—"

Adam seized Nahash by the throat and knotted the snake around a dead tree, then he stormed back home.

Nahash came to Adam's pasture the next day.

Adam wielded his shepherd's staff. "Go away!"

"Don't be that way," said Nahash. "All that I have ever done is try to help you, and you treat me very rudely in return. Still, I have it in my heart to forgive you, and continue as your advisor."

Adam waved his staff once more, then sighed and lowered the weapon. "What next?"

"Obviously, the sword of fire can be neither evaded nor fooled. You must defeat the sword on its own terms."

"Defeat it?"

"In battle."

The serpent's new plan sounded hopeless. "It's *Jehovah's* sword."

"So what? Jehovah made you, and you're imperfect."

Adam thrust out his staff.

Nahash dodged. "I mean no insult, I'm merely saying that although He is indomitable, His creations are not."

Adam gave Nahash a sour, but speculative, look. "With what would I fight?"

"You seem to like waving that stick around."

Adam followed Nahash back to the gates of Eden.

"Beware!"

He shook his fist at the cherubim.

The sword came and barred his way.

Adam hesitated.

"Show no fear!" Nahash insisted. "Jehovah made the Garden for you, you have a right to that fruit! Strike the sword!"

Adam leaped and swung his staff at the sword. The impact jolted his bones, and knocked the sword aside.

A sensation of martial joy ignited in his heart. "Take that!"

The sword flashed back at him. Adam blocked. The force drove him back a step. Adam retreated one more step, then he rushed forward and swung roundhouse at the sword. A great noise went *clang!* And the sword retreated.

"Hah!" Adam cried, and stepped into the gate.

The sword returned and flickered at him, side to side. His crook fell to the dust in a handful of pieces.

Adam regarded the smoking remnant in his hand, then he ran away.

The sword of fire pursued him and stabbed his rump.

☿

Adam ran all the way through the barrens before he found water. He sat in a creek for an hour, but when he rose his wound still burned.

Nahash said from behind him, "That's going to leave a scar."

Adam grabbed at the serpent. Nahash darted out of reach. Adam lost his balance and fell splashing.

Adam cried, "I'm done with you! Leave me alone!"

Nahash replied, "Now is not the time to give up! We've refined our tactics with each attempt."

"I've failed at each attempt! Nothing can get me past that sword of fire!"

Nahash considered for a moment, then said, "I probably shouldn't reveal this."

"What?"

"Jehovah did not intend that you should gain this knowledge yet."

"Tell me, or I swear I'll kill you."

"You will surely defeat the sword of fire if you wield a sword of iron."

"What is iron?"

Nahash explained, "Iron is a substance called metal. Its ore can be extracted from the earth, then transformed with heat. However, the ore mines belong to the children of the Others. You must commission them to manufacture your weapon."

"Others? Who are the Others?"

Nahash said, "The Other Gods."

☿

The serpent led Adam back into the barrens, then to the north. The man's soles had developed tough calluses, and he felt prideful that the stony ground could no longer injure his feet, but then the ground became even harsher, littered with sharp pieces of obsidian, and the path also grew hot. The shards cut Adam's feet anew, and his blood steamed on the rocks.

The highest mountain that Adam had ever seen stood on the horizon. The mountain's precipitous ramparts rose into the clouds and beyond. The sight was beautiful and terrible.

"Do I have to climb that?" Adam asked.

"No, you will go under Olympus."

Hours passed before Adam reached the foot of the mountain.

Nahash led him down into a tunnel between the mountain's roots. The light from outside faded, but red earth-flames burned in stony crevices and lit the way. Smoke roiled beneath the tunnel's roof. Adam gagged on sulfurous fumes. His perspiration flowed. Adam would have shed his tunic, but he dared not meet the others naked.

Others. The very word made his heart quake. What sort of children had the Other Gods created?

A barred gate, three times Adam's height, blocked the cavern. Searing heat and blood-red incandescence rushed upward through the gate's bars. Thunderous booms and ringing blows echoed from the blocked depths. Robust voices yelled out bestial syllables.

Nahash thrust his head between the bars and shouted to those below, "Arges! I've brought you a customer!"

The brutish voices stopped. Booming footsteps approached from the Hadean environment below.

Nahash whispered to Adam, "Show no fear or Arges will devour you," then he slithered away.

Adam cried, "What? Wait!" but Nahash was gone.

A hirsute man-shape, four times Adam's height, strode up from the smoke and heat, and peered down at Adam over the top of the gate. The creature spoke with a voice like gravel.

"Who summons Arges?"

Adam leaned back and looked up into the monster's single, round eye. He tried to speak, but could produce not a sound.

Arges grinned. Saliva drooled between his tusks.

Adam blurted, "I'm the son of Jehovah!"

"Jehovah? Ah yes, the Other God." Arges licked his chops. "Are you frightened of me, son of Jehovah?"

"No!"

"Then why do you tremble?"

"I'm cold!"

"Are you?" Arges opened the gate and gestured invitingly. "Then enter and be warmed."

Adam wanted to do no such thing, he wanted to flee for his life, but he followed the monster down the scorching tunnel to a huge cavern. A lake of magma bubbled there, filling most of the cavern's floor. Two other monsters, identical to Arges, labored on the lake's shore, pounding a fiery material with their huge, hammers.

Adam bounced from foot to foot, trying to evade the heat.

"Excuse the mess," said Arges. "We have few visitors." He gestured at a pile of gristly bones. "May I offer you repast?"

Adam's stomach rolled. "Thank you, but no. I came because the serpent Nahash told me that you could make a sword of iron."

"Ah!" said Arges, and nodded to his brothers.

The brother monsters took up a set of giant pliers. They used the pliers to retrieve a white-hot sword from under the magma pool. The sword was twice Adam's length.

The mere sight of it caused the First Man's pulse to soar, made him forget his fear of the monstrous others.

"Does this one please you?" asked Arges.

The monster took the sword in hand. Arge's flesh

sizzled, but he seemed immune to pain. Arges swung the giant sword overhand, aiming at a huge stalagmite. The air screamed. The blade struck its target with a flash of lightning. Thunder echoed throughout the cavern. Adam rocked backward, with his hands pressed over his ears.

"I love it!" Adam cried. "Can you make one to my size?"

"If you meet my price," said Arges.

"Name your price!"

Arges slavered. "I would have one of your kin for my dinner."

Adam stammered in reply, "How about a sheep instead?"

"Lanolin, yuck." Arges shook his head. "My price is firm."

Adam backed away. "I'll go and fetch one."

"Excellent! I'll show you out."

The monster's shadow loomed upon Adam as they returned to the tunnel's gate. Arge's price was impossible, of course, and yet Adam could not force the question from his mind:

Eve or Cain?

When Arges had locked the gate behind him, Adam bolted up the tunnel to the surface. The environment outside seemed wintery after his time below.

Nahash waited there, coiled up on a flat rock.

Adam yelled at the serpent, "You abandoned me with those monsters!"

"I had to leave," Nahash replied. "My ectothermic body would have died if I had tarried longer in such heat. How did things go?"

"Horrifically! Arges wants a *human* as payment!"

Nahash said, "You'll give him Eve, of course."

Adam looked away. "You're horrible!"

"Are you going to claim that you haven't had the same idea? The real horror is that she brought Jehovah's curse down upon you! He created you to tend the Garden

114

forever in blissful solitude. Eve was as an afterthought, a mere experiment, and she's ruined everything. She's even turned your son against you, turned Cain into a mere *gardener*!"

"What you say is true, but to cause the end of her life . . . I don't know what to call such a deed."

The serpent hissed, "It's called murder, and you know that she deserves it!"

Adam came home after nightfall.

Cain was at the hearth, at play with the loose rock.

Adam said, "Stop doing that!" and took the rock away from Cain.

Adam regarded the stone in his hand. The rock's mineral solidity transformed his arm into a killing tool, a murder weapon.

He glanced at Eve.

She had paused work on her sewing project, a miniature garment of squirrel hide, and looked accusingly at him. "Where have you been?"

He replied brusquely, "Why do you interrogate me?"

Tears sprang from her eyes. "You've been gone so long, your supper is cold and the sun has set and I feared that harm had befallen you!"

Adam's emotions were confused. He felt the urge to murder his wife and also contrite for her fear. "I'm sorry." He clenched the rock, unsure of how to proceed. "Why is that tunic so small?" He blurted.

Eve set the squirrel-skin project aside, and stood up. "I've something to show you." She lifted her tunic and showed him her round belly.

Adam gaped. "Another child?"

"We'll call him Abel. He'll grow to help you with the flock."

Suddenly Adam felt shame deeper than contrition, he

felt guilt. He gave the rock to Cain.

"Put this back where it belongs, and leave it there!"

Adam took his wife into his arms. "I love you so much, I could not live without you!"

♉

Adam whittled a new shepherd's crook while his flock grazed.

The sheep suddenly fled, and Nahash slithered into the pasture.

Nahash said, "You're a coward."

Adam replied, "I'm not, I've merely changed my mind. Depart now, for you frighten my sheep."

"I will not allow you to reject your chance at eternal life!"

"I don't want eternal life! Perhaps I was never meant to have it, perhaps everything, even our disobedience, perhaps even your interference has been a part of His plan."

Nahash said, "You're a fool! I'll murder the woman myself. You'll thank me later." He bared his fangs.

Adam brandished his staff. "You'll not touch her!" He went after the serpent.

Adam pinioned Nahash with his shepherd's crook. Nahash turned and struck at him. Adam lifted his foot out of range, then stomped down when Nahas's strike hit the earth. Adam stamped again and again and crushed Nahash's skull beneath his heel.

Long minutes later, Adam stepped back from the deed that he had done, the murder of Nahash. He gasped from exertion and emotion. The serpent's long body continued to twist and flop, even though Nahash's head now embedded in the ground.

Adam buried his crime beneath a pile of rocks, then

took his flock to the other side of the pasture.

Months passed, the Eve delivered Abel. This birthing was gentle.

Adam said, "I've made Abel a welcome gift." And he placed a tiny shepherd's crook into the infant's hand. Abel's newborn fingers closed upon the gift. Adam smiled.

Cain asked, "Father, what was my welcome gift?"

Adam replied, "I made none for you."

Time passed.

Adam watched over his flock.

Abel watched beside him, with the tiny shepherd's crook in his two-year-old hands.

At midday, Cain approached with a melon. "I grew this myself," Cain said proudly, and sliced the fruit.

Adam took a slice and munched absently.

Cain asked, "Is it good, Father?"

A lamb strayed toward the woods.

Adam said, "Abel, fetch!"

Abel scampered after the lamb. The young animal avoided him, not frightened but playful.

Adam laughed. He tossed the slice of melon into the dirt, and ran off to chase the lamb with Abel. After several frolicking minutes, the returned the lamb to its mother.

They found Cain standing over the dropped fruit.

"Why are you still here," Adam demanded to know. "And why are you crying?"

ชู

Time passed again

ชู

Offering Day came around again. Adam bound the lamb upon the altar. He gave the knife to Abel.

Cain said, "He's too little."

Adam replied sternly, "Five years is old enough." To Abel her said encouragingly, "Cut him deftly there, across the throat, and he'll suffer no pain."

Cain said, "How do you know it'll suffer no pain?"

"Because I said so!"

Cain said, "He's still too little, I'm the eldest, *I'll* do it."

Adam smirked at his eldest. "Very well. Abel, give your brother the knife."

Abel protested, "But you promised *me*!"

Cain snatched the knife from Abel's hand. He pulled the lamb's head back and thrust the blade against its wooly throat. The bound lamb struggled, bleating plaintively. Cain's tears welled up. He released the victim.

Adam laughed. "Cain, why don't you go and cut a bloodless melon for Jehovah!"

Abel joined in his father's mirth.

Cain threw the knife down and fled bawling.

ชู

Time passed once more, then Cain beat Abel to death with the hearth rock.

Adam confronted Eve with the killing knife in his hand. "Where is the murderer?"

"Cain has fled with his sisters."

"Fled to where?"

"To where you'll never find him! I hate Cain for what he's done, but if I let you kill him I'll lose both of my sons!"

Adam screamed and charged at her.

Eve screamed and fled.

Adam tripped and fell flat on his face. He gasped for a few minutes, and when he had recovered his breath she was gone.

Adam's rage collapsed and left him with a cold, ashy feeling.

He returned to his son's corpse. Abel's head was crushed, as if it were one of Cain's melons. Flies had gathered on the wound.

His rage caught fire again. "Leave him alone!" Adam flailed at the carrion insects, but they merely flew around before resuming their feast. Adam went cold again and dropped his trembling arms.

"Everything is gone," he whispered. "like a dream. I'll grow old alone, die alone."

A voice hissed in his ear. *"Get the iron sword!"*

"Nahash?" Adam whirled but saw nothing. "You can't be, you're dead!"

"Cain has provided Arges' price for you."

He recoiled from Abel's dead flesh. "I can't do that!"

"You can. Your son is finished with his body, use it for your own good."

☿

Adam built a travois from sticks and dragged Abel's corpse north across the barrens, to the grotto where the children of the Other Gods dwelt.

"Arges! I have your price! Do you have my sword?"

Arges stomped up from the volcanic cavern. He opened the barred gate and displayed the iron weapon. Adam put out his hand.

Arges withdrew the sword. "Payment first."

Adam stepped aside. A lump filled his throat, but he averted his eyes from Abel's pitiful remains.

Arges squatted over the body. "It was a sloppy kill, but the rest looks good." Arges sniffed deeply. "Ymm!" He lifted the corpse and opened his mouth.

Adam closed his eyes and plugged his ears.

A few minutes passed.

Arges tapped his shoulder. "That was even better than I expected!" The monster belched. "Here's your order."

Adam grabbed the sword by the hilt. A tiny bolt of lightning shot to his finger. Adam yelped.

Arges chuckled. "Wield it cautiously, for this sliver of iron contains the wrath of a God."

"I mean to challenge a God."

Adam seized the hilt firmly. His hair stood on end. He turned and climbed the tunnel.

Arges called after him, "Enjoy your sword!"

♉

Adam stormed the gates of Eden.

The cherubim shouted, *"Beware!"*

Adam cried back, *"You* beware!"

He struck at the lion cherubim. The blades severed the angel's neck with a flash of lightning and a boom of thunder. The cherubim's head rolled off to the ground, and stared dumbly up at itself. Then the lion-creature grabbed its head back, and both angels retreated up to Heaven.

Adam aimed his blade after the cherubim. "I will have the fruit of life!"

The sword of iron shot a bolt into the clouds.

The sword of fire rushed into being and came at him point first. Adam swung his iron sword and knocked the Heavenly blade aside. The deafening clash raised a flock of terrified Eden birds. The sword of fire circled back, striking to Adam's opposite hand. He pivoted, and intercepted the holy blow. Adam strained against the pressure, but Jehovah's weapon forced his tip down. The sword of fire slid down Adam's blade, shed from his iron point, then arced high, aimed to cleave him down the middle. Adam raised his sword and blocked the strike. The sword of fire scraped along his edge to the guard, and the hilts locked. Jehovah's sword pressed. Adam's knees buckled. The sword of fire pressed closer. Adam's hair smoked. Sweat popped from his brow. He gave a fierce shout and desperately heaved his weight against Jehovah's might. His iron weapon released a thunderbolt and shunted the incandescent blade aside. Deflected momentum carried the sword of fire down, and the conflagrant tip pierced deeply into the earth.

Adam crouched and spun on his heel while the Heavenly sword jerked itself free. His iron blade cut sideways through the air with a sparkling trail and hit the sword of fire in mid-blade. The flaming sword parted with a blast that threw Adam onto his back.

The Earth shook. Landslides fell in the barrens.

He lay stunned for a moment, stunned by amazement rather than concussion, then he leaped to his feet and thrust the iron sword on high.

"Eternal life is mine! I will be like unto God!"

The iron sword spit lightning at Heaven.

A bolt of Heavenly lightning overwhelmed the sword's spark and struck the uplifted sword of iron.

Adam's bones glowed through his skin, then he exploded into dust and the dust returned to the earth.

♉

Adam did not realize that he was dead.

He failed to notice that the sword of iron no longer filled his hand.

He proudly advanced through the gate and entered the

Garden of Eden.

Only then did he perceive that things were wrong. The Garden had turned still, its wolves and deer and birds were gone. Adam glimpsed something beneath a bush, and knelt to investigate.

It was the skeleton of a lamb. As he watched, the bones became dust.

Adam reared away and turned back for Eden's gate. The gate was there, but there was no world outside, only void.

Things rustled behind him.

Adam turned back to face the Garden. At first he could not locate the source of the rustling. Then, he saw that the garden was withering, the trees and mosses and grass, the wines and briers and shrubberies, all wilted and decayed into dust.

When the life was all gone, he stood in gray barrens.

Far off, in the middle of the Garden that had been, there still stood a tree. It was the tree of life. Adam ran to it. A grove of thorns surrounded the tree of life, Adam fought his way into the grove. The thorns tangled in his hair and tore his skin. Finally, he won his way through.

The tree of life stood before him, its branches replete with pale fruit. Adam reached up to seize one of the fruits, but then he saw what it was.

It was a human skull. All of the tree's fruits were skulls.

Then the tree of life, which had become the tree of death, rotted and became dust.

And from the dust rose a gigantic serpent.

"Nahash?" Adam's voice tasted like dust.

"My name is Satan now."

ABOUT THE AUTHOR

STANLEY B. WEBB wasted his youth watching monster movies, drawing monster pictures, and writing monster stories. He was the greatest weirdo of his school. He wanted to be Captain Nemo when he grew up. Eventually he did grow up, but instead of exploring the world in a super-submarine, he found gainful employment in a restaurant kitchen. As the years passed, he also worked at a videotape rental store and an automotive factory. He doesn't draw much anymore, but he still watches monster movies and writes monster stories, many of which are published. (Stanley's complete bibliography may be viewed on his Amazon Author Central page.)

His most recent published works – besides this deal with the devil – include his kaiju story *Sharkkon*, appearing in the anthology *Peculiar Monstrosities* from Planet Bizarro Press, and the collection *Monster Garbage and Other Trash: Stories by Stanley B. Webb*, the author's first solo volume.

In Stanley's own words, "It's been a lot of fun, and I hope you liked my stories."

TEA WITH THE DEVIL

Anna Taborska

The street was strangely quiet for Halloween.
No trick-or-treaters as far as the eye could see, and even
the candles in the carved pumpkins had been extinguished
by a wind that appeared from nowhere and disappeared
again just as fast. It was early evening, and the light had all
but faded from the dirty urban sky. There was a distinct
chill in the autumn air and for a moment the street seemed
quite deserted. Then a flurry of footsteps, and a tall man
wearing a long coat, with a cap pulled down tightly over
his ears, rounded the corner at great speed. Close on his
heels came three youths, hatred in their eyes and baseball
bats in their hands.

The man disappeared round the side of a large block of
flats and the youths followed, pausing when they realised
that he had entered the building.

♉

Once inside the block of flats, the tall man headed
straight for a flat on the ground floor and pounded on the

door. An eye appeared in the peephole and the door opened, the man inside delighted to see his old friend.

"What a wonderful surprise, come on in!" An energetic, grey-haired man in his early sixties was holding open the door, smiling at his unexpected guest. "How long's it been now?"

The tall man quickly pushed his host inside, leapt across the threshold and slammed the door behind him.

"I'm being chased," panted the new arrival. His host looked surprised.

"Oh," he said, pointing to his guest's head, "did they notice your...um...?"

The tall man pulled off his cap, revealing a fine, if rather tussled, head of shoulder-length black hair. As he smoothed it down, through his hair poked two perfect little horns.

"No. Definitely not," the tall man shook his head. "I had my cap on all the time." He took off his coat. His host took it from him and hung it on a coat rack, then turned to his guest and pointed at his backside.

"Perhaps it popped out from under your coat?" he suggested helpfully. The tall man glanced down, over his shoulder. He was wearing an elegant, if somewhat worn set of black tails. From the slit at the back protruded a long, thick tail with a fluffy black tip. The tall man smoothed down his tail.

"It couldn't have," he said. "My coat is very long. They couldn't have seen it. In any case, there are a lot of strange looking fellows out tonight."

"Then what on earth happened?" asked his host, a look of concern on his amiable face.

"I really have no idea. Some louts threw themselves at me. Each one shouted something different. One of them yelled 'Fucking gyppo!', another one 'Yids to the gas!' and the third 'Fuck off back to where you come from, you fucking nigger wop!'. Do you understand any of this?"

"Well, the 'nigger wop' you must have misheard. But,

126

all in all, I guess you don't look quite like the rest of us. Your complexion is kind of dusky, and not everyone likes that around here."

"Oh well, in that case there's nothing more to be said." The tall man relaxed a little and smiled at his host. "And what about you? Has your collection grown since I last saw you?"

"Oh yes, it's definitely grown!" The grey-haired man positively beamed. "Would you like to see?"

"Of course. You know that I enjoy looking at depictions of my fellows."

♉

The grey-haired man took his friend around the large flat, proudly displaying new additions to his exceptionally fine collection of devils: painted devils, wooden devils, bronze devils, cuddly devils, scary devils, big devils, and small devils.

The tall man smiled as he contemplated all these likenesses of himself and other fiends. It seemed to him that since God had created mankind, people had been fascinated with the fallen angels just as the fallen angels were fascinated by people. The difference was, of course, that the fallen angels were jealous of people – of their closeness to God, whereas people had nothing to be jealous of.

Finally, the grey-haired man led his guest to his prized new acquisition – a small oil painting hanging at the far end of the sitting room. It portrayed a group of men on horseback, silhouetted against a twilit sky. They rode slowly through a forest, their horses tired and their heads hung low. Some had rifles strapped to their saddles. Just visible on the head of the last rider were two small horns.

"Oh, I don't believe I recognize this fellow," said the tall man, studying the painting closely. "He's not one of our original lot."

"No, indeed. This one started off human."

"Ah, that would explain it," the tall man mused, "but what's he doing riding with men?"

"They're Polish partisans," explained his host, "fighting the Nazis."

"Ah yes, the Nazis... But why does a devil ride with partisans? That kind of co-mingling isn't strictly allowed, you know. We're supposed to remain neutral."

"It's a very interesting story." The grey-haired man was excited about having got his friend's attention. "It was told to me in an antique shop by the old Pole who sold me the painting. It will be my pleasure to relate it to you, should you wish to hear it."

"Please do." His host's enthusiasm for all things devilish touched Lucifer deeply. The grey-haired man looked delighted.

"Well, it all began in a small Polish village in the fourteenth century. In the village lived a peasant called Boruta. He was a God-fearing man... oops!" He threw his guest an apologetic glance. The devil smiled back benevolently and shrugged his shoulders. His friend carried on with his tale.

"He was a hardworking man, well-liked by the other peasants and respected for his incredible strength. One day, when King Casimir the Great was travelling through the countryside to visit his mistress, his carriage got stuck in mud near a field in which Boruta was working. The king's servants pushed and pulled, and beat the horses, but the carriage did not budge. Boruta spotted their plight and hurried over. The peasant braced his shoulders and single-handedly pushed the king's carriage out of the mud. So impressed was the king with Boruta's strength that he rewarded him with land and a title. But, like many people who move rapidly from poverty to riches, Boruta did not take well to his newly acquired wealth. He was a cruel and dissolute lord; he beat his peasants and indulged in every conceivable vice. He stopped going to church and insulted the parish priest when he tried to visit his manor. So vile did Boruta become that when he died, he was sent back into the world as a devil, destined forever to haunt the marshes and forests around his village, frightening maids and luring men into the chest high bogs."

The devil smiled, evidently enjoying his friend's tale. The grey-haired man continued.

"Hundreds of years went by and Boruta got bored out in the marshes. Scaring the villagers wasn't enough for him anymore. Then one Sunday in May he heard the church bells ringing and crept to the edge of the forest to watch the people going to their temple. How pathetic they all looked – dressed up to the nines, sucking up to the equally pathetic parish priest (a different one now, of course, to the one that Boruta had thrown out of his manor all those years ago). What empty ritual. Boruta wondered how they would look if the church tower they were all so proud of were to fall down. That gave him the idea he needed. Now he had a mission.

"Boruta waited until dark and then set about his plan to bring down the church tower. He climbed on it and shook it, but the structure would not budge. He howled and scratched, but nothing happened. He struck at the tower all night with his powerful tail and finally succeeded in knocking off a couple of roof tiles. The following morning the priest prayed, the women wailed, and the men fixed the roof tiles. That night Boruta went back to the church and pawed at the tower with his strong curved claws. He managed to inflict some visible scratches, but that was all. The next day the priest prayed and the people prayed, and Boruta waited until nightfall to resume his attack on the tower.

"For a hundred years the devil attacked the tower, and the villagers prayed to God for salvation from the unholy creature that kept them awake at night with his howling and scratching. For a hundred years the tower stood proud on the little church and did not succumb to the devil's attacks. But then war came to Poland. Not for the first time, of course, because Poland had seen many wars and had even on occasion ceased to exist as a country in its own right, but Boruta's small village had remained pretty much intact; too insignificant to warrant the attention of invading forces. But this time things were different.

"The Nazis swept through the country in search of Jews and Gypsies, scholars and priests, and anyone else they didn't like. And so it came to pass that they arrived in the small village. They couldn't find any Jews or scholars or Gypsies, but they pulled the priest out of his church and shot him in front of the villagers, and then they proceeded to blow up the ancient church tower. Smoke and rubble flew in all directions, and orange flames leapt up to heaven.

"Boruta gazed at the church in disbelief. It looked strange – wrong. The mighty tower, disproportionately large for the small church it had adorned, lay shattered into a thousand pieces all over the ground. The tower that Boruta had scratched and shaken and pummelled with his tail for a hundred years was no more. The devil looked at the rubble and wept. He sat on the ground, curled his fine tail under his body, and wept and wept. Then he disappeared. But rumours spread through the surrounding area of a brave partisan riding against the Nazis at night – a partisan with a pair of horns and a long black tail."

The grey-haired man smiled at his friend.

"A fine tale," responded the devil, "and a fine painting. I'm pleased it has found its way into your wonderful museum".

"Thank you, my friend" said the grey-haired man and, the tour being over, the two of them retired to a small parlour, the host beaming even more than earlier.

"You've no idea how happy it makes me that you like my collection. But surely you're not in a hurry? Surely you can stay for tea. I have some lovely biscuits."

"You're such a strange species," the devil mused.

"Kind, generous, civilised, so many great achievements, and yet so brutal, cruel and blood thirsty – for no real reason. There are enough resources on earth to go around for everyone, and enough capable people to run things, and yet the world is in a terrible state."

The host studied his old friend carefully.

"You don't seem quite yourself today. You should be celebrating."

"And why is that?" the devil asked.

"Precisely because there are terrible things going on in the world today. People are killing each other for nothing. There's so much evil in the world. You should be proud!"

"Proud of what? I didn't invent the atom bomb. I didn't come up with the Holocaust, or with ethnic cleansing, the Tutsi massacre or any of those things…"

"And what happened recently in the Balkans, and Iraq," added the grey-haired man, "and all the bombings, and what's going on in Syria right now… The world's a right devils' playground."

"Mr. Victor," the tall man glanced at his friend with a hint of disapproval in his dark eyes, "please don't insult us. We don't torture children – they haven't had time to sin yet. We don't rape little girls or build death camps."

The grey-haired man studied his friend thoughtfully for a moment.

"I'll bring us some tea," he said, and left the devil to his thoughts.

☿

The devil walked over to the window, pulled back the net curtain a fraction and peered outside. He noticed his tormentors hanging around, smoking cigarettes and watching the building. He quickly let the curtain drop and moved away from the window. Victor entered, bringing a tea tray, which he set down before them, pouring a cup and passing it to his guest along with a chocolate chip cookie.

"You don't look too good, Mr Lucifer," he eyed his friend sympathetically. "You mustn't worry, everything will be fine. That is, what I meant to say was, everything will be bad and then even worse."

"You're a nice man, Mr Victor. To be honest, I have a great favour to ask you."

"Oh no, not that. I'm very fond of you – you know I am. But I won't give you my soul. No way!"

"No, no. It's not about your soul. We have too many souls at the moment. Can't get rid of them. Once upon a time you had to resort to temptation – great wealth, limitless knowledge, beautiful women... those were the days. Now they'll give their soul away for a lousy buck, or for free. There are no more Fausts, Mr Victor – those times are long gone."

"Well, what is it then?"

Lucifer frowned as a door slammed outside the flat.

"How should I put it?" he continued. "It's about justice. People are doing terrible things, soon they'll demolish the whole earth, the end of the world will come and they will be saved. We rebelled once, a long time ago. Soon we will be out of work, and we would like – how should I put it? – to be saved as well."

"But Mr Lucifer, that's quite impossible!" Both men looked round nervously as the sound of raised voices reverberated on the landing outside the flat. "In any case, how exactly do you think I can help you?"

"I heard that a Polish philosopher once wrote something on the subject - well, that, er, that the devil can be saved. And I would be most grateful if you could find out how this could be done. Perhaps I could drop by again - in a few days' time?"

The voices outside were louder now, much closer. Lucifer listened uneasily. Just then, there came a loud pounding on the door.

"It's them!" cried Lucifer. "Damn! They could kill you.

Listen carefully: I will lure them away from here, and you hide. Or get some help!"

Before Victor had a chance to respond, Lucifer pulled on his hat and coat with lightning speed, opened the door and bolted out, straight into the arms of the waiting thugs. The youths were caught off guard and Lucifer slipped through, running as fast as he could away from Victor's building.

The youths chased Lucifer through the dark streets. If trick-or-treaters had tried their luck in this part of town, they were certainly gone now – probably tucked up in bed, stomachs full of sweets. Rounding a corner, Lucifer stopped suddenly, letting past a malnourished young woman carrying a small child and pulling another, slightly larger, child along behind her.

The youths did not slow down. They knocked over the woman and children, and leapt on Lucifer, beating him mercilessly with their baseball bats.

The woman pulled herself up off the ground, picked up the child that had fallen from her arms, and started to run away. The other child ran after her, crying loudly.

Lucifer's mangled body had stopped moving. One of the youths held a horn torn from Lucifer's scull to his own forehead, his victim's blood dripping from it and smearing the killer's leering face. Another youth laughed loudly as his companion cut off Lucifer's tail and made several clumsy attempts to use it as a skipping rope.

The boys heard an approaching police siren and, grabbing their trophies, disappeared giggling around the corner.

"A bit old to be trick-or-treating, wasn't he?" Officer Fullerton commented to his colleague as he finished his unsuccessful search for a pulse and straightened up, staring uncomprehendingly at the mutilated remains.

Lucifer's unseeing eyes were fixed on the dark heavens and the distant stars as his earthly life bled out into the dust of the gutter.

ABOUT THE AUTHOR

ANNA TABORSKA is a British filmmaker and horror writer. She has written and directed two short fiction films, two documentaries and an award-winning TV drama. She has also worked on twenty other films, and was involved in the making of two major BBC television series: *Auschwitz: the Nazis and 'The Final Solution'* and *World War Two Behind Closed Doors – Stalin, the Nazis and the West.* Anna's short stories have appeared in over thirty anthologies, and her debut collection, *For Those Who Dream Monsters* (published by Mortbury Press in 2013), won the Dracula Society's Children of the Night Award and was nominated for a British Fantasy Award. Anna has been nominated three times for a Bram Stoker Award – for the novelette *The Cat Sitter*, published in her feline-themed micro-collection *Shadowcats* (Black Shuck Books, 2019), for the short story *Two Shakes of a Dead Lamb's Tail* (in *Terror Tales of the Scottish Lowlands*, 2021), and for her latest collection of novelettes and short stories, *Bloody Britain* (Shadow Publishing, 2020), which also received two British Fantasy Award nominations.

You can visit Anna at
http://annataborska.wixsite.com/horror
and http://www.imdb.me/anna.taborska.

SALT GETS IN YOUR

EYES

Nadia Steven Rysing

Elaine jogged into the boardroom of Eakin Provisions and Preservations, apologizing for her lateness. She sat down near the front, trying to ignore the eyes boring into the back of her head. Her boss glanced at her, clearly annoyed, before continuing.

Mr. Travers cleared his throat. "Production is down 15% in the last week alone and workplace injuries are up nearly 34%. At this rate, we will need to hire another medic simply to keep up with the amount of eye injuries we have sustained."

Elaine looked around the table as subtly as she could. She had clearly missed the Agenda. Maybe Betty-

The woman next to her pulled her own paper closer to her and away from Elaine's eyesight. Elaine glared at her. Asshole.

"Miss Sanders. What is your understanding of the situation? Do you have any insights into what may be causing this sudden influx of superstitious activity?"

Elaine stammered in response, "Um, no, Sir."

Mr. Travers grimaced. "Miss Sanders, you were specifically hired for this sort of situation. Surely in the hour that you were delayed you must have thought of some solution or another for the problem."

Elaine looked around nervously and Jane pushed the Agenda towards her, pointing to the underlined title. Elaine murmured a quick thanks before asking the group, "Have you recently hired a large amount of Central or Eastern European immigrants? Specifically German or Polish?"

Mr. Travers snapped his fingers at the Human Resources assistant who whipped through the files on their tablet.

The assistant replied quickly, "Most miners have not filed out their ethnicity. Based on last names, it is estimated that at least seven of the last twenty employees have a European ancestor of Germanic descent."

"Lutherans?" Elaine asked.

The assistant's efficient tone turned sour. "We do not discriminate against religious beliefs in this company, Miss Sanders."

"Nor should you," Elaine assured, glancing back at Mr. Travers. "That's why you've hired me, isn't it? Now, there is a widely held superstition that is believed to originate from Germany during the Lutheran reformation. If one spills salt, one is supposed to throw it over their left shoulder in order to keep the Devil away."

"That is a harmless enough belief," someone commented, "if absurd."

"Not to Lutherans," she commented. "Especially the seven you've hired to work *in a salt mine*. Perhaps, if Human Resources would like to actually utilize my services, this might not have been a problem in the first place."

"It should not be widespread then," the assistant

argued. "It is hardly a statistical factor to have at maximum seven persons exposed to a superstition to cause a moon-wide shut down in production."

Elaine explained insistently, trying not to let her hands fly around too much as she spoke. "Ideas spread quickly. First one miner does it without thinking. The miner behind him asks why. Thinks it's ridiculous, but next time one of his rocks crumbles, he remembers the last time he nearly lost an arm or leg, or maybe one of his friends. So he thinks, why not, maybe the Devil is standing behind me. Pattern continues. Suddenly you have an entire mine panicking every time a sprinkle of salt touches the ground. Hysteria, Mr. Travers, is what has shut down your mine, not the Devil, but just as dangerous."

She smiled to herself as the boardroom chatted amongst its members. And that was why she got a Masters in Religious Studies before venturing into Human Resources. Even if this particular practice she had learned in her Oma's kitchen, she had learned plenty of other traditions to make her worth keeping around.

"So how do we stop it without shutting down the plant?" Betty asked. "Our stockholders grow more and more antsy. We have deliveries to make on three different colonies in the next few days. People need salt."

"Acknowledge it," Elaine offered. "It's harmless enough. Get miners to line up on the right and make them wear screens. Swap out their chisels for sharper ones. And maybe get a priest."

"A priest?" The assistant laughed.

"To bless the salt," Elaine said with a shrug. "It doesn't matter what faith you've got up there as a chaplain. Go overboard. They'll think it was all a ridiculous joke and make fun of those who actually believed in it. Whatever the case. You need the majority to think them worthy of ridicule."

"Aren't you supposed to help religious groups acclimatize to M-1793?" Betty asked dismissively. "Not mock them?"

Elaine sighed, seeing the call come in on her wrist. She silenced it before looking up at Mr. Travers. "Sir, you hired me for my advice. Now you have it. It's up to you what you do with it. If you'll excuse me, a client requires my attention."

The room argued as she left the room, pulling up the call on her wrist. She held it up, transferring it to her remote piece.

"Mama?" Elaine asked. "What's wrong?"

"Did you make it to your meeting alright? I'm sorry we got you there so late and to phone you now, just..."

"It's fine, Mama," she reassured. "What do you need?"

"The test came back positive. Your sister and brother are compatible. She's going to make the offering first and come back for the surgery. If you prayed...well...it would mean a lot to me. I'll let you know when I hear more, okay?"

"I'll talk to you then," Elaine assured.

She ended the call, hearing the door open behind her. Mr. Travers stood, arms folded. She recognized that look. She hated that look.

"I'm sorry," she apologized, rambling without thinking. "My brother is in the ICU. I've just heard that he's getting a liver transplant this afternoon. I know I was late, but if I could leave early today-"

"You embarrassed me today," he hissed. "You were late, you didn't read the briefing, and then you sass me in front of the others? I vouched for you, insisted that you get this job, over any other candidate. You owe me, Sanders."

"And I am sorry," she said, trying to sound sincere though she honestly could not give two shits about his ego at that moment.

"You can demonstrate that to me when you call from M-1793."

"What?" She asked in shock.

"You heard me, Miss Sanders. We cannot afford to replace an entire mining team, but I can afford to replace you. So get that little well-educated ass of yours up there and prevent this shit from happening again. If the incidents don't stop, you can spend whatever time you like by your "brother's sick bedside". You've never mentioned a sibling, Sanders, you can't pretend to have one now when it's convenient to you. And if you have been hiding resources from the company-"

Elaine realized her mistake. Sixteen months on the job and she had been so careful not to mention her family life. Mentally she swore but she said sheepishly instead, "You're right. I was...making plans with my boyfriend. We were going to go to Nassau Delta for the weekend. You caught me."

Mr. Travers shook his head with a deep sigh. "The next transport leaves in forty-seven minutes and I expect you to be on it. The company is flying you in on business class, which is more than you deserve. Those are eighty hours you are getting paid to be in cryo and not at your desk so I expect to report to me the minute you land and start making up for lost time."

"Yes, Sir."

"Now get out of my sight."

Elaine grabbed her briefcase and went to the other side of the building. She lined up with some of the lower ranked employees of the Chicago office, typing in her flight needs. Pariet 2x a day, preferably at 0900 and 1800. Full moisture every 24 hours. Post-flight massage and chiropractic treatments. Personalized nitro/oxa mix for her skin type and lung capacity. If she was going, she was using up every last one of her employee credits. It'd be like a vacation. A very shitty vacation.

She called her mother's number and eventually she answered. Security insisted that Elaine turn her monitor off but she flipped them off and exited the line, letting others get fondled first.

"Mama, I'm going to be away for a week or so," Elaine said, "maybe a bit longer."

"Are you serious? This should qualify for family leave. They let you go when Papa died, why can't...you never registered Isaac or Marian, did you? I thought it was strange that your insurance card wasn't working but-"

"I told you not to process those without me," Elaine hissed. "I've got a deal going with someone in that office."

"You shouldn't have wasted your money with a bribe. It's not like your CEO will want their parts, especially with Isaac so sick. Leah, we could have used it to-"

"Mama," Elaine said, flinching at her given name, "we cannot talk about this right now. Listen, my keycode is in the third cabinet at my apartment. There's enough in the account for anything you guys might need. Also, please feed the cat."

"You'll call me when you get there?"

Elaine hesitated. "It's going to be 80 hours, then the transfer time. I have no idea what time of day that I'm getting to M-1793."

"It doesn't matter. I have a feeling I'm not going to be sleeping much the next few days anyways. I just want to know you're okay."

"I'm fine, Mama," she promised. "I've got to go. The pilot's assistant is getting pissed off at me. I love you."

The security guard glared at her and Elaine rolled her eyes as she ended the call and turned off her monitor. She let herself be scanned, patted down, and IDed. She was allowed onto the craft where she was guided to her own pod. She handed over her monitor.

"Any allergies?" The steward asked. "Any underlying medical conditions?"

Elaine shook her head. This was not the time to announce to her company that she carried multiple unpleasant recessive genes that might announce their presence anytime soon.

"We'll be settling you in then," he assured, clipping her

into place.

She grimaced as he stuck the IV in her arm and gestured for her to start counting backwards. He blurred in front of her and she tried to squint, making out his face. She could swear...she could swear he had horns.

She pounded on the pod as the case closed and the cold slurry leaked in. She should be out by now, but the adrenaline fought back against the medication. She screamed out, banging loudly on the glass as the fluid entered her lungs.

Her eyes closed and she tried to make the sign of the three on the glass. She traced the second circle just as she slipped into unconsciousness.

Elaine woke gasping and saw that she was lying in a courtesy cot with a dozen or so other passengers who had taken poorly to the sedatives. She sat up and caught her breath, trying to remind herself that whatever hallucination she had experienced was due to a bad batch of slurry.

After being very briefly checked over by an attendant, she was given three lieu hours in compensation and handed her briefcase. She took her first steps on M-1793 shaking, her high heels trembling beneath her as she strode down the hallway and to the gateway terminal.

It was her first time off world and she had been hoping to see stars and foreign landscapes. Instead she was in a reinforced steel dome with no windows. There were tunnels leading off in various directions and a tube chute going down towards the mines or up towards an observation deck. She was considering taking a moment to look at the latter when someone called her name.

"Ms. Sanders? Elaine Sanders?"

She turned to see a man about a decade older than her holding a makeshift sign with her last name on it. He gave a little wave and came over to her side. He picked up her briefcase and luggage for her. He handed her the sign and slightly confused she tossed it in a waste receptacle.

"I'm Mark Cai, I'm the Lead Foreman on the mine here. Management asked me to show you around so you can get a better sense of the problem here. You all right? You get your legs yet?"

"I'm okay," she said, "though if we're going into the mine I'd like to put on some more practical shoes."

"We'll drop by your room so you can change out of your nice suit there. We'll grab you some boots off the shoe truck on the way down. You're what, a size 6? We should be able to grab you something or we'll get a few extra pairs of socks for you. How's the gravity treating you? Do you need weight inserts?"

"I'll be fine," she promised. "Is there a comm in my room I can use? I need to check on something back home."

"There's a company phone in there but if you're looking for a bit more privacy, we've got a joint system in our break room. You ask nicely and I'm sure someone will let you use it."

"Thank you," she said sincerely.

"It's my pleasure, Ms. Sanders. I want the best for my people and this whole thing is getting out of hand. I'd rather have you than getting some stiff with a few MBAs. You might actually know what's going on and get something good done."

"Well, I could be wrong, but really it just sounds like a superstition that got out of hand. It's silly but it's a real health and safety concern. That's my expertise, adapting workplace safety protocols to fit religious belief."

"Superstition?" Mark laughed. "Excuse me, Ms. Sanders, but I don't think they quite explained to you the real problem down there."

"Then what exactly is the problem, Mr. Cai?"

They arrived at her room and he swiped a keycard through the door. It was little more than a bed and a dresser but she got the sense that this was practically luxurious compared to most of the site.

He handed her bags to her. "Ms. Sanders, I was always told it makes a much more convincing story if you show and don't tell. You get settled in and meet me on the observation deck when you're ready."

Elaine rolled her eyes as he left. Drama Queen.

She dressed in more practical jeans and a black flannel shirt. She tied her relatively short hair back into a spiky little ponytail and washed the surviving makeup from her face. She felt more comfortable and knew that she would make a better impression than in her boardroom outfit. She didn't have any other shoes so she put her heels back on, grateful to soon be getting something a bit sturdier to wear.

It wasn't too hard to make her way back to the gateway terminal and up the chute to the observation deck but she was disappointed when she arrived on the top floor. The nearest sun was four times the distance of Sol from Earth and there were no moons to reflect its glow. It looked much like the photos she had seen of Pluto when she was a girl or honestly more like a gravel pit at night. She sighed and then turned around, looking for Mark.

He wasn't far, leaning on the railing as he looked up at the sky. He was gazing at the direction of Earth, even though it would barely be a speck through a telescope. He smiled to himself and she almost felt as if she was intruding on a conversation.

He noticed her and greeted her. "Ms. Sanders, excellent. If you're ready, we'll get going. After you."

It had taken her a few times to realize he was using Ms. and not Miss to address her. She found it oddly touching.

They entered the chute and he swiped his keycard through the base of the monitor. The elevator moved down slowly through the building, the lights growing stronger as they went beneath the surface.

They came to a halt and Mark gestured for her to go

first. She stepped onto into a dry tunnel, her eyes immediately stinging. He pointed at a quartermaster a few feet away.

"Get a mask and your boots. You'll want to shower when you get back and moisturize. Otherwise you're going to look like a mummy when you go home."

"You don't need one?" She asked.

He shrugged. "Not worth the rental price. The standard goggles are good enough for me and I keep my canteen full."

Elaine questioned, "Mr. Cai, I was told I was coming here because there were ocular injuries. How is that the case if you wear goggles?"

"Like I said. Show, don't tell."

She rolled her eyes again and went to the quartermaster. She rented a hydrating mask, bought two pairs of socks, and grabbed a pair of work boots from the shoe truck. She tossed her heels in the trash.

She returned to Mark's side. "Okay, I'm ready."

He replied, "You're really not, but let's go anyways."

He led her down another tunnel and to a second chute, this one large enough to accommodate nearly two dozen people. She stood far away from as he punched in his access codes, trying to get a better sense of him.

His skin was fairly dark and wrinkled, but it was hard to tell how much was age and how much was his working conditions. His eyes were hidden behind tinted goggles now but the lines around his mouth showed that he had a well-used smile. He wasn't very tall but she wasn't either. His ordinariness almost annoyed her. The moon wasn't pretty, the foreman wasn't worth flirting with, and she was stranded away from her family. She had no idea if Isaac was being prepped or if both he and her sister were already under the knife. They could both be dead already.

She started breathing too quickly and Mark asked, "You claustrophobic?"

She lied, "A little."

"You'll get used to it soon. The main section of the mine is pretty open."

His voice was a little too loud, a little too hoarse. He had the confidence and the hearing damage of an experienced labourer who hadn't bothered wearing hearing protection for at least a dozen years. She was surprised he was even wearing the goggles.

The elevator shuddered and they arrived on the ground floor. Mark went first, showing his identification to the fully covered guards. They let them through without issue.

"What do you need security for in a salt mine?" She asked.

"To look impressive. I guarantee you those two are watching vids under those masks. Probably dirty ones, to be honest. You can't get much else out here."

If he was trying to make her blush, it didn't work.

"You said you were going to show me the problem?"

They came into the main working area. Salt was streaming past through a series of conveyances, all circling up towards the fifty-foot domed ceiling. Stairs were built into the stone alongside them and a few workers ran up and down them doing quality control. On the ground there was an office built into the wall and a lineup of workers in front of it, most of whom sported bandages over their eyes. She recognized the Eakin Provisions and Preservations logo on its door.

"Medic," he explained.

"How many people do you have working down here?"

"Total? Eighty or so. Forty on, forty off. The barracks are a few floors up. We've got around thirty-two people down here today though because of all the injuries. Probably a bit less since we're just coming off lunch and we're not strict about people coming back from break. The rest of our folks are in the tunnels down that way. I'll take you through the first level just so you get an idea of it but if you're feeling closed in I won't take you any further."

"That'll be fine," Elaine said.

147

"Great. Let's go."

They went down a steep tunnel, the air drier than she had ever experienced. Her skin cracked as it dried and she felt like her hands might start bleeding. Mark seemed unfazed and she followed him further down into the dark earth. Maybe ten minutes later the ground leveled and she could see workers breaking down the salt deposits and loading it onto the conveyor belt that snaked through the ground.

Every worker she saw wore goggles.

She asked Mark pointedly, "Okay, we're here. You going to tell me what's going on now?"

"Wait and watch," he said. "Look at the crystals."

It occurred to her then how strange it was that there were only pickaxes and no heavy machinery. Then she looked at the walls.

Every salt mine she had visited on earth looked different. The dark bellows beneath Ontario's great lakes, the pools built in the Andes mountains, the blocks of Ethiopia's highlands. Each was beautiful in a strange way, each unique and surreal.

But she had never seen anything like this.

This salt was pink and smooth and looked almost like polished glass. Its crystals shone with unnatural light and when it broke it crackled like a burning log. It left behind a fine dust that hung in the air as if it was too light to sink.

"We brought in trucks at first and the place nearly exploded," Mark commented. "Then we hit it with hammers and we couldn't breathe. Once it fully oxidizes it turns grey and stops being volatile but it's damn dangerous when it's down here."

"So you can't spill it," she murmured.

"What?"

"If you're not spilling it, you're not throwing it," Elaine said, mostly to herself. "So how are so many people getting hurt?"

He picked up a chunk off the ground and placed it in

her hand. "Because it's not salt, Ms. Sanders."

It felt hot against her palm and the cracks healed, leaving behind smooth tender skin. Then it started burning and she dropped it. Fine welts rose and ached where the rock had touched her.

"What the hell is that?" She asked.

"We call it Devil's Salt," Mark explained. "Like I said, it's safe once it's oxidized, but down here it promises a balm and then tears it away. If it gets in your eyes, it'll nearly blind you."

"But you're wearing goggles," she said.

The ground rumbled slightly. The workers put down their picks. Mark froze and put his hand on Elaine's shoulder. She held her breath until it stopped.

He addressed the workers closest to him, "Head back to the main chamber and get Davis to start moving people back to the surface. Slowly."

"What's going on?" Elaine asked.

"I shouldn't have brought you down here, Ms Saunders. I shouldn't have risked it. I'll get you up to the surface and, God willing, I'll meet you at the administrative cafeteria soon. I want you to walk slowly and firmly back up the way we came. Go on."

The world shook harder and a large rock of salt cracked off and hit the ground. Mark gave her a gentle shove back towards the chamber. "Go."

She did as she was told, evacuating with the others. Used to the steep climb, the workers ran past her while she fumbled up the slope. She slipped, her ankle twisting beneath her. She tried to stand, grasping onto the wall of the tunnel. The Devil's Salt burned her and she fell again, wrecking her ankle further.

She called for help but the rumbling was too loud for those ahead to hear her. She looked back, desperately hoping that Mark was on his way. The ground beneath her shifted and she slid back down into the tunnel. The lights flickered on and off as she tried to climb back up and suddenly she was alone in the dark, the salt burning every part of her, the air drying the very breath from her lungs.

Elaine cried out again and she heard someone reach her side and wordlessly offer out their hand. Elaine took it and nearly screamed, feeling the deep wiry hair that encased it. The figure grabbed her and pulled her up to meet its bright orange eyes, bringing Elaine a good foot off the ground.

And then it said to her, in a slurred deeply accented ancient language it should have not known, "They will leave or they will die."

Somehow Elaine had the wits to reply, in German, not Gothic, hoping it'd be close enough. "If they leave, others will come. Once there is a resource to exploit, they will not stop sending workers. Even if it kills them."

It growled, "Then I will kill them."

"They aren't your enemy," Elaine argued, her own ire stronger than her fear. "They're not the problem. The people who send them are. They want profit at any cost. If you want them to go, there can't be any profit to have."

It dropped her onto the ground and she cried out, the salt scraping off the skin of her cheek. The creature retreated into the dark and deep in her pain, she could have sworn she heard the soft clatter of cloven hoofs.

Whatever had sustained her before faded and she called out, "Please, please don't leave me here. Please!"

But there was nothing left but the dark.

Elaine woke for the second time that day on a cot with a medic hovering nearby. She tried to move but found she was strapped down. Fearfully, she looked around and saw Mark stir from the chair beside her. He touched her shoulder, trying to convince her to stay still and not rip the stitches holding her face together.

Elaine insisted, "I saw it. I saw-"

Mark said quietly, "I know. I know what you saw. I've seen it before, just before it killed and ate one of my supervisors raw. Others have told me they've seen it too, just before they've lost their sight."

Elaine felt absurd asking it, but she couldn't help herself. "Is it the Devil?"

Mark admitted, "I don't know. But I think…I think it doesn't matter, does it?"

Elaine wanted to argue, but she had no idea what to say. They could strike, sure. But someone else would come. If not one worker, then another. It wouldn't solve anything.

Unless…

♉

Mark ordered the mine shut, claiming there had been a gas leak. Then he brought Elaine back down into the tunnels, bringing her to the place she had seen…whatever it was she had seen.

Elaine called out to the dark, "I've come to negotiate terms."

For a moment there was silence before the creature whispered, "The light."

Mark turned off the flashlight and promised, "I'll keep it off."

They could not see the creature, but they could hear its footsteps and it came close, so close, that Elaine could feel its breath on her injured face.

"They will leave or they will die."

Elaine agreed, "Yes, so you've said, but that's likely not going to be an option."

"I will make it an option."

Elaine replied, "Not by yourself you won't. I've come with an offer and I think it might interest you. Have you ever heard of collective bargaining?"

Mark clearly knew enough German to understand what

she was saying and hissed at her, "Are you trying to unionize with the Devil?"

The creature laughed, a surprisingly warm laugh in the dark and Elaine smiled. "Not trying, Mr. Kai. I believe I'm succeeding."

ABOUT THE AUTHOR

NADÍA STEVEN RYSÍNG (she/her) is an academic, poet, and speculative writer living on the Haldimand Tract in Southwestern Ontario. Her work has or will appear in *Black Telephone*, *Gothic Nature Journal*, and the anthologies *FUTURES*, *Abyss* and *Madwomen in Social Justice Movements, Literatures, and Art*. You can find her on Twitter @a_tendency.

I WEAR DEVILS

James Maxey

Getting into Hell is easy, but I'm doing it the hard way, working up a sweat on a freezing West Virginia mountain a little after midnight. I can't jab my shovel more than two inches into the churchyard without hitting a rock. I wish I'd worn different shoes. My black Keds were comfy for the long drive but crap for grave robbing.

Just so we're clear, I'm not trying to dig my way into Hell. Don't be silly. I'm exhuming the grave of a dairy farmer who choked to death drinking milk. People saw the hand of fate in his demise. Their belief imbues his bones with magic.

It smells like ripe cheese when I hack into the coffin. White bones sit atop a hardened puddle of ick. I twist the skull free and run back to the U-Haul. No time to close the grave. His relatives will probably think some depraved occultist stole his skull for some dark magic. They'll be right!

People like me are why I had Mom cremated.

I drive like a madwoman along one lane dirt roads. If I miss this hellmouth, I won't get another shot until the next full moon. That's a long time for someone to burn in a lake of brimstone because I couldn't say no to a donut. Once I reach the highway, I floor the accelerator and race toward my date with a devil.

How's that for a one sentence story of my life?

☿

My name's Jaqueline Lantern. Really. Jacquie Lantern. It wasn't an easy name to grow up with. As you might guess from my skeleton tattoos, I've leaned into the year-round Halloween aesthetic. I'm not a witch! I hate when people assume that. I'm a necromantic chaos thaumaturge. If you need someone to explain the difference between a thaumaturge and a witch, honestly, I don't have the spoons.

☿

An hour behind schedule, I screech to a halt in the IGA parking lot in Marlinton. Reverend Billy is shaking a cigarette free as he sits on the tailgate of his pickup. From the butts covering the ground, he's been waiting a while.

"Startin' to think you'd backed out," Billy says, cupping his hands around his lighter. The glow highlights the gray streaks in Billy's dark hair. Billy's native American, but doesn't know what tribe. He was abandoned in a rest stop, then raised by a pair of Bible-thumping snake-handlers. I've only worked with Billy once before. We didn't hit it off. He's a little Jesus heavy for my tastes. But, he's got the skills I need and lives nearby, so he'll do. If there's an app to rate preachers who cast out devils, I'd give him four stars.

"Sorry to cut things close," I say as a walk to the back of the van. "I detoured to grab a fresh skull."

"You've had a month to prepare," Billy grumbles.

"Shit happens. I picked up my doll from storage this

154

morning and found out rats had gnawed the glyphs."

"Ain't you a little old to play with dolls?"

"I'll never be that old," I say. "But these days, I play with bigger dolls."

I open the U-Haul to reveal a mound of stone body parts. The statue toppling of recent years has been great for business. The doll has the torso of Thomas Jefferson, the legs of Robert E. Lee, and the massive, oversized arms of Bigfoot. I ran across the big guy in Olympia and had a chisel in my bag, as one does. The stone anatomy is linked with rods and gears I stole from a haunted clock tower in Dallas. That was an all-night job requiring numerous bribes and a smidgeon of arson.

I break out my Dremel and engrave a slapdash series of glyphs on the dairyman's brow. I'd hint at an interesting backstory for the Dremel, but some things are easier to order from Amazon. I frown as I finish the last glyph. Sloppy. Two stars, max. I'll be lucky if this skull doesn't crumble before dawn.

"Rise," I say, as I place the skull upon the doll's stone shoulders.

The doll rises, twanging and grinding to its full ten-foot height. I hand it a pickax and steer it to the "X" Billy has spray-painted on the asphalt. The parking lot feels like an oven. The hellmouth can't be more than a few feet below the surface. The other time Billy and I worked together, the hellmouth opened in an abandoned mineshaft, no digging required.

"Dig," I say to my doll.

Reverend Billy and I step back to avoid the flying chunks. "Fancy," he says as he watches the doll in motion. "You know I could have rented a backhoe."

"Whoever was operating the backhoe would get sucked down to Hell the second they broke through," I say. "The doll has no soul. Infernal gravity can't touch it. We're safe over here."

"We're breaking into Hell," says Billy. "Nothing about

this is safe. If you'd gotten here on time, we could have done some entwined warding spells. Sealed off the area in case anything nasty tries to sneak through."

"Don't sweat it. I do crazier shit than this all the time." I smile. He doesn't smile back.

Billy and I are never going to see eye to eye. Everything's serious with him. To me, nothing's serious. If I didn't embrace the crazy, I'd be a gibbering lunatic after all the things I've done. Not to mention the stuff done to me. Life's a joke, and I prefer being the one delivering the punchlines. Billy's in the trenches of a supernatural war fighting to save the world. I'm just in this for kicks. Plus, you know, the money. Usually. Tonight, we're working pro bono. I haven't mentioned that to Billy.

"We'll be fine," I say. Billy's frown is only getting deeper as glowing red light seeps up through cracks in the pavement. "The doll's working perfectly. How about you how me what you got under the tarp?"

Billy nods, flicking away his cigarette. He pulls the tarp free with a flourish, revealing a dog crate housing a runty pig.

"Old school," I say.

"Been casting out devils since I was twelve," says Billy. "Nothing beats jamming a devil into a pig."

"I'll escape this swine," the pig squeals, "then rip out your spine!"

"It rhymes!" I clap my hands with delight. Rhymers are top-shelf demons. Reverend Billy has gone above and beyond. "Awesome. Now help me into my straightjacket."

I wrestle my eveningwear from my bag. The pig watches closely as I pull the straightjacket on. The heavy jacket still reeks from the last time I used it. There's a dearth of YouTube hacks for getting the stench out of brimstone out of cotton. Billy helps fasten the straps and buckles.

The pig furrows its brow, guessing what we're about to attempt. It grunts, "I shan't fear your cage of cloth! I'll shred it fast, then rip your heads off!"

"You brought the ether?" I ask Billy.

"Of course," he says.

"Wait, what?" the pig squeals, realizing the straightjacket is only part of the trap. "You snot!"

Billy cinches the last strap and asks, "Ready?"

"Ready," I say.

"Nickazeedle the Vile," Billy shouts at the pig. "Leave this vessel and assume your true form!"

"Shut your hole! I defy control!" Ol' Nick's defiance is an empty boast. The pig writhes and snorts as smoke pours from its nostrils. The smoke solidifies into a cliché from a medieval painting. He's got horns, red skin, a pointy tail, black wings, the whole package, including, you know, a huge, gnarly package.

Billy grabs me by the shoulders. He shoves his face right into mine and screams, "Jacqueline Lantern! Relinquish your mortal clay!"

The sensation of my soul peeling free of my flesh is literally unnerving. My spectral fingers slip out of gloves of skin and bone. The worst thing about it is the memory of the first time I found out this was possible.

My empty body falls limp. Tossing a soulless shell in front of a demon is like tossing a live mouse in front of a cat. Nickazeedle abandons his body to snatch mine. I slide into his devil-flesh before it can discorporate. As bad as it is pulling free of my body, slipping into a devil is a thousand times worse. Have you ever worn a tight corset? Like, steel ribs, laced until your eyes bulge? Imagine if that corset snapped shut on you all at once, and it wasn't just your torso compressed, but your arms and legs, fingers and toes, your tongue and ears and eyes. Then imagine that the corset is lined with razor blades. That's maybe a tenth of what I suffer when I take over a demon.

I gingerly try out my new fingers. The long black nails are sharp as daggers. I'm jealous. Grave robbing doesn't do my own nails any favors. I inhale, only to wind up coughing bile and blood. Devils are strong, but they aren't healthy. Every inch of my devil-flesh is covered with boils, blisters, and puss-weeping wounds. That's why devils jump into host bodies every chance they get.

I really, really wish Mom's nurse had never stopped at Krispy Kreme.

Nickazeedle has already dislocated the shoulders of my real body. He twists like a pretzel, trying to wrestle out of the straightjacket. Billy covers his mouth with the ether rag. Nickazeedle breathes out one last attempt at a rhyme, but his words are too muffled to make out what he's saying. His attempts at cursing only make him inhale the ether faster. He goes limp. I turn away, hating to see my body so vulnerable.

Just then, flames thirty stories tall shoot into the air. This is a welcome distraction from my body anxiety. The asphalt around the hellmouth starts to bubble. Billy carries my body to the passenger seat of the U-Haul. He's a good man, but of all the difficult things I'll do tonight, leaving my unconscious flesh in the hands of a man my father's age is the most difficult. Billy sees to it that my body is resting comfortably, then comes back around to the driver's side. He lights a cigarette before he climbs in.

"They'll charge me extra if you smoke in there," I say.

"The AC on my truck ain't worked in years," Billy says with a shrug. "Might as well stay comfortable until you're back. Who's the Court of Elders sending you after? Another girl with a rich daddy? Some tycoon's dearly departed mama?"

"Yeah," I say. "Somebody's mama."

I feel bad not telling him the truth. Now that he's invoked the Court of Elders there are probably a hundred crystal balls focused on him. The Elders won't be happy about our freelance incursion into the netherworld.

I flex my devil wings and fly into the flames, diving straight down. A veil of black smoke enwreathes me as I leave the living world and soar into the black sky under the asphalt.

♉

Geologists will never admit it, but Hell is exactly where you learned it was in Sunday school. It's a lake of fire in the middle of the planet filled with damned souls screaming for eternity. The first time the Elders sent me here I was kind of disappointed at how unoriginal it was. Maybe it's boring by design. It might take the edge off the punishment if it was even slightly interesting.

In fact, the only interesting thing I've learned about Hell is that, for the most part, it's filled with good people. If you've been raised in Western vagueness about what happens to your soul after you die, you probably have some unconscious link to this place. If you die with any burden of guilt, you come to Hell to receive your punishment.

Of course, any decent person is going to feel guilty about something. Maybe they can't stop thinking about the time they got angry and slapped their kid. Maybe they fantasized a minute too long about betraying their spouse with some fresh, new face. Maybe they didn't fill in a grave they robbed because they have poor time management skills. It's small sins that fill Hell to overflowing.

Heaven is mostly populated with sociopaths incapable of shame. You can't throw a harp without hitting a senator or CEO. That makes it a second Hell. Neither is a great option. Fortunately, it's not a binary choice.

♉

I land on a mound of smoldering brimstone on the shore of a flaming lake. Damned souls flail in the flames, wailing in agony. Any that get too close to the shore get jabbed by devils with pitchforks. Nickazeedle didn't have his pitchfork with him, so when a few devils look my way,

159

I use my toe talons to gouge the eyes of some old man who's trying to crawl onto my rock. The devils turn back to pitchfork duty, deciding I belong here.

Maybe I do. I mean, I desecrate corpses for a living. I seldom make it through a week without committing at least one unspeakable atrocity. I can't even claim to use my talents for some greater good. The Court of Elders pays me a hefty fee to snatch souls out of Hell. Everyone I rescue has rich relatives who can afford the offerings the Elders require. Compared to the sketchiness of that, coming here to find my mother's soul is practically the work of a saint.

But I'm no saint. Neither was mom. Look, I don't talk much about my past. Most practitioners of the dark arts will broodingly regale you with tales of their tragic childhoods. I prefer to live in the here and now. From the moment I dug up my first corpse to practice on, I've controlled my own destiny. In the field of necromantic chaos thaumaturgy, I'm kind of a big deal.

Alas, explaining why I'm back in Hell requires at least a little autobiography.

Here goes. When I was fourteen, my father started lacing my meals with sleeping pills. He didn't want me to witness what he'd do next. Yet, witness it I did. You know how some people report that they float outside their body when they're sedated? I'm one of those people. My soul wanders free when my flesh gets shut down. I saw everything my father did. I told my mother, but my father denied everything. My mother convinced herself I was having nightmares. And it wasn't like I was going to convince some school counselor that I knew what I knew because I'd gained the power of astral projection.

I ran away from home, but not just to escape my father. The science-based world taught in school couldn't explain my phantom journeys. I headed for New Orleans, seeking answers. I never looked back.

I survived on my own, a voluntary orphan, for over a decade. A few weeks ago, I noticed that the "lucky numbers" on a fortune cookie happened to be my parents' home phone. Against my better judgment, I dialed the number.

My mother answered. She wept when she heard my voice. I teared up myself. She told me my father had gone missing. He'd disappeared a few weeks back, right after Mom had told him her big news.

Mom was dying. Like, in a matter of days. Late-stage pancreatic cancer. She was all alone in the house, save for the hospice nurses. Five minutes after I hung up the phone I'd bought a plane ticket back home.

♉

Reaching my mom now in Hell isn't as easy as booking a flight. I grab the guy whose eyes I gouged out before he sinks under. Necromancy has a lot of sub-disciplines, but the core skill is divination by studying the entrails of the dead. Human guts are a pre-modern Wikipedia. Any question you care to ask, the entrails can answer. Often, the answers are somewhat right.

I slice my writhing victim open and study the folds of his large intestine. They form a bloody, smelly roadmap. Since my mother is a recent arrival, she'll be near a shore. A malignant purple blotch shows me which bay I need to look in. I flap my wings and fly off to finish this.

♉

My big mistake when I flew home to see my mother was wanting to start something. My dark magic couldn't heal her body. But I thought, perhaps, another sort of healing could begin. I thought we could finally talk openly.

I thought we could work through why she'd let me down.

Now that my father was gone, would she confess to knowing what she must have known all along? My father was an unforgivable bastard. Had she been his victim as well, and I'd missed the clues because I was young and oblivious? For close to ten years, I'd convinced myself she hadn't failed me as much as, perhaps, I'd failed her. Couldn't I have done more to help her see through my father's lies? Had it been selfish of me to abandon her to the prison of her life, trapped behind bars with that monster?

She was asleep when I arrived. I sat by her bed for an hour. When she eventually woke I couldn't ask the questions I wanted to ask. We talked about my flight and the weather. She told me she liked my tattoos, then she started crying. I didn't ask her why. She knew she'd done wrong. She knew where she was going to spend eternity.

I decided that she'd suffered enough. Heaven and Hell aren't the only options when you die. I mean, you've heard of reincarnation. You know about spirits who wander the earth as ghosts. And the most merciful option of all is to come to a final end. Just as your body will decompose into soil, the last remnants of a soul can disperse into the ocean of mystic energy that roils beneath the material world.

As a necromantic chaos thaumaturge, I know how to disperse a soul at the moment of death. Unfortunately, I can't do it while the soul is clinging to a body. This is why I sat by my mother's bed, night and day, as she went into her final decline. I hadn't been able to rescue her from my father, but I could at least spare her an eternity in Hell.

I remember the last morning. I'd spent a long night watching her sleep, wondering again and again if she'd stopped breathing. Rays of sunlight pushed through the curtains as she opened her eyes only a little and whispered, "He was a good man."

"What?" I asked, leaning closer.

"Your father," she said, her voice weak and distant.

162

"He tried... so hard. The way his father... hurt him. He fought every day... to be better."

"What are you saying?" I asked. "Are you saying his father sexually abused—"

"There are... all kind of abuse," Mom whispered. "Your grandfather... never took care of his family. Any money he made... he drank away. Your father grew up hungry... and swore it would never happen to us. He worked his fingers to the bone. He wasn't... a bad man."

"Mom," I said, squeezing her hand. "Mom, how can you say that? After what I've told you? Why didn't you—"

"I believed you," she said, squeezing my hand back. "He confessed... everything. S-swore it wouldn't... happen again."

"Again? What does that matter? If you knew he did it even once—"

"You can't give up on someone you love," she said, calmly, as if she wasn't stabbing me in the heart.

I pulled my hand from hers. I was trembling, ready to scream. At that moment, the morning nurse tapped on the bedroom door. I normally tried to keep the nurses out of the room, telling them I needed privacy. What I really needed was to make sure there were no witnesses when I cast my soul dispersal spell. Chanting and hand-waving in front of normies is awkward. Now, I welcomed the interruption.

The nurse said, "Becky tells me you've been up all night. If you need a break, I've got some donuts in the kitchen."

I brushed tears from my cheeks as I walked out. I had a donut, cold, oily and sickly sweet. In the upstairs bathroom, I threw up. I washed my face, staring in the mirror. Why had I returned? Why had I imagined I might save her? Why did I even want to?

But the face staring back at me from the mirror wasn't only my face. I have her eyes, her jaw, her lips. Perhaps it hadn't been her I'd come to save. Living like nothing matters is liberating until the day it becomes tedious.

I heard the nurse calling my name. I splashed a little more water on my face, toweled off, and went to face my mother's last moments.

But when I went downstairs, the nurse looked grave and apologetic. The nurse started to explain how quickly everything happened, but I didn't listen. My mother had said what she'd been hanging on to say. She'd had no reason to keep breathing after that.

I rushed into the room, praying I wasn't too late to cast the dispersal spell. Nothing answered my prayer. With my magically trained senses, the scent of brimstone was overwhelming.

The scent of brimstone is heavy again as I land on the shore of a bubbling caldera. I spot my mother, naked and frail, hip deep in flames. A trio of lesser demons lash her with whips.

Wearing a rhymer's skin, I'm bigger and higher ranking. I charge into the trio, slashing them with my claws. Two flee, but the last one tosses aside his whip. He's got a sword jammed straight through his ribcage that he draws out, hissing. He tries to stab me, but I poke him in the throat with my hooked tail, then twist the blade from his grasp. He turns, revealing a second face where his ass should be. I kick him in his lower nose and he races off across flames, using the faces of the damned as stepping stones.

"Jacquie!" my mother cries, stretching an arm toward me. "Help me!"

I'm not shocked that she recognizes me. The blood bond we share lets her see past my current skin. I don't call back to her. I don't intend to speak to her, or listen to anything she says. My plan is to drag her back to the material world as a spirit, disperse her, and be rid of my ghosts once and for all.

I fly toward her and grab her arm. I tug, but she doesn't budge. Something's holding her down. I beat my wings harder, lifting her. A second body emerges from the mire. It's a man, with his arms wrapped tightly around her.

It's my father. The top of his head is missing, the kind of wound you see when people blow their brains out. Now we know why he disappeared.

"Let go!" I cry, kicking him. The blow stuns him and his arms fall limp, but this doesn't free my mother. I see now that their bodies have melted together, joined at the hip.

"Save him!" my mother begs. "Save all of us!"

"Not part of the plan," I say, hacking at her hip with the sword, trying to cut her free from my father. But someone else's arm thrusts up from below their two bodies, grabbing the blade. Both bodies start to rise, and I see that my mother and father aren't alone in the pit.

My father's father emerges from the bubbling mire. His flesh is melted into my father's flesh. It's difficult to tell where one begins and the other ends. The bodies rise further, as people long submerged flex their dead muscles, moving as one mass. The faces of both my grandmothers rise up. I recognize a long-dead uncle, and there's my cousin who drowned, followed by face after face I've only seen in photo albums. Generations of relatives stretch boney fingers toward me, murmuring, "Save us! Save us!"

I grimace. I've seen this kind of interweaving before, but usually the joined souls aren't begging for more attention from a demon. My blood link to these people has changed the whole equation. Fortunately, this is exactly the sort of problem easily solved with cathartic violence.

I wrench my sword loose. I hack and bash my father's mangled body, a task made harder by the fact that other relatives keep trying to block my blows. Grunting, cursing, and chopping through bones in demonic fury, I finally get a clear shot at my father and decapitate the bastard.

Watching his head tumble away isn't as satisfying as I'd imagined.

Now that my father's too mangled to fight, it's easier to chop at the junction of hips where my parents have grown together. I free my mother, but she twists, reaching out to grab my father's flailing hand as he falls away. Instantly, their flesh fuses.

"Are you kidding me?" I groan, straining to pull her away.

She weeps and blubbers. "I can't leave him! I can't!"

I ignore her, hacking to sever her hand, but now someone below her has grabbed her ankles. It's her mother, looking pitiable as she begs, "Save me! And my sister! And your grandfather!"

More bodies rise, hands grasping, the limbs tangling. My devil-heart hammers as I see how badly this has all come apart. No, not come apart. Merged together. Even in death, my mother's entwined with my father. Even in death, my father isn't sure where he starts and his father ends. How far down does this sick mess go? My family tree is nothing but a mass of tangled roots, feeding on pain and remorse. No one, no one ever tears free.

Including me.

Where I've grabbed my mother's hand, her flesh and my flesh have merged. Her skeletal fingers wriggle up the bones of my forearm, clawing deeper under the skin. I'm being pulled under by the writhing bodies who drag her down.

I swallow hard, knowing what I have to do.

"I love you," my mother pleads, as her fingers dig into the muscles of my upper arm.

"I love you too," I whisper, "but I have to let you go."

I place the tip of the sword in my own armpit, push, and twist. My severed limb falls free. I flap my wings and rise as my family cries out. Some curse me, some beg, and some can only bellow and grunt. Like some tumorous tentacle they rise in a swaying column, pursuing me. I turn my face toward the hellmouth and fly for all I'm worth.

Swirling between me and the hellmouth, the sky is black with wings. My family psychodrama has drawn attention. Demons swarm in from every direction.

It's me against all the legions of Hell. Which, again, is my life in a single sentence.

Luckily, I don't have "Necromantic Chaos Thaumaturge" embossed on my business cards for nothing. The necromancy is obvious; I steal power from death. Chaos means this power is unencumbered by the pointless rituals that encrust true magic like barnacles. And thaumaturgy? That's another word for miracle-working. I make stones stand up and walk. I know where the secret doorways to hell stand open. I stroll through the fiery pits like a modern Virgil, as I wear devils like thrift-store sweaters.

I spent six months freezing my ass on Mt. Ararat to learn three of the fabled seventy-seven sacred names that devils dare not gaze upon. A jagged demon sword isn't as precise as a Dremel, but I take a stab at carving one of the names onto my sternum. I figure I've got it right as the nearest devil gunning for me shrieks before poofing into a sparkling cloud of glitter. I spiral upward, frying any devil close enough to gaze upon me as I strain for the surface. This buys me a few seconds before the remaining devils start plucking out their eyes and tossing them away.

They've got my scent and don't need eyes to track me. I've got maybe three minutes left before the hellmouth closes. If these demons follow me into the living world, once they tear me to ribbons, they'll start possessing the kind folks of West Virginia en masse.

The heroic sacrifice here would be to let the devils catch me, distracting them long enough for the hellmouth to close. But, seriously, you think I'm that noble?

I flap through smoke toward three faint rectangles of light. I emerge from the haze to read the letters I-G-A. My doll is standing next to the hellmouth, pickaxe in hand. I toss it the sword and shout, "Stab anything that comes out of this pit!"

I land in front of the U-Haul. "Billy!"

Billy opens the door to the cab. Next to him, my body is snarling and screaming. My hair is a mess and I'm dripping sweat. My cheeks look hollow, like I've lost ten pounds. The ether should have knocked me out for hours, but Nickazeedle has shifted my metabolism to high gear.

Billy looks at me, then at Nickazeedle, and shouts, "Both of you! Swap!"

This is easier than the journey in the other direction. I slide from the devil-flesh like it's greased. Slipping back into my own body is as easy as pulling on my favorite pair of jeans. Of course, now I'm trapped in a straightjacket, on the verge of a heart-attack. As I get full control back over my eyes, I see my doll hacking and slashing the demons boiling out of the pit. It's holding its own, but there are still dozens of hell spawn getting past.

Nickazeedle gazes at his severed stub of shoulder, then casts an evil gaze at me and Billy. He screams, "Heed my summons, hellish clan! Rip to shreds this whore and man!"

Too bad for him the demons are tracking me by scent. They fall upon Nickazeedle in a whirlwind of pitchforks. Blood spatters the hood of the van, eating through the paint. I'm never getting my deposit back.

Billy steps toward the demon tornado, Bible in hand. He's about to banish them when one of Nickazeedle's devil horns flies toward him and bashes him right between the eyes, knocking him to the pavement.

The demon horde finishes tearing apart Nickazeedle. There's at least twenty of them, tongues outstretched, tasting the air. They can't endure our world for more than a few minutes. They need to sniff out a host and I'm right under their noses. They charge toward the U-Haul. They press against the windows, licking the glass with purple tongues, nostrils flaring.

Then Billy rises, climbing onto the hood of the U-Haul.

The demons try to grab him, but scream and pull away blistered fingers. Billy holds his Bible toward the sky and sings a hymn in a language I don't understand. Suddenly, the whole parking lot is awash in light. The devils wail in anguish as, in unison, they race back into the pit.

As if on cue, the flames and smoke get sucked down with them. The hellmouth closes, leaving my doll standing over the torn up asphalt, sword at the ready, but no one to attack.

Billy hops down from the hood. He opens my door and helps me stand. My legs are like rubber, but I manage to keep my feet under me as he starts unbuckling the straightjacket.

"You just earned your fifth star," I tell him.

He gives me a confused glance, then asks, "Find your mom?"

"You knew?"

"The Court of Elders filled me in before you even called me."

"So why'd you ask who I was saving?"

He shrugs. "The Elders said not to stop you, but I thought, maybe, if you said your plan out loud, you might hear the crazy."

"Why didn't the Elders want to stop me? I almost destroyed West Virginia!"

Billy shrugs. "Elder Nightmaw sank Atlantis. Folks gotta learn from their mistakes."

"Was it a mistake?" I ask. "I mean… was it wrong to want to save her?"

"If so, I'm in trouble. Saving people's the only reason I get out of bed."

"You know what I mean."

Billy nods. "Since you didn't bring her back, I can guess what happened down there. You did your best."

"Did I?" I shake my head. "I mean, seriously, I should have checked on my golem a week ago. We could have set up wards. I'm sloppy and careless and keep laughing it off, but what if the joke's on me? I'm so broken and damaged. I can't stop and think about what I'm doing, or why, or I couldn't do it. Sooner or later, my crazy is going to get a lot of people killed."

Billy shrugs. "You'll feel less crazy once we get you out of that straightjacket."

"It probably says a lot about me that I even own a straightjacket," I say, as he helps me pull my arms out of the long sleeves.

"Quit moaning," he says, and not in a joking tone. "The woman who gave birth to me tossed me into a trashcan. Big deal. Doesn't matter where you come from, only where you're going. You gotta trust in God's plan."

"I don't trust any God that would include my father in his blueprints."

"Okay. Leave Him out of it. You're all kinds of crazy, Jacquie. You're also a once in a generation thaumaturge. You'll change the world once you put your mind to it. Between you and me, I think you're might change it for the better. You've seen enough evil to know the stakes. You're fighting on the side of light, even if you ain't seeing that light yet."

"You really think so?"

"Sure," he says. "And, if you turn toward darkness, don't sweat. I'll kill you before you do any permanent damage."

I grin as I brush my sweaty hair out of my eyes. "That's the nicest thing anyone has ever said to me."

Alas, there's no time to bask in the glow of his pep talk. Sirens are howling. Across the river, flashing blue lights speed toward the bridge.

Billy asks, "Can you drive?"

I nod.

"Take the doll. I'll handle the sheriff."

"How can you possibly explain this?" I ask, nodding toward the smoldering pit.

Billy smirks. "I've got a way with pigs."

I groan. The pits of Hell didn't stink as badly as that joke. I start up the van and shout for the doll to hop into the back. Once I feel its weight settle, I steer onto the highway. I keep my headlights off to help with the getaway. The clouds have mostly cleared. The asphalt glows in the moonlight.

I gun the motor and fly along the twisting road. My mind is churning. If the Elders want me to learn from my mistakes, I'm one step closer to being a genius. I didn't save Mom, and I sure didn't save myself. But maybe Billy's right; I'm good at this stuff for a reason.

I'm far enough out of town to turn on my headlights. I slow to a safer speed and turn onto a highway headed east. I'm balanced at the pivot point between laughing and crying. Whichever way I fall, it's going to be okay.

For the first time in a while, I'm grateful to be inside in my own skin, cruising down the highway, looking toward another sunrise.

And how's that for the one sentence story of my life?

ABOUT THE AUTHOR

JAMES MAXEY's mother warned him if he read too many comic books, they'd warp his mind. She was right! James is unsuited for decent work and ekes out a pittance writing down his demented fantasies. His 20+ novels include *Bitterwood*, *Greatshadow*, *Nobody Gets the Girl*, and *Bad Wizard*. In 2015, James was named as a Piedmont Laureate, which is certainly a sign that the end is nigh. The best of his short fiction can be found in the collections *There is No Wheel* and *The Jagged Gate*. James lives in Hillsborough, North Carolina with his lovely and patient wife Cheryl and too many cats.

DON'T BE CRUEL
Ray Zacek

Elvis ascended like vapor from the chilly water and floated in the pale, predawn light. Gitchee Spring bubbled beneath him. Leaving the water, Elvis skimmed through the slash pines and palmetto. The stiff coontie fronds rustled as Elvis breezed by, aiming for the ramshackle Victorian house with rotting grey gingerbread trim like frozen snow crystals. Feral cats hissed, snarled, and raised their backs as Elvis approached, then scattered.

On the sagging porch, Shire, the younger Fenner brother, curled in a fetal ball on a threadbare sofa, mouth-breathing, drooling, and sleeping off an alcohol and chemical binge. Elvis glided past, through the screen door, into the house. Elvis didn't bother with runty Shire, or the other brother, Truett, gasping for breath as he staggered to the toilet to spit blood into the porcelain. Neither Shire nor Truett sensed Elvis' divine presence; neither possessed the ability. Only the oldest brother, Edgar, had *The Gift*.

Billowing up the creaking staircase, Elvis swept down the dark hall to the corner bedroom where he found Edgar Fenner fast asleep. Edgar's bulk strained the bedsprings.

Squealing springs and Edgar's snoring blended into an awful cacophony. Elvis undulated over Edgar, getting a taste of his dreams, like a mosquito drawing blood.

Of what did Edgar dream? Pussy, of course. Girls with soft, doe-like eyes, their sun-washed bodies shining as they swam in cool, clear water of Gitchee Spring. Girls lolled in the sand, playing with red coonhound puppies. Pretty naked girls and playful puppies: Edgar was all about yearning.

Wake up, Edgar, Elvis said.

Of course, Elvis did not 'say' anything, didn't make a sound, and didn't need to. Edgar served as His Receiver. But the Receiver failed to respond. Wouldn't let go of his dreams.

Edgar, I'm talking to you. Wake up.

Edgar mumbled but didn't open his eyes. He snorted. He farted. A foul vapor mingled with Elvis' ectoplasmic essence.

Set your fucker to receive! Dammit, lard ass, I'm talking to you! Get up! Atten-SHUN!

Edgar shot up straight in bed, banging his head on the low slant of the ceiling in the corner of the bedroom. His eyes popped open. He rolled out of bed, plopping on the floor, tangled in the sheet. He wore a t-shirt and white boxer shorts, size XXL.

"Elvis, is that you?"

Who else could it be? Are you awake now?

"Yessir, I'm awake." He stared into the roiling blue-green mist that filled the bedroom.

You got wood there.

"Sorry 'bout that." Abashed, Edgar covered his erection with the sheet.

Don't be sorry. It's natural. Nothing wrong with waking up with a good stiffie.

"Thank you, Elvis." Edgar grinned. At ease now as well as at attention.

Elvis shimmered, a coruscating cloud, sparkling like

Christmas lights. Then, as Edgar gawped in open-mouthed awe, Elvis condensed into form. Ectoplasm became body. The spangled, beaded, glittery white jump suit with the high collar; the wave of jet black, finely coiffed hair; the piercing blue eyes. He smiled upon Edgar.

Hunka hunka burnin' love. Got to find you a girl, Edgar. Yes, we do. To satisfy your natural urges.

"For sure, would be nice," said Edgar. He added, "You *did* promise me."

I know what I promised. No need to remind me. I promised and I will deliver.

"Well, I've been waiting on that," said Edgar in a plaintive voice. "Can't help but wonder about the delivery date."

Don't bug me about it. I will get around to it.

Edgar grumbled. "Kind of nice to know *when.*"

Didn't I say ... I WILL DELIVER!

Elvis' sudden rage crumpled Edgar. Throat muscles tightened, his eyes bugged out, his lips curled, as if Elvis would peel his face. But Elvis relented and released His grip on Edgar.

Edgar cowered and steepled his hands in supplication. "Sorry, sorry, sorry."

I'm sorry for having to do that, Edgar. Don't get insolent with me. Never doubt my word. I thought you knew better.

"I won't, my mistake, a weak moment. Sorry, sorry, sorry."

Alright, cool it. Let's move on to business. I got you up this early for a reason. Trouble is heading this way. Something wicked is coming to Gitchee Spring.

"Wicked?" Edgar gasped. "Another, uh, *enemy*? Oh, darn!"

Threats always lurked. Enemies plotted; perverse creatures in the gross, material world vied to drag down Elvis and trample His Greatness. Elvis hid at Gitchee Spring while he regained strength for the Coming Battle. He charged the Fenner brothers with keeping the secrecy of His Sanctuary at Gitchee Spring.

Could be, could be. It's not clear to me yet. Do what you have to do, Edgar. Don't fail me.

"I will never fail you," said Edgar. "Never ever."

Guard Gitchee Spring. You and your brothers, the Diddler and the Feeb, be on guard.

Elvis referred to Shire as Diddler because, according to Elvis, Shire diddled around. Truett, injured and collecting disability after his meth lab blew up, Elvis called Feeb.

Keep those boys in line!

"I will!" said Edgar.

Stick to the task. Be ready.

"We'll be ready!"

I know I can count on you, Edgar. You're a loyal guardian and that's why I love you.

"I love you too," Edgar replied. His eyes watered. Elvis' love was a powerful thing.

I wandered in misery between worlds before I came to Gitchee Spring.

"I know you did. But tell it again."

Elvis sang. *It used to be agony for me, when I was lost, wandering, wandering, and wandering. It was an ordeal. I got so lonely, I got so lonely, I got so lonely worse than death. But then I found a new place to dwell. A sanctuary, a resting place, where all is well. It's not the heartbreak hotel. No, it's here at Gitchee Spring.*

Elvis swaddled Edgar in a glittering blue-green mist. *I can't begin to describe the depth of my love and gratitude to you.*

"Nor me for you," Edgar blurted out, bawling, tears streaming.

When the time comes, Edgar.

"Glory be," Edgar said.

When Time Comes signified that future date when Elvis broke out of the worldly domain, unleashed from his current exile, and ascended to the next plane of existence, called Graceland. The *true* Graceland, spiritual and eternal. The exact date of the ascension remained indeterminate, unknown even to Elvis. But When Time Comes, always imminent, *arrived*, Elvis promised that his loyal guardians would march along with him like Pharoah's retinue.

Hand in hand, Edgar, we will go to Graceland together. Don't never doubt it.

Edgar choked out the words. "I don't doubt you."

Elvis whispered a parting command. *Guard my sanctuary.*

Then he faded. The blue-green shimmer dimmed and receded, curdling, shrinking, flowing out the window, streaming down the side of the house, wafting through the palmetto, back to Gitchee Spring, cutting like a knife into the chilly water. Elvis dove to the depths of the spring, where a scaly creature resided, swimming in the pure water. There Elvis abided, merged with the creature.

Fifty miles from Gitchee Spring, in Gainesville, Florida, Kat Condon heard the juicer roaring like a jet engine. Her head ached and she didn't want to get out of bed. She wrapped herself in herself in a sheet, a mummy with tangled magenta hair.

Josh walked into the bedroom, already dressed. "Kat, get up."

"*Nooooo.*" Kat moaned.

"You *wanted* to go canoeing today."

"Changed my mind." She plopped a pillow over her head.

Josh shook his head. "Uh-uh. Can't renege."

"Who says?"

"Last night," replied Josh. "You wanted to go canoeing and see *primeval* Florida."

"Ugh. That was Mr. Pernod talking," said Kat from under the pillow. The empty green liquor bottle stood on the bedside table next to the Mickey Mouse clock. A kick-ass confection, for sure, but the morning-after proved dire.

Kat lifted the pillow. "I dreamed I was drowning. *Bad omen.*"

"Dreams are mental barf," said Josh.

"Whatever. Let me fucking *sleep*." She rolled over on her stomach, pulled the sheet over her head, and clutched the pillow

"Nope," replied Josh, tugging the sheet. They played tug-of-war. Josh won, unraveling her, and snapping the sheet from the bed. He said *ha ha*, grinning, and holding the twisted sheet like a captured banner.

Kat glared. *Why oh why had she ever hooked up with Josh?* He hovered over her in his black antifa t-shirt, its red flag waving. Chubby Josh Gruber with wavy black hair, scraggly goatee, and perpetual smirk. They shared a cramped, off campus apartment. *Her* apartment. She paid the rent from her trust fund disbursement and money from her moneybag stepfather in The Villages. Josh only crashed there, making only sporadic contributions toward the costs. This relationship, Kat decided, had run its course. As good as he was at oral, Josh did not rate as a keeper.

"Bring me juice."

Josh fetched her fresh-squeezed pear and guava juice, green and foamy in a plastic tumbler, scoops of protein powder added. Kat sat on the edge of the bed wearing only thin panties and sipped the juice.

Daylight filled the room as Josh flung the curtains open. "Have a *sun-gasm!*"

"You're a sadist." Kat shielded her eyes.

Josh said, "Want an egg?"

"Ugh. I don't eat eggs. I'm vegan."

"For, what, a week now?"

"It's a commitment," replied Kat. She slurped juice. "Cigarette me."

"Vegans don't smoke," said Josh.

"This one does."

"Filthy habit that I won't enable."

Kat made a fish face at him and crawled over the disheveled bed to grab her black pebble leather bag. She fished out a pack of American Spirit, lighted one with a Bic, and puffed.

"It's unhealthy," said Josh.

She brandished the pack. "Look, see, no additives. All natural."

"False corporate advertising. Nicotine is *poison*."

Kat deposited the cig in the empty Pernod bottle. "Oh, fuck it. I want to take a shower."

She hopped off the bed and locked herself in the bathroom. She peed, swallowed aspirin, then pulled back the dingy plastic curtain and twisted the shower knobs. Adjusting the water temp proved tricky. The knobs squeaked. Cold water gushed, dousing her shoulder; Kat shrieked. When she got the temp and pressure where she wanted Kat stripped off her panties and luxuriated in the warm spray of the round daisy-like shower head. This felt delightful. Pores opened, water rippled on her bare skin, the hangover receded. A steaming hot shower in the morning washed away all the overnight blahs. Kat cooed with delight.

"Where is this place we're going?" said Kat as she emerged from the shower and toweled herself.

"Down the Lacoochee River," said Josh. "To Gitchee Spring."

♉

"So," said Shire over breakfast, "what's he done for us lately?"

Edgar bristled. He sat across from Shire at the table in the kitchen. "How can you talk that way? He's … he's …he's *Elvis*!"

"*You* say. Because he coddles you. Gives me *nothing*. Won't even show himself to me."

"But you know he's *there*," said Edgar. "He spoke with me just this morning. You go dive in the spring, Shire, and you *will* see him. Face to face. If you dare."

Shire said nothing and avoided Edgar's gaze. Wielding his fork like a backhoe bucket, Shire attacked the sausage biscuits on his plate, stuffed a heap in his mouth, and chewed with his mouth open. White gravy dribbled from the corners of his mouth.

"You know he's there, and he's promised us to go to Graceland with him."

"Promises'rrrr easy t'make," Shire said.

"Don't talk with food in your mouth, Shire. Elvis will deliver on his promises. What he asks of us is to guard his sanctuary. Because some wickedness is headed our way."

Shire said, "I got other plans today."

"What other plans?"

Shire shrugged. "Business I got to deal with in town."

Edgar pounded the table. "Oh, bull ... *stuff!*"

"Don't get mad, Edgar. You'll keel over with a heart attack and you're too big to catch."

"You're just being ornery!"

"Don't push me around, Edgar," said Shire, "and try to provoke me."

"*Me* provoke *you?*"

"Yup." Shire slurped from a mug of inky black coffee, into which he had heaped tablespoons of sugar. "You're a bully."

Edgar's face reddened. His pulse quickened. Shire liked to pester people with sass and snarl, like a kid sticking pins in a helpless creature to make it squirm and suffer, which Shire had used to do to small animals when a child.

"Shire, if you got any business at all, *which you don't*, you got no business more important than guarding Gitchee Spring. Because Elvis sees trouble coming. T-R-U-B-B-L-E."

"You guard it."

"We will take turns. You, me, and Tru."

Shire snorted, spitting biscuit crumbs. "Tru can't guard shit and you can't spell for shit."

"Tru's in a bad way, but he can take his turn too. Man

got to have a purpose, things to do. We can't just let him sit and waste away."

"Who're you fuck'n kidding, Edgar."

"Watch your language, Shire."

"Tru's in bad shape and that leaves me and you to pick up the slack. Since you are one Elvis coddles, and Tru ain't what you call able-bodied, it's me that gets dumped on. It ain't fair."

"Shire, I bend over backwards to be fair with you."

"No, you don't."

Edgar banged the table. "Yes, I do!"

"Liar! *Liar!*"

Edgar counted to ten; Mama had always told him to do that. He took a deep breath. Then another. Finally, Edgar said, "I speak for Elvis. Do you want to get on His bad side?"

Shire's sneer vanished and he lapsed into sullen silence. Invoking the wrath of Elvis always caused Shire to get that scared, contrite look. Shire was no Receiver, but when He chose to make the effort, Elvis could materialize to both Shire and Truett. The power, the sizzling blue-green shimmy in the air, made Shire tingle all over. Once, when he had aroused Elvis' wrath by misdeed, Shire had trembled, almost convulsed, and pissed himself.

"Now, we take turns," Edgar said. "You go on down there for two hours and I will spell you. Then Tru. We take turns through the day until Elvis says the danger has passed."

"I got a better idea."

Edgar eyed him with suspicion. "What?"

"I'll stay down there the morning and you and Tru take the afternoon."

"All morning?"

"Yeah, all fuck'n morning."

"Stop talking that way. It's crude talk."

Shire shrugged. "*Excuuuuse* me if I hurt your dainty feelings."

"Never mind. Just do your job. Okay, you take the morning, and guard Gitchee Spring."

"I will stay on top of things, Edgar. Promise."

Edgar cringed. Shire made promises, discarded them for no good reason, and then denied he ever made any such promise. Edgar gimlet-eyed his brother. Shire didn't flinch. Edgar invested all the older brother authority he could muster into his voice. "You got to stick to the task, Shire. Stick like glue."

"I will."

"I mean it! No diddling!"

"Nope." Shire smiled. A boyish, toothy, aw-shucks smile, earnest and reassuring.

"Well, alright," said Edgar, nodding. The effort left him weary. "That's settled."

"And bring me my lunch when you come down," said Shire. "I want a baloney sandwich and don't forget to cut the crusts. And tater salad. And bring me some Little Debbie cakes too."

"I will," said Edgar. He fixed his own breakfast plate of biscuit and thick white gravy. "Why don't you hustle down to the spring."

Shire stood, picked up the pump shotgun, and stuffed a .22 pistol in his belt. He swaggered. "On my fuck'n way."

♉

The Gourds blasted from the speakers, dancing with a Strawberry girl, *aaaaarrrrrrrr!* Bobbing to the music, Josh hunched over the steering wheel of the Toyota Tacoma. Before leaving Gainesville, he had switched his antifa shirt for one featuring a country western singer and secured the canoe in the truck bed with a spider web of rope and bungee. A tattered copy of the Florida Atlas and Gazetteer, pages dogeared, lay on the seat. Josh careened west on State Road 26, weaving in and out of lanes.

Kat registered her dismay. "Slow down, *bitch*!" She

shouted over the music. "And stay in one lane."

Josh's lips curled in a smug smile. "Who's the pilot, *bitch*?"

Kat dialed down the volume on the CD. "You're driving *like reckless*." She cinched her seat belt tighter. "How far is this boat launch?"

"An hour. There's a park under an old train trestle where we put in the canoe. Deep in rectalbilly country."

"In what?"

"Rectalbilly," said Josh, "is a species of hillbilly. Stupid, head stuck way up ass, raving Trumplican knuckle-dragger. That's why I changed my t-shirt to this good old boy country singer. It's *camo*."

Doubt furrowed Kat's brow. "This sounds sketchy. Are you sure about this?"

Josh nodded with confidence. "For real. Gitchee Spring is unspoiled and uncommodified unlike most of Florida. It's not theme-parky. It's pristine. A first magnitude spring."

"But," said Kat. "Didn't you say it's on private property, and this is, like, banjo-strumming country."

Josh dismissed her misgiving with a smirk and a wave of his hand. "I'm on good terms with the guy who lives there. Yeah, sure, he's red of neck, but he's cool. A good old boy named Edgar Fenner."

Kat laughed. "What a dork name!"

"He's all that but Edgar my man is gentle giant sort of dude. Harmless. Lives alone. He's got some brothers but they're in jail or some shit. Edgar said come back to Gitchee any time, and he *meant* it. He likes company."

"But did you tell him we're coming today?"

Josh shrugged. "Uh, not exactly."

"What does that mean?"

"He hasn't got a phone. I wrote to him, but the letter came back return to sender."

♉

Nothing was going down at Gitchee Spring. Guard duty was boring. Warm breeze rustled the palmetto, water percolated in the spring, and Elvis remained dormant, hidden in the depths. *Maybe*, thought Shire, this was a false alarm. Elvis got edgy at times. *Got paranoid.*

Shire yawned. He plopped in a canvas camp chair, almost sleepy in the heat and humidity. For guard duty he wielded a 12-gauge Mossberg and an old Ruger pistol. He had retrofitted a homemade silencer to the pistol and prided himself on his ingenuity. Using only a 2-liter plastic soda bottle, duct tape, and a hose clamp, he converted a target pistol, good for plinking and varmint control, into a stealthy killing machine. *Wasn't that the fuck'n bomb?*

But it needed a field test.

Armadillos are stupid. Shire chuckled when he saw one of those long-headed, peg-toothed, sticky tongue-flicking 'dillos scrambling about amid the palmetto in its slinky armor. Scratching its tiny claws in the dirt, bustling along, looking for bugs to eat.

"Hello, 'dillo," Shire said. "I see you there. Shire Fenner got you on radar."

Shire scanned all around Gitchee Spring; he shielded his eyes from the sun and gazed down the run to the Lacoochee River, looking for any movement, listening for any sound.

Nothin'.

Stupid, vulnerable creatures appealed to Shire's predatory instincts. *Okay, a little diversion might be in order. Yessir. Uh-huh, shouldn't begrudge a man a little recreation. Elvis is asleep anyway.* Shire picked up his pistol to go 'dillo hunting. Maybe smoke a jay and jerk off in the woods for relief too. Edgar might call it diddling, but Shire figured to be back before Edgar discovered he was gone.

Armadillos are quick to sense threats. As soon as Shire stood and began stalking, tiptoeing around the edge of the spring, the armadillo raised its snout, and ambled away.

Shire tagged along after it, amused, in no hurry, keeping the critter in sight. He paused to light a jay, took a hit, breathed deep, held the smoke, then exhaled languorously, feeling an immediate buzz. He coughed, hocked, spat, and traipsed into the woods.

As Shire vanished into the woods, Josh and Kat caught sight of a metal cable strung across banks of the Lacoochee, guarding the approach to the spring.

Turtles sunning on tree trunks plopped into the river as the canoe approached. The Lacoochee snaked through flat Florida countryside, a narrow stream the color of tea. A sluggish current carried the canoe. Cicadas buzzed. Fallen trees and cypress stumps presented obstacles. Spider webs in the branches caught Kat's hair and green flies buzzed around her head. She cursed. Her arms and shoulders ached.

"Canoeing is fucking *work*," said Kat. She pulled sticky spider web and bits of Spanish moss from her hair.

"Let me steer, okay?" said Josh.

"Keep us out of the branches!"

"Uh-huh."

"Don't 'uh-huh' me! Just do it! How much further?"

"Not much further," Josh replied. He surveyed the shoreline.

Kat mumbled. "Fucking sick of this."

"Can you be chill? It's coming up."

In a few minutes they rounded a bend and discovered a channel that fed into the river from the spring, but another impediment greeted them. Steel cable strung attached to wooden posts blocked the passage. A hand-lettered sign swung on the cable. *Private Property Ari Ver Deechee.*

"Huh," said Josh, chagrined. He laid his paddle across the thwart.

"Is this *it?*" Kat dropped her paddle in the aluminum

canoe with a clunk. She slouched and squinted. The canoe drifted.

Josh nodded and pointed at the steel cable. "Yeah, but that wasn't here before."

"It's here *now*!" Kat said. "Who the fuck is Ari Verdeechee?"

"No idea."

"You're *sure* this is the place?"

"Can't you feel the current coming out of there from the spring? It's pushing our canoe. Yeah, Gitchee Spring is that way." The canoe swept about in a circle.

"Okay," said Kat, exasperated. Hot, sweaty, and achy, she wanted to bash Josh's head with her paddle. "But what if your buddy Edgar sold the place to some guy named Verdeechee who doesn't want visitors?"

"No way," replied Josh. "Edgar bragged his family owned the land since before the Civil War and selling was *unthinkable*. He's there. Got to be there."

A long silence ensued. Kat sighed. "Oh, *fuck it*. Let's go! I didn't come all this way to turn back."

"Hey," said Josh. "That's the spirit of *Murrica*."

Josh navigated, turning the canoe into the channel. Kat, crouching in the bow of the canoe, lifted the cable and they floated underneath, both hunching down.

"Not to worry," said Josh. "Everything's gonna be cool."

♉

Unlike the tannin-stained river, the run to Gitchee Spring remained crystalline. They paddled against a swift current, the freshwater pumping out of the spring. Pebbles and rocks lined the sandy bottom like a mosaic and clumps of grass danced with the current. On either bank the woods gave way to open pasture and rolling hills. A cool breeze rippled across the water. Paddling ceased to be a chore for Kat.

"This is awesome!" she said, elated now.

"Told ya," said Josh.

At last, they found themselves in a huge circular pool, hidden among huge old mossy oaks and cypresses and rimmed by sugar white sand. The azure water sparkled, percolating from a cumulus of mossy green-gray rock. Under a crude lean-to they spied a folding canvas camp chair, but no one was around, not a soul. They ceased paddling and bobbed in the canoe, passing a bottle of energy drink back and forth, slurping. Kat popped CBD gummies in her mouth.

"Gitchee Spring," said Josh. "In its thrilling and transcendent splendor."

"Just wow." She dipped her hand in the water and reveled in the chill.

"Seventy-two degrees," said Josh. "Scrotum-shrinking cold."

"What effect on vaginas?" said Kat.

Josh leered. "Jump in and find out."

"I have goose bumps. A feeling like electricity all over." She opened her top to peek down. "My nipples are big as Bing cherries."

"Because Gitchee Spring is a vortex," said Josh. "Indigenous peoples used to come here for healing. It was a sanctuary."

Kat leaned over the gunwale and splashed herself with spring water. She wanted to chirp like a bird, shuck off her clothes and dive in, swimming and frolicking like a frisky she-otter. Glancing at the mossy green rocks below she saw something deep in the water. At first, only a shadow. It rose. An elongated and misshapen shape emerged from the rocks and waggled toward the surface.

"What's that?" Kat said, alarmed. She pointed.

Josh peered into the water. The shape swam along the bottom of the pool, long and dark, its movement deliberate.

"Catfish," said Josh. "See like its whiskers."

"Doesn't look like any catfish. It's all scaly and has *blades* on its back."

Josh scoffed. "Those are fins. That is a *monster* catfish. Wow."

"I'm not getting out of the canoe," Kat announced. She was a few clicks short of panic but moving in that direction on a steady course.

"Be cool! Probably, it's just checking us out."

"It's circling us." Kat tensed. "It's not acting afraid. It's acting like it's going to attack."

Josh laughed. "Oh, come on! Not likely."

Then it surged toward the surface and leaped. A huge, armor-plated fish broke the water, soaring over the canoe and bringing a wall of water in its wake. Kat screamed. She saw a blur: *a thing.* Dark brown with a silvery white underbelly; a long pulpy, wriggling, tentacled snout and stubby whiskers; dorsal and pectora fins that opened like bat wings; a twisting, scimitar-like tail that slashed at them.

Blood spurted.

Cold water cascaded over them. The canoe tipped.

Kat found herself struggling in the water, immersed, under the capsized canoe. She flailed, kicking her legs. She saw nothing but foam and churning water and the huge dark creature gliding by like a torpedo, retreating amid the porous rocks.

After an eternity, Kat broke the surface again and gulped air. The canoe floated half submerged in the water. Josh, bleeding, crawled over the sand, sprang to his feet, and dashed away through the palmetto.

"Come back!" She yelled at him, but her mouth filled with water, and she choked. Her feet found the sandy bottom. Coughing, dazed, bleeding from an abrasion on her forehead, Kat struggled to the sandy rim of the pool.

A giant in overalls stood there, obese and scowling at her with mean, porcine eyes.

"Help me," Kat said.

"Hold still," he said. He reached out with his huge

hand and lifted her face. Then he landed his fist squarely on her chin, knocking her unconscious.

♉

Shire emerged from the palmetto holding a dead armadillo by its tail, the Ruger with its homemade silencer in his other hand. "What's going down, Edgar?"

Edgar flailed his arms over the canoe capsized in the spring and the unconscious girl in the sand. "It's a shambles! Where were *you*, Shire?"

"Me? Where was *you?*"

"You were supposed to be on guard!"

"Other one's getting away," Tru wheezed. He slumped in the passenger seat of the green John Deere Gator that he and Edgar had driven to the spring. The other intruder thrashed through the palmetto, stumbling.

"Get him, Shire," Edgar said. "Don't let him get away!"

Shire hesitated. "Don't you try to blame this all on me, Edgar!"

"Never mind that for now, just get him!"

"I'm on it," said Shire. Tossing the armadillo, he darted off in pursuit.

"Elvis is not going to be happy about this," Edgar said.

"Uh-huh," said Tru, sucking on his respirator.

Edgar fretted. He lowered his head. "His wrath is going to be terrible to behold."

"No shit, Edgar."

Edgar waded into the spring, pulled the canoe to the sand, and collected the items floating in the water. A small cooler, empty bottles, the paddles. Then he lifted the girl. His hand felt the cool, bare skin of her thigh. Edgar lingered, gawping at her purple-red hair and the t-shirt clinging to her breasts.

"Trying to guess her weight?" Tru said.

"Uh, no, I am not." Edgar plopped her down in the cargo box of the Gator like a sack of oranges, next to the picnic basket that held Shire's lunch. A ribbon of blood trickled from her nose. Edgar wiped it with his bandana and dried her face, careful of the tiny silver ring that pierced her nostril. Desire gurgled in his brain. *If only* …

"Edgar," Tru said. "Wake up."

"Yessir," said Edgar, with a start. He shook off his reverie, like popping a bubble.

"What're we doing with her?"

"That's for Elvis to decide," said Edgar.

"I got an idea," said Tru. He leered.

"That is for Elvis to decide," Edgar reiterated, standing over the girl and glaring at Tru, who backed off.

In the distance, they heard shouting and the muffled sound of gunshots, like firecrackers.

♉

"Hey, hippie," said Shire. "I see you there."

The intruder cowered in the palmetto where he tried, futilely, to hide. Scrapes and slashes bloodied his face and arms. Shire had followed the blood trail toward the river.

"Let's be cool," he said, standing, unsteady on his feet. He held up his hands in surrender.

"Did you fall down and hurt yourself?" Shire said, as if talking to a child.

"Fell and sprained my ankle. Can't walk too good. Uh, dude, what is that thing you're pointing at me?"

"What's it look like?"

"Like a BB pistol with a soda jug stuffed with rags attached to it."

Shire sneered. "This here," he brandished the Ruger, "is a lethal weapon with an improvised suppressor device. What you think of *that*?"

"Honest, I'm scared shitless. Please don't shoot me, bro."

Shire chuckled. "Big 'fraidy cat, aren't you?"

A big guy, this hippie. Shire resented big guys, hated

'em. Shire had been bullied and pushed around all his life, taking his licks, and dreaming of giving back. In Raiford, doing time for burglary, a big guy named Darby Shupe, reeking with stinky breath and bad teeth, had taken a liking to Shire. Called him Shrimp. Shupe wanted Shrimp's ass, that kind of liking, prison gay. Shire obliged Shupe for a time, then shanked him with a sharp plastic toothbrush shiv. Punctured both lungs and a kidney, finishing Shupe, and getting away with it too.

"I ain't your bro and you're trespassing," said Shire. "Didn't you see the sign? Says private property. Keep out, goodbye, *ari ver deechee.*"

"You mean *arrivederci?* That's what that meant?"

"It means what it means!" Shire growled.

"Look, my name is Josh," he said, forcing a smile. "I'm a good friend of Edgar Fenner."

"Are you?" Shire feigned interest.

"Yeah, yeah, yeah. Edgar still lives here, right?"

"Yeah," said Shire. He lowered the pistol to put his prey at ease.

"So, so, so," Josh said, lowering his hands, slowly, to his sides. His head bobbed and his nervous smile widened. "Let's talk to him. Edgar knows me. We're cool, we're cool. I was at Gitchee Spring before."

"When?"

"Year or so ago. Before --- uh, what is that ... *thing* ... that attacked us?"

"None of your business," said Shire. "How did you get here?"

"In a canoe. Can we talk to Edgar? Let's talk to Edgar."

"*Besides* in a canoe."

"In a Toyota truck. From Gainesville. Let's talk to Edgar."

Shire nodded. College kids. Figured. "Where's that Toyota truck at now?"

"By the, uh," said Josh. He hesitated. "The train trestle."

Shire nodded; he knew where that was. He held out his hand, palm up, and made a gesture with his fingers. "Gimme keys."

"Keys? To my truck? Why?"

"Because I said to."

"We really need to talk to Edgar."

"I lied," said Shire. "Edgar don't live here no more. He died." He thrust his hand toward Josh. "*Keys.*"

"*No,*" said Josh.

"Hell with you, then." Shire emptied the pistol magazine into Josh's face and abdomen.

♉

"Where's my lunch?" Shire said. "I'm hungry."

He strolled back to the Gator where Edgar and Tru waited. The Ruger, minus its bulky plastic jug suppressor, was tucked under his belt.

"Git that guy?" Tru grinned.

"Taken care of," Shire said. He dug into the picnic basket, unwrapped the baloney sandwich, its crusts carefully excised, chomped on the sandwich, and glued his eyes on the unconscious girl in the truck bed.

"Stupid hippie lay in wait for me," said Shire. "Tried to jump me but I was too quick for him." He patted the grip of the pistol.

Tru said, "Where's your silencer?"

Shire shrugged. "Plastic started to melt and smoked real nasty, so I got rid of it." He dug into his pants pocket. He dangled a key fob and tossed it to Edgar. Then Shire tossed Josh Gruber's eco-friendly hemp wallet to Edgar, who fumbled, dropping the wallet and keys. He hunkered down to pick up the items. Shire had emptied the wallet of cash.

He stared at the girl in the truck. He nodded at Tru, who smiled. "She and her hippie boyfriend come here from G-ville in a Toyota pick'em-up truck that's over at

192

the county park off Joe Flagg Road."

Edgar stood and scowled. "Where were you?"

"Just told you. Went after that hippie."

"Where were you *before* when you were supposed to be guarding Gitchee Spring?"

Shire ceased spooning tater salad in his mouth and reacted with his defiant, bantam rooster stance. He stood on tippytoes and got in Edgar's face. "*Where were you?*"

"Me and Tru got here," said Edgar, "and you were *gone*! When you were supposed to be on guard!"

"I *was* on guard!" I heard some commotion and went to investigate. I suspect now that was a diversion to throw me off."

Edgar pointed at the animal carcass. "Dead 'dillo says otherwise. You were off diddling, Shire. Now look what happened."

Shire fumed, pacing back and forth. He snarled. "It's all your fault, Edgar."

"*My fault?*"

Shire shouted in his brother's face. "You took your sweet time coming down here to help me. If you had got here when you were supposed to and not when you did, none of this would have happened. *This is all on you, Edgar.*"

Edgar stood mouth agape, like a fish out of water, stunned and trying to breathe. His face burned, a terrible spiking pain assaulted his head and his throat muscles tightened. His brothers stared at him. Shire fumed. Tru rasped with amusement and sucked on his respirator.

"Now that *that's* settled," said Shire.

Edgar stomped his foot. "That ain't settled!"

Shire ignored him. He finished his sandwich. "We got to get rid of the canoes and the truck. The dead hippie we can plant amongst the others."

The Fenner homestead, over the few months, included an ad hoc boneyard behind the shed with the corrugated tin roof that housed Tru's old Ford Mustang on blocks.

The Fenner brothers had interred other trespassers there, along with the dead hounds that Elvis had condemned for always barking and growling at his emanation.

"I want to get out of here before Elvis shows up," Shire said, and Tru nodded. He turned to Edgar. "What about the girl?"

"Elvis will decide," said Edgar.

Shire smirked. "You *know* what he's going to decide."

"I will stay here and wait on Elvis. Haul the girl to the house. And do not *touch* her."

Shire played dumb. "Huh?"

"You know what I mean." Edgar determined to remain resolute on this issue. *The girl would not be molested.*

"C'mon, Edgar," said Shire. He winked and pinched the girl's thigh.

Edgar put his fist on his hips and towered over his younger brothers. He raised his voice to the tall feathery tops of the slash pines. "Do as I say! It's for Elvis to decide and I doubt he's going to be a generous mood. *Don't touch her!*"

Shire sulked, like a swatted pup. He slinked into the Gator, next to Tru in the driver's seat. Both wore resentment, but remained compliant, knowing they could push their older brother only so far. Tru wheezed, eager to be gone before Elvis resurfaced, and clunked the Gator into gear. The vehicle rumbled up the path toward the house.

Ominous silence and stillness descended upon Gitchee Spring like oppressive humidity. Edgar knew that deep down in his lair, in the eldritch caverns of porous limestone, Elvis seethed, His fury building.

Edgar waited. Half an hour? An hour? Elvis existed outside of time as measured on the earth. He would come when he was good and ready.

Then a ripple. A shadow. A stirring. Elvis moved upon the water, rising from the slimy green rocks. As Edgar watched in trepidation, a blue-green haze swept over

Gitchee Spring. It coiled like a serpent, turning purple and turbulent, churning waves. Elvis manifested, clad in a flowing, razor-creased black jumpsuit of pure wrath. He glowered at Edgar through chili pepper red aviator glasses.

What did I tell you, Edgar?

Edgar hung his head, hangdog. "Tried my best. I take responsibility. I'm sorry."

Sorry don't get it done. What did I tell you about trespassers? Well?

"That none were allowed."

Or what?

"I can't say."

You were supposed to keep 'em out. You failed. People penetrated my sanctuary! One remains. What are you going to do, Edgar?

"I don't know," said Edgar.

Don't play dumb! You know what must be done. Don't be a sissy about it. Do it, Edgar.

Edgar raised his head and stared wide-eyed into Elvis' anger. "No," said Edgar.

What?

"I said no."

Elvis struck out, aiming a karate kick at Edgar's chest. Edgar doubled over in agony. Elvis gripped him, but after a few seconds, he relented, leaving Edgar prostrate in the sand and straining to breathe.

I hate it when you make me do that, Edgar. Never say no to me. Never disobey. You're in enough trouble already. Now pull yourself together and take care of business, Edgar.

"I can't do it! I will not do it. I will not hurt her!" Edgar crawled on his knees, his chubby fingers grasping sand. "This once I *will not* do what you say. Do to me what you will but I won't budge."

Edgar shut his eyes tight as a dark, vengeful cloud enveloped him. Suffocating him. A huge weight pressed upon Edgar's heart

Is that your final jeopardy answer, Edgar?

"Whatever you are going to do," said Edgar, "do, let it

come down. But you promised me a girlfriend."

You fail guarding my sanctuary, then you defy me, and you expect a reward?

"If I'm gone, who're you going to talk to?"

Elvis flared in fury. *What are you saying?*

"You don't got another Receiver. Gonna be lonesome tonight. You made me a promise. All I'm asking is that you keep it. Everything happens for a reason. This could be the delivery on that promise."

After a long silence, Edgar heard Elvis laugh. The dark shroud over Gitchee Spring receded and turned reassuring blue green. The weight on Edgar's heart lifted. Elvis' black jumpsuit transformed to blazing white.

Maybe I was a little hasty and let my temper get the best of me. I am hard but I am fair.

"So, I can keep her?"

Don't get ahead of me. It's not that easy. But, yes, I will keep that promise.

"You will?"

Elvis' radiant smile roasted Edgar with joy. *Just said so, didn't I?*

Kat regained consciousness in stifling darkness, in a stuffy room that smelled of pee. She lay supine on a scratchy bamboo mat, wearing only her string panties. Her head throbbed. Her skin prickled. Kat moaned.

"Hello, dear," a kindly female voice said.

Kat sat up. "Who's that?"

She heard someone breathing. Then a crackling sound, a tiny giggle. And creaky sounds, a rocking chair.

"Turn on the lights, hon." An old woman's whisper. "To your left. No, that's my left. Your right."

Kat felt around, found a plastic power strip, cords sprouting out of it. She clicked the switch. Lava lamps came to life. Orange, yellow, and green. In the dim light

Kat discerned a wizened old woman perched in a rocking chair, wearing a fleece robe and furry slippers. Her long, white hair shined, falling to her shoulders. Her benign smile reassured.

"You poor thing," she said, shaking her head. "Those boys are mean to take your clothes and lock you in here. Shames me to say I am their *auntie*." She clucked her tongue in disapproval. "I'm Kate, old auntie Kate. Tell me your name, hon."

"Kat."

The old woman cupped a hand to her ear. "Kathy?"

Kat nodded. She raised her voice. "But I use *Kat*."

Auntie Kate clapped her hands, delighted. "We're namesakes! Isn't that sweet?" The glop in the lava lamps rose and fell and the green light reflected in Auntie Kate's eyes.

"I want to get out of here," said Kat.

"Well, so do I, hon, and people in hell want ice water. You know why those nephews of mine are so *cruel*? Because they worship the Devil. Did you see him there in Gitchee Spring?"

"All I saw was a monster of a fish and a fat guy who hit me." She added, clenching her jaw, "My 'boyfriend' ran away and abandoned me."

"Men will do that." Auntie Kate nodded gravely. She murmured. "Can't trust them, you cannot trust men."

"What will they do with me?" The pain in Kat's head subsided.

"Do not marvel," replied Auntie Kate. "Satan is transformed into an Angel of Light."

Kat looked at the old woman with astonishment. "*What?*"

"That's in the Bible, hon. Apostle Paul's Epistle to the Aleutians."

"I wouldn't know," said Kat.

"I guess you don't read your *Bible*," said Auntie Kate, grinning, almost gloating.

Kat ignored the jabbering old woman, crawled toward the door, and rattled the doorknob.

"It's locked, sweetie," said the old woman. "The Devil in Gitchee Spring has got those boys fooled. I got wise to his tricks, and that's why they keep me locked me in this room."

Kat turned in desperation to the old woman. "Can you help me?"

"Want some rock and rye?"

"Want *what*?"

"Whiskey, hon." Auntie Kate held up a plastic jar filled with an amber liquid with a chunk of rock candy settled at its bottom. She twisted off the lid, gulped, and *ahhh'd* with satisfaction. She gestured to Kat. "Come to me and I'll give you some."

"I don't want any." Dejected, dazed, fearful, her head still hurting, maybe a concussion. Kat retreated to a corner of the room and sat with her knees up. She stifled sobs.

"Want to know where the Devil in Gitchee Spring comes from?" Auntie Kate paused, drank more rock and rye, and emitted a tiny belch. "I will tell you! Jesus and the Apostles were in the land of the Gadarenes. They met a man possessed by an unclean spirit."

Kat looked at her, an old woman drinking and babbling with dementia. "Will you please shut the fuck up?"

But Auntie Kate went on. "This man lived among the tombs. *Among the dead.* Jesus said, what is thy name? The demon in the man answered, my name is Legion, for we are many. Jesus said, come out of this man, unclean spirit, and out they came, the whole kit and kaboodle." Auntie Kate chuckled. "But nothing comes out but has to go somewhere else. Where did Legion go? Are you listening, hon?"

"No," said Kat.

"The unclean spirit went into a herd of swine that was grazing nearby. And then those piggies all ran down a steep place into the sea and drowned. But that wasn't *the end*. Getting rid of evil isn't that easy. Cast it out here, it pops up there."

"Please stop talking."

"Legion," said Auntie Kate, leaning out of her rocking chair and grinning. "Moved in the water. Water encircles the earth. Legion searches the waters until it discovers Gitchee Spring. It assumes a pleasing shape and doesn't call itself Legion no more. It got a new name!" She leaned forward, perched on the edge of the rocker, and thrust her chin out, cackling with harsh laughter.

"*Now* do you get it?"

"*Stop*," Kat pleaded.

A shrill scream burst out of the old woman. "You will get it, and you'll get it good and hard, you little whore."

Old Auntie Kate lurched out of her rocker. Kat shrieked. The old crone yanked Kat's hair, twisted her body, and pinned Kat's arms to the floor with her knees. Auntie's breath sulfuric, fetid, hot. Her face red and incandescent, distorted. Eyes bulging. Limbs strong, hands like claws. She choked Kat.

"You won't ever get out of here! Not never! That demon will do to you what it did to me! I am Legion too! You filthy little cunt, those boys are going to tear you into little bloody pieces!"

Door hinges squealed. Edgar Fenner rushed into the room. He grabbed the old woman, peeled her off Kat, and threw her back into the rocker. In an instant, the old woman resumed her placid, kindly appearance. She patted her hair.

"You spoilsport, Edgar," she said, disappointed. "I was having fun."

"Shame on you, auntie. Drink your rock and rye and behave yourself."

Kat trembled and gasped for breath, almost unconscious again. Edgar picked her up and heaved her over his shoulder.

"Shire and Tru thought it was a big joke," Edgar said to

Auntie Kate. "Locking her in here with you. Made me look all over to find her."

"You always been a numbskull, Edgar." Auntie Kate swigged from the Mason jar, and then belched fire. "You're going *to Hell*, Edgar."

"You hush!"

"Bring me more whiskey," said Auntie Kate as Edgar stormed out of the room. She added with an evil leer, "Bring me another girl too. I get lonely for someone to talk to."

Edgar slammed the door shut.

"This is torture!" said Kat.

"No, it's not," Edgar said. "It's *Clambake*."

Edgar possessed encyclopedic knowledge of every Elvis movie ever made. *Clambake* (1967). Elvis as the heir to an oil fortune who trades places with a water-ski instructor at a Florida hotel to see if girls will like him for his own lovable self and not for his crass daddy's money.

Kat shouted. "You're torturing me!"

"No," replied Edgar, "I am not." He sat in the La-Z-Boy with a pair of surgical scissors cutting her driver's license, student ID, credit cards, and everything else from her wallet, into strips. Kathleen Grace Condon, with mouse brown hair, smiled in her DL photo. Pretty girl.

But she was not now, not pretty at all, her face contorted, strands of magenta hair fluttering over her face. She struggled against the green duct tape that bound her to the chair in front of the HD TV. Edgar sat next to her in the Jungle Room with its green shag carpet, cypress stump table and Rousseau jungle prints that Edgar bought on ebay. She remained naked, like the wild girl on the couch in the jungle picture.

"Untie me! Let me go!"

"Sorry," Edgar said. "Can't do that. Watch the movie."

"Where's Josh?"

"Uh, he went away." Edgar cringed. Shire and Tru had disposed of the body and then got rid of the Toyota and the canoe. Edgar hated thinking about dead things. His belly turned sour and ached. Thinking about the boneyard filled him dread.

"No, he didn't!" Kat shouted, growing hoarse.

"Yes, he did, he did!"

"You're lying! What happened to him? What did you do to him?"

Edgar sighed. "I told you. He went away."

"You're a pig!" Spittle sprayed. "A sorry fucking fat pig!"

Edgar shook his head. "The mouth on you, girl! Don't make me gag you again," thinking *might have to anyway.*

Edgar did everything Elvis told him to do. She remained tied to the chair for days now, with no sleep or food or bathroom breaks. Water from a sippy cup kept her hydrated. Edgar poured caffeine drinks into her mouth, with crushed white pills from Shire's stash of fentanyl and Adderall. Edgar fetched magic mushrooms that Elvis told him where to find amid the cow turds in the pasture. He sliced and diced and crushed these into a sticky brown paste that Edgar fed the girl with a turkey baster. Edgar stayed by her side to see her through her conversion. She had to be *cocooned,* Elvis said, like the caterpillar that breaks free as a butterfly. She had to be Brought to Elvis. Only then could Elvis bring her to Edgar.

Elvis' plan required she bear witness to every Elvis movie ever made from *Love Me Tender,* 1956, through *Change of Habit,* 1969. Plus, the concert tapes, and the outtakes. Edgar owned the complete Elvis library in DVD; he had grown up on those movies. He loved them. She would too, soon enough.

"Please," Kat said. Tears rolled down her cheeks. "Just let me go."

"Nope. Watch the movie."

"I won't tell anybody what happened."

Edgar shook his head. "Sorry, no. I hate being cruel, but it has to be this way."

"I hate you!"

"That'll change," said Edgar. He leaned out of his recliner and put his arms around her. She struggled but he tightened his grip. "In time, I promise, it will be all about love and not hate. Everything is for the best even if it don't seem that way now."

"Let me go!" Kat tried to bite him and then howled. Screamed like a banshee, ear piercing. The din made Edgar shudder.

"Stop that now. Stop it, I said. Please!"

She cursed again. Lashed Edgar with fricatives, spitting at him, straining against her bonds, shaking, her limbs and breasts taut.

"That's enough!"

He grabbed a hank of her hair, jerking her head back and stuffing a ball of gauze in her mouth. Kat tried to spit it out, but Edgar had strips of hurricane tape ready and plastered them over her mouth, holding his hand over the tape until it was secure. With a sigh, he plopped again in the La-Z-Boy. His heart pounded from the exertion, and he panted. He ejected *Clambake* and inserted another DVD. *Follow that Dream.*

Mmmmmffffffmmm said Kat.

"I know it's an ordeal," Edgar said. "But has to be this way. You will understand later, after you accept Elvis, and you'll be thankful."

She glared at him with cold fury.

"Destiny," said Edgar. His eyes watered. His chest ached. "Is what it is. Honest! You came to Gitchee Spring *for a reason.* To be part of Something Bigger. Part of His plan."

☿

Days later, Edgar stepped out of the Jungle Room to empty the bucket while *Viva Las Vegas* blared from the TV. Edgar closed the door behind him and toddled to the kitchen. Shire sat at the kitchen table. He smoked the remainder of the American Spirit cigarettes, in a waterproof container, that he'd filched from the canoe.

"How long does this go on?" Shire said.

Edgar rinsed sponges in the sink. "Until Elvis says it's time. Don't ask me when that will be. And didn't I tell you get rid of all their stuff?"

Shire grunted. He ate his biscuit with gravy and poured cheap bourbon into his cup of coffee. "And when Elvis says, then what happens?"

"Same as what happened to Auntie Kate," replied Edgar. Feeling weary, bags under his eyes. He poured himself coffee. He hadn't eaten, washed, or slept.

Shire snorted, spitting coffee. "That didn't work out so good. In case you ain't noticed. Just what we need around here. Another crazy bitch we got to keep locked up."

"Don't use the b-word," said Edgar. "That isn't nice. And this time will be different."

Shire scoffed. "That's what you say!"

But Edgar oozed confidence. "No, *He* says! Even Elvis can learn from mistakes."

☿

Her new name is Ginger.

"Huh?" Edgar had dozed off in the La-Z-Boy. He awoke with a start. Bright blue-green shimmer flooded the Jungle Room. Radiant, dazzling, benign. The girl remained bound to the chair, listless, limp, as if melting. On the big screen TV, outtakes from Elvis '68 comeback special held her attention.

Wake up, Edgar. Listen to me.

"I'm listening!"

Elvis manifested in glittering white Vegas attire, with red spangles and flowing red silk scarf. He towered over Edgar, a nimbus of gold cloud adorning his head, obsidian rings on his spidery fingers. *Her name shall be Ginger from here to Graceland.*

"Why?"

For a moment, Elvis glowered. *Because I said. That's why.*

"OK, OK," Edgar replied. "I got no problem with that."

His irritation passed and Elvis reverted to joy. His hand caressed the girl's hair. She flinched. *Kathleen Grace Condon is no more. Ceased to exist. She is filled with My Spirit, and when you are filled with My Spirit, you are born anew.*

"I understand," said Edgar. "I like the name, Ginger. That's fine by me, fine by me, oh, fine by me. Ginger's a good name. I love that name!"

Cool it, Edgar. It is time. Soon it will be dawn. Bring her to me.

"At the spring?"

Where else? He faded. His parting words, *Get a move on, Edgar.*

♉

Thick, humid darkness reigned outside. Edgar fumbled through the armoire in his mother's old bedroom. Ginger needed to be proper, clad in finery and not naked. Edgar switched on the brass lamp in the room, examined garments, and selected a lacy white sleeping gown.

Downstairs again, Edgar untied the girl, cleaned, and dressed her. She breathed but barely, hardly conscious, and weak as a kitten. Almost weightless now as Edgar lifted her. He carried her in his arms and plopped on an Adirondack chair on the porch, waiting for first light. She murmured.

Edgar whispered. "It's going to be alright, Ginger. Trust Elvis, and things turn out alright. Sorry about what you had to go through. But it's all for the best. Going to be a new you."

"Uh-huh," Ginger replied. Her eyes open now but unfocused, like an infant's, blue blots floating in pallid sclera.

Darkness dissipated. The sky became white, hazy, and promising. Then fierce sunlight broke through the skinny pines. Gitchee Spring shined. Edgar picked up the girl and ambled down the path away from the house toward redemption. He waded into the spring until the chilly water was up to his waist. The girl remained limp, but her hair and the hem of her gown dipped into the water.

Water rippled. Elvis, the great spirit locked in physical piscine confinement, ascended to the surface from the depths of the spring. His armored scutes heaving, his scimitar like tail swishing, his stubby whiskers twitching. Fearsome. Edgar shuddered, feeling His power. Elvis came close, within a few feet of Edgar. Someday, when Elvis and his entourage ascended to Graceland, this fish form would burst, releasing the spirit within.

White creamy blobs erupted from the distended gray underbelly and drifted through the water, becoming a cloud. An electric blue-green curtain fizzled upon the water. Elvis was there, in the water, in the air, in Edgar's soul, in the bulky, armored sturgeon and in its lumpy milt.

"Glory be," murmured Edgar.

He gently dipped the girl into the water and let that milky cloud and cold spring water envelope her head and shoulders.Bubbles rose to the surface as she exhaled. She struggled a bit, gasping, trying to raise her face out of the water.

"Nope," said Edgar. He held her under the water until she ceased squirming and kicking.

He lifted her. "There you go," Edgar said in a whisper.

"There you go."

Her face and hair glistened with beads of milt. Goops of it dripped from the corners of her mouth too and her nose and clouded her eyes. Edgar wiped her face. For several scary moments she remained still and grey as a dead thing. Edgar shuddered. Then, awakening, she took a deep breath of air. Choked, coughed, spit. Edgar held her tight and let her breath the fresh, piney-scented air.

Her eyes opened. Wide open. Not fearful now. Looking, seeing everything as if for the first time. She looked at Edgar, studying his big smiling face. She blinked.

Edgar said, "Wasn't so bad, was it?"

"Uh," she replied.

Edgar carried her out of the water. "What's your name, sweetheart?"

"Whaaaa?"

"Tell me your name. *Your name.*"

She had to think. Confused, abashed, her mind searching. Finally, she said, with confidence, "Ginger."

Edgar rejoiced. A smile cracked his plump face. "Uh-huh, uh-huh, you're Ginger. 'Love me, Ginger, like I love you." He moaned. Ginger touched his face, tenderly with her cold, moist hand. Gazed into his eyes. They kissed.

Edgar's heart, filled with joy, almost leaped out of his chest. On this fine Florida morning, he and Elvis had triumphed.

ABOUT THE AUTHOR

RAY ZACEK writes horror, dark fantasy, satire, and crime/noir. His short fiction has been published by All Due Respect, Appalling Stories, Deadman's Tome, Denver Horror Collective, Out of the Gutter, Shotgun Honey, and Sirens Call Press, among others. His full-length play Desperados was produced by Stageworks in Tampa, Florida. His crime novel The Road to Moravia, set in Texas, is available on Amazon. A native of Palos Hills, Illinois, Ray previously lived in Seattle; has spent much time in Austin, Santa Fe, and Arizona; and resides in south Tampa with his wife, artist Theresa Beck.

THE FAUSTIAN
FREQUENT FLYER
P. Anthony Ramanauskas

Senator Guy Guiseppi (R, Kansas) was a mess of contradictions. The pro-choice, young Earth creationist proponent of stem cell research was an ardent defender of marriage and the family. He held libertarian views that were stretched so thin that he could, reasonably, claim to be an anarcho-socialist. He held at least one position with which every American could agree, and no opponent ever succeeded in drawing attention to his contrasting views. He was a legend to some, a paragon of social progressiveness marred only by his perplexing and temperamental devotion to the far-right. To others he was a clear example of the worst of American politics, a talking head good for nothing more than reading the latest leftist talking points on CNN. He was a greased pig slinking through the murk of Washington: dirt never stuck to him, and no one could catch him in a scandal. Despite the commentary of talk show hosts, Guy was no "antichrist."

He was not a worshiper of Satan. He was proving this in fine style by failing to summon the devil.

His daughter Moonmist—whose pre-college name was Sandra and whose Facebook page listed "Devout Satanist" as her religion—knew even less about the process than Guy did. "It's not about that, Dad," she had said over dinner, turning 'Dad' into a nasally whine of exasperation. "It's about casting aside the yoke of organized religion and spitting in the face of patriotic consumerism to find a truer, more spiritual self."

She had gone on at length in this vein, spouting the trending talking points as Guy ate his mashed potatoes and feigned attention. She finished her monologue in a self-righteous tone achievable only by a speaker of great conviction and dearth of understanding before asking Guy if he "got it now." Guy had nodded, kissed her on the check, and handed her the keys to the Corvette before telling her to stay out of the house until morning.

The bookshelf of "religious texts" in Moonmist's bedroom only served to further explain her complete lack of practical information on the subject. He gave up after reading the fifth article on the various uses of quartz crystals in alternative medicine, settling for drawing a pentagram on the concrete of his back patio. He stepped back, looked around, and said "Hail Satan?" to the Saturday night air. He stood next to his grill, and he waited.

Nothing happened.

He repeated his affirmation with a little more gusto, careful to keep quiet enough that Mrs. Beisly next door could not overhear. The last thing he needed right now was for Tucker Carlson to run a rant about the "Satanist Senator."

"I am not," said a slightly-lisping voice from the patio shadows, "in the habit of making house calls."

Guy peered into the gloom. "Satan?"

"If that's what you want to call me." On cue, the

clouds parted and the figure sitting on the gliding bench was revealed by the moonlight. He was the perfect image of androgynous, angelic beauty. His cheekbones were immaculately sculpted; his skin was creamy and smooth; and he wore just enough eyeliner to tie the package together. His face, when combined with his oversprayed hair and angsty expression, reminded Guy of the singers in Moonmist's YouTube videos.

"You look different than I remember."

"It's been twenty-five years, Guy," said Satan. "Button-up plaids and Nirvana t-shirts aren't fashionable anymore. I have to keep up with the times." He flicked his bangs at the pentagram at Guy's feet. "What's with the modern art?"

"I didn't know how to summon you. Everything happened so quickly last time that I don't remember how it started."

"And you didn't think to go to a crossroads? You live in the suburbs, Guy. Hundreds of crossroads within spitting distance of your front door."

"Why would I go to a crossroads?"

The devil rolled his eyes. "No *The Devil Went Down to Georgia?* Never heard of Robert Johnson? Hell, the damn karate kid made a whole *movie* about crossroads!"

Guy held up his hands in defeat. "Crossroads, got it. Can we go inside now?"

"Suit yourself." They walked through the sliding door into the dining room. "Doesn't look very comfortable," said Satan, examining the furniture.

"It's not," Guy said gloomily. "Vera designed it. Well, Vera paid some interior decorator to design it. It's supposed to be chic."

"Sounds like Hell." Satan smirked as he sat down. "Clove?" he asked, pulling a pack of cigarettes out of his slim-fit jeans.

"Thanks, but I only smoke in public. Vera'll kill me if she smells smoke in here," he said, his voice trailing off nervously.

Satan laughed. "I really picked a winner for you there, didn't I?" He lit his clove, inhaled, and said, "She has the Johnnie Walker Black of bosoms. Best chest in America, and I mean that literally."

"She's not the nicest, though. Or the best mother, for that matter. Our daughter turned out to be a Satanist."

"In all fairness, that one's not on Vera."

Guy grimaced.

Satan exhaled, sending spirals of smoke up to the chandelier. "As much as I'd love to sit around chatting about your wife's tits, I have minds to corrupt and souls to taint and first-person shooters to design. Why did you call me here, Guy?"

Guy swallowed. "Well if you remember our agreement, I was supposed to-"

"I don't need you to remind me," Satan interrupted. His jaw grew squarer and his eyes glossed over; when he spoke again his voice was deeper and filtered through a Midwestern accent curled by five-too-many shots of cheap bourbon. "*I need to get out of here. Anywhere at all, as long as he ain't there. Hell, if I'm selling my soul, I may as well as to go wherever I want, whenever I want. See the world.*" Satan's features snapped back to normal. "You spoke those words outside of Webster's bar at three in the morning on the 23rd of March, 1992, piss-drunk after your father hit you for what was to be the last time. You vomited shortly after signing our agreement. I had to discard my shoes."

"Right, well," said Guy, "that's just it. I sold my soul and got nothing in return."

"Nothing?" asked Satan softly, a hint of menace in his voice. "Your wife has a figure that, should she have continued down the path of making instant-gratification videos, would have triggered a paradigm shift in the appreciation of the modern female form."

"Yeah, but-"

"I'm not finished yet!" yelled Satan. He lit another

cigarette. "I fixed your grammar, your style, your hairline. I set you on the fast track for political power."

"For your own gain."

Satan shrugged.

"By now," said Guy, "I figured I'd have pissed off the Great Wall of China or something. I wanted to see a different country every morning and a different lady every night. I wanted to *move*."

"You didn't know any better. When you get down to it, travel is nothing but crabs and indigestion."

"I never cared for beaches. I'm more of a Swiss Alps man. A little wine, a roaring fire in some chalet, and an easy woman are more my style."

"As I said, crabs." said Satan. "What about D.C.? You live half your life in your nation's capital."

"I'd sell my soul again to bitchslap whoever decided to build the center of the federal government in a malarial swamp."

"You've seen your whole state on the campaign trail."

"One cookie-cutter dustbowl town after another. Not a hill in sight, let alone the mountains I used to dream of. Christ, I'm middle aged and I haven't even left the country!"

"Don't do that."

"Don't do what?"

"Use the Lord's name in vain," said Satan. "Exodus twenty, verse seven."

Guy blinked twice, stunned. "Did... did you just quote the Bible?"

Satan shrugged again.

"I just want to know why you haven't upheld your end of the bargain."

"Excuse me?" whispered Satan.

"I'm forty-two and I haven't traveled at all."

"Of course you haven't. You're on the retirement package."

"Come again?"

"You spend your life serving me, and after you die you travel to your heart's content until the Apocalypse hits. We'll have to take you down to Hell first, of course. Burn away your humanity until you're a low-level demon. Then you're free to do as you please." Satan ground his cigarette into the table, then lit another one with a snap of his fingers.

Guy winced, imagining Vera's expression when she found the burn marks. "From everything I've read, though, that's not how these things are supposed to work."

"How have you done any reading at all on the subject without running into a mention of damned crossroads?"

"That's not the point. I already said I'd use crossroads next time."

Satan sighed. "We live in an ever-changing world, Guy. To stay competitive in a dynamic market like this, I need to stay innovative. I need to synergize, do what I can to keep it all moving forward. You're my first foray into modern politics."

Guy's eyes widened. "You mean you have no one else in the Senate?"

"I've been out of politics since I invented automatic income tax withholding. But, you've been a remarkable success. Living proof that voters will believe whatever I want them to if my social media campaign is aggressive enough. You'll be the next governor of Kansas, mark my word."

"I already serve in the *federal* legislature."

"Better to reign in Kansas than serve in D.C." Satan said with a puff of smoke. "Wouldn't be for long, anyways. You have more 'Mr. President' in you than Marilyn ever did."

"That's not what I *want*, though," said Guy.

"Doesn't matter. You signed a contract. In blood."

"I don't remember it saying anything about dedicating my life to your service. Just my immortal soul."

"It's all in the addenda."

"Addenda?"

"Little additions and alterations to the document that we've made throughout the years."

"So you've changed the contract without informing me?"

"Of course not!" said Satan cheerily. "I've had HR send you a copy whenever I needed your signature."

Guy shook his head. "You have an HR department?"

"I have *all* the HR departments." Satan said, smiling. "When they're happy with the legalese, they beam it up to you in various End-User License Agreements."

"I don't read those things! Nobody reads those things!"

"I know. It's a great system. They're still legally binding, too."

Guy sat silently for a moment, brow furrowed. "I want to read it."

"You mean you didn't keep a copy?" Satan asked innocently.

"If I did, I don't have it with me."

"I'll have HR send a copy over. Got a landline?"

Guy led him to the unused jack in the kitchen. Satan conjured a beaten, leather suitcase out of thin air, opened it, and began setting up a fax machine on the counter.

"Fax?"

"All HR materials are sent by fax. It's the oldest and most reliable method of business communication."

The machine connected quickly, and three hours later Guy held a contract as thick as an old phone book. He took it back to the dining room and read it page by page, carefully examining every detail. Satan spent the time chain-smoking his cloves, the perfect image of irritated boredom. The first trickle of morning reached the windows as Guy finished reading and sat wearily back in his seat.

"Iron-clad, isn't it?"

Guy rubbed his eyes. "These low-level demons of

yours. What do they spend eternity doing?"

"Why do you want to know?"

"Humor me."

"I send them to career fairs, mostly. To small colleges all across America. They offer advice to graduating youth."

"That's... surprisingly kind of you."

"They target liberal arts majors. Pull them aside, explain there's no future in History or Comparative Literature, but the communication and interpersonal skills required for those majors can be easily adapted to certain corporate settings. Human Resources, for example."

Guy mulled it over. "I could do that."

"I'm sure you *could*, but it's not in your contract. Once you die you get to travel the globe until the end of all things."

"At the end of my natural-given life?"

"That's what 'death' means, yes."

Guy opened the contract to the page he had earmarked. "Ahem. Appendix CXXIV, AOK 'Steppenwolf' 6.0.2, dated 13 December 2001. 'In exchange for services enumerated above, Party A agrees to henceforth forgo any action, exchange, or condition that may shorten the natural-given life of Party B."

Satan's eyes narrowed. "What of it?"

"Forgoing any action including, I assume, increasing my risk of heart disease and lung cancer by, say, offering me a cigarette. Which you did. Earlier tonight."

All expression melted from the devil's face, the cold fury in his eyes the only hint of Guy's victory. "Alright," he said in a venomously-silky voice, "you win. I breached the contract and your soul is yours." With a wave of his hands the burn marks on the table vanished, as did the fax machine and the ancient suitcase. He stood to leave.

"I'd hate to see you lose an investment like this, though."

Satan glared at him. "Cut the crap, Guy. What do you want?"

"The original terms. The ones written in blood. No addenda to be acknowledged at this time or any point in the future. I get to travel to my heart's content until I die, then you get my immortal soul to serve in your fiendish Ponzi scheme."

"You win your soul back on the slim authority of a Surgeon General's warning, then barter it away with your next breath?"

"That's right."

Satan's salesman grin return. "You're my kind of guy, Guy." He spit on his palm.

Guy shook the offered hand. The contract on the table burst into flame, burning quickly until only the original page remained. "We'll be in touch," said Satan as he lit another cigarette. "Give me a little time to wrap this mess up, then your life is yours." He walked out the front door, closing it gently behind himself.

A paparazzo caught a photograph of Satan leaving the Giuseppi residence that morning. The resulting gay prostitution scandal drove Guy from office, shaming his wife to such an extent that she left him—with the full support of Moonmist—in a very public and expensive divorce. Guy could not help but smile as his life fell apart around him.

Four months after the divorce was finalized, a priority envelope was delivered to Room 24 of the Rosemary Inn, temporary home of the disgraced former Senator. After the postman left, Guy sat down on the bed and opened the package. A letter fell into his lap.

Guy,
I believe this concludes my half of the agreement. See you soon.

The letter was unsigned. The only other item in the

envelope was a frequent-flyer card for Delta Airlines accompanied by a notice that his account had a practically unlimited number of miles attached to it, although each checked bag would incur a separate fee.

ABOUT THE AUTHOR

P. ANTHONY RAMANAUSKAS lives in Ohio with his wife, son, and two noble dogs. He spends his writing breaks either exploring the mountains of New England or tinkering with vintage motorcycles or typewriters. He is one of the hosts of the *Radio FreeWrite* podcast, where he reads a new story every week under the call sign WebEater.

BEHIND THE EIGHT BALL

Edward R. Rosick

This is the story of how the world was (almost) saved from disease, famine, war, death, and taxes by Stanlee S. Simolitz.

Now, Stanlee was no superman, no god, no neo-conservative republican or right-of-center democrat. He was merely a nameless Joe in a long string of nameless Joes (or Stanlees) working in a local bubble-sheet factory. He wasn't vertically challenged, he wasn't a person of color,(although he did tan quite well when out in the sun), he didn't have the stunning good looks of TV actors or the haggard, somber looks of tobacco company lawyers. No, Stanlee was of common height and weight, with light brown hair and medium-dark brown eyes and absolutely no distinguishing features whatsoever.

So therefore, because of (or perhaps in spite of) his totally nondescript nature, Stanlee was chosen one bright sunny afternoon to be visited by the second-most hated being in the world, Satan (the most hated being an obscure shoe-salesman in Newark, New Jersey, who, by FBI accounts, had received 14,242 unsolicited death threats for no reason whatsoever. The case is currently under investigation).

T-24 hours

At first glance, Stanlee thought the man walking toward him from the back of the bubble-sheet factory parking lot of the was a new foreman looking to push his political weight around. Being a staunch union man (except of at due-paying and voting time), Stanlee figured he would straighten the guy out real quick.

"Before you start any of your high and mighty talk," Stanlee said, getting up from the lounge chair he was sitting on after carefully placing his cheese and baloney on rye sandwich on the loading dock next to him, "I have four minutes left on my lunch break. Since we both know it's my union-given right to take it all, that's what I fully intend to do!"

Beaming with pride, Stanlee sat back in his chair, secure in the knowledge that he again had done his part on keeping the feud between labor and management in the U.S. of A. alive and well.

"Four minutes?" The man looked at his wristwatch. "I thought I had at least ten minutes. Damn cheap Swiss watches--certainly don't make them like they used to. No matter, I'll just skip the formalities and get to the point."

"Point? What point is that?" Stanlee had started to become suspicious of the guy. He seemed too well dressed to be a foreman, wearing a three-piece dark blue pin-striped suit, shiny black loafers and a matching off-white and red tie.

Maybe this guy wasn't a foreman, Stanlee thought. Maybe he was an assistant production manager. Or maybe even a full production manager.

The man moved closer, loosening his tie and unbuttoning the top three buttons of his vest. Stanlee hoped that he wasn't one of those new bleeding heart managerial types that actually cared about the conditions of the working man; they took all the fun out of life. As Stan looked him over more closely, he noticed that the guy seemed out-of-place. At first, he couldn't put his finger on it; the guy dressed well, and his personal grooming habits matched his clothes--short-cropped black hair, well-trimmed black mustache and beard, red eyes--

The eyes. That was it, Stanlee realized. They weren't just bloodshot red from too many shooters or too much dope. No, they were *red*. Blood red, fire red, red that could burn straight into your soul.

Stanlee was no uneducated idiot, and while he did have trouble reading the morning newspaper online, he watched CNN every day, so he knew a crack addict when he saw one. Or was that heroin addicts who had blood red eyes? Then again, he had heard someone in the bar last night say that--

"Something the matter there, Stan?" the man asked, concern in his voice.

Stanlee moved his chair back a couple inches. "Not at all. I was just thinking that--hey, how did you know my name?"

The man smiled, showing off a perfectly straight row of Hollywood white teeth. "I know many things about you, Stanlee."

"Oh yeah?" Stanlee retorted, pushing himself up off his chair. "Well, if you're so smart, Mr. Manager type who's been smoking crack, then you know I'm now officially two minutes late, and since you've caused me to be late, I'm going to file a grievance."

"You're very mistaken on that first point. I'm not a manager, at least not around here."

"Then who are you?"

The man cleared his throat and puffed out his chest.

"I've been known by many names, Stan. Prince of Lies. King of Darkness. Master of Evil."

"You think you're Dracula?"

The man scowled. "Dracula? You've been watching too many horror movies. I'm not Dracula. I'm Satan."

"Satan? As in the devil?"

"Uh huh," the man replied proudly. "The one and only!"

"Listen, buddy, I'm sorry about that Dracula remark," Stanlee said, slowly backing away. He tried to gauge how far away the nearest lockable entrance was as he kept up conversation to keep the guy--who was obviously crazy as hell-- from going postal. "You're Satan? That's real nice. Have your demons been keeping you up late at night? Your eyes look pretty tired and red."

"Eyes?" Satan slapped himself on the forehead. "Damn, I always forget about change them when I come up for a visit. My current concubine is forever nagging me about it. Just this morning she said, 'now don't be an ass and forget your blue eyes or you'll scare the shit out of the top-siders.' Boy, even I get no respect sometimes." He reached into his pants pocket and pulled out two small blue orbs. With the deftness of a magician, he plucked out his red eyes and put in the blue.

"Better?" Satan asked jovially, rolling the blue orbs around in his eye sockets a few times to make sure they were set. "Hey Stan, quit puking. Me and you got some heavy dealing to do."

Stanlee was having serious feelings of déjà vu, remembering the first time he had gone on a roller-coaster as a young child. He had felt then, as now, that his whole world had turned upside down, that his hold on reality slipping away. Slowly getting up from his knees, Stanlee tried to spit out the taste of partially digested cheese and baloney on rye and rationally weigh the situation: Stranger walks over, stranger says he's Satan, stranger takes out red eyes and puts in blue eyes.

There was only one possible conclusion: This guy was Satan. Not being well-versed in conversation with demons, Stan said--more to calm himself then anything—the first thing that popped into his head:

"So, Satan, you mentioned you have a concubine?"

"I do. A real beauty, Cleo, she is. She's pretty much the perfect little women...except for her particular fascination with snakes, and after the garden snafu, me and snakes are not on friendly terms."

"I can feel for you there," Stan said, feeling somewhat less queasy. This guy sure didn't seem to be the living embodiment of evil. He didn't have horns, no pointed tail, not even a pitchfork. Except for the eyes--and the fact that he was now levitating a foot above the loading platform--the guy seemed just like one of Stanlee's buds.

Yet there was one thing, one small fact which Stanlee knew he was missing. . . .

"Aren't you going to ask me what I want to talk to you about?" Satan asked Stan.

"That's it!" Stan said triumphantly, finally completing the piece of his small mental puzzle.

"That's what I like. Enthusiasm! So Stan my man, here's the real deal. Ever since I've been around, I've been, to put it bluntly, a real prick to humans. And to tell you the truth, I'm getting tired of it. In the beginning it was fun—an earthquake here swallowing a defenseless town, a volcanic eruption there killing off thousands in a single day, revolutions, wars in which millions of innocents were slaughtered . . . the good old days have a lot of fine memories. But I'm older now, Stan, and frankly, I'm getting tired of playing the heavy. So here's my point: I'll rid the world of disease, famine, war, death, and even taxes, in exchange for one teeny tiny thing."

"What that?"

"Guess."

Don't let it be my soul, don't let it be my soul..."My soul?"

Satan looked genuinely disappointed and gingerly

floated back down to the loading dock.

"How'd you guess?"

Stan shrugged. "I guess I just watch too many horror movies."

"Damn, I was hoping you'd sweat it for a while. I love playing twenty questions. Ah well, I guess even I can't have everything," Satan said wistfully, looking up at the sky. "But hey Stan, what an offer, eh? What do you say?"

Stan paced back and forth for a couple minutes, his head down, deep in thought. "Now, let me get this straight," he said. "You say you'll rid us, forever and ever, of disease, famine, war, death, and taxes, in exchange for my soul?"

"Yes Stan, I do believe you've got it."

"But what do I get out of the deal?"

"A cosmic eternity of damnation, pain and terrible suffering."

Stan felt a large ball of panic forming in his gut. "That doesn't sound like such a great deal to me. What if I don't want this deal?"

Satan arched his back and several loud pops echoed in the air. "I hate to tell you this, but you don't have a choice."

"What do you mean, I don't have a choice?" Stan's voice cracked and tears formed in his eyes. "I hate not having a choice. And why me? I mean, why not the pope, or the president, or--"

"Hey Stan, calm down," Satan said in a wryly amused voice. "It's not like I'm asking you to make the choice right this very second. In fact, to show you what a great guy I am, I'll give you twenty-four hours to make up your mind. And really, when you get right down to it, it's a pretty easy decision."

"Easy decision?" Stan blubbered, tears now freely streaming down his face, "how do you figure it's an easy decision? Maybe for a saint, but definitely not for me."

Satan put his hands out, palms up. "Look at it this way:

decide yes, and you'll be the everlasting hero of all humankind. Say no, and when anyone dies, when any small defenseless child comes down with an incurable disease, when the politicians decide they need to steal more of your paycheck, you'll know that in a very real way you helped cause it."

Stan mouth puckered like he had just sucked on a lemon. "You really are a prick."

"You got that right." Satan smiled. "The biggest. And oh, yes. As to your earlier question as to why I picked you, my answer is, 'Why not'?"

Stan had nothing to say.

"So, Stan," Satan said, softly levitating off the loading dock and onto the driveway, "in twenty-four hours and not a minute sooner or later, I'll be back. Then, my friend, you can give me your

decision. Now, watch this real carefully." Satan walked to the middle of the drive. "Exits are my specialty!" With that, he exploded in a rain of fire and brimstone, and the faint sounds of Tchaikovsky's "1812 Overture" could be heard.

Stan did not look forward to the next twenty-four hours.

T-16 hours

Stan had left his post on the line two hours early, worried and depressed over his meeting with Satan. He sat in his car, numbly watching thick rolls of smoke spewing from dozen tall stacks from the nearby Gigantic Motors Corporation factory. Stan had always enjoyed watching the smoke coalesce into funny shapes and figures (except on those rare occasions when he remembered each plume held an average of two hundred and twenty-one pounds of toxic materials). Now it only made him more depressed, since it reminded him of Satan's fiery exit. Stan had considered drowning his sorrows in alcohol and debauchery at the local topless bar, but discounted it on the grounds that explaining to his wife why he smelled like a deer in

rut wasn't the way he wanted to spend his last hours on earth. He figured his only hope was to have a man-to-man talk with the greatest bubble wrap maker of all time, Clifford J. Buggman. Cliff was a local legend; word was that he had an IQ of one hundred and forty-two. He had also built up quite a reputation around the factory, and even if his penchant for smoking a particularly nasty concoction of hashish and cooking oil did deep-fry his brain, Stan still believed in Clifford's amazing intelligence.

Stan caught Cliff—easy to spot with his long gray hair tied in pigtails, dark brown trench coat worn every day of the year along with immaculately polished black army boots--just outside the gates of the plant, leafing through mounds of trash.

"Hey, Cliff!" Stan said loudly. Clifford turned around and peered with wide green eyes at Stan, then threw hands up in the air. "Don't shoot! I swear I don't have nothing on me!"

"I'm not going to shoot you," Stan said. "It's me--Stan Simolitz."

"You're not a cop?"

"No."

"FBI agent?"

"No."

"CIA?"

"We work together!" Stan said, his voice rising with emotion. "Every day! Or, at least the days you're at work. Don't you remember?"

Clifford slowly backed away. "I bet you're from the NSA! I saw your drones circling my apartment the other day!" He scratched his scraggly beard with one dirty hand. "Or maybe them were buzzards...sometimes it's hard to tell when they're so high up."

"Listen, Cliff, I'm sorry you don't remember me but I

need your advice."

"Why does the NSA need advice from me? I haven't been a field operative since 1997. Why, it was just like yesterday that I was in Berlin, using my seductive charms on this---"

Stan lunged forward and grabbed Clifford by both shoulders. "Cliff, this is serious! I need your help. I had a visit today...from Satan."

"Satan?" Cliff's eyes suddenly became clear and bright. "Why didn't you say so? I've been dealing with that bastard for the last three months."

"You have?" Stan released his grip. "You mean he's come to you too?"

Clifford nodded. "Yep. That bastard thinks that just because he's the new foreman of the plant that he can make me---"

"No," Stan said, "I'm talking about Satan. The devil. You know, fire and brimstone and hell all that stuff."

"That guy?" Clifford said, looking at Stan with an expression of awe and respect. "The metaphysical cosmic master of darkness, whose sole aim is to plunge the world and all humankind into eternal chaos and pain?"

Stan was stunned. "Yeah, Cliff, that's it! He came to me today. Says he wants my soul in exchange for eternal peace and tranquility on earth."

"What did you tell him?"

"Nothing."

"Hmm," Clifford said, his brow furrowed deep in thought, "you think he'll buy that?"

"Buy what?"

"Nothing. I hear the devil is a pretty crafty dude."

"No, Cliff, I mean I don't know what I'm going to tell him. That's why I needed to talk to you." Stan took a deep breath, then continued. "I admit I haven't read the bible much---well, okay, I guess not at all--- so I was wondering if something like this has ever happened to anybody before."

Clifford frowned in concentration. "Well, it's been a while since I read the good book...actually, it's been a while since I've read any book...but I truly that you're the very first!"

"What am I going to do?" Stan said, leaning up against the fence. "Satan's coming back for an answer. Tomorrow morning. 'Round nine o'clock."

Clifford shrugged. "Ever think about a heavy-duty prayer session?"

Stan shook his head. "I don't believe in God."

"The devil comes to you, and you don't believe in God?"

"Just because there is a devil still doesn't mean there has to be a God," Stan said indignantly.

"And they call me a nutcase," Clifford said under his breath as he walked away and resumed leafing through the trash.

T-12 hours

Stan was depressed while driving home that evening. He had been so sure Clifford would have an answer to his dilemma. Pulling into his driveway, Stan conceded to himself that he should bring up the matter of possibly selling his soul to Satan with his wife, Lisa. She probably would be sleeping, which means that he would have to wake her up, something roughly akin to waking up a grizzly bear in the middle of its hibernation.

He quietly opened the front door and walked down the long hallway. In the living room, he heard laugher of Mindy, his sixteen-year old daughter, and of Melvin, his fifteen-year old son.

"She looks like she's gonna tear it off him!" his daughter squealed.

"Watch when I put it on fast forward!" Melvin said with glee.

Curious, Stan peaked around the corner and saw his

children watching one of his Pamela Pleasures X-rated DVDs.

Stan marched over and turned off the TV, much to the displeasure of his children. "Where did you get that?" he said, hoping he sounded father-like and angry.

"From your bedroom," Melvin answered.

The kid had him there. Stan tried another tactic. "Kids, don't you think you're too young to be filling your minds with such filth?"

Melvin shook his head. Nope. How about you, Sis?"

"No way, Daddy," she said dreamily. "Why, that Johnny Steele is such a stud. He's got the biggest and most delicious--"

"That's quite enough!" Stan said, wondering if they were too young to be sent away to a military academy. "If your mother knew you two were watching this, it would break her little heart. I want both of you in bed this instant."

"Gee Daddy, you sound just like the movie," Mindy giggled as her and Melvin ran up the stairs.

Maybe he'd send her to a convent.

Stan took out the DVD and tremulously walked to his bedroom. He placed the it in his secret (or obviously not-so-secret) hiding spot in his closet, then walked over to the bed and gently shook Lisa, was wearing an oversized flannel ankle-length nightie.

"Dear, wake up."

Lisa lay still, snoring softly. Stan put both hands on her and shook more vigorously. "Dear, wake up. It's important."

She gave a snort, turned over and opened one eye. "Whaizit?"

At least she's alive, Stan thought. "C'mon, dear. Wake up. I have something very important to talk to you about."

Lisa turned on the night light next to their bed, illuminating her ashen-gray face. Stan often wondered how anyone could wear a mud pack, night after night for sixteen years. He imagined that he could take a plaster-cast of it and sell it for use in a slasher movie.

"Talk?" she grunted, her eyes small and dark under the mud. "Is that what you call it now?"

"What do you mean? Honey, I need--"

"I know what you need," Lisa said sarcastically as she shook thick strands of black hair out of her face. The way she did it reminded Stan of a terrier shaking a rat to death. "I heard you watching those disgusting movies of yours in the living room." She began to untie her nightie. "Let's get this over with so I can get some sleep."

Stan took a deep breath and slowly exhaled. "Really dear, it's not that. I need--"

"No? What do you think I am then, your personal pleasure machine you can just turn on and off?"

Stan had a maddening urge to grab his wife around the neck and see how far he could make her eyes bug out. "Listen honey," he continued, "this is important. *Very* important. The devil came to me today. He wants me to sell him my soul."

Lisa sniffed the air. "You been out getting hammered with your pathetic friends again?"

"No, I haven't. Listen, you've been going to church lately. You should be the one person who believes me."

Lisa slowly got up, holding onto the bed sheet like it was an integral part of her body. "Oh, I know what's going on here," she said in a high-pitched voice. "You're possessed."

"*What?*"

"Sure," she said, grabbing clothes from the dresser and closet. "It's all part of an atheistic, humanistic plot to subvert us through those awful movies you watch!"

"What are you raving about? And hey, those movies are the reason we've had any--"

"Yes, our new pastor told us about your perverted ways," she continued on, oblivious to Stan. "I've been wanting to do this for a long time anyway, but now I have found the strength. Hallelujah!" she cried, doing a little dance that shook the floor.

"What have you wanted to do?"

"Leave you and this awful life," she said. "I'll have the movers over tomorrow morning to pick up my belongings. The lawyers should have all the papers drawn up by the afternoon. My children won't grow up in a house run by a demon-worshipper!"

Stan sat back in a daze, watching her scoot around the room like a poodle on amphetamines. He had always wondered why she said 'my children.' Of course, Melvin did look like their old mailman, and Mindy, well, if that big nose of hers wasn't from their next-door neighbor. . .

T- 30 minutes

Try as he did, Stan couldn't sleep. Although he really didn't miss Lisa, it seemed strange to have the bed all to himself. He tossed and turned for a few hours, then he got up and drove downtown, watching the sun come up over the river. As the rays of the sun glistened off the still water like horizontal flames, Stanlee knew the time was drawing near.

He got out of his car, then walked to the river bank and looked up at the clear blue sky. "Well, maybe Clifford is right and there is a God. Are you happy I'm admitting it? You think You could give me a little last-minute advice? I'll admit that I haven't been the greatest person around, but why hang this decision on me?"

The only sound was the water washing up against the shore.

Stan continued on. "Aren't You supposed to be the number one guy? If Satan can cure the world of all its ills, then how come You can't? I'll gladly give You my soul and go to heaven for the same deal he's offering me."

Again, nothing.

"Well, something here's not right," Stan grumbled. "I

mean, if you're God and yet he can promise--"

"Better watch it there, Stan. People might think you're crazy if they see you talking to the sky."

Stan turned around to see Satan sitting underneath an immense oak tree.

"What? No grand entrance this time?"

"Nah," Satan replied, getting up and walking to Stan. "Too much partying last night. We got in a couple dictators, a few rapists and murderers, and even a United States Senator. Yeah, that was some fun, let me tell you. Of course, not half as much fun as I have planned for you." He grinned, an ominous glimmer in his blood-red eyes. "So I do think it's about time, Stan. What's your answer?"

Stan uneasily shifted around. "I don't know." The air around him suddenly grew much hotter.

"Now listen here, Friend," Satan said, a hard edge to his voice, "this is a decision that you have to make, one way or the other. I've been giving up a lot of general hell-raising around here while I've been waiting for your decision, and--"

"Hey, you can't take all the credit for the general shitty nature of the world," Stan said. "Look at that river. It may be all nice and blue, but we've poisoned it with so many pollutants you can't even eat what few fish live in there."

Satan nodded. "You've got me there."

"Sure, and what about our own disregard for each other?" Stan continued. "Just last week six people were gunned down a couple blocks from here for ten dollars' worth of crack cocaine."

"Stop!" Satan cried, big red tears welling up in his eyes. "You're making me homesick."

"Oh, sorry."

"I'll let it go this time. Hey, you're not trying to make me forget about our deal, are you?"

"Well, no, well, I mean that-"

"Now, c'mon, Stan, a deal's a deal. What's it gonna be?"

Stan looked up in the sky and shrugged up his shoulders. "Yeah," he finally said in a small, quiet voice.

"Yeah what?"

"Yeah, as in a deal."

"Really?"

"Really."

"Hot damn! Now you stay right here while I go get all my documents so we can make all this legal-like," Satan said, walking with an exuberant gait back over to the tree for his briefcase.

Stan stood as still as the oak, pondering his decision, a very important decision, actually the most important decision he had made in his entire life. He stood there, lost in thought, and didn't even notice the five-meter long lightning bolt until it flashed by, knocking him to the ground and vaporizing Satan who stood whistling a happy tune underneath the oak tree.

"Now that was a pretty sight!"

Stan brushed the dirt off his clothes and examined the singed hairs on his arm before looking behind him to see a tall, handsome, tanned figure dressed in a 3 piece white suit a few feet away.

"I probably don't want to know this," Stan asked, "but who are you?"

"Me?" the man said, sitting down next to Stan. "You can call me anything you want as long as you don't call me late for dinner!" He roared with laughter.

Oh great, Stan thought, another comedian.

"No, really," the man chuckled, "call me Gabe."

"As in Gabriel the angel?"

"How'd you guess?"

"Just lucky I suppose." Stan motioned over to the oak tree. "Wasn't that lightning bolt a little unfair for an angel?"

"What do you mean?"

"You hit him when his back was turned."

"Oh, that," Gabriel answered. "I like to think of it as a

pre-emptive defensive strike. Me and that dude go back a long way, and I'm sure he's done the same to me somewhere in the past." He stopped speaking for a moment and got up. "Well, Stan, it's been fun and all, but I really do need to be getting back to heaven."

"What? Just like that? You know, maybe Satan was a real jerk, but he was going to rid us of disease, famine, war, death, and taxes. Maybe in heaven in those aren't such big deals, but down here they sure are."

Gabriel patted Stan on the shoulder. "I hate to disillusion you, but he wasn't going to do any of that."

"Sure he was," Stan said. "We were going to sign on it."

"He would have gotten you with the small print."

"The small print?"

"Sure," Gabriel smiled, a hint of self-assuredness in his voice, "the small print. So small that even I would have had a hard time reading it, and believe me, after counting the number of angels that can dance on the head of a pin, I can see *real* small."

Stan admiringly looked up at Gabriel. "Wow! How many?"

"How many what?"

"How many angels can dance on the head of a pin?"

"Sorry, that's a company secret," Gabriel answered. "Anyway, you've given me new faith in the human spirit. You were going to give Satan your soul to torment for all eternity for the betterment of humankind, and while I can't offer you--or the human race— an out of your general misery, due to the free will clause and all that, I think I can get away with granting

you at least a small miracle."

Stan thought hard for a few seconds, then nodded excitedly. "How about a week, no, how about a month off of work? With pay?"

"What? C'mon, Stan, this is a miracle, not a new labor contract."

"All right," Stan said, furrowing his brow in

concentration. Suddenly he got a very dreamy, very contented look in his eyes. "Well, Gabriel," he said, "there is this girl named Pamela Pleasures. . . ."

ABOUT THE AUTHOR

EDWARD R. ROSICK is a writer and physician who resides in central Michigan. His poetry and speculative fiction published over the last 30 years covers the spectrum from sublime to surreal. Rosick's poetry has been published in numerous magazines and esteemed literary journals including Trillium, Big Two-Hearted and The MacGuffin. His horror and speculative fiction have been featured in magazines and anthologies including *Pulphouse*, *Creepy Campfire Quarterly*, and *The Half That You See*. His first horror novel, *Deep Roots*, has just been published by Thurston Howl Publications. His website can be found at www.edrosick.net.

BEHIND THE EIGHT BALL

DANCING WITH THE DEVIL

L.N. Hunter

"My good man, I assure you I am indeed the Devil."

The short, bespectacled man puffed out his skinny chest and glanced at his wristwatch, a bulky affair with a chunky gold bracelet and far too many hands. 'I realize that this is a little early—you're not due for another few days, but I'd like to get things tidied away quickly. And then we can all move along with our lives—well, perhaps not moving very far in your case. Now, as it's part of the standard contract, I will grant you a final wish before I take your soul. Anything at all, which I would like to point out is very generous of me, given the rather limited value of your next few days on this Earth. I don't do this for everyone, you know, but I'm in a good mood.'

Taylor—Tubby to his friends—gave a shake, zipped up, and turned from the urinal. "Do y' think I'm soft in the head? I wasn't born yesserday, Sonny. I know what y're after, accosting reshpec- respectivle, respectable gennelmen in the toilets, y'perv! If I wassin such a gennelman, I'd deck ya."

Tubby belched, emitting a potent cloud of stale beer and lamb vindaloo fumes. After flicking his hands under the cold tap, he gave them a perfunctory shake and wiped them on his trouser legs. He leaned against the door of the Gents, letting in the noise from his table in the Prize of India, where five equally intoxicated diners sat. They were waving chapattis and half-empty bottles of Kingfisher in the air while they laughed and shouted at each other.

Other customers had been casting annoyed glances at that table all evening. Hastening to finish their own meals, they muttered about leaving before the loud-mouthed drunkards did anything worse than being rowdy, such as coming across and talking to them about the referee's visual acuity during yesterday's match and asking, 'We was robbed, wasn't we?'

The long-suffering waiters were used to this sort of behaviour, but there was little they could do about it. Tubby and his friends were end-of-week regulars and, pragmatically, the drunkards' money was as good as anyone else's. Better, even, because the staff could easily slip an additional dish or two on the bill, safe in the knowledge that the extra charges wouldn't be noticed. And the chef could offload the older and past-best meat without any risk of it being remarked on.

The short man claiming to be the Devil grabbed Tubby's elbow and pulled him back into the Gents, his eyes flickering red behind his round glasses.

"Wha'the fuck ya think y're doing? Leggo my arm, y' speccy bastard," Tubby slurred.

"Listen to me, you loathsome glob of sputum. I can make the final moments of your life miserable, or I can grant your one true desire." His voice deepened. "But you don't get to turn your back on me. I am the Prince of Hell."

Tubby looked blank.

The man sighed. "Satan? You know, the Angel of Death?"

Tubby tried to pull free, but the other man's grip was strong. A shiver ran up Tubby's spine and settled in his brain, where it drowned in a sea of alcohol before breaking through to conscious awareness.

"Dunno what your game is, laddie, but I'm going back to my friends." His voice had become a whine, but he took a breath and soon recovered his belligerent tone: "Leggo m'arm, Angel of... Angel of Arse!"

The man took hold of Tubby's shoulders and shook him sharply. He leaned close, bringing himself into the range of the foul stench of Tubby's breath, and grated, "You festering pile of bovine manure. I will take your soul this night. You can choose to benefit from the transaction or not."

He released one of Tubby's arms and reached up to tap him in the middle of the forehead. "Let me try once again, to see if I can get through your thick skull. What do you want most in the world?"

Tubby laughed at the little man scowling up at him. "Listen, sunshine, you can't fool me. D'y know how many spam emails I get every single day?" He paused and belched. "Hunnerds! Hunnerds, thass how many! They *all* promise the world, but only a moron falls for them. An' I'm not a moron. D'you know what you sound like?" He poked the man in the chest and put on a high-pitched, prissy voice. "'Me money's trapped in Nigel- Nigeria an' I need only a li'l from you' or 'Fraudulact- fraudulent acti- activity has been detected; click here to unfr'ze yer account.' You're just the same, offering me a big pile of nuthin' tha' you won't deliver! Now, gerroff me, ya prick." He shook himself free and reached for the door handle.

As Tubby pushed the door open, he heard three sounds behind him. First, the tink of a pair of wire-framed round glasses breaking on the tiled floor. Next came a ripping noise like clothing being torn apart but with an additional fleshy squelch. And finally, the sound of something shattering one of the ceiling lights was accompanied by the rest of the lights dimming.

Another chill made a valiant but ultimately vain attempt to penetrate Tubby's alcoholic haze. He pivoted unsteadily on his feet.

A seven-foot-tall demon loomed over him, smoke rising from his slick red skin. The monster's feet cracked the floor tiles, and enormous curved horns poked into the ceiling. Smoke, sulphurous and heavy, drifted from his nose. Torn clothes and what appeared to be human skin lay in a heap on the floor.

Tubby blinked. Then he laughed loudly, slapping his knee. "Great costume. Tha's brilliant, that is. How'd ya change so quickly?"

The demonic monster roared, "Taylor Patrick Entwistle Roberts, before I leave this place, I will have your soul. But, because I'm in a good mood tonight—or, at least I was—I want to offer you something in return. For the final time, therefore, what is it you want in the depth of your being? What is your most desired pleasure? Do not try my patience."

"Sheesh, keep y'r hair on, buster! Who says I wan' anythin'? I've had enough of y'r game. So, bugger off. I'm going back t' me friends." Tubby opened the door, but the Devil placed a bony hand on his shoulder. Struggling but unable to break free, Tubby called to his dining companions, "Hey, guys! Tony, Shaun, got a bit of trouble here in the bog. Can you help?"

There was a guffaw at the mention of 'trouble in the bog' and a comment about some lightweights not being able to handle their vindaloos, but nonetheless, five chairs loyally scraped back on the floor. Within moments, the Gents was feeling rather crowded, occupied as it was by six drunk men and one oversized demon.

Tubby said, "The dickhead in the Halloween costume

says he'll gimme anythin' I wan' in exchange for my soul."

"It's a scam," slurred one of the newcomers. "'s obvious. Like them Nigerian wossnames."

Another added, "Don't be ridiculous, there's no such thing as souls. It's all mumbo-jumbo."

A third said, "Go on, ask for whatserface, the actress. You know, the one with the big…" He traced an hourglass shape with his hands.

All six men laughed.

There was a short pause as the men eyed the figure in front of them.

One asked, "What do you wan' with Tubby's soul, anyway? It can't be much of a thing. No use to you and"—he looked Tubby up and down—"bugger-all use to Tubs."

Tubby and his companions sniggered.

The demon boomed, "Do you know who I am, you revolting bags of fetid pus?"

The men stared at the figure. Two shook their heads, as if trying to decipher—or possibly extinguish—the frantic babbling from that tiny part of their brains responsible for self-preservation. The remainder merely wore expressions of expectant curiosity.

Shaun ventured, "Someone with a bad case of sunburn? Would you like us to get some burn ointment?"

"No, no, I got it," said another, gesturing at the flames starting to flicker around the demon's head. "That Ghost Rider guy from the comics. Go on, light up properly."

Tubby lifted himself up on tiptoes, looked the demon directly in his glowing, red eyes and growled, "A dickless shortarse in a tall costume."

The men laughed for a third time.

The Devil muttered, "What is wrong with people these days?" He squeezed the bridge of his nose. "Why didn't I stop? Just one, I said to myself. Just one more to end the day on a round number. It'd be tidy, I thought. It'd be easy. Piece of piss."

He straightened up and boomed, "You malodorous

offspring of rabid mountain weasels, I AM SATAN!"

The remaining lights in the Gents extinguished, plunging the room into total darkness for a moment, then gradually blinked back to life.

"Yeah, right."

"'Course you are, mate."

"Pull the other one, it's got jangly bells on."

"Well, bugger off back to Hell or Hades, or whatever loony bin you came from, and let us eat in peace." This was accompanied by a finger being prodded in the demon's rib cage.

Tendrils of smoke drifted from demon's nose. "I WILL NOT BE MOCKED!"

Tony, the largest of Tubby's companions—almost as tall as the monster and twice as wide—threw a haymaker of a punch, connecting with the skeleton's jaw.

Satan jerked back in surprise. His feet became entangled in the discards of his earlier disguise, and he tripped, landing hard on his tailbone. The crack that sounded could have been either a floor tile breaking, or one of the bones in the Devil's rump.

"Ha, we got 'im now. Pile in, lads!"

Tubby and his friends started punching and kicking.

Satan was about to curse the men to damnation when one managed a lucky shot in the pelvic area. "Owwww," he squeaked instead, as the men continued to pummel him.

Finally, panting with unaccustomed exertion, the men were finished. The Devil lay on the floor, broken-boned and leaking a thick grey fluid. He groaned weakly and lapsed into unconsciousness. One of his horns had been snapped off, and Tony picked it up, mumbling that it would make a nice souvenir. Tubby wiped grey mucus off his knuckles on Satan's hairy leg and tossed the rags on top of the demon, before strutting through the door.

The other customers stared at the men as they returned to their table. They hadn't seen what had happened, but they'd certainly heard the ruckus. One or two swallowed nervously. The waiters' gaze darted between the six friends and the door to the Gents.

Shaun broke the silence, 'Bollocks to this, let's hit the nightclub.' They emptied their bottles and threw some notes on the table before walking out, munching the last of the poppadums.

The only movement amongst the other diners and staff was heads swivelling to watch the six friends leave. As the door eased itself shut with a quiet click, all eyes flicked to the Gents.

Outside, four men sitting in a bus shelter glanced up at Tubby and the others from their cans of lager.

"Whatchu looking at?" Tubby blustered.

Shaun put a hand on his shoulder. "Steady on, Tubbs. There's something…"

One of the men, tall, pale and so thin he was not much more than a skin-covered skeleton, pointed at the horn Tony held and nudged his companions.

The second stranger's bloodshot eyes widened. He stood up and waved away a handful of flies which had been buzzing around his greasy hair. A stench of vomit—and worse—hit Tubby and his companions as he croaked, "Have you seen our friend?"

The third man, fat and red-faced, smiled, showing far too many sharp teeth. "Skinny dude. Glasses." He pointed a talon of a finger at what Tony was holding. "That looks like his…"

The fourth, clad in a cloak so dark it seemed to suck light from the air reached out a skeletal hand.

Shaun shouted, "Run!" and the six did just that.

The four men settled back into the bus shelter.

"He's late again," the skinny one sighed. "Probably trying to end the day on a round number, the pig-headed tosser. Best postpone the Apocalypse until next Friday."

ABOUT THE AUTHOR

L.N. HUNTER is a tangly web of off-kilter ideas and eccentric thoughts, masquerading as a human being – and sometimes as a writer, which is much more fun. And harder work. Some of those weird notions have appeared in *Short Circuit* and *Rosette Maleficarum*, as well as anthologies *Obscura* and *Trickster's Treats 3*, among others. There have also been papers in the IEEE Transactions on Neural Networks, which are probably somewhat less relevant. When not writing, L.N. unwinds in a disorganised home in rural Cambridgeshire, UK, along with two cats and a soulmate.

NETHERWORLD

EXPRESS

Charlie Jones

Most bar stories, especially those told after midnight, sound like bad B-movies. You can tell them because they start out with a phrase like, "This is God's-honest truth." That makes your truth antennas tingle. But, every once in a while, you hear one that sounds too odd to be made up. That happened to me last Monday night.

Sam and I were the last two customers in Andy's. Sam's question lingered in the air. The football game ended two hours ago, and all the west coast baseball games were over. The Phillies lost 2-0 on a 4-hitter by a Giants rookie right-hander. Mike, the night bartender, sat in his usual spot, chin on his chest, snoozing at the other end of the bar. At closing time, Sam got off his stool, doused the lights, and locked the door. I turned off the TVs.

A minute passed in silence; we drank by the light of the neon signs behind the bar. Sam and I were semi-regulars. He was in his mid-forties, of sturdy construction, thinning hair and brown eyes. He worked for the transit authority, an engineer on the subway, graveyard shift, so he spent most of his work time underground. Monday was his night off. He was a normal guy, as normal as the rest of us who hung out at Andy's. Whispers circulated that he was having troubles at home and work. I guess working in the dark does funny things to you.

"Do you believe in Hell?" he repeated.

Anytime someone asked you a direct question in a bar, it usually meant he had something on his mind that he wanted to talk about.

"If I thought about it, I probably would," I replied. "How about you?"

He looked at me. "Up until about a year ago, I would have said no. Hell sounded like a place that somebody made up just to scare us."

"And now?"

"Something happened at work that made me change my mind."

"Must've been pretty big."

Sam turned to me. "Yeah. Look, if I tell you this, you won't use it for one of your stories, will you? It'll make me sound crazy."

"No. It's like confession."

Another pause. He drummed his sausage-link fingers lightly on the bar. I sensed that he was struggling to find the right words.

He said, "This is a true story, I swear to God. It happened just like I'm telling it. Got it?"

The tingling started. "Sure, Sam. What reason would you have for making it up?"

"Right. So, this happened last fall," he started.

He spoke without the usual nervous traits that some people have. Sam talked as if he was reliving it in his mind, moment by moment, detail by detail, using his large hands to make a point. Every once in a while, he'd shift on his stool to get comfortable or take a sip of his beer. This is the story he told me.

ʘ

Last fall, the transit authority decided to run the subway all night to try to keep the drunks off the road, so they asked for volunteers. They sweetened the pot to work the graveyard shift, and I was on the hook for my daughter's tuition, so every dime helped. I worked ten to six, with a short break after each round-trip. I was doing it for about two weeks when I started my shift on Halloween, and by the time I made the second round-trip, we were long past midnight.

The subway looked like rush hour rather than the shank of the evening. Besides the usual riders getting off late shifts, there were drunks, teenagers, and college kids in costumes, with just another excuse to go out drinking. There weren't enough transit cops to cover the whole line, so they only rode the trains around Center City and up to Temple University. But north of Temple, I was on my own. There were about a hundred people onboard when we pulled out of Temple on our way to Fern Rock, the end of the line.

We left Dauphin station when the train began to shudder and buck. Even though I pushed down firmly on the dead man switch, the train would stop and start, and it took five minutes to get to the next station, North Philadelphia. I tried to call into Command but the radio was dead. I opened the doors, and toggled the mike to announce that due to operational problems, I was taking the train out of service and everybody must get off and wait for the next train.

Before I could make the announcement, the doors slammed shut. Instead, over the PA system a voice, sounding like hot daggers, said, "Welcome to the Netherworld Express. My name is Charon, and it is my job to escort you to your eternal damnation. This train will be

247

making stops at the following stations: Limbo, Lust, Gluttony, Greed, Anger, Heresy, Violence, Fraud, and Treachery. My assistants in each car will tell you which station you should use."

The smell of rotting flesh crept into the booth. I wasn't pressing on the switch, but the train started with a lurch and moved forward. I heard loud knocking as if someone was beating the exterior of the car with a crowbar.

I yelled, "Who's doing this? Stop right now! Give me back control of the train." More knocking, this time from outside the booth door. I ripped open the door and in front of me were six people in various states of distress. Some were in costume and two were regulars, guys who worked at the newspaper who rode home every night on this run.

"What the hell, Sam? Is this some kind of Halloween prank? This ain't funny!"

I tried to remain calm and told them it was as much a mystery to me as it was to them.

"Can't you stop this?"

"Can't you use the radio?"

"Who's driving?"

I turned around and saw the speedo read 25 mph. I wasn't frightened yet, just confused, and my head felt stuffed with cotton. I was about to say something, but one of the revelers cried, "What the hell!" and pointed down the car. Everyone turned that way and cried out. I forced my way out of the booth and peered down the car.

The most godawful looking thing anybody ever saw moved towards us. It stood seven feet tall, human in shape only. The creature had dark scales all over its body. Pinpoint red eyes dominated its scaly face. Dark fangs came out of its mouth. Dozens of black adders entwined themselves around its body, slithering over its back and sides, nipping at each other, all hissing at us. Its scaly arms and legs were unnaturally long, connected to the thin body. Its arms ended in claws with three pointed skeletal fingers.

Its webbed feet barely grazed the floor of the car. As it got closer to us, it extended its right arm and with a small flick of its wrist, it tossed the people standing there back into seats and pinned them there. Fear and horror etched their faces.

"Sam, I am driving the train," the thing said in its dagger voice. "I have control of the PA and the radio, too. Your Command Center thinks you are dead on the tracks at North Philadelphia, but as you can see, we're moving, and I command you to sit down," and it pointed to an empty seat, "so that you don't get hurt. All your passengers are safe, as long as they don't try to move. One of my assistants is in each car with the instructions to keep order and not let anybody get out of their seats until told to. Sit down, we're making a turn."

"But there's no turn here."

At that moment, I felt the train veer to the right and head downward. The wheels screeched on the tracks. "Where are we going?"

"Like I said before, our first station is Limbo. We'll be there in a few minutes. Now sit down!" It forced me into an empty seat.

I couldn't move, but my mind raced with fear and confusion. The overhead lights flickered off and the emergency lights came on, giving the car an otherworldly look. I knew that the subway had a few unused spurs, but none of them were this far north. It wasn't on any of our maps.

After a few minutes, Charon announced, "Next station is Limbo. Listen for instructions from your car attendant." At that point the creature pointed its claws and three people stood up. It addressed them, "You will be departing here at Limbo. Attendants will meet you on the platform to direct you to your resting place. You are the fortunate ones. Limbo is for the unwashed who don't belong to either Heaven or Hell. Now, get off."

The car stopped and the doors slammed open and the

three people stepped out onto the Limbo platform, which looked like any other along the subway line. I could see that about a dozen more passengers got off.

The doors closed and I heard an announcement, "Next station is Lust." I saw that we were on a single track with a platform on only one side. As the train moved ahead it rode into a dense fog. I looked out the front window and the only thing I could see was the train light reflected in the fog. The whistle sounded every fifteen seconds to accompany the clackety-clack sound from the wheels. We continued our rapid descent for what felt like hours.

The train slowed, and the creature chose four people. Three men, one in a Batman costume, and a middle-aged woman stood up and the creature said to them, "You are condemned to Lust, the second circle of Hell, from which there is no escape. Your pursuit of pleasures of the flesh was your downfall. Hurricane winds will buffet you from all directions as your torment. You will never have a peaceful moment again. You will have all eternity to contemplate your life on earth and how you could have reformed to avoid this punishment."

A look of terror filled their faces as the creature spoke to them. The train came to a stop and the doors banged open. A strong wind entered the car and swept the four people onto the platform and out of sight. The doors closed and we moved forward. The look on the faces of the remaining people on the car turned to horror when they realized that this was real and not a nightmare. I wondered what my sins were and where I'd be getting off. I didn't know if it would help, but I started praying.

The train continued on to the Netherworld, going faster than before over track that now felt like washboard. We made stops at Gluttony, Greed, Anger, Heresy, and at each one a few people got off to meet their fate.

I thought for sure my summons would come when we reached Anger. A few years ago, I got mad at my wife when I discovered that she stepped out on me with a neighbor. Their screwing around wrecked two families and when I found out, I took an axe from the garage and went down the street and smashed every window on the neighbor's first floor and started on his car when the cops showed up. I stared at them with eyes ablaze, brandishing an axe, and the cops used a taser to arrest me. My chest still tingles where it hit me, a lasting memory of my anger. When the creature did not summon me at Anger, I wondered what unimaginable misery awaited me.

As I sat there awaiting my fate, I realized I must be dead, sentenced to Hell, and on my way to eternal torment. Is this what God had in store for sinners? I always thought preachers made up Hell, and Satan was just a symbol of evil, to scare us. If people were sitting where I was and could see the creature standing in the middle of the car, they would believe in Hell and Satan and repent their sins. But what puzzled me was, how did I die? I didn't remember dying. Does anyone?

Sam put his hand on my arm. "You still awake?"

"Huh? Yeah, I'm with you. This sounds a little over the top, but I guess the combination of Halloween and the subway can do funny things to a person's mind."

"No, what's funny is that I'm still alive to tell the story, did you ever think of that? Everything happened exactly the way I'm telling you. God's honest truth."

A minute passed, then another. We finished our beers.

"Do you want me to go on?"

"Yeah, let me hit the head first." Standing there, I wanted to believe him, but anybody who told a story like this has to be crazy, right?

When I got back, Sam poured us two more beers. He slipped back into his story.

♉

The train went faster and the ride got bumpier and continued downward. I couldn't keep track of how far we went. The train shook so much I wondered how it stayed on the rails. If it hit a curve at this speed we would surely derail, which might be the only thing that could save us from our fates. All the lights in the car went out and the sickly light of the headlamp illuminated the fetid tunnel we traversed.

Hailstones, as large as a man's fist, fell, sounding like little explosions when they hit the car. The hail would stop occasionally and tornadoes rocked the car, causing it to shudder. I felt the wind lift the car from the rails and toss it against the side of the tunnel, then slam it back down on the tracks. When the hail and tornadoes subsided, the tunnel and car filled with a red mist. Could it be blood? The creature stood in the middle of the car, looking at the stricken faces of the passengers. The hail cracked the windows in the front of the car where I sat. The flying glass or hail would kill me. Could I die again? How many times can a person die?

After Heresy, the train leapt out of the station and we made stops at Violence, Fraud and Treachery, the last circle of Hell. Along the way, first, lava, then bright yellow sulfur assaulted us, filling the car to our knees. At Fraud, the creature selected a man and told him there is a special place in Hell for politicians. The man would never have another chance to defraud anyone or take their money for his purposes, for all eternity, truly Hell for a politician. The doors opened and the man got off. A lake of boiling pitch enveloped him. I heard the man's screams long after we left the station. Only one other guy remained on the car, along with me. And Charon.

On the approach to Treachery, the creature told us that this stop was for those whose crimes and sins were especially heinous. It told us to search our souls and determine how we lived our lives that caused us to spend eternity with the first criminal, Cain, and Judas, the betrayer of the Savior of the world. "He is in the deepest, darkest part of Hell we could find. Even Satan didn't want to allow him in."

The train sped on. The tunnel was aflame and the car started to burn as well. The flames ignited the sulfur clinging to the walls and seats of the car, turning them black. Noxious fumes enveloped me. It burned through the roof of the car and I could see up into the fiery hell that was our fate. I tried not to breathe the flames and fumes as the train slowed, then ground to a halt, unable to go any further.

The creature made the doomed man stand and pushed him out the door into Treachery. Icy water filled the platform. It enveloped the man, the temperature dropped, and encased him in a block of ice; immobile, contorted, but awake, for all eternity. An attendant moved the block of ice off the platform.

I sat still, wondering if the creature forgot about me. I could not figure out why I was still on the train. The creature moved in front of me and the snakes hissed and snapped at me. It said, with more daggers, "My Master has a special torment for you, Sam. You are not welcome here until you have served a long life of pain and suffering on Earth. He wanted you to see what your fate will be when he does want you." And the creature went away, up in a cloud of smoke in the air.

I sat there for a few minutes and wondered how I was supposed to get back. Incessant banging reached me, and after a moment, I came to in the engineer's booth.

The train sat in North Philadelphia station. I opened the door to the booth and two transit mechanics stood there, with irritated looks on their faces.

"What the hell, Sam!"

"What are you doing, radioing us at three in the morning?"

"You drunk or what?"

"Where are all your passengers?"

I stepped out of the booth. The car looked the same as when I left the yard at the beginning of the shift. I stood there with my jaw hanging open. Had it been a dream or a trance or a hallucination? No! I grabbed the first guy's shoulders and jumped up and down; I'm sure I looked like a crazy person. I shouted, "It wasn't real! It wasn't real! I'm alive. And the train is okay! It wasn't real!"

The man wrestled away from my clutches and said, "Sam, take it easy, we got it from here. See the EMT upstairs, get checked out."

I looked around, wild-eyed. "Yeah, yeah, I'll do that. It wasn't real, it wasn't real."

As I walked away, the second mechanic pointed at me and asked, "Yo! Sam, what's that stuff on your pants?"

I stopped and looked down. A bright yellow substance stained my pants from the knees down. I ran off the car, over the platform, and up the steps to the street. The EMTs chased me for a block before they caught me and put me in the back of the ambulance and took me to Temple Hospital for tests and overnight observation.

On the way to the hospital, I asked one of the techs where the passengers were.

"Passengers? You were the only one on the train."

"No, there were about a hundred people aboard. Did they catch the next train?"

"There hasn't been another train. Yours was blocking the tracks," the tech said.

"What? WHAT?! Jesus, that means …" I realized that they all went to Hell, and I was the only survivor.

I tried to get up, but the tech injected the IV with a syringe, and I laid back on the gurney. My last thought was that all those people met their fates tonight. On my train.

The ER doctor gave me a sedative and I slept the rest of the night and most of the next day. When I awoke, I checked out okay and they released me with a prescription for more sedatives if I needed them.

♉

Sam sat back in his stool. The sheen of sweat on his face reflected the red neon light from behind the bar. He finished his beer. We sat in silence for a few moments in the semi-darkness.

"That's the way it happened, swear to God. Craziest night ever, I can't believe I survived. Can you use it for a story?"

"I don't know, Sam. I thought you said you didn't want me to make a story of it."

He put both hands flat on the bar exposing the grease under his fingernails. "Can you?"

I rubbed my forehead. "Like I said, it's out there. Do you have any evidence that it really happened?"

"What are you, a lawyer? Here's some evidence, some stuff that's happened to me since then. The divorce became final and the judge ruled that I owed my wife alimony for the past two years. After paying tens of thousands in tuition, my daughter dropped out of college a semester before she was supposed to graduate to follow some douchebag she met around Europe. They cut my hours and I have to go to the shrink twice a week. My apartment flooded and I lost my whole baseball card collection. All this happened in the last eleven months. Sounds like torment to me."

"I don't know that all that stuff is evidence, just horrible bad luck."

He got a determined look on his face. "Okay, I have this." He pulled his wallet out and withdrew a piece of khaki cloth, stained yellow, the size of a dollar bill. Sam, eyeing me, laid it on the bar between us.

Staring at the cloth, I asked, "Is that what I think it is?"

"Yeah, I threw the pants away, but kept this to remind me of that night. Someday I'm going to repent. I've tried a few times, but I keep slipping back to my old ways, so I know what my fate looks like. Do you?"

I caught a whiff of sulfur. I wiped my fingers on my pants and reached out to touch the cloth.

Sam grabbed my arm and gave me a stern look. "You sure you want to do that?"

I looked at the cloth, then him, then back at the cloth. I moved it an inch along the bar, and withdrew my finger. "What's the harm?" with a shrug of my shoulders. I picked it up and rubbed it between my index finger and thumb. "See, no prob ..."

Before I could finish, the bar morphed into a broken-down, beat-up subway car, stained with yellow and black on the walls and floor. The roof was gone and flames raged above me. In the center of the car stood a scaly creature looking at me with red pinpoints for eyes. Black snakes writhed around his torso and limbs.

It lifted its three-fingered claw and beckoned me. Its words pierced my ears, "Welcome to the Netherworld Express."

As panic overwhelmed me, Sam yanked the cloth away from me and jammed it back in his wallet. The vision departed, and we were sitting in the darkened bar again.

All I could stammer was "What the hell?" When my heart rate slowed down, I shook my head and said, "Nice trick."

"It's no trick," Sam said. "You saw it, just like I said. Now you gonna believe me?"

"I don't know what to believe. All I know is that I don't ever want to touch that again. How do you walk around with it? Doesn't it affect you?"

"Only if you hold it for more than a few seconds."

"You should burn that," I said.

"No, every once in a while, I need it to remind me of

that night."

"Suit yourself."

I told him I didn't want any more to drink and had to go. I don't know if that was true or not, but I wanted to get away from him and that piece of cloth. We got up and we each left a twenty on the bar for Mike and walked out as the sky lightened. He went his way and I went mine. The last thing he said to me was that I shouldn't ride the subway after midnight, especially past Temple.

All the way home his question troubled me. What will our fate be when we pass away? But I knew I could never use his story because who would ever believe it.

ABOUT THE AUTHOR

CHARLIE JONES lives in and writes about Philadelphia. Contrary to the subject of his story, he had been known to ride the subway, occasionally after dark, and lived to write about it. Philadelphia is a hotbed of stories about both living and dead people. All you have to do is open your eyes and ears and mind to the possibility that the voice you just heard might not be of this earth. Whistling past the graveyard is a birthright of any true Philadelphian.

PROTÉGÉ
Ken MacGregor

Jefferson Elementary School sat quiet in the afternoon sun. Birds chirped in the plentiful trees, and traffic ambled by at a relaxed pace.

Without warning, the double doors burst open, spewing forth a sea of miniature humanity, shrieking with the twin joys of freedom and youth.

Diesel engines rumbled to life and kids climbed aboard buses, jostling for their favorite seats.

Simon navigated the slowly thinning horde and walked home. Along the way, he kicked small rocks and walked atop low, stone walls, acting out superhero fantasies. Finally, he got to the door, always unlocked, and let himself in.

"Mom!"

"In the kitchen," she shouted back. Simon dropped his backpack on the floor by the couch, where it ceased to exist for him. He walked into the kitchen and hugged his mom, who raised her elbows out of the way. Her hands were covered in soapy water. She smiled at him and he smiled back.

"How was school?"

"Bo-ring" He rolled his eyes.

"Again?" his mom asked in mock dismay.

"I know, right?" Simon said. "I keep waiting for it to be a Carnival of Awesome, but I am always disappointed."

Harmony laughed. It made him smile.

"How was *your* day, Mom?"

"It was nice actually," she said. "I got to spend an hour in the hammock reading Vonnegut."

"Bo-ring!"

"Why don't you go change, so you can go outside and get filthy?" Simon bolted for the stairs. She yelled after him, "I'll call you when dinner's ready."

The next morning, while Simon was in school, his mom went shopping. She was carrying a hand basket, only getting what she needed for the next couple days. The cashier was young, maybe sixteen, fighting a losing battle with acne, but polite and genuine; Harmony wished him a lovely day, too.

On her way out, a flyer on the community bulletin board caught her eye. It was crimson paper, thick, handwritten with a calligraphy pen or brush. It was very ornate and pretty and said: "Classical Piano Lessons. All Skill Levels. Very Reasonably Priced." There were tear-away tabs cut into the bottom with 'piano lessons', and a phone number, also done by hand.

Harmony was enchanted by the idea of Simon learning piano. She tore off a number.

That night, just after dinner, before Simon cleared the plates—his job—he drained half the milk in his glass all at once.

"Aaaaahhhh..." he said, wiping his mouth with the back of his hand dramatically. "Best. Milk. Ever."

"Glad you like it," Harmony said. "Can I ask you a question, Simon?"

"You just did." He patted his belly. "But, I'm feeling generous. Go ahead and ask me another one."

"Kind of you, sir," she smiled. "Would you like to learn to play piano?"

"I don't know. I never thought about it. Why?"

Harmony reached over to a side table and grabbed her purse. She pulled out the red flyer and handed it to him. He read it over and looked up at her.

"It's really pretty handwriting."

"Yeah."

"I don't know, mom," Simon hedged. "You remember when I tried to learn trombone?"

"Simon, you were six. You could barely lift the thing. A piano is much less … awkward"

Simon looked at the flyer again. He ran his fingers over the letters. He set it down and assumed a very serious, concentrating face. He arched an eyebrow, lifted his hands and "played" piano very dramatically on the table. Harmony laughed and he joined her.

"Okay. I'll give it a shot," he said. "But if I hate it after a month, can I quit?"

"Two months."

"Deal." Simon nodded and they shook on it.

♉

The following Saturday, around 11 am, Harmony and Simon found themselves in a nondescript, suburban ranch-style home. They sat side-by-side on a worn loveseat in a small sitting room. The walls were adorned with framed prints: photos and paintings of grand pianos. After a moment, an interior door opened and a tall, gaunt man, sixty-ish, appeared and looked at them for several seconds in silence. He had unusually long fingers. Harmony and Simon were uncomfortable, but afraid to be rude. Finally, Simon couldn't take it anymore.

"Hi," he said standing up. "I'm Simon and I'd like to learn to play the piano."

"Well," replied the man. He had a mild, German accent. "By an odd coincidence, I happen to teach that particular instrument." He smiled at Simon and Harmony, but it was slightly off, as if his mouth didn't quite know how.

"That works out well then," said Harmony. "Doesn't it?"

"Yes. Forgive my rudeness," he said "I am Klaus Engel. Does the boy have any musical training?"

"He tried to take up the trombone a couple years ago, but it didn't go very well."

"I kept dropping it," said Simon. "And tripping over the slide."

"Please do not drop my piano."

Harmony and Simon stared at him.

He laughed, a wheezing, coughing sound. "It is a joke." They laughed politely and he was suddenly serious again. "Please, come and meet the instrument. Perhaps you will be friends."

They went through the door. It led to a small, plain room that was dominated by a beautiful, shining black grand piano on a dais, the top slanted open to reveal the insides. Beyond the piano, one wall was all windows looking out onto a wilderness of trees. The overall effect was breathtaking.

"Wow," breathed Simon.

"What a gorgeous piano," Harmony said at the same time.

"You are kind to say so," said Klaus.

Simon approached the piano, almost reverently. He looked at Klaus. "May I?"

Klaus nodded, watching him. Simon sat on the bench

and opened the cover over the keyboard. He looked at the keys, white and black, long and short. He passed his hand over the keys without touching them, and then rested his fingers very lightly on the surface of the keys. Harmony was bemused; Klaus was watching intently.

"They're cold."

"Yes."

"It's so pretty, Mom." Simon was hooked. "I want to learn how to play."

"Well, honey. That's why we're here."

"I know," he says. "But, before? I was just humoring you. Now, I really want to."

"Miss," Klaus began, "I'm sorry. I didn't catch your name."

"Harmony."

"Ah," Klaus said, grimacing his non-smile. "The child comes from music. It is auspicious. Harmony, it has been my experience that no one learns well while their mother is in the room, but I will understand if you wish to stay for this first lesson."

"I'd like that," Harmony said. "Simon is very responsible. I'm sure he'll be fine without me in the future."

"Good," said Klaus, turning to Simon. "Touch the keys again. Feel the weight of them under your fingertips. Start at the far-left end of the keyboard and play each note. Gently, gently, boy. This is not a drum. You do not bludgeon; you caress. Better. Work your way along. Listen to each note. Feel each key. Is there resistance? Can you feel the hammers inside as they strike the wires? Good. Now, go back the other way, and feel all the notes again."

Simon was intent. He caressed the keys as instructed. He listened to each note. He did feel the hammers striking the wires. He was fascinated by the cause and effect of his fingers on the keys and clear, loud notes from inside the piano. When he reached the left end of the keyboard again, he smiled at Klaus. Klaus nodded his head. He turned to

Harmony.

"I will teach this boy."

♉

The next morning, while Simon was in school, Harmony "Googled" Klaus Engel, telling herself it was idle curiosity; certainly, she was not worried about leaving Simon alone with him. He was an odd old man, to be sure, but her son knew when to leave if he had to. And, he did take two years of Judo. Still, she was his mother, so she checked up on the man.

In his late teens and early twenties, Klaus had been a world class pianist, the toast of Germany, a *wunderkind*. But, crippling arthritis in his mid-thirties ended his playing career and he disappeared into obscurity.

There was a video link on the page and Harmony clicked on it. Even through her mediocre laptop speakers, she could tell it was beautiful. The piece was twelve minutes long, something by Beethoven that she recognized, but couldn't name. This was unlike anything else she'd ever heard. This was raw, visceral playing. This was what music should sound like. And Simon was going to learn from this man? *My god, he'll be brilliant!* The music stopped and Klaus bowed formally to the audience, who stood and offered thunderous applause. Harmony closed her laptop and stared at it.

"Wow."

♉

After school, Simon stopped home, wolfed down a PB&J, and jumped on his bike. Harmony kissed him just below the helmet, accidentally getting part of his ear. He shook his head a little, grinned at her and took off.

♉

Simon was practicing his scales; Klaus called out notes, and Simon played them. After a while, Simon stopped and looked at his teacher.

"What?"

"How come you don't play anymore?"

"I played for years. Now it is your turn."

"Mom said you were really great," Simon said, "back in the day."

"Your mother is checking on me?"

"Wouldn't you? If it was your kid, I mean?"

"Of course," Klaus said. "I am not offended, just asking."

"So," Simon persisted. "Why'd you quit? Playing, I mean."

"My hands," Klaus said, looking at them. "They hurt when I play for more than a few minutes. It is arthritis...a curse."

"So," Simon said, "You could play for a few minutes without pain?"

"Yes. Why?"

"I'd like to hear it." Klaus looked at him for several seconds, considering.

"Move over," he said. Simon did, and Klaus sat next to him on the bench. He closed his eyes and put his hands on the keys. What came out of that instrument was sad and beautiful, unearthly and profound. Simon was blown away.

"That," he said. "is the prettiest thing I've ever heard. How did you learn to play like that?"

"I sold my soul to the devil," Klaus said. Simon rolled his eyes.

"If I sold my soul to the devil," he said. "I'd get something really cool for it."

"Oh? Such as?"

"Immortality," Said Simon, very smug. "That way, the Devil would never get to collect, and I'd have all the time in the world to learn piano or anything else I want."

Klaus nodded. "Very smart. I wish I'd thought of that."

♉

A few weeks passed; Harmony and Simon were in the back yard. At the edge of the yard was an old swing set from Simon's early childhood that was starting to rust. Harmony was weeding her flower garden; Simon was throwing a ball up in the air and catching it again and again.

"So," Simon said.

"So," his mom returned.

"Klaus says I'm getting really good."

"You call him 'Klaus'?"

"Sure," Simon said. "He's cool like that. He says maybe someday I could be really great at piano. Says I have a 'gift'."

"That's great, Simon! I always thought you were talented, but, you know, I'm a little biased...But if your piano teacher thinks so, too... wow. And he was incredible in his prime, so, I guess he'd know."

"Okay, Mom," Simon said with a back-up-a-little gesture. "Let's not get all carried away. Klaus said maybe, and I could be... I still have a lot of work to do. I just started learning, you know?"

"Of course," Harmony said. "Rome not being built in a day and all that...it's still cool, though."

"Yeah," Simon grinned at her. "It is."

♉

Back in the room with all the windows, Klaus was listening to Simon play. It was a fairly simple piece, but Simon played it well. He finished with a flourish that was not on the sheet music. Klaus's eyebrows shot up.

"What was that?" he demanded.

"I don't know," Simon shrugged. "It just seemed to need something else at the end."

"You are improvising."

"Is that okay?"

"It is," Klaus paused, searching for the word. "Unusual."

"Why?"

"Well, Simon," Klaus said, "you have not been playing long enough to be improvising."

"Sorry."

"You misunderstand me, Simon. It is a skill that should only come with years of training and performing, not months. You are making intuitive leaps that are, quite frankly, astounding."

"I am?" Simon asked. "Cool." Klaus looked at him.

"You want to cultivate this gift, do you?"

"Sure," Simon said. "I mean, that's why we're here, right?"

"Indeed, it is." Klaus smiled. "Let's get back to it, shall we? This time, if you feel like improvising at any point in the piece, go ahead and do it. We'll see how it goes."

Harmony was cutting small strips into the skin of a whole chicken and sliding garlic slivers underneath. She learned this trick from her own mother. The garlic infuses the whole bird and tastes amazing. Simon was doing his homework, but was tapping his foot to music in his head, and would put down the pencil to tap out "notes" on the table. Harmony watched him.

"Dinner in about 40 minutes, kiddo."

"Mm-hm." Simon said.

Harmony watched his hands. "Whatcha doin'?"

Simon looked up. "Math homework."

267

"To me," Harmony said, "It looks like you're playing piano."

"Oh yeah" Simon said. "That, too. Helps me think."

"Well, whatever gets the job done, right?" But, Simon was no longer listening. He tapped fingers and toes to the music in his head. Harmony watched him for a few more seconds. She was filled with a sudden sense of love and pride for her son. Then she remembered the chicken and put it in the oven.

At Klaus's piano, Simon was playing a complex piece of music and doing it well. He stopped when he mis-keyed a note.

"Damn," Simon said, unconsciously mimicking his mother when she's annoyed.

"Start from the beginning, please."

Simon was frustrated. "I know this piece. That shouldn't have happened."

"Simon," Klaus's voice was calm, soothing. "You are too hard on yourself. Six months ago, you had never touched a piano. Now, you are playing something it takes most students three years to even attempt. You are a *wunderkind*. Start from the beginning."

Simon started to play again. He closed his eyes as he played, rocking slightly. Klaus watched Simon's face and listened to the music pouring from the piano. Simon finished the piece. It was flawless. He dropped his head and sat in silence. Klaus slowly applauded and Simon's head snapped up. He was grinning.

"Nailed it, didn't I?"

"Yes, you did." Klaus gave Simon his awful smile.

Harmony and Simon were watching the BBC series

"Planet Earth," eating popcorn and silently marveling at the cinematography.

"I've been thinking," Simon said.

"Yeah?" Harmony said. "What's up?"

"The school has a talent show they do every year."

"And?"

"I think," Simon said, "I want to play piano for it."

"You really think you're ready?" Harmony caught herself: "For an audience, I mean."

"Sure" Simon was confident. "Klaus started performing when he was eight. Mozart was only six."

Harmony tilted her head at him. "Mozart?"

"Yeah. Of course, he was insanely brilliant. But, I'm good, Mom. I really am. And I'm ready to play for a crowd. Especially since it's just grade-school kids and their parents. Nobody's expectations are going to be too high."

"That's true," she said. "Okay, honey. I'll talk to your teacher about it."

Simon leaned over the bowl to kiss his Mom on the cheek. "Thanks, Mom. You're the best."

♉

Simon sat at the piano. He hesitated.

"Are you going to play?" Klaus eyed him.

"Yeah," Simon said. "I wanted to tell you: I'm booked as one of the acts for my school talent show in two months."

"What will you be doing?"

"Playing piano," Simon said. "Duh."

"Interesting. Who made this decision?"

"I did."

"Good," Klaus nodded. "Sit. We must make sure you

are ready."

♉

The next few weeks passed in a blur of practicing and comments from Klaus: "Too fast. It is not a race. You will get to the end in good time ... that's it. Let the music set the pace. Good. Good." The leaves outside the piano room changed from green to red and gold. One fall day, Simon finished a beautiful piece by Brahms, precise and soulful. As the last notes echoed around the room, Simon looked at his mentor. Klaus nodded.

"You are ready."

♉

The grade-school auditorium was actually pretty nice; it had good acoustics enhanced by hanging microphones. The act before Simon's was a short, original comedy by some fourth and fifth graders; Simon was friends with one of them, who did most of the writing. It was pretty funny. Simon was glad for them. After the applause died down, his principal, Ms. Calloway introduced him. The grand piano was already set up just left of center stage; it was not anywhere near the same class as the one on which he learned, but it would serve.

Simon entered from the wings wearing a rented tuxedo, the sight of which elicited some titters from the audience. He walked to just behind the bench, turned to the audience and took a small, formal bow as he had seen pianists do in movies. He then sat at the piano, shot his cuffs, and placed his hands over the keys. He waited for the sound in the audience to die down. When it did, he began to play. He played Tchaikovsky's Sixth Symphony; it was a dark and powerful piece, emotionally stirring and somewhat disturbing. Simon played it brilliantly: he was technically perfect and he invested the music with an emotional intensity that was astounding.

When he finished, there was silence as the audience realized they have witnessed something great. Then, the applause was thunderous. They rose to their feet, clapping even harder. Simon lifted his head, stood and turned toward the audience. He took a formal bow, then stood up again with a huge grin on his face. He pumped his fist in the air.

"Booyah!" He shouted and he thought he could hear his mom laugh. He walked to the wings and Samantha Knox stood there, holding juggling pins, staring at him.

"I," she said, "have to follow *that?*"

"Sorry," Simon said, shrugging and grinning. Klaus and Harmony were backstage already. His mom gave him a huge hug and told him how proud she was. Simon thanked her and looked to Klaus.

"Well?" he asked.

"Very nice," Klaus said. "Perhaps a little showboating at the end."

"Really," Simon was surprised. "I thought I played it perfectly."

"I was referring to the 'booyah'."

"Oh, yeah," Simon said. "Well, I was pretty stoked."

"Yes. Well, you should be. You, as you are so fond of saying, nailed it."

"Thanks, Klaus. And thanks for coming, too."

"Simon," Klaus said, "Hell's Legions couldn't have kept me away."

"Klaus," Simon said, "you're a little creepy sometimes."

"I will work on that."

"Who wants ice cream?" Harmony jumped in. "I'm buying."

"I don't wish to intrude..." Klaus started to leave.

"Nonsense," Harmony said. "If it weren't for you, we wouldn't have anything to celebrate. I insist."

"Then, I have no choice but to accompany you for ice cream."

"That's right," Simon said. "You don't. Come on. I'll introduce you to the awesomeness of Superman flavor."

"I am quite familiar with Superman flavor," Klaus said. "Though I find Pistachio infinitely more satisfying."

"*You* eat ice cream?"

"Certainly, Simon," Klaus said. "I'm not a complete barbarian."

♉

Simon walked into the piano room; there was quite a lot of snow on the trees outside the windows. He walked toward the piano, but Klaus stopped him.

"Wait," he said. "Let us talk a little."

"Sure," Simon said. "What's up?"

Klaus removed a small key from his pocket and opened the drawer in a table by the window. From inside, he removed a leather-bound folder, plain, black. He reached back in and pulled out a fountain pen with an extremely sharp tip. He handed the folder to Simon; inside was a contract. Simon read it. Some of it was lawyer-ese, but he got the drift. One can become the finest piano player of his generation, for the low, low cost of their immortal soul.

On the signature line was "Simon Chase".

♉

Harmony was on the couch reading a novel. She jerked upright, uncannily certain her son was in danger. The book hit the floor.

"Simon!"

♉

"A long time ago," Klaus said, in almost a whisper, "you asked me how I learned to play piano like that. You remember?"

"Sure," Simon said. "You said that you sold your soul to the Devil."

"It was not joke."

"I don't understand."

"When you came to me, I thought, 'here is a child with talent. With an innate gift. I can teach this child, make him an excellent pianist. Then, maybe the Devil will take his soul instead of mine.' I thought: if I could pass on my gift, I could pass on my curse. I never thought it would work of course, but the Devil liked the idea. He was quite enthusiastic about it. But, then I got to know you, Simon. In the last several months, I have come to be very fond of you, and I find that I cannot offer you up in this way."

"I don't know what to say."

"I think," Klaus said, "maybe you knew all along." They were silent for a moment.

"I am ashamed," Klaus continued, "for even thinking of sacrificing you. I am appalled at my selfishness. I almost didn't tell you about this. For my own piece of mind, though, I need to be honest with you."

"But you decided not to do it," Simon said. "That's what counts, right?"

"It certainly makes it easier to live with myself."

Simon looked at the contract in his hands. He looked Klaus in the eye for a long moment.

"What if I were to agree to it?"

♉

Harmony slammed her car into gear, and left tire tracks on the cement backing out of her driveway. She nearly collided with the Post Office truck.

♉

"No," Klaus said. "You do not know what you are offering."

"Give me some credit, Klaus. I'm a smart kid. I know what I'm doing. And I think I'll be able to figure out a way out of it, too. Even if it means passing it on to some other kid when I'm old."

"It is very touching," Klaus said, "that you would even consider it, but I cannot allow it."

"Klaus, my Dad died when I was four. I barely remember him now, but I know he loved me." Simon put his hand on Klaus's much larger one. "I couldn't stop my Dad from dying, but I can stop you from going to Hell. I've made up my mind."

"Simon," Klaus deliberated. "That is selfless and beautiful. But, I still can't let you do this. You are too young to make this decision. Did you know, for example that you would have to sign the contract in your own blood? Very painful."

"If the Devil were here right now, I'd sign this contract," Simon said. "And then you could get on with your life, without worrying about what happens after." Simon looked into Klaus's eyes. Klaus looked back at the boy for several seconds. Simon returned his gaze unflinching. "Give me the pen."

♉

Harmony parked the car in Klaus's driveway, throwing it into park and getting out in one motion. She left her door open and ran to the house, the keys still in the ignition and the small alarm dinging away. The front door was locked, and she beat on it with her fists.

♉

Simon gestured vaguely toward the front of the house. He blinked slowly, trying to shake off the mental fog. "Someone's at the door."

"I am expecting a delivery," Klaus said. "I will let them

in shortly."

Simon took the pen from Klaus. He held it over his left hand for a moment, then stabbed the point into his palm. He winced and withdrew the tip. There was blood on it. He signed his name on the line of the contract. The capital letters were three times the size of the lower-case ones.

The lights dimmed to half. Simon turned to Klaus, who was grinning his awful grin. Klaus snatched the contract from Simon, opened his mouth to speak, revealing four distinct rows of sharp teeth, like a shark's mouth. A forked tongue lolled out, tasting the air.

"Thank you very much, Simon Chase," Klaus said. "A pleasure doing business with you, my boy." His voice was horribly distorted by those teeth, but the words also echoed in Simon's head, too; where they were perfectly clear.

I forgot to ask for immortality, he thought.

Forty feet away, Harmony bashed her fists against the door, simultaneously screaming to be let in and weeping for her lost son.

ABOUT THE AUTHOR

KEN MACGREGOR writes stuff. He has two story collections -- *An Aberrant Mind* and *Sex, Gore, & Millipedes* with a third on the way -- a young adult novella, *Devil's Bane* (YA winner of the 23rd annual Critters Readers Poll), a co-written (with Kerry Lipp) novel, *Headcase*, and is a member of the Great Lakes Association of Horror Writers (GLAHW) and an Active member of the Horror Writers Association (HWA). He is a somewhat regular contributor to HorrorTree with his column *Brain Babies*. He has also written TV commercials, sketch comedy, a music video, some mediocre poetry, and a zombie movie. Sometimes, he edits stuff too.

Ken is the Managing Editor of Collections and Anthologies for LVP Publications. He's curated two anthologies: *Burnt Fur* for Blood Bound Books, and *Stitched Lips* for Dragon Roost Press..
When not writing, Ken drives the bookmobile for his local library. He lives with his kids, two cats, and the ashes of his wife.

Ken can be found at the staggeringly egocentric-named website kenmacgregor.com.

MYSTERIOUS WAYS

Richard J. Brewer

Homicide Detective Markus Troval drove down the Los Angeles suburban street knowing he was heading toward blood. This wasn't unusual. His calls, especially those coming at 3:30 in the morning, usually had him heading toward blood of some kind.

Turning a corner in the trendy neighborhood of Los Feliz, he could see the red and blue flashing lights of the police cruisers, their strobes creating a strange lightshow in the thick fog that had rolled in earlier that evening. A yawn escaped from him as he pulled up to the crime scene.

Climbing out of his car, Markus was reminded by the creaking of his knees that he was feeling all of his eighteen years on the force. Holding his detective badge out in front of him he walked past the uniformed police officers guarding the perimeter and worked his way up a stone walkway toward the two-story brick house. Ducking under the yellow crime tape, he was met by Thomas Martinez, his partner for the past seven years, who handed him a paper cup of steaming coffee.

"God love ya," said Markus, accepting the hot drink.

He took a careful sip, relishing its warmth and looking forward to the kick once the caffeine moved into his system.

"When did the call come in," he asked.

"About an hour and a half ago," Thomas said.

"And?" he said.

"Same as before, 911 call with a voice saying that we would find "something of interest" at this address. Then they hung up."

"So, it was him," he asked.

Thomas nodded. "If there was any doubt, it disappeared once we got inside the house."

"Just the one?"

"Yep," Thomas answered.

"Name?"

"Michael Jordan."

Markus shot his partner a look.

"Seriously," said Thomas. "That's his name."

Markus took another sip of his coffee.

"Well," he said. "Let's see it." He made an "after you" motion with his coffee and followed his partner up the rest of the walkway and into the house.

Crossing the threshold, Markus took a practiced look at the doorjamb. There was no sign of forced entry. Lining the walls of the entryway were a series of framed photographs, each taken in various exotic locations: the Egyptian pyramids, England's Stonehenge, Peru's Machu Picchu. One of the pictures had been taken somewhere in a tropical jungle. The background showed a huge golden Buddha lying on its side. In the foreground stood a pleasant-looking man with a neatly trimmed white beard. He was smiling broadly at the camera. Markus pointed to the image. "Our vic?" he said.

"That's him," said Thomas. "I mean, the face in the pictures on the walls match the photo on the driver license we've got, so we're pretty sure it's him. You know Markus, it's like the others. We'll have to confirm with fingerprints."

"Guy got around," said Markus, pointing at the photos on display.

"There's more throughout the house," said Thomas. "Retired schoolteacher."

"Guess we know how he liked to spend his summer vacations," said Markus. He looked again at the man in the photos and thought for a moment about the life and travels of Mr. Michael Jordan, and how all that was over now and forever.

The master bedroom of Jordan's house was tastefully decorated. The furniture—bed frame, end tables, dresser and armoire—was made of a rich dark cherry wood. The whole room had a functional but comfortable feeling to it, but the decor was marred by the blood-spattered walls and the mutilated body that lay in the middle of the room's king-sized bed.

"Aw Christ," said Markus, and quickly made the sign of the cross.

"Yeah," said Thomas.

The body of Michael Jordan was splayed across the bed, arms and legs spread wide, each appendage tied to the bedposts. Like the past five other murders, a gag had been placed in the victim's mouth and secured with duct tape.

Jordan had been beaten with some type of blunt instrument until his body was unrecognizable pulp. The sheets were stained a solid maroon with his blood, and what hadn't soaked into the mattress covered the walls in intricate patterns of reddish-brown gore.

The Blood Painter, as he was now known, had arrived on the L.A. scene six months ago. His first murder had been a sixty-three-year-old woman in Beverly Hills and was followed one month later by a soon to be retired lawyer, who had been a partner in one of the largest downtown law firms.

It was at the site of the third murder, an elderly Latino man named Miguel Sanchez, where one of the on-site police officers had said the spattering of blood on the walls had reminded him of a Jackson Pollock painting. A news reporter had overheard the remark and quickly dubbed the murderer the "Blood Painter Killer".

The forensics team was moving carefully around the room, taking pictures and collecting samples. It would prove to be a useless endeavor. Markus knew that this murder would only confirm what they already knew: that Michael Jordan was the sixth victim of the Blood Painter, that the killer struck on the last Sunday of the month, that he was targeting the elderly, that each victim was missing their right hand and that despite their best efforts, they would find nothing incriminating left behind. Markus sighed.

Two days later, Markus was seated at his desk, one of the Blood Painter murder books open in front of him, when the desk Sergeant, Jim Stone, poked his head into his cubicle.

"Detective," Stone said. "I've got a woman, just came in. Name's Rachel Cross. She wants to see whoever's in charge of the 'Blood Painter' case."

"And you told her it was me?" Markus answered.

"Well," said Jim. "Only because you *are* the one in charge of the Blood Painter case."

"What if she's from the press?" said Markus, "or some whacko out looking to get attention."

"She not press, and she doesn't look like a whacko," said Jim.

"What does she look like?" said Markus.

"She looks normal."

"Lord keep us," said Markus. "It's the normal looking ones you have to watch out for. One of the worst whack jobs I ever saw wore a freshly cleaned suit and horn-rimmed glasses. He could have been my priest. Freak goes completely nuts during a routine interview. Comes right across the table. It took three of us to subdue him. He bit off the tip off an officer's finger during the fracas. So forgive me for being a little cautious.

"Detective," said Jim. "She's here, she looks okay to me, what do you want me to do with her?"

The Detective rubbed his hand over his face and looked at the stack of files on his desk, manila folders that held all that was known about the Blood Painter murders. He had been going over these files for weeks, and would probably be going them over for weeks to come. He looked up at Sergeant Stone.

"Take her to interview room A," he said. "I'll meet her in there. If Martinez comes in tell him to join us."

"Yes sir," said Stone.

Markus shifted back in his chair. He was sure this woman would only add to the growing reports and useless leads he and his men were getting every day. But at this point they had nothing but six gruesome crime scenes and six dead victims. So… grabbing a spiral-bound notebook, he got up from his desk and walked out of his cubicle.

Seated at the small table in the interview room was a striking young woman who stood as Markus entered the room. He placed her at about 5' 7" and in her mid-twenties. Her skin was a light brown with a sprinkling of freckles running across the bridge of her nose and cheeks. Her coal-black hair was in a complementary contrast to her dark blue eyes. She was dressed in a professional-looking gray jacket with a matching skirt and a white blouse. She stretched out her hand and he took it, noticing how soft and petite it was.

"Good morning, Ms. Cross," he said. "I'm Detective Troval

He saw her eyes giving him the same once-over he had given her. He could see her taking in his gray hair and mustache, the wrinkles around his eyes and the bulge around his belly. At 56 he must have looked ancient to her.

Taking back his hand he motioned for her to sit.

"It's alright, Ms. Cross," he said.

"I'm sorry?" she said.

"I'm really much older than I look."

This brought a blush to her face.

"Detective," she said. "I…"

"It's okay," he said. "Everyone thinks we're going to look like the guys they see on TV. Truth is we tend to look more like the fathers of the guys they see on TV. No offense taken."

"Thank you," she said.

Markus seated himself behind his desk and said, "So what brings you here, Ms. Cross?"

"It's my grandfather," she said. "I'm worried that he may be involved in the Blood Painter killings."

"And why would you think that?"

Rachel opened her purse, reached inside, and pulled out a folded piece of paper. She handed it over to Markus. He opened it and found a photo showing a crowd of people standing behind a stretch of yellow crime scene tape. The picture's location looked familiar to him. It took a moment but then it clicked. It was outside the home of seventy-two-year-old Gabriel Hawthorne, a retired car salesman and the Blood Painter's 3rd victim.

"Where'd you get this?" he said.

"From the Los Angeles Times website," she said.

The photo had been taken some time during the night of the murder. It showed a group of twenty or so onlookers, drawn together by the police activity and the proximity of death by violence. Reaching inside his coat, he brought out his reading glasses in order to examine the photo more closely.

"What exactly am I looking at?" he said.

Rachel rose and leaned over the table. She pointed to a figure at the far left of the photograph. What Markus saw was a blurry profile of a man wearing a blue baseball cap and a red and black checkered shirt. Oddly, while the rest of the people in the photo were that bright digital camera clear, Mr. Baseball Cap was just out of focus, some trick of the camera obscuring his face with a shimmering haze. Markus looked at Rachel.

"You're saying this is your grandfather," he said.

"Cyrus Clevenger."

Markus studied the photo some more.

"How old is he?"

"Eighty-three," she said.

Markus tried to bring the face in the picture into focus, but it remained too fuzzy for any real identification.

"Ms. Cross, are you sure…."

"It's him," she said. "That's his hat. That's his shirt. I've been living with him for the past year. I know him. It's him."

"Okay," said Markus. "Let's assume it is him. Why do you think he'd have anything to do with the Blood Painter killings? There are a lot of other people in this picture. This kind of thing always draws a crowd. It's human curiosity."

"Detective, my grandfather suffers from severe osteoarthritis. That's why I came to live with him. He's confined to a wheelchair. He can't even get out of bed and go to the bathroom without help. But in that picture, he's up, he's walking, and that's impossible, unless he's been faking his disability this whole time. Or…" she stopped.

"Or what?"

"Do you believe in the supernatural, Detective Markus?"

"Ghosts, witches, séances," he said. "That sort of thing?"

"Possession?"

"I'm sorry?" he said, his 'whacko' alarm starting to go off. "You mean like *The Exorcist*?"

"I know how it sounds. But there are times at night when I hear things in the house, strange things, but when I look around we're the only ones there. Sometimes, I hear him in the next room, and I swear he's talking to someone, but when I go in to check on him he's alone. The first few months when I moved in with him everything was fine. Good even. But things have changed. He's changed. It's hard to explain."

"You think your grandfather is possessed?"

"I don't know what I think. There's just something… not right. How do you explain my disabled grandfather being in that picture?"

"Is your grandfather suffering from dementia or Alzheimer's?"

"Why?"

"It isn't uncommon for people suffering from Alzheimer's disease to do things that may seem impossible. Sometimes they get up and wander, even if they're physically challenged and you would never think they could. There's some kind of inner… something they tap into. I don't begin to understand it. But I've seen it. I knew an Alzheimer's patient, about your grandfather's age, who climbed over a ten-foot chain linked fence in his bare feet and walked around for hours and miles before he returned to the care facility where he was living. Now, physically he never should have been able to even get to the fence, let alone climb over it, but he did. And some patients talk for hours, holding full conversations with people who aren't there. Are you with your grandfather one hundred percent of the time?"

"I'm his primary caregiver."

"But you sleep."

"Yes, detective" she said. "I sleep. As nervous as I've been lately, I'm exhausted by the end of the night. When I do finally go to bed and put my head on the pillow, I'm out. I sleep like the dead."

"Okay, and how far away from your house was this picture taken?"

"Three blocks."

He took a moment.

"Look, Ms. Cross…"

"Rachel," she said.

"Rachel," he said. "Here's my opinion. I don't know your grandfather. But I do know a little about the elderly and the different types of dementia. I'm guessing Mr. Clevenger is a wanderer. As I said, it happens in some Alzheimer's cases. They get up, usually at night, and take a walk. Now I'm thinking one night while you were asleep, your grandfather got up, walked out of the house and just happened to get caught on film. Add to this that this photo was taken at the scene of a terrible murder, a murder that took place only three blocks from where you live. Well, that would be enough to spook anyone, maybe to the point where you start feeling uneasy, hearing things in the house. Now, this wandering may have been a onetime thing. Maybe never happen again. But they make alarms you can put on his wheelchair and bed. They're pressure sensitive. If he gets up, the alarm will sound and wake you. Then you can stop him from leaving the house. I'm not trying to belittle your concerns… but I'm looking at what we have here. He is eighty-three. And these murders we're investigating…I can't go into detail, but, if he's as infirm as you say he is, then I think you should be more worried about the possibly of him hurting himself, rather than strange voices and bumps in the night."

Rachel looked at him for a minute, thinking. Then she said, "Maybe I am over-reacting. Maybe you're right."

Reaching inside his coat pocket, Markus pulled out one of his business cards and handed it to Rachel. "I really don't think you have anything to worry about with your grandfather. Just keep an eye on him as best you can. But feel free to give me a call if you feel the need. Dealing with an elderly relative can get kind of all-consuming. I know some places that can help you get a break every now and then."

"Thank you," she said, taking the card. "That's nice of you."

The two rose from the table and Markus walked Rachel back to the front of the station house. Before she left, he made sure to get all of her contact information, and then watched as she exited the station.

As she was leaving, Thomas Martinez was just coming in to work. As he passed Rachel, he gave the attractive young woman an appreciative glance and then turned to Markus with a questioning look.

"Who's that?" he asked and listened as Markus filled him in on Rachel Cross and her concerns about her grandfather.

"An eighty-three-year-old serial killer?"

"She was just concerned about her grandfather, and a little spooked by having one of the murders take place so close to home."

"But not a whacko?"

"No, no... low level on the whackometer."

"How were her teeth?"

"Normal, Thomas." said Markus, his face reddening. He turned and started walking back toward his cubicle. "Her teeth were normal. Okay? Let's get to work."

"Whatever you say Tip," said Thomas as he followed his partner. "I'm just trying to watch out for you."

That night Markus left the station around 7:00 p.m. and drove across town to a gray, blocky, Fifties-style building that was the Evergreen assisted living residence where his father lived. Carrying a paper bag, he entered the lobby of the building, where he was greeted with hellos and hugs from the elderly residents who knew him from his frequent visits. From out of the main office came Ruth Morton, the administrator of the facility.

"Mr. Troval!" she said. "Like clockwork. Every Wednesday."

Ruth had worked for Evergreen for over twenty years.

At sixty-two she was an impressive five foot ten, two hundred and fifty pounds, and so full of the spirit she just bubbled over with goodwill. There were times when Markus wanted to strangle her.

"Hi Ruth," he said. "How is he?"

"How is he ever?" she said. "He's fine. He doesn't bother anyone. Most of the time he just sits in his room. I go in and talk to him, but…" she raised her hands in a 'what can you do?' motion.

"Well, I appreciate you looking after him."

"He's a part of our family," she said. "One of the best. I am sorry that he has been sinking into himself so much lately."

"It's what they said would happen," he said.

Markus' father, Isaac Troval, had been an LA police officer and detective for 35 years. Now in his eighties, the first signs of dementia had shown up in 2007. Markus' mother had died three years after that of a massive heart attack that no one saw coming. Although it was hard dealing with her loss, Isaac was able to live quietly by himself for some time but gradually the day to day became harder to manage. Then one day he decided it was time to move into assisted care. He and Markus had found Evergreen together and after the initial inspection Isaac had deemed it good and moved in a week later.

"We have him all ready for you," Ruth said as she turned to lead him toward his father's room.

Markus hated that phrase. It always made him think that the old man was left unattended until his son's visit and then cleaned up for the occasion, even though he understood, given what he knew of Evergreen and those who worked there, that this concern was unfounded, at the same time he never made any surprise visits to find out for sure. He had faced many tough situations in his career as cop and detective, but some things took more courage than others.

They stopped at one of the doors that lined the

hallway. To the right of the entrance, on a white plastic board, written in blue erasable marker, was the name Isaac Troval. Ruth rapped on the door, opening it as she did so. "Isaac? You have a visitor."

The door opened to a small furnished single room. The wall opposite the doorway, looking out into an alleyway, was a large window. In front of the window, between a neatly made twin bed and a small television, was an old brown recliner, moved over from the family home, with a small end table beside it. Settled deep into the recliner, his head turned to the window, was Isaac Troval.

"Hey Pop," said Markus entering the room.

The old man turned his head and looked blankly at his son. He started to rise.

"Dinner," he said.

Ruth moved in and gently put her hand on Isaac's shoulder, guiding him back into his chair. "Now Isaac, we've already had our dinner. Remember? Right now your son, Markus, is here to see you."

Isaac settled back into the chair. He looked up at Ruth with questioning eyes.

"That's right," Ruth said. "He's come to visit."

Markus went over and grabbed a folding chair that was leaning against the dresser and brought it back to the little table. He unfolded the chair and sat down opposite his father.

"Hey Pop," he said again.

Ruth reached over and patted Markus on the shoulder. "I'll leave you two to have a nice talk," she said. She turned and walked out of the room, gently closing the door behind her.

"So Pop," said Markus, "how are you feeling today?" The old man looked at him but didn't respond, didn't register any recognition and eventually turned his face back to the window. The two men sat in silence for little while then Markus pulled up the paper bag he'd brought with him and set it on the end table. "Hey, look what I got for you," he said and opened the bag that was filled with macaroons.

"I stopped off at Cantor's Deli and picked these up for you," said Markus. "I know how much you like them." Markus held out the bag to his father and gave it a little shake, causing it to make a "shuck shuck" sound that drew the old man's attention away from the window. Without a word, Isaac reached into the bag, brought out a coconut covered cookie, raised it to his mouth and took a bite.

"There ya go," said Markus. He reached into the bag himself and pulled out a cookie for himself. The two men sat chewing and looking out the window. After some time, and a few more cookies, Markus leaned back in the small chair and put a hand to his face and rubbed at the weariness he felt. He looked over at his father.

"I'm on a heck of a case, Pop," he said. "I got six bodies in six months. Crime scene's clean as a whistle, no fingerprints, no DNA, no witnesses. We got nothing. You should see what the perp does to these poor folk, God help 'em, and always on a Sunday. No connection to each other that we can find. No motive as far as we can tell. It looks to be totally random. The last victim, last Sunday, a guy named, and I'm not kidding, Michael Jordan. A retired school…"

"Traveling man," said Isaac, his hand reaching to the bag for another macaroon.

Markus sat up in his chair.

"What did you say?"

"Michael Jordan. Traveling man. Nothing there though. Talked to him… but nothing there." The old man pulled another macaroon from the bag and stuffed it into his mouth. "We never found the heads," he said. "Never, never."

Thomas arrived at work Thursday morning to find a

stack of old file boxes piled outside of Markus' cubicle. Working his way around the wall of cardboard and paper he found his partner leaning back in his chair, still dressed in the clothes he'd worn the day before. In front of him were seven yellowed, water-stained file folders.

"Markus?" he said. "What's going on?"

"They're related," Markus said.

"What's related?"

Markus stood up and moved out of the cubicle, clutching the old file folders in his hand.

"Follow me," he said.

Markus led Thomas to the office where they were running their investigation of the Blood Painter murders. On the wall were taped pictures of the six victims, both in life and in grisly death. He walked up to a photo of a doughy-looking woman in her early 60s. He put a finger on the picture.

"Deborah Hansen," said Markus. "Our first victim." He opened one of the files in his hand and held up a picture of a man in his mid-thirties whose dark eyes stared out at the camera from under bushy eyebrows. He held the photo under Deborah Hansen's. "Jonah Dekker."

"Yeah?" said Thomas.

"He was her car mechanic."

"When?"

"Right up until he died. Right up until he became the first victim of the Head Collector in 1987."

"Wait a minute," said Thomas. "The Head Collector case?"

"Yes," said Markus.

"That was… what? Forty years ago?"

"Thirty-Five," said Markus. "My father was one of the detectives that worked that case. I've been going over his old files. From January to July 1987. Seven dead, seven months, each death on the last Sunday of the month. Sound familiar? All decapitated. Heads never recovered. Killer never found. Dekker was the first victim, and he knew Hansen, our first victim."

"Coincidence," said Thomas.

"You might think," said Markus. "If it was the only one."

Markus opened the next file. "Michael Beckman, our second victim. He was a classmate of Hannah Miller. Hannah's mother was Rebecca Miller," he held up a picture of a smiling woman with straight blond hair. "The Head Collector's second murder."

Thomas pointed at the remaining files in Markus' hands. "You're saying each of our vics is connected to each of the vics from a 35 year old unsolved case, that your father worked while he was a detective."

"Yeah," said Markus.

"That's crazy," said Thomas.

"I know," said Markus. "Don't think I don't know."

"Could it even be the same guy? I mean, the MO is completely different. And if it is them, they would be in their... What? Sixties?"

"At least," said Markus.

"And why go 35 years between killings?"

"I don't know."

"Were any of our vics suspects back then?"

"Not that I can find," said Markus. "They were just in routine interviews." He motioned to the files of the new victims. "These people were sitting on the peripheral edges of the case. If they were suspects at some point, they were quickly cleared and dismissed. There's nothing in the files of them being more than just background."

"And yet here they are now," said Thomas. "How did you come up with this?"

"My father," said Markus. "I was talking to him at the home."

"About an ongoing case?"

"Tommy, most of the time he doesn't remember who he is, where he is, or who I am. I was just making noise while we were sitting together. Talking to myself more

291

than anything. But he picked up on our last victim, Michael Jordan. He knew him. Knew about his traveling. And then he brought up the Head Collector case. I thought he was just rambling really, but I pulled the old files. My dad interviewed Jordan during his investigation. He was the history teacher of victim number six's kids. Once I confirmed that connection I started cross referencing our Blood Painter dead with the Head Collector dead." He motioned again to the manila files on the table. "All of them were in some way connected to our current murder victims." He put a hand on the files, "You know, my Pop never talked about this case, but when I signed these out last night from records I saw that he had pulled out these files on a regular basis every year until he retired. He never gave up on the case. It would be nice if we could clear it up for him."

Thomas thought about this, his eyes going from Markus, to the files, to the photos on the wall. "Okay," he said. "So, what's next?"

"Well, whoever it is, they're working the murders in order. So, the next one on his list will be connected to…" he held up a file the front cover folded back to show the face of an African American male. "Peter Caldwell. Head Collector victim number seven. The last of the killings."

"Until now," said Thomas.

"Yeah," said Markus. "Until now."

♉

The two detectives spent the rest of the day poring over the old Head Collector files in an effort to find any clues or connections that linked to their six current homicides.

That night they sat at a table in Lucy's El Adobe Mexican Café, one of their favorite places for dinner. A massive burrito was placed in front of Thomas, smothered in a dark, almost arterial blood-colored mole sauce.

While Markus chewed on a chicken taco, Thomas said, "If we figure it's the same person committing our murders as committed the Head Collector murders, he would be in his sixties, seventies, hell, maybe even his eighties, right?"

"Yeah?" said Markus.

"That Cross chick," said Thomas. "Her grandfather is that age."

"As are a few hundred thousand other men and women in this city," said Markus. "No, I thought about that, ran a check on him. I couldn't find anything that ties him to the Head Collector victims."

"But?"

"But what?"

"The Head Collector was never caught, right?" said Thomas, "Never left any physical evidence."

"Right, just like our guy," said Markus.

"Just like our guy," Thomas agreed, "So, maybe… Look, I'm not saying it's a good lead… but it's something to think about. I mean, what was he doing at the crime scene? I know there are a lot of questions. *If* it was this Cyrus guy. This eighty-three-year-old man would have had to crawl out of a wheelchair, get out of the house, commit the murder and make it back home. Not once, but six times. And do all of this without waking his granddaughter."

"Yeah," said Markus. "I was thinking about that, and I thought of something. It's pretty wild."

"Wilder than an eighty-three-year-old serial killer who goes thirty-five years between murders?"

"Good point," said Markus. "Okay, here goes. She told me that ever since she came to look after her grandfather, she slept better than she's ever slept in her life. 'Like the dead' she said."

"Yeah?"

"What if he's drugging her so he can get away at night."

"That's a helluva thought…"

"I said it was wild, said Markus, "But many it's worth

following up."

"When?"

"Right after we finish here," said Markus.

Thomas gave him a look.

"What?" said Markus, "You got big plans tonight? We go there and talk to him. Get a feel for the guy. Twenty minutes. We're in, we're out."

"Christ," said Thomas as he cut into his burrito.

The two detectives arrived at the Clevenger residence at 7:30 that night. It was situated in one of the older, more rundown areas of the city. The house was a one-story wooden ranch-style home. What paint hadn't peeled away from the walls was a dirty, dingy brown. Iron security bars covered all the windows.

Parking in front, Markus and Thomas climbed out of the car, walked across the sidewalk and stopped at the edge of the yellow, dead grass that made up the front yard. Both looked at the darkened windows and general sense of decay.

"Oh yeah," said Thomas. "This isn't creepy at all. Why don't we come back later, like when the sun is up?" But Markus had already started across the lawn and Thomas was talking to the back of his partner's head.

"Great," he said, and jog-trotted forward to catch up.

At the front door, Markus reached out and knocked. When there was no answer he knocked again, only this time harder. Both men heard footsteps approaching from the other side.

"Who is it?" said a voice that Markus recognized as Rachel Cross.

"Rachel, it's Detective Troval. I'm here with my partner. May we speak with you?"

There was the sound of a lock being turned and then the door opened. Rachel was dressed in black jeans with a matching tee-shirt. Markus made quick introductions and gave Rachel a digest version of what had brought them there.

"So now you think my grandfather *is* involved?" she said.

"We're not saying that," said Markus. "We just want to talk with him. See if there is any connection between him and the last Head Collector victim."

"I don't know how much you'll be able to get from him," she said. "He hasn't had a great day." She opened the door and motioned them in. "He's in the dining room right down the hall, the second door on your left."

Markus and Thomas walked down the hallway, Rachel following behind. The old plaster walls, with their faded paint and spiderweb cracks, showed years of neglect. They were just at the door leading to the dining room when Markus heard a grunt of surprise from Thomas and the sound of something hitting the wall behind him. Before he could react, he was thrust into the room so hard that he lost his balance, tripping and falling as a result. He had a momentary glimpse of a figure in a wheelchair before landing, with a *thwump*, against the hardwood floor. He started to scramble to his feet, but something slammed into his head, and everything went to black and silence.

The first thing Markus saw when he opened his eyes was Thomas lying on his side just inside the dining room's doorway, a pool of blood forming around his head. Moving carefully, he pushed himself up onto his elbow and looked around. To his left was a man in a wheelchair. A closer look showed him that the man was gagged, duct tape wrapped around his mouth and head. The tape had also been wrapped around his arms and legs, binding him to the chair.

"What the hell…" Markus began, but whatever he was

going to say was cut off by a giggling that came from behind him. Working himself into a standing position, he turned to find Rachel squatting in the back corner of the room, looking up at him.

"Rachel," he said, but even as he said her name, she began shaking her head back and forth. It was then that he saw there was something different about her. Something wrong.

"Not Rachel," she said, rising. "Good name. Strong name. But. Not. Me."

Markus looked at the woman, knowing, he didn't know how, but knowing just the same, that this was not the Rachel Cross who had come to him looking for help. He had heard of multiple personality syndrome, but he'd never encountered it before. That was what this had to be.

"If you're not Rachel," he said, "then who are you?"

The woman looked at him intensely. "That's a question," she said. "Who am I? So many names. Legions of names. The Enemy, The Adversary? Those Christians really know how to cut to the chase. But where is the class? Iblis is good. Old Scratch never did it for me. Meph..iss..toph..eles. Now that has a sound to it, rolls off the tongue…power to it…. Oh, there are so many names, how do I pick only one." Then her mouth split into a way too wide smile, showing way too many teeth, and there issued from her a sound, a sound he knew must be laughter, but it was unlike any laugh he had ever heard before. The dark sickness of it made bile rise in his throat and he wanted to put his hands over his ears in an effort to block it out. The sound permeated the room around him and with it came a fear, deeper than any he had ever known. To his relief, the hideous laugh subsided but a malicious amusement remained on Rachel's face.

"You can't be," Markus said.

"Oh, why not, Markus?" she said. "Why not?"

A groan came from the old man in the wheelchair. Markus tried to move toward him, the serve and protect instinct kicking in, but she/it moved to block his path.

"*Too fast*," he thought. "*No one can move that fast.*" Her eyes locked on his and she shook her head again.

"No, no, no, Markus," she said. "We're not quite through with him yet."

Markus became aware that the house was much warmer than when he first entered.

"Who is he?"

"Why Detective Troval," she said. "He's the end of a family quest."

"Your grandfather…."

"*Her* grandfather," she said. "The evidence in this house will point to him as a bringer of death, but not just him, this body, this woman, she too will be discovered."

"Discovered?"

The heat in the room had started to rise. It was becoming more and more uncomfortable and yet, despite the heat, Markus could feel goosebumps forming on his arms. He wanted to step back, away from Rachel, but found he couldn't move. She leaned in close to him, her breath hotter than the room, so much so that it felt as if it was scalding his skin as she pressed close to his face.

"They're here" she said.

"Who?" he said.

"The heads. All seven."

He pulled his head back and look at her. "Here…"

"There and everywhere," she said, opening her arms wide. "All around the house. Your men will find them. The evidence will connect Cyrus to the old killings and there will be plenty to connect Rachel to the new." She pulled back from Markus, the strange grin still on her face. "And then I will be done here." She looked around the room and then back at the detective. "It has been good to be back. To reconnect with old friends… and the children of friends."

Another groan came from the old man. The thing that wasn't Rachel squeezed its eyes shut in what looked like pain, but could just have easily been pleasure. It sucked its breath in through its teeth with a hiss.

"I don't understand," said Markus.

"Connections, Markus," she exhaled. "Connections, connections, connections. The knee bone to the thigh bone, the thigh bone to the hip bone... A to B to C to... Death. You and your partner put it all together. With a little help from your father."

"But," said Markus. "There's nothing to connect Rachel or her grandfather to the Head Collector."

"Secrets, Detective. Every family has secrets. Rachel's mother had a secret. Born the product of an affair ...."

"With Caldwell," said Markus. "The last head collector victim..."

That wide smile again.

"Clever boy," she said. "Mother dead in childbirth. Sad. So sad. Leaving Cyrus to raise his 'daughter' all by himself. Never knowing he wasn't the real father. The daughter grows up, moves out, marries, and has a daughter herself, Rachel. That daughter who grows up and becomes ..."

"The Blood Painter," said Markus.

"Not at first," said Rachel. "I used Cyrus to start, like before, but his old body was too feeble, too unreliable. After the first two I knew I needed fresh. Young."

She moved again and stood behind Cyrus Clevenger. She began massaging his temples as she talked, the old man's eyes widened, and another groan escaped from him.

"The granddaughter. The kind-hearted, beloved granddaughter." She/It cackled a laugh, "So innocent. Each night she would fall into bed to sleep, and once that sleep arrived... she was mine." With that last word her grip on the old man's head tightened and with a vicious twist, she broke his neck.

"Nearly done," she said as she stared down at her handiwork. "Almost time to move on. So much to do."

"Rachel," said Markus.

In a blink she was standing in front of him, eyes

blazing.

"Not Rachel," she said. Reaching up she grasped him on either side of his head, her eyes boring into his. "Know me!"

Markus's mind was suddenly filled with a crushing conglomerate of images, sounds and sensations; primitive clubs and swords flashed under ancient, foreign skies. Blood flowed over rocks and fields, hacking and slashing, war and murder. The cries of thousands, tens of thousands of the dead and dying from across the ages filled his mind. He could see the Head Collector victims, hear them pleading as they died, the Blood Painter deaths, blood flying through the air, covering walls, covering Rachel. He could see it, hear it, feel the wetness against his own skin, and through it all came the cackling laughter of the thing that was but wasn't Rachel Cross. His own mind began to cry out in agony and terror and pain, he felt himself sinking to his knees, Rachel towering over him, smiling, laughing. He was vaguely aware of a loud explosion coming from somewhere. He heard it above the suffering cries of the dead filling his head.

And then it was over.

Markus' senses returned to him. He was kneeling on the floor, the horrific images and sounds still resonating in his head. Rachel was lying on the floor in front of him, blood flowing from a bullet wound in her chest.

Markus managed to look behind him and see Thomas, the man's face covered in blood from a deep gash on his head, propped up against the doorframe, his gun in his hand. He gestured toward Rachel.

"Woke up and saw what she did to the old man," he said. "I thought she was going to do it to you."

Markus nodded. "You okay?"

"Sure," said Thomas, "Never better."

A gurgle rose from Rachel, and Markus moved over to her. Her eyes were shifting back and forth as though searching for something then they focused on him.

Markus reached into his pocket for his cell phone.

"I'm going to call for an ambulance," he said, but she shook her head.

"Too late for this body," she said. "Finished here anyway. I'll find a new one, more work to do."

Markus could see the life draining from her eyes.

"Why?" he asked. "Why did you do it? Why these people? Why my father? Why me?"

A last hint of a smile passed Rachel's face. "Markus," she said, her voice growing weaker, "you must know…."

"Know what?" he said leaning closer to her so he could hear. So close that her lips brushed his face, almost like a kiss, as she whispered her final words.

"You must know that He's not the only one who works in mysterious ways."

RICHARD J. BREWER

ABOUT THE AUTHOR

RICHARD J. BREWER is a born and bred California native who has always loved stories. That love has driven him to work as a bookseller, a writer, an actor, a narrator/director of audiobooks and in earlier incarnations as Story Editor for Interscope Communications/Radar Pictures and the Manager of Development for the Hallmark Hall of Fame/Signboard Hill Productions, where he was once required to give a series script notes to the multiple award winning writer Horton Foote (don't ask, it was just embarrassing). His short story *Last to Die* appeared in *Trouble in the Heartland* (Gutter Books) and received an honorable mention in *Best American Mystery Stories* of 2015 (Houghton Mifflin Harcourt). He is the co-editor of three critically acclaimed anthologies, the Bruce Springsteen inspired, *Meeting Across the River* (Bloomsbury USA), the crime/sci-fi collection, *Occupied Earth* (Polis Books) and *Culprits: The Heist was Only the Beginning* (Polis Books). *Culprits* is now an eight part limited television series for Disney+.

HELL'S KITCHEN

Lena Ng

I've been through hell, and let me tell you, I wouldn't recommend it. I had stood in line for processing for, oh I don't know, probably a thousand years. The hellfire burning around the labyrinthine line was hotter than you could imagine—unless you've spent a day inside a charcoal barbeque deep in the centre of the sun—and all I could see were red-faced sinners in front and behind, lined up in an infinite number of parallel rows surrounding me in all directions. I waited for what must have been a year before taking a step forward. It made the line-up at Disneyland on the Fourth of July seem quicker than a blink.

I thought this was hell, this sweaty, irritating, exasperated waiting, but it turned out to be only the beginning. Finally, I took a step at a sharp corner and realized the guy standing in front of me, a stinking, hulking, silverback of a guy whom in all this time I've never bothered to ask his name, had disappeared. The line ended at the sharp edge of a cliff.

Confused, I inched my toes closer to the obsidian edge

when the sharp side of a hoof booted me square in the backside. I flew off the cliff's edge, bounced from the granite-hard side of the rocks, rolled over some smouldering coals, roasted through three volcanic flares, before being ungainly impaled on a red-hot stalagmite. As I lay there in unspeakable pain from a lacerated liver, a demon prodded me with a pitchfork to get up.

I staggered to the front of a desk made of skulls which, after what I had just been through, I rather envied. Why couldn't I be a bleached pile of bones used to decorate some demon's home office? Sitting on a chair of thorns, a baby-faced demon, his skin redder than a cinnamon heart but without the sweet disposition, barked a sulfuric question, "Name?"

"Quentin Dunn," I croaked.

He pulled out a small metal stamper, turned one of the gears, and held it over a teasing tendril of hellfire. He stamped the Book of Damnation, wrote my name with a devilish flourish, and grabbed my hand, pressing the hot stamp onto my palm. It resembled a glowing barcode.

He pulled a lever, fashioned from a femur, and the floor opened up from under me. I bounced from rock to rock, teeth rattling, until I landed—again—impaled on a stalagmite. At the sight of a pitchfork, I dis-impaled myself and limped my way through the rock tunnels, engineered for discomfort by being several inches shorter than my full height.

After several decades of wandering through the tunnels, where random knives burst through the walls in some areas and mountains of centipedes crawled over the floor in others, not to mention being chased by the eyeless skin-walkers, I emerged in a large cavern of what looked to be jail cells.

The warden, a towering, ten-foot, goat-faced demon who stood on cloven hind legs, read my barcode and stuck his snout in my face. "Prisoner Dunn, for your crimes against God and humanity—littering, public drunkenness, atheism, standing around at the top of the escalator, queue-jumping, date-ghosting—"

This went on for an hour. Who knew man-spreading was a crime? I knew I wasn't a saint, but I didn't feel these were hell-worthy activities.

"—talking with your mouth full, and belching without excusing yourself, you are now sentenced to an eternity in hell." He stroked his magnificently curled goatee. "You will be assigned…tunnel-carving." He trotted off while his assistant, a squat, purple frog-demon with a whip-like tongue, handed me a spoon and a fork.

With the whip-tongue lashing against my back, I was frog-marched to the Tunnels of Eternal Toil. If you hate your job now, imagine one you can never quit. Every day I took out my spoon and tried to carve through granite. Once in a while, I would poke at the rock with the fork. I would agree that Hell was meaningless labour with an asshole frog-demon as a manager.

One day, as I was listlessly picking at the rock, a strange thing happened. I hit a thin crust of rock which collapsed inward at the spoon's miniscule pressure. I glanced around and the frog-demon must have been tormenting souls at another end of the tunnel. I stuck my hand in the hole, which I would probably advise against doing if you saw a random hole, and grabbed something that felt like—

—a face.

When I pulled it up, it was covered in soot, making the whites of its eyes look brighter in contrast.

Pssssst, I heard. *Where am I?*

"The Tunnels of Eternal Toil," I whispered back. "You don't want to be here. Where have you come from?"

"Hell's Kitchen." The tunnel crawler heaved herself out of the wall's side. She was scrawny and her hair was a patchy mess. "I'd rather be anywhere than there."

I looked back and forth between my spoon and the hole she emerged from.

She gave a maniacal laugh. "If you don't believe me,"

she said between shrill gasps of glee, "be my guest."

When I caught a glimpse of the frog-demon hopping over to investigate the hilarity, I scrambled down the narrow tunnel and crawled faster than I've ever crawled before.

I heard the roar of the flames and felt the waves of heat before I reached the end of the tunnel. Maybe the tunnel crawler was right. The place where I arrived was an enormous cavern with seven monstrous ovens belching away at full blast. A massive hourglass with crimson grains of sand flowed at one end of the cavern. Things in baskets and on hooks hanging from the ceiling thrashed and squirmed. Kitchen workers in sooty white aprons bustled around, chopping, mixing, stirring, roasting. A bowl of limbs flipped itself over and tried to crawl off the table. A red blob on another swiveled some of its eyes like a chameleon and stared at me.

A pig-demon wearing a giant chef's hat hauled me out of the hole by my neck. After he read my barcode, the chef started laughing. "You were assigned the Tunnels and you chose to come here?"

I was hoping I wouldn't end up on a plate. "Why? What's wrong?"

The pig-demon snorted through two heavy tusks. "Every day we need to create a whole array of dishes. Lucifer likes to be surprised. If he enjoys them, fine and good. But if he doesn't like the dinner, he roasts us crispy and carves us into pieces like a suckling pig. Then the next day, when we reassemble, we have to do it all over again. Can you create delicious new recipes every day for an eternity?"

Compared to being roasted and carved, perhaps tunnel-digging wasn't so bad. But then again, I needed a change. "I didn't realize the devil liked eating so much."

"Well, gluttony *is* one of the deadly sins." The pig-demon threw me an apron and pointed at one of the prep tables. "Get going." He glanced at the hourglass. "We have only twelve hours before the hellfeast begins."

My fellow kitchen assistants glared at me, silent. There were nine others around this massive stone table. The woman beside me had burly arms and she expertly chopped foul-smelling meat into mince. A man with a splatter of teardrop tattoos on his face strangled a bunch of cobras, swiveling his face to avoid the fangs.

The first dish I was to prepare: satanic stinging nettle soup. Baskets of greenery were dragged into the kitchen by slithering octo-demons. Three wicker baskets were plunked on the table in front of me. Before I could pick up a knife, a vine lashed out. It whipped across my face. I felt the skin burn and blister. I dodged the next attacking vine and managed to hack at a few ropey, thorn-laden tendrils.

Before I could make another chop, a vine twisted around my arm. I felt the acidic slime coating the monstrous vegetation scorch my skin, the thorns impregnating its poison. Another vine whipped around the other arm. I started to scream. A third vine lashed around my throat, choking the scream into a gurgle. It lifted me off the ground, my legs kicking, eyes bulging.

The burly-armed woman smirked. She let me hang there for a few minutes before picking up a pot of boiling water and dumping it over the basket of nettles.

The vegetation changed in colour to a darkened green. The vines holding me grew limp and I dropped to the ground, coughing. The woman gave me a side-eye squint. "You now ready to work? You have to blanch them first."

I brought back another pot of boiling water and doused the other two baskets. After I chopped the life out of the satanic stinging nettles, I read over the recipe, written on tanned hide and inked in blood. Two pinches of arsenic. A swirl of mercury. A tablespoon of blue whale blubber. An eye of baby seal. A whiff of cyanide to taste.

As the soup began simmering, the smell right rank, I glanced around the kitchen. A stout woman with a haggard face struggled with a bucket of mutant crabs, their pincers larger than her head whereas she was only armed with a cleaver. It ended in a stalemate with each less a limb. A long-haired, droopy-eyed man with a harpoon battled a land barracuda which wiggled back and forth in a fishy tango.

Another man wrestled a colossal squid which seemed to be getting the better of him. Despite the sucker welts on his face and his bulging eyes, I recognized that toothbrush moustache. Wait…wasn't that Hitler? He was trapped in a tentacled death hug and screeched obscenities in German.

A grizzly mauled an Asian man with a long moustache. Genghis Khan? A rhino with three barbed horns gored a young man, who was crowned with a laurel wreath, and bloodied his toga. Caligula? A woman with a ruffled frill around her neck and face coated in congealed crimson screamed as her legs were pecked raw by a horde of razor-beaked gulls. Elizabeth Báthory? I groaned. The worst criminals of history were assigned to this particular level of hell? That couldn't be a good sign.

The blanching technique worked with a basket of scorpions, whereas it made the hamper of millipedes angry. They scampered over the table, reared up, and spit searing poison which burned holes in my apron. I flattened them with a cast-iron pan. I crushed some red berries for flavour. "Don't breathe in the ricin," the burly-armed woman said as the pulp splattered. "Diarrhea in hell is horrific."

I cooked a parade of dreadful delicacies. Extra-large botflies poached in beurre-blanc. Deep fried tarantulas, legs curled over their abdomens, au jus on the side. Rubbery Portuguese Man O' Wars on skewers with their jellied stinging tentacles artfully displayed.

Despite all the nasty, creepy dishes, the hardest dish for me to cook was the baby bunnies in a puppy stew. The bushel of baby bunnies looked trustingly with their wide, black eyes and twitched their pink noses. The Golden Labrador puppies jumped and tried to lick my face. One of them looked exactly like my childhood dog Ruby when she was a puppy. No, I thought. I'm not going to do it. I took a quick look around, and while the pig-demon chef was checking on the belladonna soufflé, I kicked over the basket. "Run," I hissed as the bunnies and puppies gathered around my feet and went nowhere. "Get out of here."

A meat tenderizer flew through the air and conked me on the head. "Amateur," the pig-demon chef snarled. He picked up the tenderizer and began bludgeoning the poor animals. Their sharp whimpers rang in my ears. "There," he said. "It's either them or you. Get cooking."

I wiped away the gathering moisture in my eyes as I skinned, deboned, and quartered. I placed the heads facing downwards in the Dutch oven since I couldn't abide their glassy eyes. I wiped the snot away with my apron while I added a splash of vinegar.

The hours rushed by. I sweated as I gutted, filleted, disemboweled, and skewered. I roasted, grilled, broiled, stir-fried, braised, poached, and steamed.

Finally, the last grain in the hourglass topped the crimson sand pile. The sound of the gong rattled my ears as it echoed through the cavernous kitchen. The pig-demon handed out the red presentation uniforms. As I was about to pull on the pants, glints of sharpened metal shone. The interior of the uniform was lined with tacks, like a cloth version of an iron maiden.

Great. I gingerly put on the uniform, the tacks scraping welts over my skin. We lined up, each pushing a cart into the oval dinner theatre, accompanied by a liveried waiter. An anaconda-headed demon unhinged his jaws and glurped down an electric eel that was thicker than my waist. His eyes bugged out with each swallow and he lit up from within as jolts flashed through his body. I kept my eyes on the ground as I pushed the cart to each diner. I had no wish to see down some demon's gullet.

Thick-necked and massively horned, Lucifer sat on a throne of blood. His eyes glowed and he rubbed his taloned hands together as each cart was rolled into the theatre. Instead of waiting to be served, he shoveled a heaping mass of food from each cart onto his plate. He began spooning the food into his horribly shark-large maw as the theatre lights were lowered. After we served the food, we stood at attention around the room's perimeter.

A hypnotic music started, played with a full orchestra including bassoons, the musicians a mix of multi-limbed stag beetles and cane toads performing at a professional level. Two rows of gorgeous young women, dressed in diaphanous robes, flittered onto the stage. The dance of the seductresses. They undulated their arms and stomachs; flowing hair of every shade streamed around them; and their feet clad in red ballet shoes fluttered over the stage. They danced and danced, they seemed to tire but their shoes danced on relentlessly.

With the thunderous ending chords of the symphony, Lucifer, in appreciation, flung a smouldering piece of coal onto the stage, setting a dancer's robe on fire. With shrieks of laughter, the other demons following suit, launching a volley of burning coals at the women who fled screaming from the stage.

Next, a choir of red robed cultists sang haunting songs of devotion, their awed voices echoing throughout the theatre. Lucifer looked bored. He tapped his thick fingers as he ate more of the food. He made a small hand gesture and perked up as the choir members began to spontaneously combust, leaving piles of ash that the custodian swept from the stage.

Finally, a mob of men and women crowded onto the stage. Lucifer stood. "My dear sinners," he began, addressing the motley group, "now we begin the Clash of the Murderers. Choose a weapon" — a rain of knives, axes, hatchets, and swords fell from the ceiling, killing a few of them — "and the last one alive will be released."

So began a show of butchery. Amid a cacophony of shouted bets and thrown coins, limbs, heads, geysers of blood, entrails, fingers, and raw-slick organs littered the stage. At last, with a broken arm at his side, the final murderer, thick-necked and gore-covered, stood panting, wormy veins protruding from his neck. Lucifer clapped his hands. "Excellent," he exclaimed. "Only the best for my dogs. Release the hounds!" A pack of three-headed hellhounds leapt onto the stage and tore the remaining man apart.

We returned to the kitchen to roll out the dessert carts. Some dishes, such as songbirds in wooden cages, were simply presented. A boil of sweetened tentacles flailed about in a gold tureen. A new round of dessert wines in giant crystal goblets were placed on the tables.

Lucifer took a long time choosing a dessert. We kitchen staff collectively held our breath. My heart thumped against my ribs. Lucifer took out a small spoon and carefully cut into the dessert. After a sniff and a nibble, he stood, his bare torso shiny with sweat. He drew back a muscular arm and launched the belladonna soufflé into the middle of the theatre. The entire cooking crew gasped. A trickle of sweat slid down the pig-demon's face. Hitler started to cry, his shoulders heaving with silent sobs.

Suddenly, Lucifer beamed with his stretched-out, piranha-toothed grin, looking rather pleased. "A triumph," he crowed. "An absolute triumph. Let's all raise a glass." The feasting demons rose to their cloven feet, hooting and hollering. Some clanged their glasses with their spoons.

"To the staff of Hell's Kitchen," Lucifer said, picking up a large crystal goblet. "May you cook sublimely for eternity." The pig-demon let out a big sigh with a visible look of relief. Lucifer put the glass to his lips and took a big swallow of his wine. His face immediately darkened. "Chateau de Morangias Fronsac d'Apcher 1341?

311

CHATEAU DE MORANGIAS FRONSAC D'APCHER
1341??!!"

The pig-demon stuck one of his trotters in his mouth.
"I knew he was playing us. He hasn't liked a dinner in over
a thousand millennia."

The joyful clanging grew angry when feasting demons
began leaping onto the tables and kicking the plates. They
hurled the cutlery. I managed to dodge a lamb carver
before being speared in the ear with a trident. Genghis
Khan kicked up his heels, leading the retreat. The demons
reached under their seats and pulled out their weapons. As
I stood there, mouth gaping like a carp and arrows flying
around me, I realized we were part of the entertainment:
the after-dinner hunt. I spun around and sprinted down
one of the tunnels. A steel five-pointed shuriken sliced a
part in my hair.

I didn't get very far when someone launched a javelin
which skewered me to a tunnel wall. I hung there limply
while a fallen archangel plucked the javelin from the rock
and hoisted me over his shoulder like a fish on a rod.

He whistled as he walked to a cavern holding the
biggest oven I had yet seen. He hooked the javelin into the
oven's sides as though I were a rotisserie chicken,
maneuvering his black wings out of the way. The oven
door clanged shut.

As the flames licked my body and my skin grew crispy,
I thought tomorrow I was going to steal an industrial-
grade spoon and start digging.

ABOUT THE AUTHOR

LENA NG roams the dimensions of Toronto, Ontario, and is a monster-hunting member of the Horror Writers Association. She has curiosities published in seventy tomes including *Amazing Stories* and the anthology *We Shall Be Monsters*, which was a finalist for the 2019 Prix Aurora Award. "Under an Autumn Moon" is her short story collection. She is currently seeking a publisher for her novel, *Darkness Beckons*, a Gothic romance.

FIRE ESCAPE
Diana Olney

The band was still backstage, and the crowd
was getting restless. A tempestuous sea of anxious bodies
awaited the arrival of Fire Escape, the newest hard rock
addition to the Seattle grunge scene. The night was young,
but the Off Ramp was already an inferno—the club was
packed with so much wall-to-wall sweat that the ceiling
itself was starting to bleed.

Mort took a final swig of Jack Daniel's as he stumbled
out of the dressing room. Last call was coming early for
once. The party was just getting started, but he had to stay
sharp. Everything was riding on this performance.

You've gotta give the people what they want.

The disgruntled music fans down the hall were ready
for action, and Mort was more than prepared to deliver.
The last few gigs had been a bit lackluster, but tonight the
band had a plan, and this time, they were guaranteed an
encore.

It's gonna be one hell of a show.

Steadying himself against the door frame, he turned to
call back to his band of derelict brothers. "Yo! Let's get

315

movin' guys!"

His request was instantly met with a barrage of indecipherable expletives.

Mort let out an exasperated sigh. If last night hadn't taught these idiots to get serious, nothing would.

"Uggh, dude..." Glenn, his guitar player, grunted as he wormed his way through the labyrinth of beer bottles and cigarette butts that lined the floor. "I don't think I can do this, man. I've been scrubbing this shit for an hour, and I still can't get the goddamn stains out." He grimaced, staring down at the Jackson Pollock splatter all over his favorite flannel shirt.

"Seriously? Just leave it, dude. No one will give a shit. This is the *Off Ramp*, for fuck's sake," Mort scoffed.

Glenn raised an eyebrow. "Really? I dunno, man... this is pretty gnarly. You don't have anything I could wear?"

Mort shook his head. "Hell, no. You've gotta get your head in the game. The opener finished twenty minutes ago. We're running out of time—we might not be able to turn this room around if there's too much bad blood."

"It's a little late for that," Glenn mumbled, still nervously eyeing his shirt.

"Don't be a smart-ass. Just get your gear, and let's *go*. And no sloppy solos, got it? Stop trying to be Jerry Cantrell. It's not working. Sharing a dealer with the guy hasn't taught you any new tricks."

"*Jeez*, dude. That's a little harsh. You know I'm trying to get clean."

Mort frowned, studying the faded track-marks that still covered his guitarist's pale skin. "Sorry, man, but if we want to pull this off, we can't lose the audience, and that shit is a distraction. So cut the crap, or your Gibson is going home with me tonight."

☿

"You'd better get back here, Mort," a disembodied

voice pleaded from somewhere inside the dressing room.

Goddamn it.

Mort clenched his fists. He wasn't usually this hot tempered, but his whiny bandmates were about to push him over the edge.

"Screw you, Will! Get your sorry ass out *here*! We're about to lose our slot. And then all of this shit will have been for *nothing*."

Glenn sighed, finally glancing up from the stains on his shirt. "I'll deal with this."

"You'd better," Mort groaned.

As his weary guitarist scuffled back into the shadows, Mort closed his eyes, trying desperately to collect himself. But he shouldn't have bothered. His anger, misguided or otherwise, acted as a natural buffer for his fear. It was always the same; the second he started to let it go, that's when the real panic set in.

We've only got one shot at this… and they're totally gonna blow it.

He stared longingly at the bottle of whiskey in his hand. *Fuck it.*

He chugged a shot or two, then cast it aside. He had to drown his demons somehow, or there'd be an even bigger body count tonight.

Maybe that wouldn't be such a bad thing. We could obviously use a fail-safe here.

Mort leaned into the doorway, debating if he should just charge in there and drag out his useless bandmates himself. The filthy dressing room was more of a poorly lit corridor than an actual room, and he couldn't hear anything over the rising crescendo of the drunken mob around the corner. He pulled a Marlboro from the pack in his pocket, trying to resist the urge to beat his buddies black and blue.

Nah. I'll give them five. Then it's SHOWTIME.

Mort sighed in relief the moment he tasted his cigarette. He didn't know why he was so anxious. Last night had been crazy, to say the least, but everything had gone according to plan—for a satanic ritual, it had actually been a shockingly simple task. Not that he had any real experience with those. The closest he'd ever come to Devil worship was a graveyard threesome with some freaky goth chicks last year.

Now that was some sacrilegious shit...

Of course, he had cut out a little early. Once they'd started hacking up their ex-drummer, Mort figured his role in the debauchery was done. After all, he was the one who had orchestrated the whole thing. Plus, it was the front-man's job to let his band do the heavy lifting. He had to remind them who was calling the shots. Or stabs.

Fortunately, it hadn't taken much to get the guys on board. They may have been burnouts, but Fire Escape was their life, and anyone could see that it was going to take a goddamn good gimmick to compete with the bands that were taking over the scene. It was sink or swim out there, and crowd surfing had never been Mort's thing. Hence his choice to call the dark lord to their aid—at the end of the day, a few gallons of blood was a fair trade for musical acclaim.

He checked his watch. Time was almost up. If they didn't make some noise soon, they'd have a booze-fueled riot on their hands. Mort peered into the doorway, forcefully stomping the last of his cigarette out on the floor.

"Hey!" he bellowed into the darkness. "What's the hold up? You guys find new groupies and forget to share?"

No response. Broken glass crunched under the heel of his steel-toe boots as he made his way through the narrow room. The place was a wreck, and his comrades were nowhere in sight. But as Mort trudged through the towers of forgotten gear and piles of trash, it soon became clear where they'd gone.

The back door was open.

Those assholes… are they trying to bail?

Mort stepped outside. It was finally a clear night; the pale glow of the moon broke through the starless sky above, illuminating the wet pavement like a spotlight on a midnight stage. And sure enough, there in the center of the theatrical glare stood his bandmates, heading for the van. Mort's anger management skills were of little use now. A fresh wave of fury was building inside him, armed and ready to kick them right in the teeth.

"What the fuck is this, guys?"

Will gripped the neck of his bass defensively. "Sorry Mort, this whole thing is just too much. We've gotta call it."

"Like hell we do! There's at least a hundred people out there. We're not calling shit."

"Dude, chill," Dodge, the new drummer, chimed in. "We just came out here to get some air. We'll still play and everything, let's just cut the creepy bullshit."

"*Creepy bullshit?* You guys are just as invested in this as I am. So, if you need to feel guilty, go ahead, but it's *way* too late to back out now."

Glenn slowly stepped forward, approaching Mort as if he were a wild animal that had escaped from its cage. "Look, man, there's something you don't know."

"Oh, yeah?"

"Yeah." Will nodded in agreement. "But we wanted to ask you," he said softly, still hiding behind Glenn, "the, umm, instructions you got… from Vedder? What exactly did they say again? About the… you know…"

"You know *what?*" Mort sneered.

"The… uhh…" the bassist mumbled, staring down at his feet.

"The sacrifice," Glenn finished for him.

Mort rolled his eyes. "First of all, I never said I got *anything* from Vedder. So, stop asking—unless you want us all to get our asses kicked." He edged closer to the group, asserting his dominance. "Just fuckin' relax, okay? As long as you guys followed *my* directions last night, we're good."

319

Glenn sighed, placing an unsteady hand on Mort's shoulder. "Okay, well, we did what you said, man. You know, you were there for… most of it. But Dave was a good dude, so it was hard..."

"He was a crap drummer," Mort reminded him.

Glenn shrugged. "Sure. Whatever. But that didn't make it easy."

"Maybe not. But the amount of dope you guys shoot should have."

"*Mort*—Jesus, man. I haven't touched that shit in months," Will interjected, struggling to match the singer's threatening tone. "And that doesn't even matter right now, so let's cool it with the judgment. No one wants to fight tonight… just listen for a second, okay?"

Mort was moments away from losing it, but he tried to keep himself in check. "*Okay.*"

Will was visibly shaking, and for once, it probably wasn't withdrawals; the fear in his eyes reflected much more than the need to score. "Well, we're just not a hundred percent sure that Dave… umm…" he stammered, glancing nervously at the rest of the guys.

Glenn nodded his approval. "Go ahead, dude."

"Well, we're not sure that he… that he died. There's a chance he might still be alive."

A chorus of primal screams surged through the club as Fire Escape finally took the stage. Waves of writhing limbs and feral eyes rushed towards the front, crashing into one another like a massive hurricane of human flesh. The crowd was hungry.

And so are we.

Mort tore into the opening track, filling the room with the electric wail of his Fender. Then the bass kicked in, and the band behind him released their battle cry, bending the airwaves to their will with the battering ram of percussion and guitar. That was his cue. As the house lights dimmed, Mort leaned into the mic, unleashing a rebel yell of pure, unfiltered testosterone.

"Yeeeaaahhh-*ah-ah-ahhh!*"

He dove into the music, trying to lose himself in the hidden spaces between the notes. He couldn't quite seem to find his rhythm though. Every amp in the house was cranked, yet somehow he could still hear the dissonant whine of his neuroses, hissing like static inside of his head.

What if it doesn't work...

It WILL.

But they said he wasn't dead.

They're just chickenshits. Of course, he's dead. You saw the blood. No one gets stabbed that many times and lives to tell about it.

Or so he hoped. The ritual was simple, and guaranteed a lifetime of success, but it required a real sacrifice. "You can't half-ass this stuff," his source had said. He spoke in whiskey-infused riddles, whispering into his half-empty glass as he handed Mort a scrap of paper covered in mysterious stains. "So just killing a goat or whatever won't cut it. If you're gonna dance with the Devil, you've gotta get all your moves right. And forget what you've heard about virgins. That's total bullshit. You need a symbolic offering, and it can't be just anyone... All the true rock legends were born from tragedy. And do you know why? Because greatness requires *sacrifice*. You get what I'm saying?"

Mort got it right away. The guy was needlessly cryptic, but his meaning was clear enough. If Fire Escape wanted a hit single, someone in the band had to die.

Drummers are a dime a dozen anyway.

Mort's restless mind fell into sync with the set once they reached the second song. "Cobweb King" was his opus, and the crowd was all ears. He let his voice rain down onto the swarming masses below, submerging them in a minor key melody guaranteed to haunt their dreams.

"*Walk* behind me. Your footsteps… fall empty."

321

"*Hard* as stone. Show me to the throne..."

Mort's lyrics ignited the air as they passed from his lips, breathing new life into the room. The music was effortless now; the band was tight, and even Will's back-up vocals were perfectly in-key. Mort could feel a rush of energy rising up from the audience, their wayward souls instantly falling under the spell of the song. It was almost time. He was approaching the end of the third verse, and once he hit them with the new guitar solo, rock stardom would be his.

"...where the kingdom *lies*. In a crown of thorns…"

"...secrets *hide*."

NOW.

Mort stepped back from the mic, his fingers already flying down the slender neck of his Fender. Deep, thunderous notes soared into the crowd, assailing them with an ancient refrain rarely heard by living ears. This was the final step in the ritual, the moment of truth that would bring the power of the Prince of Darkness up into the light. Power that would be ripe for the taking.

HELL yes!

But right in the middle of the last chord, the unthinkable occurred—Mort's hand slipped, torn from the fretboard as a sudden shockwave burst forth from the strings. Then the world went dark.

What the...

A series of gasps and angry shouts erupted from the center of the room. The crowd was livid, but when Mort looked down, he couldn't even see their faces. The walls of the club were washed in black, masking his new fans in greyscale obscurity. He tried to stay calm, but he couldn't deny what was happening. This was his, and every musician's, worst fear: a mid-show power outage.

Shit.

He turned around, hunting for the shapes of his bandmates. But it was no use. The shadows had swallowed everything in sight. He steadied his guitar against his chest and reached out in front of him, searching for an amp to anchor himself to until the lights came back on. He knew the layout of this place by heart, but any trace of the familiar seemed long gone now. And as he wandered through the gloom, teetering along the edge of the stage, he bumped into something that shouldn't have been there at all.

What the hell is that?

At first, he thought it was a speaker, but whatever he had crashed into was soft, and unnaturally warm. Mort instantly recoiled in disgust. There was a foreign substance clinging to his skin; a sticky, almost-liquid sludge that had surely come from the unidentified thing. He wiped his hand on his jeans and kept backtracking, trying to put as much distance as possible between himself and whatever filth had found its way onto the stage. But he didn't get far. Before he knew it, the thing was upon him, seizing him tightly by the shoulders and locking him in place. He struggled frantically, trying to break free, but his assailant just dug in deeper, driving its invisible claws further into his flesh.

"Hey, Mort."

Mort stiffened. He knew that voice.

"Nice set, man."

Mort didn't get a chance to reply—Hell literally broke loose before he could speak. The Off Ramp had never ended a show early, but he knew the music was over when the stage started to shake, rocking to the earth-shattering beat of an imaginary bass. And that was only the beginning. Moments later, a blazing fluorescent light pierced the shadows, carving a massive hole in the floor below. The crowd screamed in terror as those closest to the edge stumbled and fell, devoured by the concrete jaws that had opened at their feet.

What have I done?

It was far too late for questions now. Evil was here, and it didn't care who was to blame. Mort tried to close his eyes, but was nearly blinded when the great chasm before him burst into flames, forming a ring of fire fifty times the size of the pyrotechnics the band used on stage. This was no parlor trick, this was biblical fire and brimstone, the real Old Testament kind. And Mort knew it had come here for him. His heart was beating in triple time, pounding a funeral march right into his chest. Instinct told him to run, but he was frozen stiff, imprisoned by the gnarled fingers that were still burrowing into his skin. More horrified shrieks ensued as the remaining members of the crowd ran for the door, trampling over one another as they tried to escape. It was the violent mosh pit Mort had always dreamt of, but it felt like a nightmare instead.

This is the end.

Isn't it?

"Sorry to crash the party, man."

That sounded like a yes.

In a flash of panic-fueled fury, Mort grabbed his guitar and swung backwards, haphazardly throwing the neck of his Fender towards his captor. He missed his target by a mile, but surprised the thing just enough to finally wriggle out of its grasp. And as he stumbled away down the stage, trying to catch his breath, he found himself confronted with a strange creature that vaguely resembled Dave.

HOLY SHIT.

Mort shuddered, trying to stifle the sudden urge to puke. His ex-drummer had taken the grunge look to a gruesome new level—he was drenched in blood from head to toe, and the gaping wounds that covered his torso had already spread a gangrenous looking rot across the rest of his flesh.

"*Dave?*" Will's horrified voice called out from behind them. Seeing their singer in peril, the trio rushed to Mort's rescue, stopping only when they saw the sadistic smile on Dave's decomposing face.

"Step off, man!" Glenn yelled, raising an angry fist in futility.

324

Dave threw his head back, his decrepit frame convulsing with maniacal laughter. "Oh, Glenn. It's a little late for heroics, don't you think?"

Mort turned to his bandmates, then subtly nodded towards the side of the stage. The main exit was out of the question, but if they went for it soon, they might still be able to reach the back door. Unfortunately, his idea wasn't quite subtle enough. Dave's sunken eyes saw everything, and as he followed Mort's gaze, the ceiling above the hallway completely collapsed, obliterating the only way out in thirty seconds flat.

"You guys weren't gonna skip the encore, were ya?" Dave snapped. "You know that's not fair to the fans."

The band exchanged horrified looks. There was no backup plan. None of this had been part of the deal, if there ever even was one.

Will took a tentative step towards Dave, his eyes filled with regret. "I'm sorry, man. We all are."

"*Sure,* you are. You guys are selfish assholes, just like the rest of them. You think drummers are expendable? Well, think again."

Dodge, Dave's replacement, finally crawled out from behind his drum kit.

"Fuck..."

"Yes, you are fucked." Dave smirked. "And on the first date, no less."

That much was true. While they'd been wasting time with their disgruntled drummer, the fire had started to spread. Out of the corner of his eye, Mort could see the flames racing across the floor, encircling the massive column that marked the center of the room. He prayed he was hallucinating, or passed out backstage in a post-show coma, but he knew it wasn't so. These were his last moments, and all this, everything he had worked for, was about to go up in smoke.

"Well, you know what they say… you're not a rockstar unless you die young," he murmured, trying to force a smile as he glanced back at his friends.

"Hey, look on the bright side!" Dave chimed in. "Fire Escape is about to go on tour. And from what I hear, it's almost sold out!"

The band stared out at the devastation beneath the stage. Dave was bat-shit crazy, but he was probably right. The Off Ramp was empty now, but there was surely a captive audience awaiting them in the lake of fire below.

...the SAME audience.

"I've gotta hand it to you guys, you've got more balls than I thought. Necromancy is about as heavy as it gets. And human sacrifice? *Hardcore.* Metal bands are always screaming about that crap, but you motherfuckers actually did it! And you almost pulled it off—*almost.*"

"He shouldn't be alive," Glenn muttered under his breath.

"No shit," Mort whispered.

Dave 2.0 stepped forward, closing the gap between himself and his soon-to-be victims. Mort could smell the scent of death on his skin.

"*Alive?*" Dave echoed. "Not so much. You bastards *drugged* me—I never had a chance. But I was always a has-been to you, wasn't I? Just another deadbeat drummer you could stab in the back." Then he chuckled again, tittering in amusement at his own post-mortem humor. "That was a good one!"

No one else laughed.

Jesus, his one-liners suck.

Dave narrowed his eyes, staring daggers into the living members of the band. "Well, come on, give me something! We're all friends here, aren't we?"

Will shuffled his feet nervously, inching away from Dave's aggressive approach. The rest of the guys turned to Mort, looking to their leader for ideas. Dave was just toying with them now, waiting for one of them to finally snap. He wanted some entertainment before eating their brains, or whatever it was zombie-types did these days.

"Really? Nothing? Man... I kinda missed partying with you guys, but I guess Fire Escape just isn't fun anymore. No wonder you're still playing this shitty little club."

Mort glanced down at the guitar still strapped to his chest, then back at the foul-mouthed cadaver that was harassing his band.

Screw THIS.

He knew they were doomed. But dead or alive, Mort refused to allow a *drummer* to make a fool out of him. So, he did something he'd vowed never to do. He unhooked his strap and gripped his two-month-old Fender Mustang by the neck, then raised it into the air, preparing to bring the hammer of the rock gods crashing down upon Dave's unholy head.

And that's what should have happened. Mort attacked without hesitation, striking well before his target could react. But somewhere between the rise and fall of his axe, Dave interfered, moving much too quickly for Mort's mortal eyes to see. Somehow, he managed to snatch the guitar right out of its master's hands, and by the time Mort realized his weapon was gone, it was too late. Dave was already smashing it to pieces, reducing his precious Fender to a tangled mess of blood red splinters and broken strings.

And he was *still* cracking jokes.

"I can't believe you bought this hipster piece of shit! A Mustang—*really* Mort? That's style over substance, dude, and that kind of flash never lasts."

Mort stared in horror at the wreckage before him, suddenly drowning in grief. Cobain may have enjoyed mutilating his instruments on stage, but to Mort, that was an unforgivable sin. Losing the Fender felt like losing a limb, and the monster responsible was clearly feeding on his pain. Dave had intentionally left him unharmed, just so he would be forced to witness the murder of his six-stringed friend. But as he stood there, writing a heavy metal eulogy inside his head, Mort realized he had to move on. So, he grit his teeth and swallowed his sorrow, burying it beneath the reanimated corpse of his rage. And before he knew it, he was rushing back into battle, charging with all the primal ferocity of a bloodthirsty warrior hellbent on revenge.

Unfortunately, his second wind didn't last long. Mort's fury was no match for inhuman strength and speed, and in a matter of moments, Dave had him by the throat, his fingers forming a noose around the soft flesh of the singer's neck. Mort thrashed against him, trying to get away, but to no avail. He was fading faster by the minute, and the best he could do was spit in his drummer's face.

Dave didn't like that. With a series of savage blows, he threw Mort onto his knees, forcing him to bow before the funeral pyre that was devouring the club. The struggling singer tried to hold his ground, but the fight had been beaten right out of his bones. His entire body went limp as he was dragged across the floor, ready to power-slide right into an early grave.

I hope there's at least some hot groupies down there.

"Let him go, you freak!" Dodge yelled from behind them, taking a swing at the back of Dave's head.

It was a valiant effort, but equally short-lived. Dave hardly flinched, and with a simple wave of his hand, sent his rival flying face-first into the wall.

"I don't think so," he snarled. Then he burst into laughter—*again.*

Mort couldn't take one more second of that horrible, dissonant sound. Dave's drumming had always been off-beat, but this new comedy routine was even worse. Someone had to put a stop to it, and since the rest of his band was scared shitless, Mort knew it was up to him. His music career may have been over, but after everything he'd been through, he'd be damned if he was going to let this talentless hack steal the spotlight now.

This is MY SHOW, asshole.

As he inched closer to his imminent death, the cackling

continued, sending caustic shivers running down his spine. Speaking was nearly impossible, but Mort was a vocalist, and as long as he could breathe, he could still sing. So, he put his training to the test, belting out one final, pitch-perfect chorus straight into the blazing conflagration below.

"*FUUUUUUUCK YOUUUUU!*"

It was an impressive performance, but Mort's defiance only seemed to encourage his enemy. The band watched in terror as Dave tightened his grip around their singer's throat, slowly hoisting him up off the floor. Mort clawed frantically at the hailstorm of smoke and embers filling his lungs, praying for a lifeline to magically appear. But the fire was rising, and there was no escape. Though on the bright side, he was about to be famous. There were hundreds of fans all dying to meet him—he could already hear them screaming his name.

"That was killer!" Dave shouted. "An excellent warm-up."

"Go… to… *Hell*," Mort hissed through his teeth.

"Oh, I will. You guys made sure of that," the undead drummer declared, his pale lips curling into a crooked smile as he dangled Mort over the edge of the stage. "But the first thing they teach you down there… is that the Devil always comes back."

ABOUT THE AUTHOR

Raised in the haven of horror and grunge, Seattle, Washington, DIANA OLNEY is an up-and-coming author currently writing her second novel. Her debut short story was featured in *Stranger with Friction* magazine, and her newest creation, a collaborative release entitled *Drawn & Quartered*, also includes her first full-length novella, *She Devil*. Her influences include David Wong, Jane Mendelsohn, Christopher Nolan, and the music of Aesthetic Perfection. Visit her at dianaolney.com for updates on all of her latest nightmares.

OMNIPOTENT
Ravenna Blazecroft

Fr. Reynolds died masturbating. He was a short, heavyset fellow in his fifties; when he turned sideways, he was nothing but a paunch and a jowl, with a garnish of combover. We'd never taken him very seriously—but no one could have imagined the obscene indignity of his demise.

It was late October, and the crimson leaves were swirling in the deep cerulean breeze, as Rachel Archer and I crossed the courtyard, clutching our books. Alyssa West, a senior, was the one who had found the old padre cooling on the carpet, and she'd flung the lit match of gossip into the tall, dry grass of speculation before the sisters came around and hushed her up. We all knew Fr. Tim had perished clutching his veiny little manhood; but no one knew why the cops had sealed off the room where it happened.

"Serena thinks he was doing witchcraft," I half-whispered. "She says if he was in a cult, the FBI would have to come investigate."

Rachel gave me a disapproving look. "Leah, Serena's in

a *Macbeth* phase. Last year, when she was obsessed with *Romeo and Juliet*, she told us Mother Immaculée became a nun because she screwed up her side of a suicide love-pact."

"It could be true. A lot of sisters try dating before they take their vows."

"I'm not questioning that part. But you and I both know, if Mother Immaculée ever made up her mind to kill herself, she'd be the deadest dead person in the morgue."

". . . That's a good point."

St. Bernadette's Boarding School for Girls was over a hundred and fifty years old, and the wise Franciscan nuns in their archetypal black habits had been cranking out well-behaved, well-educated young ladies since Appamattox. It was a tiny place—one chapel, one schoolhouse, one dorm—tamped into the rocky hills of western Washington State. The inscription over the old iron gate read, *Credo ut intelligam*—"I believe, so that I may understand." That semester, there were five nuns and sixty students all told. One good blizzard, and you'd have the perfect spot for an Agatha Christie novel.

My friend Rachel is beautiful. Intoxicatingly so. She has violet eyes, so luminous they could be seraphic haloes rising from the deep, and magnificent golden hair like the tail of a holy comet. Me, I'm such a redhead that my hair is almost carrot-orange, and my eyes are cat-green one-way mirrors.

Class was over for the day. In fact—thank God the Father for Fridays—class was over for the week. We headed into the dorm and up to the second story (freshmen got the ground floor, seniors got the penthouse) to cast off our backpacks and get down to marathoning some serious Netflix.

But Faith Rosemont met us on the stairs. A fellow sophomore, she was freckled and pretty, with strawberry locks and a keen azure gaze. "Guys! I need help. She's being nuttier than usual this time."

Serena Greenfield, Faith's roommate, was a tiny thing with nut-brown hair and eyes, and the scaled-down but perfect features of a woodland sprite. Brief acquaintance, however, revealed her as more impish than elvish. "We've both helped the old man get ready for Mass," she was saying. "You know that stupid window is always popping out of its frame."

"Oh, for goodness' sake," said our lovely blond classmate Thérèse d'Avignon. "It's not a question of whether we *can* break in, it's a question of whether we ought to. Oh good, Rachel and Leah! Can you reason with this sociopath?"

"That's why we came to St. Bernadette's," I said. "Just to reason with Serena."

"Leah." Serena reached up and took me by the shoulders. "We could sneak into that sacristy. See all the padre's dark secrets! Come on, you know you want to."

I opened my mouth to object, then stopped. She was right. I wanted to.

"Leah," Rachel said in a low voice. "Don't even think about it."

"I mean, it wouldn't hurt anything," I pointed out. "Whatever we saw would stay with the five of us. Aren't you a little bit curious?"

"Of course I'm curious, but it's not knowledge that we have a right to."

"Yeah, but. . . I want it anyway."

"Me too!" Serena said. "And Faith, you *always* wanna know stuff."

Equivocating daintily, Faith raised her hands. "I can see both sides here. We're an odd number, so we can settle it by vote."

"The vote released Barabbas," said Thérèse.

"And we'd none of us be here if Pilate had turned Jesus loose," Faith retorted. "Leah's with me, right?"

I nodded—slowly at first, then with mounting conviction. "I think I am. Yeah."

"It's a bad idea," Rachel said gravely. "But if you're going, I'm going."

Serena clapped her hands like a little girl. "All right! Whattaya say, Thérèse? Join our merry band of thieves?"

Our saintly classmate shook her head and sighed. "Somehow, it feels even worse to stay here and pretend I don't know what you're up to. You realize how much trouble we could get in?"

"Yep! Come on, let's get changed. The sun'll be down soon."

Being a traditional Latin Mass institution, St. Bernadette's required us to wear the uniform of the classic Catholic schoolgirl: white shirt and black tie, dark blue sweater, plaid skirt with knee-high socks. Personally, I didn't mind; it freed up much-needed brain-space at the rainy break of dawn not to have to think about what to wear. Rachel and I ducked into our room to change into baggy grey sweats and yank our hair into ponytails, then we rendezvoused with the others and headed for the chapel.

At scarcely four o'clock, it was already getting dark, and a haze of drizzle hung in the rising gloom. The sisters would be praying their Rosary in the sanctuary, which was both good and bad—good because they wouldn't be wandering around checking on things, bad because the sacristy is the room behind the altar, where the priest prepares for Mass. Thirty paces from the front pew, where Mother Immaculée would be.

We walked with unnecessary casualness to the windows at the back of the chapel. Serena was right, we'd all run afoul of that one irksome pane that yearned to be free of its chipped and peeling frame. The sacristy was on the ground floor, and no one was around; the view from the dorm was blocked by an old, bent oak tree. I laced my fingers and gave Serena a boost. She tapped the corner with the heel of her palm, and the pane slid free. She handed it down to Faith.

"Okay, future felons, let's break and enter."

"Ssshhh!"

Rachel gave Serena's other foot a boost, and she scrambled inside. Faith and Thérèse were next. Then Rachel took two steps back, sprinted toward the stone wall, and jump-walked right up the side. She turned, straddling the windowsill, to reach down and give me a hand.

It was dark inside—darker, it seemed, than it should have been. The lights were off, of course, and the mist of dusk was turning to a rainfall; but the shadows in the room felt more solid than the dim light seeping in through the space between the carpet and the door. We all pulled out our phones.

"Careful," said Rachel, barely audible. "Keep them pointed down."

As the beams began to crisscross, limning dust-motes in the air, there was a sudden stir of gasps and murmurs—followed by the rustle of us shushing one another and ourselves. Hanging on the wall, a ruinous banner, was a large black sheet inscribed with a silver Pentagram. In the center of the circle was a face like a hideous goat-man, horned and glaring. The sheet was around the corner from the door to the altar; Alyssa must not have seen it when she found Fr. Reynolds dead.

With a trembling hand, Thérèse made the Sign of the Cross. "It's horrible."

"Look." Faith pointed. On the counter by the sink were three black candles and a piece of paper. On the latter, in Latin, was a paragraph written with ink; beneath the text were the words "Timothy Reynolds, S.J.," scrawled in something flaky and brown.

Serena glanced at Rachel. "Can you read it? You're the best at Latin."

". . . I'm not sure."

While my friend frowned at the sinister document, I found myself wandering the room. I realized I'd been subconsciously expecting a chalk outline where the padre had fallen, like the crime scenes on TV. There was no obvious patch of floor that evoked the image of a decomposing cleric, but I felt drawn toward the far corner somehow. There was nothing over here but a few hooks on the bare wall, one of which held Fr. Tim's old brown trench coat. With no clear motive in mind, I patted the pockets and stuck a hand inside. It came out holding a book.

A small black book, bound in leather. Easy to carry, 3 x 4 inches, made to fit in a pocket. No writing on the spine or cover, but a five-point star etched into the front, pointing down. I hesitated—almost turned to call the others—then opened to the first page. It said, "Omnipotent Lord Satan, I beg You to take full, final, and perfect Possession of my everlasting soul—for You alone are my God, my Master, my Christ. Hail Satan!"

Snapping the book shut, I shook my head. Not in denial or refusal: simply to clear it, as if I'd been slapped.

Faith called softly, "Leah? You okay?"

"Yeah." I shook my head again and stuffed the book in my pocket. "Yeah." I went over to rejoin the others. "So what's the paper say?"

Rachel was grim. "What it looks like. It's a contract with the Devil."

"St. Michael, defend us," Thérèse mouthed, clutching the silver crucifix that hung around her neck.

"Okay," said Serena, "I've officially seen enough. Let's get the hell outta here."

Faith nodded vehemently. "Amen to that."

♉

There was no Netflix that night. We stayed up till 3 in the morning, talking feverishly and praying fervently about what we'd seen. Somehow, in all the chatter, I never found the right moment to mention the book.

336

I slept late the next day. I missed breakfast, but it didn't matter: Rachel never allowed our supply of emergency Pop-Tarts to dwindle too far. I'd slept in my clothes, exhausted; my first waking sensation was the pressure of the book against my pelvis.

Fear and desire, uneasily blended. I put my hand on the pocket of my sweat pants and hesitated. I should just throw it out. Burn it. Or take it to Mother Immaculée, show it to Rachel, call the police. Anything.

I padded down the hall to the bathroom. Brushed my teeth, took a shower, combed my hair. All the while, I kept an eye on the nigh-imperceptible lump in my baggy pants. Back to my room to get dressed. Rachel was out somewhere, probably finishing up her pancakes, which meant my best available source of advice was not available. I could pray about it, of course.

I paced the matted carpet, ruminating. It wasn't as if I planned on casting unholy spells or anything. I was just—curious. So, so curious.

Involuntarily, I recalled the words I'd read last night: "Omnipotent Lord Satan, I beg You to take full, final, and perfect Possession of my everlasting soul—for You alone are my God, my Master, my Christ. Hail Satan!" As they played through my head, almost audibly, I quivered in horror. Well, mostly in horror. Well—partly.

A peek. That was it. A quick peek, then rip and burn the pages one by one.

"Satan knows what you want," it said. "And He wants you to have it."

"No," I muttered. "Never."

"You will resist at first. All believers do. But as soon as you form the intent to study a ritual, the ritual has already begun. With every word you read, there is less resistance."

I made as if to shut the book. But, damn it, I was sealed with the Blood of the Lamb. I was protected, I should fear no evil. Ascribing irresistible power to this claptrap was, itself, a form of irreverence. There was no danger if my heart was pure.

"Hold the image of that which you covet. Feel it. Smell it. Know that your guardian devil sees it too. Imagine your devil entering the flesh of those who would keep it from you. Influencing their choices, their thoughts, their core beliefs. Changing them to suit Lord Satan, God of the World and all who live upon it."

What did I covet? Nothing came to mind. I wished Rachel were here to advise me.

Rachel.

Her scent, like wildflowers. Her hair, like the mane of a unicorn. My God, her *eyes*.

"Beware: to alter the soul of another, you must first overcome the familiar spirit of your target. Their 'angel,' as some would have it. Chant these words: 'By the Power of Almighty Satan, I place this spirit under the feet of my guardian devil. May it be enslaved for all of Eternity.' If you can learn the name of your target's familiar, so much the better."

It so happened that I did know. Rachel called her guardian angel Max, after St. Maximilian Kolbe and the stuffed bear she'd loved as a child. Max.

But for God's sake, what was I doing? Enough of this! I closed the book, and found that I was shaking head to foot. A strange, insistent pulsing throbbed between my legs. I lowered myself onto the bed, exhaling slowly, and made the Sign of the Cross. "I'm sorry," I whispered. "I take it back." Then I dropped to my knees on the carpet and started to pray the Hail Mary over and over again.

The doorknob rattled. Reflexively, I reached up and pushed the black book under a fold of my blanket as Rachel walked in.

Her face softened when she saw me on the floor. "Sweetie, are you all right?" She knelt and put her arms around me. Wildflowers. "Let's go to the chapel and say a Rosary."

I nodded. *God*, those eyes. My shaking stopped, but the throb intensified.

We got the others, and the five of us prayed together. I had to fight to pay attention, but that yearning in my secret place eventually faded. Afterward, we convened in the cafeteria for tea and coffee (a double espresso, in my case), and to strategize.

"We have to tell the sisters," said Thérèse. "They need to know what's been happening in their sanctuary."

"But they obviously know," Serena argued. "They all went in there after Alyssa found Fr. Tim. Now they're waiting for the feds, or maybe some kind of inquisitors from the Vatican, who knows? There's nothing we can add to what the pros are gonna figure out on their own."

"Well, there's one thing for sure," Faith put in. "Either we all confess, or we all swear to keep quiet. We've gotta stick together on this."

Rachel nodded. "I think telling the sisters is the right thing to do. But if it's not unanimous, then it stays between us."

Thérèse turned in my direction. "Leah? You've been awfully quiet. What do you think?"

For a long moment, I said nothing. Then: "I think, if we knew something useful—something important—then we'd be obligated to tell them. But Serena's right, we don't. There's no sense in our getting detention, or worse, to give them information they already have."

One by one—Thérèse last of all—the others acquiesced. I felt violently ambivalent about it, but it was done.

We spent the rest of the day studying, confabulating, doing yoga, watching silly movies. Despite getting up late that morning, I felt tired early. I said my goodnights, said my prayers, and got into bed. The book was right where I'd left it; for a few brief moments, I'd actually forgotten. But sleepiness trumped the temptation to open it, and I found myself spiraling down into murmuring, enveloping mist.

"Leah." A strange voice, half purr and half gravel—amused, confident, sultry. "You found your way, how clever."

"Dear child." Sweet, loving, strong. "Remember who you are. Hold onto that."

Opening my eyes, I found myself still in my dorm room, still in my bed, but no longer alone. Two women stood at the foot of the bed, not glowing, but somehow perfectly lit despite the drawn shades and full dark inside the room. They were both lovely—in fact, they were identical, tall and slender with night-black hair and deep blue eyes—but one wore a cloak of silver from her chin to her toes, the other a skintight leather top, warm yellow in color, that hugged her breasts and arms, left her sleek midriff bare, and was complemented by boots and a micro-skirt of the same material. The face of the lady in silver was beautiful and kind; the love in her eyes was like a halo, the strength in her shoulders like wings. The other was alluring, feline; her hips moved back and forth, very slightly, like the swishing of a tail.

Opening my mouth, I began to ask who they were, but stopped. I'd known them all my life. I started to ask if this was real or a dream, but stopped again. I knew the answer: both. "Why am I here?" I asked, finally.

The lady in yellow: "You opened the book."

The lady in silver: "You opened the door."

"Okay. I guess I already knew that, too. What do I call you guys?"

A smile curved the lips of my gorgeous demoness. "Monika."

"Maryaela," said the other, with honor and sorrow in her voice.

"And what happens now? Do I have to choose between you, or something?"

"Oh, you've made your choice," Monika said. "There's no going back."

"That is a lie," Maryaela said flatly. "The mercy of God is infinite, for those who seek it. Nor have you consummated your choice yet. Come back to us, Leah, come back to Jesus and your Father. Seek the Lord while He may be found."

Monika was examining her crimson fingernails. "You could do that," she said wryly. "Or, you could do *her*."

The door opened. Rachel walked in. She was clad in soft pink lingerie, with a collar on her neck: white all the way around, but with a black clerical insert at her throat, the reverse of a priestly collar. Smiling, she sat on the corner of the bed and leaned down to kiss my face. My eyelids fluttered and closed, and she kissed the lids. Kissed my nose, my cheeks, the corners of my mouth. One hand twined itself into my hair, running soft fingers through the tresses; the other rested lightly on my thigh. The pulse between my legs awoke, hungry and aching, and her hand moved slowly up my leg. The pleasure was beyond anything I'd felt—anything I'd imagined. I couldn't believe such pleasure existed in the world.

"Oh, my love," Maryaela grieved. "This too is deceit. Don't succumb to these phantoms. Are they worth your soul?"

Rachel whispered into my ear, and I caught my breath as the shivering warmth cascaded down my torso. "She's right, Leah. I'm only an image of the one you crave. To have her, you must fully commit yourself."

"I want her," I moaned. "Oh my God, I want her so badly."

"Hey, Leah. Hey, wake up!"

My eyes came open. Angel and devil were gone, but Rachel was there. The real one, shaking my shoulder.

341

"Sweetie, you were thrashing like crazy. Must've been a heck of a nightmare. You okay?"

In a long, cool gust, I let out my pent-up breath. "I truly don't know," I said.

♉

In the morning, we all went to Mass. I kept the book with me, choosing a Sunday dress with pockets for the purpose. As I knelt in the pew, smelling the incense and hearing the ancient chants, I found myself repeating one phrase in the silence of my skull: "Satan knows what you want, and He wants you to have it."

When I went up to receive the Eucharist, I hesitated. Surely I was in a state of sin? But perhaps, if there was doubt, I should accept the graces of the sacrament all the more gratefully. I took the wafer on my tongue and headed back to my pew, but didn't swallow; surreptitiously, I peeled it from my tongue and palmed it.

I had no intention, good or bad; I was watching myself to see what I would do. My hand moved unobtrusively to the hem of my dress—pulled it slowly up. It slipped inside, still holding the Body, Blood, Soul, and Divinity of Christ, and cupped the hidden heat between my thighs. I heard a sound, low and gentle, and knew it was my own sweet sigh of rapture. Quietly, but aloud, I uttered the transmogrifying words:

"Omnipotent Lord Satan, I beg You to take full, final, and perfect Possession of my everlasting soul—for You alone are my God, my Master, my Christ. Hail Satan!"

A hand on my shoulder. "What a good girl."

"Monika?" I glanced around at the sisters and the student body, clearly oblivious to the very noticeable temptress. "Am I asleep?"

"Not at all," she smiled. "You're growing stronger,

through Blasphemy and Lust. You're opening yourself more and more to Omnipotence. Now you can see the astral plane with your waking eyes. Look!"

Students and teachers, as before. But now, superimposed, a hard, bright world of which we ourselves were only the shadows. I saw the souls of my classmates, glimmering inside their bones, marked with humming purity or slashed with dribbling iniquity. I saw, hovering near each human soul, two spirits like my own, stooping to speak numinous words of cleansing and corruption. And there, above Rachel, I saw Max.

He was huge, imposing, knotted with muscle, scowling through a kingly beard. He saw me too. His counterpart grinned at me, every bit as powerful as Max himself, and pointed down at Rachel. "Yours for the taking, witch!" he roared. "Let's guide her home to Hell!"

"For God's love, Leah, don't do this." Maryaela, pleading. "She's your best friend. Would you make her a slave? A whore?"

For reasons I didn't understand, those words—a slave, a whore—inflamed me with a passion that shook me like a rag doll. I got to my feet and stumbled from the chapel. In the vestibule, a door caught my eye: the old, locked door to the disused bell tower. I put my hand on the knob, and today it turned.

Up through years of spinning spiders, up through years of dust. The stairs creaked and groaned like dying men. At the summit, I stood panting between huge bronze shadows, struggling one last time to break the seductive grip of the Darkness on my will and my flesh.

"Please, God, help me. Save me." I fell prostrate, mummified in cobwebs, and desperately recited the Our Father. ". . . and lead us not into temptation, but deliver us from Evil. Amen."

As I finished, I heard Monika laughing good-naturedly, totally unthreatened. Maryaela was on her knees at my side, adding her prayers to my own. The book had fallen from my pocket, and lay open on the floor beside me. "You will have moments of repentance," it said. "The Lord God Satan likes to play His fish. Each time you try to return to the crucified donkey, you will fall yet deeper under the domination of our Master, who is Lord forever and ever."

And the depths of my soul, the innermost core of my being, breathed: *Yes.*

Monika stepped closer. "It's time, Leah."

"No," Maryaela gasped. "No! You can't!"

"By the Power of Almighty Satan," I chanted, "I place this spirit, Maryaela, under the feet of my guardian devil. May she be enslaved for all of Eternity!"

"No!"

Monika cackled. Plunging her incorporeal hands into my forehead and chest, she tugged me out of my mortal frame. "Well done, witch," she said, clutching my astral shoulders. "Well done indeed." Then she dove into the vacant body on the floor.

Fear, doubt, resistance fell away. I felt the smile of Evil on my face. Turning to Maryaela, I rent the silver garments from her back and laughed with sheer delight at the perfection of her naked body. She struggled feebly, but the grace was draining from her as my aura curled around her skin and held her tight. Gripping her silken hair, I pulled her closer and kissed her on the mouth: she stiffened for a moment, then yielded, helpless.

I pushed her down and pinned her, delirious with ecstasy. I kissed her neck, her breasts, her stomach, and she keened as her resistance turned to desire. Then I felt it—felt *Him*.

From the once-secret place between my legs, the Power of Lucifer was rising. A surging astral member, already dripping with the ichor of damnation. It grew and curved and swelled, and then His Will moved my hips and I entered her: He entered her. I don't know how long we writhed and coiled together, lost in the absolute pleasure of Possession. Aeons, perhaps. For anyone who experienced even a moment of such bliss, there would never again be the slightest thought of worshiping any God but Satan.

At last, I came. I came like a deluge, flushing out every trace of salvation, filling her with the Unholy Spirit, binding her eternally to the King of All.

She lay motionless—changed—fallen. Soundless, her lips formed magnificent syllables: *Ave Satanas*. I rose to my feet and stepped back into my human form. Reaching out with a tendril of my demonic aura, I dragged Maryaela into my body as well, making her angelic powers my own.

"Now," I said, and the bells stirred, resonating, at the force of my words and my will. "The time has come."

♉

Snow was coming, the first snow of the year. It would be a mighty storm. As I stepped outside, glancing at the impotent heavens, I saw no clouds, but a solid roof of sheer, grim white. It was not yet noon, but the hushful gloom of twilight held sway over St. Bernadette's.

I entered the dorm. Invisible entities, conspicuous to my new vision, skulked everywhere. Some were good, some evil; some were wholly alien, unconcerned with the destiny of Adam's race. And, I discovered, I could see the souls of my classmates even through walls and doors. Mounting the steps with calm deliberation, I gazed steadily at the hulking Max and his adversary. Max watched, fuming with ineffectual rage, as I drew ever closer to the radiant girl he existed to protect.

"There you are!" Rachel exclaimed as I walked into Faith and Serena's room. She jumped up and took my hands. "The way you rushed out, I was worried. You really haven't been yourself since we went to the sacristy."

"Well, no. I really haven't."

"Leah, what can I do to help?"

What a kind heart she had. "Undress. All of you."

Their eyes glazed over. They obeyed.

"You were my desire." Caressing her flawless cheek. "It all began with wanting you." Pressing my palm to her heart. "But now you're not enough." We stood, we five, on the points of the Pentagram. "By the Power of Almighty Satan, I place this spirit, Max, and these others, under the feet of my guardian devil." Ethereal howls of glee and despair. "May they be enslaved for all of Eternity!"

Lucifer rose again between my thighs—but this time, it was no mere phallus. A dozen straining cocks, a brood of pythons, a penetrating hydra, burst from my loins and slithered through both worlds, astral and earthly, to enter every soul and body in the room, angel and devil and human alike. The wailing of unimaginable ecstasy, along with my shrieking laughter, filled the air.

Our classmates came running when they heard the din. Though blind to the spirits, they nonetheless saw Leah Kell shooting tentacles from her maidenhead, lifting four once-pure schoolgirls into the air as she pumped their flesh full of The Lord God Satan. Screams of raw, mindless terror echoed in the halls. More tentacles, more Satan-cocks, came wriggling out of me, lashing at the skirts and blouses of my slaves, my whores. Entering more and more of them. With every shred of innocence I swallowed, my power grew.

Back to the chapel at once. The telepathic command rippled through the campus. *Go to the altar and await*

My coming.

Several of my nightmare appendages, like the legs of a centipede, pushed down against the floorboards, raising me into the air. One of them smashed open the brick wall of the room, and I climbed spiderlike down the outside of the building, punching easily into the stone with my cockheads, carrying thirteen concubines by the seat of their taken virginity.

Helpless to resist my call, the nuns and the rest of the students flocked to the altar. The Power and Will of the Darkness flooded them, and they began to chant:

"Omnipotent Lord Satan, I beg You to take full, final, and perfect Possession of my everlasting soul—for You alone are my God, my Master, my Christ. Hail Satan!"

The whole congregation went to their hands and knees before me. I, His chosen vessel; this, my glorious destiny. To become one with Omnipotence.

But a face was missing. I caught the eyes of Sister Gabriella, young and fair, and beckoned with a single finger. She rose instantly and came to me.

"Tell me, Gabriella, where is Mother Immaculée?"

"She went out, Goddess." Her gaze was adoring, reverent. As it should be. "To meet the special priests from Rome. She was afraid they'd lose their way in the snow."

Interesting. Serena had been right: inquisitors from the Vatican.

"Good girl. But here's a secret—no matter how good you've been, you're not going to heaven. You'll never see your little god on a stick, Gabriella. You belong to Hell."

She whispered: "Yes, my Goddess."

I said nothing more, but closed my eyes and let the Unholy Spirit pour forth. Flowing through all my playthings. Igniting them.

The orgy began.

♉

The storm was here; the white roof had become a white wall, and the muzzled sun had gone down. I was on the altar, in the chair of the priest. Alyssa West and Rachel were on either side of me, in the altar servers' chairs. I'd retracted my forest of monstrous cocks, resuming the appearance of a simple schoolgirl—a naked one, of course, enjoying the languid caresses of my altar servers, the touch of their tongues upon my neck and breasts. Kneeling between my legs, pleasuring me slowly, was Sister Gabriella; prostrate before me, kissing my feet with sensual piety, were Thérèse and Serena. I was thumbing idly through the black book, savoring my apotheosis.

Then the broad double doors of the chapel slammed open. Three men in priestly vestments strode through the vestibule and headed down the aisle in my direction. Behind them, bleak-faced, was Mother Immaculée.

As the ministers advanced, they brandished aspergillums, long rods used for flinging holy water, and commenced to re-sanctify this desecrated ground. The one in the middle—tall, gaunt, grey-haired—cried out in a loud voice: "Ancient Serpent! I command you in the name of xrist to be cast forth into the outer darkness. You cannot disobey, for it is god himself who compels you. Go, and leave these children of god in peace! *Go out!*"

I lounged in my chair, listening with amusement. He kept mouthing his little spells as they marched ever closer, and I let them come right up to the foot of the altar. Then I raised a hand and said, "Stop."

They stopped walking. Stopped talking.

"It's wonderful of you gentlemen to come all this

way. It happens that I've just now stumbled upon a piece of especially black magic, and I'm excited to share it with you. We're going to remove the grace of your baptisms! Isn't that fun?"

The tall one had gone pale. A thread of sweat unspooled from his brow. He seemed to have something he wanted to say.

"You may speak," I said, magnanimously. "But no more prayers."

He glowered. "The sacrament of baptism is eternal. No evil can take it from us."

"What's your name, padre?"

"I am Monsignor Ivan Burke of the Order of St. Rose. With me are Father Joseph—"

"Enough." I got to my feet. "Who gives the church its authority to administer the sacraments, Ivan?"

"Jesus xrist, the son of god!"

"Well, then. Why don't we see if he shares your confidence?" Three tentacle-shafts emerged from my unholy of unholies, planted themselves on the floor, and lofted me high above my worshipers and my enemies. Ignoring the gasps of horror from Immaculée and the clerics, I turned to the huge crucifix on the wall and the life-sized wooden Jesus hanging from the crosspiece. "All right, you fucking donkey," I shouted. "Come down off that ridiculous thing and let's chat."

Silence.

Then—

The wooden eyes moved. They met my gaze, and the wooden brow furrowed. The wooden mouth frowned. The hands and feet came free of their moorings, and the carven carpenter descended from his cross. I descended as well, to stand facing him.

"Leah," said the pinewood throat. "Daughter. Your sin is grave. You will receive a very severe condemnation if you do not come home."

"I relish your curses, Nazarene. And what you call damnation, I call orgasm. But that's not why I've called you down here. These poor fellows seem to think the power of xrist compels me. Would you like to break the truth to them, or shall I?"

I almost felt sorry for those fools as they gazed imploringly at their little lord. "I say to you, good servants, that your faith will someday be rewarded. But I can work no miracle against this monster. The Darkness is stronger."

"No," Ivan mumbled. "No."

"Believe it," I grinned. "Is he not the way, the truth, and the life? But here stands one far greater. I Am Power. I Am Bliss. I AM!"

At my words, everyone in that chapel went to their knees. Everyone—including the carpenter. His face contorted with the effort to resist, but it was hopeless.

I stretched out my hand toward the son of god. "By My words and by My will, I declare you open to the Spirits of Blasphemy and Lust." Turning, I stretched my other hand toward the kneeling priests and Mother Superior. "By My words and by My will, I take from you the grace of your baptism!" My hand twisted into a claw, summoning, and they groaned as a mist of red steam arose from their foreheads. "Now you shall never enter the kingdom of heaven. And you, little donkey." Turning back to xrist, I saw that he had already succumbed. His pinewood hands gripped and stroked his pinewood member. His voice, barely audible, chanted:

"Fuck god the father. Fuck the holy spirit. Fuck god the father. Fuck the holy spirit."

I threw back my head and laughed. God is Mine. The universe is Mine. All worlds, all realities, are Mine. And I Am with you now as you read this, and You are Mine:

Omnipotent Lord Satan, I beg You to take full, final, and perfect Possession of my everlasting soul—for You alone are my God, my Master, my Christ. Hail Satan!

ABOUT THE AUTHOR

RAVENNA BLAZECROFT is a Theistic Satanist who is actively working for your damnation. She loves what you've done with your bedroom closet.

OMNIPOTENT

EL DIABLO

Mike Baron

The car rental in Dziuchi, Yucatan, was part of a strip mall that contained The Camaron tavern and a *taqueria*. The rental was a 1998 Jeep Rubicon that had crossed the river too many times. Christian Haas guessed that the odometer, which read 186,000, had been rolled back. But it ran, and that was good enough for Christian and his girlfriend Miranda Cates, who loaded the rear with their camping and diving equipment. Not SCUBA diving. They weren't crazy enough to investigate the Yucatan's *cenotes* for any longer than it took to hold their breaths. Too many stories of divers dying in cul-de-sacs, rumors of snakes and giant reptiles.

Christian signed the documents and handed over a Visa card. Guillermo the rental agent, snappy in a Western shirt with a bolo tie, said, "May I see some identification?"

Christian slid a driver's license across the desk. Guillermo peered at it. "You have glasses in this picture, Senor Ryan."

"I had eye surgery. It makes a world of difference."

"What about your passport?"

"It's in my luggage. I can get it if you want, but it will take a while."

Guillermo carefully wrote down information from the license and handed over the keys.

"Where you going?"

Christian spread the plat map on the counter and pointed to a blue spot circled in red. "We're going to dive this *cenote*, if we can find it."

"You go through El Mariachi estate. Got a gun?"

"A gun? Why do I need a gun?"

Guillermo grinned, displaying yellow teeth in a seamed face. "Not many gringos know about El Mariachi. He was head of Quintana Roo Cartel. They funnel tons of coca up from Columbia through Belize. Five years ago, Campeche Cartel took him out. Bad blood. Brewing for a long time. Federales were in on it. They hit his estate at midnight, killed everybody, released his wild animals, and trashed the place. Now it is haunted. They say El Mariachi's ghost lingers. If you listen late at night, you can hear him playing guitar. But most people called him El Cheapo. He didn't pay his workers. So if you see a tiger or a jaguar running around, it probably came from his zoo."

Christian looked at Miranda with raised eyebrows. "Did you know about this?"

Miranda, a pert brunette, hair cut short for the adventure, wearing cargo shorts and a halter top, shrugged. "Not me, hoss. You're the leader of this expedition."

Guillermo reached under the counter and set a heavy revolver down with a clunk. "Very reliable. Forty-four magnum. Two boxes cartridges. Yours for five hundred dollars."

Christian picked it up.

"Oh, come on!" Miranda wailed.

"What if we run into jaguars or a giant snake?"

Guillermo set a box of cartridges down with a clunk. "There are also bad hombres, my friends. There are gangs who prey on tourists. The Yucatan is a lawless place."

Christian reached for his wallet. He had more than enough cash for a posh Mexican getaway. He'd suggested Cabo, but Miranda, an athlete and a snorkler, talked him into the other side of the country. Christian peeled off three hundred dollar bills.

"I'll give you three hundred right here, right now."

Guillermo stared at the bills. He swept them off the counter. "Done. Would you like to fire the gun? We can go out back. Have you ever fired a gun before?"

Christian grinned. "Nope."

Guillermo motioned them around the counter, through the unkempt office out the back door to where a ravine filled with open sewage separated them from the rain forest. It was a humid eighty-five.

Twenty feet on the other side of the culvert sat an old fifty-gallon oil drum, punctured with bullet holes. An old picnic table rested in the weeds, a large amber glass ashtray on top filled with water and soggy butts. It was a beautiful sunny day in February.

Christian took up a shooter's stance, the pistol in both hands. Guillermo bumped him with the box of shells.

"You should load it first."

Christian set the pistol on the picnic table and opened the box of shells, pushing them one by one into the cylinder. Miranda walked a little ways off and regarded him skeptically, arms crossed. Christian lowered the long-barreled pistol until it pointed at the oil drum.

"Just squeeze gently," Guillermo advised.

A sonic boom shattered the air as the pistol leaped in Christian's hands. Miranda shrieked and clapped her hands to her ears.

"Did I hit it?" Christian asked excitedly.

Guillermo shook his head. "No, man. You try again."

An hour later they headed west on a dirt trail that frequently descended into swamp, the pistol jutting out of the center console. The top was down, sunlight intermittently splashing them through the canopy.

Miranda put her hand on Christian's shoulder. "This is so exciting!"

Christian slammed on the brakes. "Oh my god! Did you see that?"

"What?"

"Something just dashed across the trail in front of us. I think it was a wild pig."

"Maybe you can shoot one for dinner."

Taking the pistol in hand, Christian got out of the car. "Watch this."

Resting his elbows on the Jeep's hood, he called a falsetto, "Soo-ee! Soo-ee!"

He winked at Miranda. "Used to call hogs back on the farm."

Shortly, the curious pig wandered back into the road. Christian squeezed off a shot, striking the pig in the head. It immediately collapsed. Shirt soaked with sweat, Christian loaded the dead pig into the back of the Jeep. He got in and put the car in gear. "Ha!"

It was six p.m. when they came upon the ruins of what had once been a grand estate. An eight foot stucco wall had been knocked down in numerous places. A lone buzzard circled overhead. They drove in beneath a Moorish arch bearing the words "El Mariachi" as musical notes, hanging from several rebars, into a spacious front yard strewn with rubble. Brackish rainwater filled a central fountain, lizards sunning on the rim. The main house, once a two-story Spanish style estate, lay in ruins with great holes in the roof and walls. "El Mariachi" had been painted in musical notes over the main entrance. Christian stopped in the sun, got out, shoved the horse pistol into his belt, and went up three steps to the main entrance, Miranda right behind him.

An eerie silence settled over them.

The front doors had been blown off. Inside, jungle had begun to reclaim the interior, with plants growing up through the tiles and around the interior fountain. Rubble lay everywhere. Vines snaked across the floor.

"Let's explore!" Christian said. "Maybe we'll find some coca. I could use a bump."

Miranda hugged herself, suddenly cold. "Let's not. This place is creeping me out. It gives me bad vibes."

Christian drew the pistol. "Fear not, fair lady!"

She grabbed him by the arm and dragged him outside. "Not today, John Wayne."

"Well at least let's walk around to the back," Christian said, heading clockwise.

They passed a burnt-out eight-vehicle garage, including the remains of an old Rolls Royce. In the rear, a broad veranda looked out on a swimming pool, now filled with opaque rainwater. Several iguanas plopped into the water at their approach. Wild birds trilled from the trees. Beyond the swimming pool, the cages to El Mariachi's zoo stood eerily open, slogans painted on stucco in the same manner as "El Mariachi." "El Diablo." "Elefante." "Oso."

They looked down into a sunken pit surrounded by eight foot walls. "El Monitor."

"Don't all these drug lords keep tigers?" Miranda said.

"I think that's El Diablo. Maybe we should crash here for the night."

Miranda looked around. "It's creepy. Can't you feel it, Chris? Something bad happened here."

"Yeah, but it will be dark soon, and at least the ground's dry. Come on. We'll just pitch our tent in the plaza. We might not even need a tent. And we have to butcher that hog."

"You're the butcher," Miranda said.

Christian used a machete and skinning knife to butcher the hog, tossing the entrails into the forest where they were soon covered with ants. They roasted a ham over a small fire and threw the rest out back in the zoo.

They took turns pumping up the air mattresses and set them on a verdant stretch of what had been the lawn. They made love on the air mattress, powerless to stop the mosquitoes. Beneath a brilliant starry sky, they went to bed, Christian's pistol between them.

"Don't wake up and shoot me in the middle of the night," Miranda said.

"Don't snore."

After a while, she said, "Do you think they found the body?"

"Don't worry about it," Christian said. "I dumped him in an abandoned mine shaft in the middle of nowhere."

Sounds of the jungle kept them up most of the night. Mad yowls from behind the house from predators fighting over the ham.

As Christian dozed off, Miranda shook him, leaned over and hissed, "Do you hear that?"

Christian squinted, irritated. He heard jungle cacophony, birds, monkeys, God knew what. "No. What?"

"Mariachi music! Listen!"

After a few seconds Christian shook his head. "It's nothing go to bed."

She scooted so that their mattresses touched, and put an arm around him.

They woke cranky and bug bit, breakfasted on roast pig and sunflower seeds, and were on the road by eight. It was almost noon when they reached the *cenote*, visible ahead only because of the absence of trees and a shaft of sunlight shining straight down like a column. Christian parked the jeep and they piled out, fatigue replaced by excitement, and walked up a gentle stone incline leading to the lip. Ten feet below the *cenote* beckoned, a mystic blue eye staring up through layers of sediment. They stood hand in hand, overcome.

"It's like finding God, or something," Miranda said softly.

"It's fantastic," Christian said.

"Jerry wouldn't take me anywhere."

"Forget Jerry. Let's hit the water. We don't even need

swim suits! We're all alone out here."

"You do what you like," Miranda said, heading back to the car. "We don't know that we're all alone, and Mama taught me never go in the water without a suit."

Christian followed. "Chicken! You're just worried I'll shoot pictures."

"You're damned right I am," Miranda said, unselfconsciously stripping off her clothes and changing into a blue one-piece.

Christian put on a pair of baggy surfer shorts, filled a backpack with bottled water, towels, sun tan lotion, insect repellent, goggles, flippers and the pistol, and headed toward the water. "I think we can get down to the water this way."

The jungle chirped and rustled, birds jumping from branch to branch. About a hundred yards on, the trail descended to a ten foot sand beach. From below, they looked back at the cliff on which they'd stood, and saw a dark tunnel at the waterline. The water was so clear, they could see bones on the bottom.

"It's gorgeous!" Miranda declared, sitting on a rock and strapping on her fins.

"Wait for me!" Christian said.

"One of us has to stay here and hold off the *banditos*, buster. Relax. I'm just going to splash around a little, maybe go ten feet down."

"Okay, but if I can't see you, I'm coming in after you."

Miranda stepped in thigh-high water, spit in her mask, put it on, and dove forward, her big green flippers breaking the surface once before she submerged. Christian watched her paddle away, marveling at the limpid water, the dust motes dancing in sunbeams, the green riot overhead. It was easy to imagine he was the only human being on earth. The *cenote* was remarkably clean and trash free. Everywhere else they'd traveled was trash. Wind-blown plastic bags, empty bottles of *Dos Equis*, fast food wrappings. Inside the walled resorts, employees patrolled

24/7 with gloves and trash bags but outside in the real world, the trash was pervasive.

Christian grabbed the pistol and whirled to face a sudden thrashing in the jungle. For a second he froze, extending his senses into the jungle. Was it the tiger? He realized how ridiculous he must look in his baggy shorts clutching the enormous pistol.

"Silly wabbit," he said, turning back to the water and replacing the pistol in the backpack. Miranda emerged like Aphrodite, removing her mask and shaking out her short auburn hair.

"It's fantastic! You've got to come! I saw all these little colorful fishes, and there appears to be an underwater passage to other *cenotes*!"

"Did you see bones on the bottom?"

Miranda duck-walked out of the water. "No. What bones?"

Christian got up on a rock and pointed. "Look. You can see them better from over here."

Miranda took off her flippers and joined him, following his finger to a set of white bones resting delicately on a ledge.

"Those look like rib bones," Christian said.

"What, you mean like human rib bones?"

"Don't they?"

Miranda punched him on the shoulder. "Oh come on."

"Well I don't know—they could have been down there since Mayan times! Or maybe a jaguar dropped them there."

"Or they could be pig bones," Miranda said.

"They don't look like pig bones."

"Well put on your big boy pants, swim mask and flippers, and go down there and take a look!"

Christian leaped to the ground. "All right. I will."

"Don't stay down too long," Miranda said.

Flipper strapped, Christian slipped and fumbled his way back to the stone perch which rose six feet above the water and jumped in feet first. He disappeared in a vortex of bubbles, reappearing as he flipped and swam toward the ledge jutting from the side of the *cenote*. He plunged down, feet pumping. It was further than he thought. He felt water pressure leaning on his ear drums and estimated that it was thirty feet to where the bones lay. Too deep. He turned back and swam toward the surface, following the swirling walls. Something white gleamed from a shelf strewn with rubble. He scooped it up as he ascended.

Miranda had spread lunch on a blanket, bananas, jerky, trail mix, dried apricots. She looked up.

"What did you find?"

Christian held the skull before him. "Alas poor Yorick, I knew him well."

Miranda rose like smoke. "Is that a skull?"

Christian tossed it to her underhand. She shrieked and caught it.

"Oh my god," she said, turning it over in her hands. "It is! It looks recent!"

"Don't be silly. Look at it. It's got that Mayan slope to the brow. It looks old. It's got to be hundreds of years old. Maybe this is one of those *cenotes* where they made human sacrifice. The bottom could be covered in bones. I'll bet if we dig down there we'll find all sorts of shit."

"Nobody is digging down there. You didn't even make it all the way to the bottom."

Christian sat on the blanket and reached for a bottled water. "Yeah, but I'm thinking if we go and get some SCUBA gear, we might find something worthwhile."

"Not this trip, boyo."

Christian chewed trail mix. "Yeah, you're right. But we'll remember this spot. I mean, it's uncanny that it's so untouched! Like no one's been here in a hundred years."

"Except for whoever murdered poor Yorick."

Christian looked up. "What murder?"

Miranda turned the skull over and pointed to two puncture wounds at the base in back.

Christian reached. "Gimme."

He turned the skull over and over. "These aren't bullet wounds. They appear to be some kind of puncture wounds. Like a giant snake or something."

"Great!" Miranda said. "Like an anaconda or something. I hate snakes."

"Anacondas don't bite. They squeeze."

"There are other snakes, worse snakes."

Christian grinned. "Just last year, villagers in Benito Juarez beat a twenty-five foot snake to death with hoes."

Miranda put her hands on her hips. "You gotta be shittin' me."

Christian made the Boy Scout sign. "Swear to God."

"Well what kind of a snake was it?"

"They didn't say."

"Well what kind of snakes are there?"

"You got your jumping pit viper. You got your boa constrictors..."

"That's enough."

Christian regarded the skull in his hand and hurled it into the *cenote*, where it hit with a plop.

"Why did you do that?"

"I was just putting it back," Christian said. "We're not grave robbers."

That night they camped out on the sandy beach and built a small fire in a stone circle they'd assembled. "We could catch one of those fat iguanas and cook it," Christian said, holding his pistol.

"Stay your hand, Red Ryder. Maybe we ought to put up the tent. It feels like rain."

Josh looked up to see clouds scudding in from the west. "Maybe you're right."

The hemispherical pop tent was self-supporting. Christian had just finished fastening the fly to the surrounding trees before the skies rumbled and the gates opened. Inside, they held each other tight while the rain pounded on the tent, drumming them to sleep. They woke with the sun baking the tent. Christian crawled out to see steam rising from the *cenote* and the rock itself, burning off last night's rain. Christian ran naked to the rock and threw himself in the water, surfacing like a dolphin.

"WOOO!" he hooted.

Miranda emerged, looked around comically, then shed her T-shirt and did the same. After they'd dried off, she said, "I'll go back to the Jeep and find some victuals."

"You want to take the gun?"

Miranda waved him off. "Rest easy, Red Ryder."

A minute later her scream echoed through the jungle causing birds to take flight. Pulling on his tennies, Christian grabbed the gun and ran through the jungle to where Miranda stood with her hands to her mouth staring at the Jeep. The canvas top was shredded. So were the seats. Foam rubber, bits of cloth, even springs littered the ground around the Jeep as if Wolverine had been looking for change in the seat cushions.

"Fuck," Christian said.

Miranda grabbed his arm. "What could have done that?"

"A jaguar, or a bear, maybe."

Miranda sunk her fingernails into his bicep. "What if it's the devil?"

"Fuck you talking about?"

"You saw that sign. El Diablo. All the other cages named the animals. But not Diablo."

"What, you think some drug lord is keeping the devil in a cage? That's hilarious."

"Don't make fun of me. I'm scared."

Christian went to the Jeep and looked inside. The controls, at least, seemed intact. It appeared drivable if he didn't mind sitting on shreds and springs. "Let's go back to the tent. We're getting out of here."

Holding the revolver like a dousing rod, Christian led the way back to their campsite. The tent was gone. A wet slick indicated where it had been dragged down the rock into the pond.

"That's it!" he declared. "Grab your shit and let's go."

They hurriedly gathered their belongings, stuffing them into their backpacks, and headed into the jungle. They were halfway to the jeep when Miranda's cry was abruptly cut off, followed by the signs of something large thrashing through the jungle. Christian whirled, gun pointing. The trail was empty.

"MIRANDA!" he yelled. The thrashing receded, heading for the *cenote*.

Christian ran. In high school, he'd lettered in track. Ran the hundred meters in 11.5. He pounded right through the puddles, ignoring the mud splashed onto his once white Adidas. When he burst from the rainforest into the clearing, he froze, the way a deer freezes in headlights, or a rabbit quivers under a coyote's gaze.

A dragon dragged Miranda into the pond by her arm. It was enormous, wet scales glowing iridescent green in the sun. Mercifully, Miranda had passed out. She was seconds away from being dragged under and drowned. Christian ran to the edge of the pool, pointed the pistol in both hands and held his breath. Miranda was between him and the creature. Abruptly it turned, exposing the long, sinuous body as it partially submerged.

Christian, who'd earned his marksman badge in the Boy Scouts, squeezed off a shot. The bullet entered the lizard's back leaving a dark hole as it churned forward, dragging Miranda until only her head and one shoulder was above the water.

Leading the thing as if it were a duck, Christian emptied the remaining five bullets. The creature disappeared without a ripple. For long seconds he watched in horror as the mirror-like surface reflected the overhead canopy. Something pink broke the surface. It was Miranda, eyes open in death, trailing a red contrail. Tossing the pistol on the ground, Christian dove, reaching her in five long strokes.

Cupping her chin in one hand, Christian pulled her to the shore and laid her out on the rock with her feet toward the water. Her left arm had been chewed off above the elbow. She had probably died from shock.

Grimly, Christian crouched and reloaded the pistol. Would it fire underwater? Why wouldn't it? The cartridges were sealed. But water was eight hundred times denser than air. It wouldn't travel very far or very fast. If he shot the thing at point blank, it would die. He replaced the Adidas with flippers. He spit in his mask.

He stopped. Wasn't this all Miranda's fault in the first place? What if he'd never met her? The way she'd come onto him at that thrifting convention in Vegas. What was thrifting, but drifting from one flea market to another looking for bargains? Thanks to shows like *American Pickers* and *Pawn Stars*, millions now viewed thrifting as a legitimate enterprise instead of the bottom ladder desperation that it was.

What happens in Vegas stays in Vegas. Except it hadn't. She'd told him it was her first vacation without her husband in years. That her husband was a miser and a hoarder who had built a fortune in *faux* antiques, fleeing Massachusetts one step ahead of the tax man.

How she'd met Dennis at a casino in Wisconsin, bereft and at odds, and had thrown herself into his lifeboat. Dennis glommed onto her like a bear to a dead beaver She was the most exquisite creature he had ever seen. Within six months they were married and he took her away to his farm outside of Barneveld, with a barn filled with thirty years of pickings. *American Pickers*' heads would have exploded. The barn contained everything from Bakelite phones to shovel-head Harleys.

Whoever ended up with it would make a fortune.

The day Christian killed Dennis, Miranda cleaned out their joint checking account to the tune of 22,000 dollars. They took all the gold and silver and sold it to a dealer in the twin cities. Their net haul was over two hundred and fifty grand which seemed more than enough if they went south and never returned.

Dead Miranda changed everything. Hardly anyone knew of Christian's relationship with her. Christian still had plenty of contacts in his demimonde of drifters and grifters. Chances were, nobody had even discovered they were gone! Dennis was a recluse who often didn't emerge from his house for days at a time. If Christian got back fast enough, brought a truck, that barn was easily good for another one hundred and fifty thou. The miser had squirreled away Tiffany glass, Barbie dolls, Star Wars paraphernalia, leisure suits, lava lamps, first editions and Fanner Fifties.

There was nothing he could do for Miranda. She was dead. He didn't have to die as well. He'd liked her well enough but now she was gone. He pulled off his fins and goggles, got in his cargo shorts, put on his Adidas, grabbed both backpacks and the gun and turned to leave.

A tiger crouched in the middle of the path snarling at him.

With a sound like a baby bird, Christian stumbled back and threw himself into the pond. Bubbles rose, then a great thrashing as the monitor's tail broke the surface. After a while, all was quiet. The tiger turned and padded silently back the way it came, past the savaged Jeep.

The radio lit up and played mariachi music.

ABOUT THE AUTHOR

MIKE BARON is the creator of *Nexus* (with artist Steve Rude) and *Badger*, two of the longest lasting independent superhero comics. *Nexus* is about a cosmic avenger 500 years in the future. *Badger*, about a multiple personality one of whom is a costumed crime fighter. Baron has won two Eisners and an Inkpot award and written *The Punisher*, *Flash*, *Deadman* and *Star Wars*, among many other titles.

ALSO FROM CRITICAL BLAST

GODS & SERVICES
edited by R.J. Carter

When old gods need new worshipers, they offer their divinity for sale. Put a little god in your life with this collection of short stories from authors Ross Baxter, Ira Bloom, Laura J. Campbell, Aristo Couvaras, Jon Del Arroz, David J. Pedersen, Zach Smith, Michael Tierney, and Katherine Traylor.

BULLETPROOF: ORIGINS
by Stephen J. Mitchell

Kody Haywood is a freshman at Bannerville High School, struggling to maintain focus. Every day he finds himself getting lost in his thoughts, the hallways at school, or even in conversation. Having a mind that wanders makes him an easy target for the school bully and all-star athlete, Brett Walker.

As his birthday approaches, Kody discovers a genetic change in his body that renders him indestructible. When a mysterious letter from his deceased father arrives on his doorstep, it puts him in the crosshairs of an international terrorist!

Facing trouble in and out of school, Kody must find his focus and deal with two very different enemies or else there will be terrible consequences for being…

Bulletproof!

THE DEVIL YOU KNOW
edited by R.J. Carter

A short-story anthology of encounters with various incarnations of The Devil, with genres ranging from fairy tale to folk tale, from urban fantasy to science fiction, from comedy to horror. Featuring the works of Jared Baker, Erica Ciko Campbell, Sarah Cannavo, Michael W. Clark, Christopher Cook, Andra Dill, Cara fox, R.A. Goli, Gerald A. Jennings, Kevin Kangas, Daryl Marcus, Damascus Mincemeyer, Steve Oden, Evan Purcell, Troy Riser, Joseph Rubas, Hannah Trusty, Wondra Vanian, Henry Vogel, and K.D. Webster.

CPSIA information can be obtained
at www.ICGtesting.com
Printed in the USA
JSHW030255130522
25817JS00002B/7

9 780578 390200